MOTHER HENS

Also by Sophie McCartney

TIRED AND TESTED: The Wild Ride Into Parenthood

MOTHER HENS

Sophie McCartney

Harper
North

HarperNorth
Windmill Green
24 Mount Street
Manchester M2 3NX

A division of
HarperCollins*Publishers*
1 London Bridge Street
London SE1 9GF

www.harpercollins.co.uk

HarperCollins*Publishers*
Macken House
39/40 Mayor Street Upper
Dublin 1
D01 C9W8

First published by HarperNorth in 2023

1 3 5 7 9 10 8 6 4 2

A catalogue record for this book
is available from the British Library

ISBN: 978-0-00-847533-8

Printed and bound in Great Britain by
CPI Group (UK) Ltd, Croydon

For Nate – who I made, grew and birthed at the same time as my book baby. And for my husband, Steve, for always putting out... the bin.

Prologue

Prologue

I often used to wonder… what makes seemingly good people do horrifically bad things? Hatred, greed, jealousy, a cup of tea made with the milk added first? Just how far can a person be pushed before finally snapping and shoving someone back… over a cliff?

Cascades of loose coppery stones flurry downwards past his flailing feet as they desperately try to find their footing on the crumbling edge of the never-ending scorched abyss. God, it's breathtaking up here, almost as beautiful as those bright blue eyes of his, which are now burning even more brightly with shock and betrayal under the searing heat of an Arizona sky. Dilated pupils foolishly attempt to penetrate the remaining fragments of my enraged soul and, as they do, I wonder… is it really too late for him? For us? For a margarita? If there was ever a time to be tanked, this is most definitely it. Although the events unfolding before me are happening in a matter of split seconds, in the vengeance-thirsty sandstorm of my mind time is as still as my stone-cold heart. Water slowly trickles from places I didn't even know were capable of perspiration and two wet boob-shaped orbs of sweat are now visible on my shirt. He was always a breast man, and I wonder whether God might see this last cheap thrill before the bitter end as a final act of kindness? A good deed that will perhaps result in a bit of time shaved off my eternal damnation? Unlikely, given the *number of deadly sins committed: lust, envy, pride, wrath. And now look at me, about to break one of his Ten Commandments too: thou shall not kill.*

Without warning, his bloodied hand lurches towards mine – catching me off guard and causing me to stumble forwards to the edge of nothingness. Maybe we'll both go down together in a blaze of glory? Destined to spend eternity with one another, like he always promised. In this moment, however, as those magical fingers of his fleetingly graze against my own for the very last time, I remember everything. The way he made me feel – the fire, passion, lust – but also the lies, venom, manipulation, and his ability to destroy a life without hesitation or regret. I see him clearly for what he is… a beautiful monster, an apex predator, and king of chaos.

With the lightning-quick reactions of someone who's been burnt by a flame, my hand instinctively jerks away. As I watch that once heart-stopping, knicker-dropping handsome face of his slip into the sun-scorched void, my mouth curls into a slow and satisfied smile. Finally, he's out of our lives and into the afterlife, forever.

As it turns out, the catalyst for unspeakable callousness is actually very simple. A human being's greatest downfall always has been – and always will be – love.

But now… love is dead, and so is the king. So what next?

Long live the fucking queen.

1

Domestic Bliss

It never snows any more in December, does it? Of course that doesn't stop the annual festive tradition of every British tabloid rag madly speculating on the odds of a festive flurry, a bit like that psychic octopus who predicted the World Cup results. Apparently the chances of Cheshire getting a white Christmas this year are 2-1 but, on looking out of my kitchen windows at the clear sky and bright winter sunshine cracking the garden flags, I decide this must be a reference to the county's middle-class cocaine addiction. All down to global warming, I suppose: the weather I mean, not the drug-taking. I like to do my fair share though: of helping the planet, that is… not snorting coke. Once I had an awful reaction to Night Nurse and it very much put me off trying anything harder. Safe to say, the only line I'm happy to participate in is an orderly one at the Marks & Spencer checkout.

Assessing the midwinter mudbath of what, pre-kids, used to be the rather picturesque and pristine girly-garden of my cosy semi-detached home, a nice fluffy layer of snow would certainly help to mask the unkempt slew of deflated footballs, pink plastic tat, and slalom of dog poos I'm yet to psyche myself into clearing up. No, it would seem, in more ways than one, I'm no longer any good at maintaining my lady garden. I can't quite put my finger on the reason why, but I don't feel especially Christmassy this year. Possibly it's down to the unseasonably warm temperatures or, more worryingly, is it because of the strange and unshakeable niggling sensation that's been brewing in my stomach all morning? That said, maybe, just maybe, my festive fretfulness is actually down to the fact that today, along with Jesus, I'm celebrating my birthday. Yep, Cara Stringer, you are now thirty-seven years young. Fuck. Where did the time go? There's a part of me that knows I should be eternally grateful for the happy and healthy existence I've already had on this earthly plain, when so many others haven't had the same luxury. But there's a bigger, more self-centred part that's already obsessively googling 'Botox near me' and 'dry vag… menopause?' At just three short and terrifying years away from the big 4-0, a complete nervous breakdown, along with a bottle of lube, is pending.

After a morning of letting the kids open all two of my cards (which they made themselves), I've come to the realisation that birthdays past thirty, and as a parent, are generally pretty shit. In your twenties, you think age, much like the PTA, will never catch you. Shuddering at my almost unfamiliar reflection in the patio window – first signs of silvery greys nestled amongst my recently 'lobbed' mousy brown hair, tired eyes, with bags large enough to fit the weekly big shop in, staring back – I consider myself well and truly caught. Just another year, I try to reason with myself. It's time to be grateful for being alive and to enjoy the added benefit of today, it being socially acceptable to get hammered at 7am. Amen to that, JC. As I drain the dregs of my fourth mimosa, my perimenopausal pity party is interrupted by a completely different type of festive w(h)ine.

'Why do we *always* have to go to Nannie's for Christmas?!' Benjamin, my seven-year-old, and most vocal about anything and everything these days, especially at the prospect of our impending family outing to my parents' house.

To be fair, on this occasion, his protests are 100% valid. No one enjoys the annual pilgrimage to watch my mother soak up the Christmas spirit (anything 40% proof) or witness my stepdad becoming increasingly less tolerant of her dancing round the kitchen to Mariah Carey in her underwear. Let me tell you, every year without fail, you can cut the air with a knife – sadly, the same can never be said about the cremated turkey.

Regardless of this, off we go on our annual trip to watch this pair of geriatric caged tigers taking chunks out of one another: mainly due to a case of my eldest-child guilt, and because it's cheaper than a family pass to Chester Zoo. With a love–hate relationship to rival Marmite, I live in constant fear of receiving a phone call to say he's caved her head in with the £3 bottle of Chardonnay she carries round like a third child, and has buried her body under the patio. It would be horribly upsetting for all concerned, but I'd get it and probably still provide him with an alibi, and then sign him up to a dating app. As stepdads go, I did quite well.

Taking both my mum, Camilla, and me on when I was a grumpy eight-year-old, he was sturdy, dependable, and emotionally available – a stark contrast to Camilla's inattentive, selfish, and flaky approach to parenting. My 'real' dad or, as Mum liked to call him, 'sperm donor', disappeared without a trace when I was seven – no goodbye, no note, no nothing. Like he dropped off the face of the planet. I'd thought the world of him. Camilla, however, had not. As a child, I'd lose count of the number of arguments they'd have ending in her losing her temper and throwing something at him. I don't blame him for going, but he's never tried to contact me since. That's the bit that hurts the most. Don't get me wrong: I love Camilla, of course I do, she's my mum. The woman selflessly grew me in her womb as though she were a walking petri dish, only to torpedo all 10lb 3oz of me out of her body, ripping her V to her A in the process (something she reminds me of regularly). But two peas in a pod, we are not. Like it or not, we're bonded for life, our fractious relationship held together by an invisible thread of history, emotional blackmail and an inescapable IOU for bringing me into this world. One thing's for sure though: I'll never be like her – apart from 7am drinking – but today is *totally* an exception to the rule. Isn't it?

'Here's the thing, Ben,' I foolishly attempt to reason with the mini face of fury flailing about on the floor before me, 'I don't particularly want to go either but, you know as well as I do, we don't have a choice. Nannie claimed this day as hers thirty-seven years ago. It matters not that God gave his only son to save the world. She gave her only vagina to deliver me, and no one's been allowed to forget it since. So we'll go, open some weird presents she's last-minute-panic-bought on the internet, feed rock-hard poultry to the dog, and smile politely while counting down the time until we can make our escape. Ok?'

'It's not fair! I want to stay here!'

Assessing my unimpressed frowning face (people who claim their wrinkles are laughter lines evidently don't have children) he stops thrashing about on the floor like a trodden-on grass-hopper, opting instead to go for a textbook move straight out of the parent manipulation manual given to all children at birth: sad puppy dog eyes.

'Pleeease!'

Unfortunately for him, I'm a tough crowd. 'Sorry sweetheart,' I faux-sympathise, completely disregarding the pleading baby blues inherited from his father, 'but life's not fair.'

There's a semi-accepting grunt in my general direction, but still no movement.

'Anyway,' I cheerfully remind him, hamstrings straining with the weight of having to deadlift 30kg of limp child off the kitchen floor, 'it won't be *all* bad this year because Auntie Connie's coming too, and you know how much she likes to buy you horribly age-inappropriate presents that'll no doubt either impale or traumatise you!'

Yes, fun old Aunt Connie. I say old… but, annoyingly, my half-sister is only twenty-seven, and has as much of a grasp on responsibility, and impractical gifts likely to result in the loss of an eye, as I do on viral trends that don't require Imodium. On hearing the name of his second-favourite human EVER (his first being some god-awful YouTube star with a voice more irritating than intestinal worms), Ben's face instantly brightens. 'Do you think she's bought me Fortnite?!'

Ah, the eternal optimist. You see, to my son, I am a complete fun-sucking she-devil who has cruelly prohibited his impressionable young mind from being exposed to the violence and horrors of any video game that's not Mario Kart – although don't get me started on the Italian bloke's blatant disregard of the Highway Code. Not a fan of violence, the only head shots I want him taking are selfies with me, so I can cry over them when he's a teenager and hates me. Plus, gaming is all online now, isn't it? You don't know who the hell they're talking to, which is a terrifying prospect to any parent who grew up in the nineties where the dodgiest bloke you came across in a video game was Doctor Robotnik and the aim was collecting gold rings, not dodging paedophile ones.

In a bid to manage his already wildly out of control expectations, I attempt to talk him down. 'Oh, I doubt it, sweetheart. Auntie Connie won't even know what it is. The closest she's got to Fortnite was her two-week stint on *Love Island*, which I'm sure she'll happily tell you all about once she's stopped crying about being dumped for Ariana Grande's personal assistant's UK dog walker. Do Mummy a favour, will you? Go and make sure your little sister hasn't got the Sharpies out again while I find Daddy, and sort my face out.'

Ever hopeful that later in the day he'll be able to fire a virtual crossbow directly through the forehead of one of his school friends, he happily bounds off with a spring in his step and murder in his heart. Boys, young ones and fully grown ones – until my dying day, I will never truly understand them. Speaking of which…

'Dom!' I bellow, from the kitchen. Where *is* he? These days he's harder to track down than the latest PlayStation a week before Christmas Eve. It's pretty hard to lose a guy in a house this size – yet off he sloped to the bathroom, phone in hand, over an hour and a half ago and has been AWOL ever since. Pouring a fresh mimosa, I'm fairly suspicious I know exactly what he's doing on his own upstairs. Nothing, not even the great Lord himself, so it would seem, stops grown men playing with their balls for ninety minutes.

'Dom?!' I call again, plodding up the stairs and making my way across our bedroom towards the Jack-and-Jill bathroom. 'Are you still in here? I need a wee!'

My husband's job as a professional football manager, and the endless hushed calls that go along with it, always grate on me so much more over the holidays. I've never understood the allure of Boxing Day matches and why people choose, of their own free will, to freeze their nips off watching twenty-two blokes running up and down a pitch' over the joy of wearing elasticated trousers and inhaling After Eights.

Stupidly, in my younger days, I always thought my exciting new wife life would be akin to the TV programme *Footballer's Wives,* but with slightly less crushed velvet furniture and fewer fake-tanned babies. That, however, was before I truly understood what the National League was. Think Premier League, but then keep heading down through all the levels until you hit the basement. Once there, open the trapdoor and you'll find Trafford Rovers, the jewel in Manchester's crown… or at least the really small cubic zirconia next to Manchester City and Manchester

United. Sure, those clubs have money, world-class players, and stadiums that don't resemble cow sheds – but they don't have the strategic mastermind, genius tactician, and hot-stuff-to-my-muff Dom Stringer running the show.

Glamorous, it is not. Long hours, shit pay and, without fail, every Christmas Day is dominated by pre-match training and tactics. The rest of the year isn't much better. The kids and I seldom see him, especially lately, and I've spent more time solo-refereeing in soft-play centres, children's birthday parties, petting zoos, and shopping centres than I care to recall. Of course there are some perks: the endless swanky events… that I'm never invited to; match-day catering… if you like cold chips and a warm pint; and, last but not least, inauguration into a special society governed by a sacred rule that football comes above all else in life… including the arrival of it. Yes, while Dom was two goals down, knee deep in a match, I was two midwives up, elbow-deep in my snatch, birthing Ben.

Admittedly, there's a lot I wish I'd known before signing a lifetime contract but, in all truthfulness, there's nothing I'd ever change. Everyone has a calling in life and, while mine was to give up my career to stay at home raising our two beautiful children (and googling reasons for my saw-dusty faff), his is the beautiful game. No, I could never begrudge him his passion, his brilliance, his everything. Naturally, I was unsure when he asked me to effectively become a 1950s housewife. I'd spent so much of my life striving to be independent it felt alien to be giving it all up because I was growing something inside me that felt, well, like an actual alien. But one look at newborn Ben and I knew Dom was right to talk me round. Childcare was so expensive, and he had such big dreams that mine felt mediocre by comparison, so who was I to stand in his way? You see, football is what makes him shine, what fuels that gloriously effervescent charisma of his. After all, it's what attracted me to him in first place – well that, and his bloody gorgeous face. Personality is, of course, of the upmost importance in any relationship, but so is a face you never get tired of sitting on. Tall, brooding, with impeccably carved cheekbones perfectly offset by an ever so slightly crooked nose (a lingering reminder of his own playing days), he possesses just the right balance of playboy pretty and captivatingly craggy.

Speaking of the dapper devil, the bathroom door swings open and out he nonchalantly swaggers, cheeks flushed and spraying himself in a cloud of Hugo Boss cologne. Even after twelve years of marriage, I still like to take a minute and appreciate what a magnificent specimen of a man he truly is. Water from his freshly washed sandy blonde hair trickles freely down his neck, and my eyes can't help but follow as it dances downwards past his clavicle, flirtatiously flowing over the undulating, rock-hard ridges of his annoyingly well-defined-for-forty-one abdominal wall, before being absorbed by a strategically placed *Beauty and the Beast* bath towel – the bulge of what lies beneath perfectly aligned with poor Lumière the Candledick. Out of all the women in the world, to this day I still can't believe he chose me. His imposing six-foot frame combined with intensely serious face would make him an absolute shoe-in for a Viking era shampoo advert. However, born and raised in south London, the most Scandinavian thing about Dom is his ability to construct IKEA flatpack furniture. Which to be fair, is still sexy as hell. Why is it that men age so much better than women? The greys in his stubble are undeniably sexy. The greys in mine, however, make me look like a donkey from the school nativity.

'All ok? You've been ages,' I ask, scuttling past him, hoicking up my dressing gown, and plonking myself on the loo. I often think back to our early dating days and laugh at how refined I tried to be in his presence: once actually leaving his swanky London pad in the dead of night for a number two in the twenty-four-hour McDonalds on Clapham High Street, happy for him to think I was off out for a quarter-pounder rather than expelling something from my body of the same weight and colour. Nowadays, thanks to many years of marriage, and the nearest twenty-four-hour fast-food joint being ten miles away, our boundaries are next to non-existent.

'Yeah, sorry babe,' he says, somewhat flustered, his boy-about-town cockney accent making every term of endearment sound as though he's about to blow the bloody doors off something. 'Fucking Harry's injured again, fucking groin strain! Can you believe it? Physio reckons he's going to be out for six weeks.'

Funnily enough, I can believe it. Harry Jones is twenty-one, handsome, and has more money in his back pocket than the average part-time plumber. My money's on that very prominent groin of his being strained by scoring with an aspiring Instagram model behind the Slug and Lettuce bins. Flushing the chain, I eye Dom suspiciously as he takes one final look at his phone, a broad grin spreading across his face.

'What are you smiling at?' I ask, heading to my dressing table to begin speed-applying mascara. 'Something vulgar on the dads' WhatsApp group again? Honestly, you lot are worse than a bunch of teenage boys!'

He laughs guiltily. 'You got me.' He throws his phone onto the bed and pads across the carpet to wrap his long, strong arms around me. 'How's my birthday girl doing?' he growls seductively into my ear, before nuzzling his stubbly face into my neck. 'I've just realised, I haven't given you your present yet...' The earthy smell of his aftershave washes over me as his Disney towel conveniently drops to the floor, Lumière now replaced by the rampaging Beast.

Giggling at his unrealistic hopefulness, but also wondering what's brought on the sudden friskiness, I'm quick to shoot down his advance. 'Probably for the best that you re-wrap it for now.' I nod my head towards the landing. 'Little eyes and ears are close by. Unless you fancy forking out for the years of childhood therapy required after seeing Daddy playing leap frog with Mummy over the John Lewis ottoman?'

'But I'll do that thing you like,' he smoothly counters, taking a lesson out of Ben's book and attempting those all-too-familiar puppy dog eyes.

'What, put the bin out?' I mock. 'You're on!' Smiling, I turn my back on him – it's lovely to feel wanted, but whose birthday does he think it is? The only sausage I'm planning on eating this morning is one that's grilled and in a bap.

It's at this point, with timing impeccable as ever, and proving my point perfectly, Ben barges into the bedroom, accompanied by his three-year-old hell-raiser of a sister who, to be fair, he has in an impressively firm headlock. While Dom desperately scrambles for his towel, I make a mental note to limit the amount of unsupervised time my eldest has watching *WWE* videos on YouTube. I dash across the room to separate the two of them before Nancy's oxygen levels diminish.

'MUUUM, look! *She's* done a bad thing!' Ben complains, throwing his little sister under the proverbial bus as only a big brother can.

'Benjamin, firstly, you know the drill with Nancy. Snitches get stitches. She'll seek her revenge when you're least expecting it, and then you'll be sorry. Secondly, please can we refrain from physical violence? Today is going to be difficult enough without you getting arrested for GBH. That's grievous brotherly harm in case you're interested.'

Swearing under my breath, I make my way back to my dressing table wondering how it's possible to love your kids implicitly while also fantasising about being a childless free spirit living her best life on a hedonistic party island where her only responsibility is having to try every incredibly potent cocktail on the poolside menu. Slapping on foundation as though I'm plastering a wall, I realise we're most definitely going to be late.

'Oh fucking hell!' Dom swears loudly, and with the enthusiastic gusto of a drunken sailor.

'Language!' I chastise, whipping my head round once more to eyeball the incredibly distracting trio hampering my efforts to leave the house any time this century. Having only just got over the horror of Nancy cheerfully calling a kid at nursery a shitnugget, we most certainly don't need the 'F' bomb added to her repertoire of pre-school profanity. Now free of Hulk Hogan's vice-like grip, curtains of messy blonde hair have parted to reveal her tiny and beautiful little face along with what appears to be a very large and very unfortunately phallic-shaped horn, complete with ejaculating sparkles, scrawled on her forehead.

'FUCK!' I scream, in absolute horror. 'Is that permanent marker?'

'Language, Mummy!' mocks my unhelpful husband.

'I'm a unicorn!' shrieks Nancy, in delighted glee.

'No, you're not!' yells Ben, in condescending disdain, before pointing towards his father's crotch and concluding, 'You're Daddy's extra leg!'

Pulling on his trousers with tears of laughter rolling down his face, Dom leans down to me. 'Merry birthday, babe. At least the unicorn got his happy ending… you got this, yeah?'

'No!' I object. The only thing I've 'got' is a small child with a dodgy dick tattoo on her head, but I'm swiftly interrupted by him swooping in to kiss my half-open and protesting mouth. As the softness of his lips presses into my own, prickles of white hot electricity course through my nervous system – but, instead of experiencing desire, I'm once more struck by the same stomach-lurching pangs of anxiety I've been batting off all morning. As his tongue gently flickers against mine, a disconcerting coolness creeps over my skin, causing the hairs on my neck to stand on end like the hackles of a rabid street dog.

Abruptly pulling away from his embrace, my muddy green eyes lock firmly with the cool and familiar azure of his and, reaching out to touch his cheek, I take a few seconds to examine the contours of his face, scanning for the smallest indication of a problem.

'Why are you being weird?' he asks, avoiding my stare and turning his back as he fishes a tracksuit top from the wardrobe.

'Oh, it's nothing…' I blag, noting the rapid change in his tone and sudden frostiness. 'Just wondering what other joys today has in store for me.'

'Listen Cara Stringer, supermum of the highest order, and protector of public order,' he life-coaches me while once more picking up his phone and absent-mindedly flicking through its contents. 'You're head of the PTA. If anyone can deal with a room full of irritating knobheads, it's you.'

Ain't that the truth, I think as he fondly pats me on the head as though I'm an ageing family pet, and heads off to say a hurried farewell to the kids.

'Love you!' I call behind him as he leaves the room, but, with eyes already glued to the glow of his screen, he's down the stairs and out of the front door without so much as a glance over his shoulder.

Turning back to face my mirror, I take a long hard stare at the woman before me. Her reflection is so very different from how it used to be: ballsy, confident, a woman who was going somewhere other than to the playground and back. Now all I see is an out-of-touch thirty-something mother of two who's treading water, and fighting her constant fear of not being good enough by going out of her way to do anything for anyone. You're overthinking this, Cara, I tell myself, swallowing down a mouthful of uneasiness. You know you are. It's not like last time. We're just super-busy, I try to rationalise. Dom has matches to plan, training sessions to attend, players to buy and sell – I have parent rep meetings, school traffic patrols, and fancy-dress days to organize, in between a mountain of housework and after-school clubs taxi runs. We just need to make more time for one another; keep the romance alive and all that jazz.

Feeling bad for shooting him down just now, I realise all my oversensitive gut is picking up on is marriage guilt – like mum guilt but you substitute enduring soft play with foreplay. The problem is, I conclude, while attempting to wrangle both my eyebrows into position, once you've lived through one marital blow-up, if you continue to look hard enough, traces of explosive will always remain. You see, there's always a taint that lingers in your mind, and paranoia. What was once shiny and fresh, no matter how hard you scrub, will never be the same as it was when it was brand new. A red wine stain on a woollen carpet, an oil mark on a dry-clean-only silk blouse: sure, with enough effort, they'll fade over time to some degree – other people probably will never even notice – but you'll always know it's there. You just have to learn to live with it.

'Stop it!' I shout, serving a warning to both myself and the kids who are trampolining on my bed.

'Right, you lot, down NOW!' I command. 'We do not need the addition of a green stick fracture to make Christmas any more painful than it already is. Ben, downstairs and get your shoes on. Nancy, go get Mummy's nail varnish remover. You are not leaving the house like that, do you understand me?'

Nodding in resigned defeat, she scurries off into the bathroom while I head downstairs to refill my mimosa glass and grab a scouring pad. Stopping once more at the patio windows of our perfect little family home, I look up at what was, only an hour earlier, a calm, blue sky. A chill runs down my spine as ominous as the dark plumes of clouds that now loom on the horizon. Necking my drink as giant droplets of rain begin to lash against the glass, my heart sinks. I was wrong: it looks as though a storm's brewing after all.

2

The Flab Four

'SHOES, COATS, NOW!' An hour later and we're still no closer to leaving. I've come to the conclusion it's easier to evict a child from the depths of your uterus than it is to remove them from a house in a timely manner.

After being shouted at repeatedly by a furious Nancy because of my failure to know who some bloke called Tod was ('Babybel Cheese's daddy, Mummy!'), I've given up attempting to educate her on why we put shoes on the correct feet and have left my incredibly 'free-spirited' three-year-old to do whatever the hell she wants. Life with a daughter, I've discovered, is all about picking your battles, and then choosing the appropriate level of bribery required to win said fight.

The front doorbell rings, sending Ruby, our beyond bonkers cocker spaniel and furry member of the motley crew, into a *Hound of the Baskervilles* barking frenzy.

'Ruby! Shhh, it's Grandad! IT'S GRANDAD!' Shooing her to one side, I climb over the mountain of discarded shoes and Lego strewn ready to skewer the newly barefoot, and open the door to Big Ray.

'Hiya Dad, come in,' I say with an exhausted smile, leaning in to kiss him on the cheek. 'Mind the dog doesn't… ' and with that a blur of red fur flies past his legs and heads straight towards an elderly lady with a walking frame on the opposite side of the street, '…escape.' Every fucking time.

'I'll get her! Happy birthday, love!' he shouts while jogging towards a yapping Ruby and apologising to the petrified pensioner who's just had five years she really couldn't afford to lose knocked off her lifespan.

Back in the kitchen, Ben is still nowhere to be seen. Nancy now has her shoes on her hands, but in some sort of small mercy at least they're on the correct sides.

'Gamdad!' she squeals in delight, standing up and taking a running jump at my dad's crotch as he enters the kitchen with a naughty but delighted-looking dog under his arm. The child can perfectly pronounce the word *brioche*, so I'm almost certain the mispronunciation of her grandfather's name is a strategic bid to melt his heart, secure her place as his favourite, and gain a few quid in the process. Bending down to kiss her head and slip her a fiver, he clocks her new facial tat which only seems to stand out more after half an hour of aggressive scrubbing by a Brillo pad.

'What the bleeding hell is that on her forehead?'

'I know, I know, ok? It's a unicorn…'

'A unicorn? Looks like a gigantic co—'

'…cker spaniels, hey, who'd have them!' I quickly finish, taking Ruby from him.

After packing practically the entire contents of my house into Dad's car, along with a dog and two car-seat-resistant children, and having fielded a multitude of questions regarding the exact numerical value of infinity, all while Dad sat eating a pack of fruit pastilles and telling me a long story about two people I don't know – we're finally ready to go. Slamming the rear passenger door mid-Nancy's request to know what animal you'd get if a pig and ladybird had a baby, I'm a hot, sweating mess, despite the now very cool temperature and howling wind blowing torrential rain right underneath my flapping dress. Climbing into Ray's ageing maroon Saab and strapping on my seatbelt, the thought that this isn't even going to be the hardest part of my day is enough to make me sob.

Pulling out of our drive and past all the brightly coloured lights on Eaton Road, I look back at our gloomy and non-festive sash windows with a pang of guilt that our own efforts aren't up to the same national-grid-buckling standards half the street seems to have adopted this year. Peer pressure from the highly informative neighbourhood WhatsApp group (normally reserved for missing cats, suspicious-looking youths, and inconsiderate dog-foulers) resulted in me panic-buying some fairy lights from Amazon but, as Dom's been too busy of late to even get his penis up (this morning's anomaly aside), their box, much like mine, remains untouched.

My thoughts are interrupted by the ping of my phone. Rummaging through the crumb-laden portable sandpit I call a handbag, I'm ever hopeful that it's Dom texting to say there's been a Christmas miracle and he'll be finishing early. Locating my old iPhone 11 underneath a collection of half-open tampons and receipts from at least three years ago, I peel a tacky Chupa Chup stick from its cracked screen and am momentarily disappointed to see it's sadly not my husband messaging. The good news, however, is that the message is from a WhatsApp group consisting of my three absolute long-term besties: Jac, Debs, and my larger than life first cousin Amy, collectively known as 'The Flab Four'.

Jac: 'Cara, happy birthday babes! And merry Christmas to one and all! Hope you're all having good

ones. Kevin has an STD, and Perry has just told me to
go fuck myself… but joy to the world and all that!'

Ah, Kevin and Perry, otherwise known as Jake and Henry: Jac's
teenage twin sons and my justification for wanting my precious
baby boy to stay small and non-pubescent until I'm well into my
eighties. I want the endless tissues littered around my house to
be filled with snot and nothing else for the foreseeable. Jac's
much more resilient than I am though. Emotionally as hard as
nails, she takes the daily battles, strops and name-calling from
the humans she spawned with a pinch of salt… alongside a shot
of tequila and a slice of lime. Another ping…

Jac: 'BUT I do have some good news…'

Her third message contains no word. Instead it's just a picture
of her hand, complete with one of the biggest engagement rings
I've ever seen, causing me to scream so loudly Ray nearly drives
us straight off the road and into a ditch.

'Jesus, Cara! What's the matter with you?' he yells, gesticulat-
ing wildly at the road and then back to me.

'Jac's engaged – look!' I gush, thrusting the image of her
jewel-encrusted finger under his nose as the car once again
swerves to the opposite side of the road – narrowly missing a
now-not-so-smug Christmas Day jogger.

'About bloody time!' he says sternly, waving an apology to the
runner who returns his gesture with a middle finger salute. 'That
Phil lad should have done right by her years ago, getting her
pregnant out of wedlock like that and not having the common
decency to make an honest woman out of her. Poor girl's been
waiting on that proposal longer than Charles waited to get his
arse on the throne.'

'For the last time, Dad,' I begin to lecture, while typing my response. 'Just because *you* were born in the 1950s, doesn't mean that we're still living in them, ok? She didn't want a shotgun wedding; they were happy as they were and then life just got busy. Don't be such a dinosaur!'

Cara: 'OH MY GOD JAC! CONGRATULATIONS! THIS IS THE BEST NEWS EVER!'

It genuinely is. If ever there was an occasion for using shouty letters and an excessive amount of exclamation marks, this is most certainly it. I could not be happier for my best friend. I love the woman as though she's blood and, if I'm being honest, 99% of the time she's preferable to certain members of my actual family. Her happiness is my happiness. The hardest-working bitch on the block. Most nineteen-year-olds who find themselves unexpectedly up the duff with one baby, never mind two, might be blown completely off course in life, but not this absolute hustler of a queen. One year after the boys were born, she'd swapped the NCT for the GMP – Greater Manchester Police. A total natural with a pair of handcuffs, she stuck two fingers up to everyone who doubted her ability to have it all by quickly rising through the ranks from 'bobby on the beat' to crime-fighting inspector extraordinaire, kicking the arses of many men – criminals and colleagues. Despite us both being the same age, one day, when I grow up, I aspire to be just like her: someone who genuinely has her shit together and doesn't spend her whole life pretending so that others won't judge her many inadequacies. A straight shooter (with opinions, and a taser), but with a gloriously gooey centre, she's the kind of girl everyone needs on speed dial – especially if you're the type of person who finds themselves in questionable legal scenarios. Speaking of which,

I see the words 'Amy is typing…' pop up at the top of my screen and wonder what heartfelt message of love and best wishes my cousin is going to bring to the virtual table…

Amy: 'Yes you slaaag! I'm so fucking happy for us, because you know what this means, right? A MOTHER-CLUCKING HEN PARTY! And if it ain't hot, or full of cock – I'm not coming!

PS… Cara book a bikini wax in now. That married bush of yours will take months to cut back.

PPS. Congrats.'

Ah, there it is. You can always count on Amy to bring the sentiment. It's part of her charm – along with being harder to shake than headlice. Inseparable as kids, we couldn't have been more different if we tried – she was bold, bolshy, and always had particularly poetic panache for profanity. I, on the other hand, was quiet, shy, and determined to learn the theme tune to *The X Files* on my recorder. Despite her traumatising me with her overly graphic insights on the birds and bees, pinning me down to force-feed me my first fag, and chemically burning my scalp while trying to highlight my hair with Domestos, we were as thick as thieves. 100% personality and with zero fucks given about what anyone thinks of her (which is fortunate as most people think she's off her bloody rocker) she's blessed with a superhero ability of being able to say what everyone else is thinking, without being completely ostracised or punched. *Of course* a wedding will be lovely and we're all super-pleased for Jac, but deep down the three of us are probably more excited by the thought of walking down the aisle of an Easyjet flight to somewhere sunny than we are by a trip to the local registry office. Three days of unadulterated, unleashed and under-the-in-fluence hen do fun? Yes please!

This is exactly what I need, I think, as Ben shoots Nancy in the eye with a contraband Nerf gun he's managed to smuggle into the car (a screaming fit of ear-piercing decibels ensues). No kids, no husband – a total break from normal life, responsibility, and school parents texting me 24/7 to ask what the lunch menu is this week. Bliss. The prospect is so tantalizing I can practically feel the sand between my toes and jugs of sangria cascading down my throat. Also, if I know Jac as well as I think I do, which of course is *very,* then I'm pretty sure I know where we'll be going and it's not doing much for my already increasing levels of giddiness…

Jac: 'Thanks Amy, I think… Ok. How do you all feel about… IBIZA?!'

'YES!' I shout, fist-punching the air in delight, causing Ray to curse me once more and my shocked kids temporarily to stop squabbling, 'Oh, I'm going to Ibiza!' Stamping my feet in the car footwell with excitement: it's happening, it's finally happening! A complete Ibiza virgin, I've been waiting most of my adult life to tick this one off my bucket list of things to do before I hit forty – when the chances of me being refused entry at the border for being too old and pathetic will be significantly higher.

Another 'ping' from the group chat:

Debs: 'Oh my God, oh my God, oh my God! CONGRATULATIONS JAC! This is amazing! Sorry, late to the party, I'm ovulating and I've just asked Will to go into the bathroom and have a wank into a cup because I'm one more bout of cystitis away from celibacy. Do you reckon I can just kind of shoot it in afterwards? Oh and Ibiza? Absolutely!'

With Debs being the prolific over-sharer that she is, I feel as though I'm more knowledgeable about Will, and well, his willy, than I am of my own husband's. The Flab Four, all of us friends from our high school days, however, is a safe space for talking all things cervical mucus, vaginal douching and sperm-enabling protein shakes. You name it, I think we've quite possibly heard it, cackled about it, and then sobbed into our pinot grigio over it. I seriously don't envy the pair of them... Debs and Will have had a rough ride on the baby-making journey, and the urinary-tract-infection-inducing friction occurring in the bedroom is now spilling over into their marriage. Sadly, I remember the feeling all too well... Dom and I went through a similar phase of unsexy sex when trying for Nancy, and I honestly think baby-making is the least amount of fun you can have with your clothes off.

Another ping...

Jac: 'You've got this, Debs. Just lay back and think of England... preferably its rugby team. Failing that, Cara – can she borrow one of those syringes that come with Nancy's Calpol?'

Amy: 'As much as I love discussing Will's spunk, can we move onto more pressing matters... IBIZA DATES! My diary is as wide open as Debs' legs are about to be...'

Saying a silent prayer that Jac will reply telling us the wedding will be this coming summer, I mentally calculate how many Christmas calories can realistically be crammed in before the strict healthy eating regime starts on the 1st January (and ends on the 3rd).

Jac: '*Hate to break it you ladies… We're thinking of July… two years from now. SORRY! We've got the extension to do…'*

God damn it! I internally rage. Bloody extensions. They are the bane of middle-age existence. If you're not spending your time saving for them, you're spending your existence cleaning up after the mess from them. Still, at least it gives me time to eat some more Toblerone, write a lengthy childcare instruction manual for my husband, oh and save up… Ibiza is crazy expensive and I'm not exactly flush at the moment, although Dom keeps telling me that's about to change – he's been moving money in and out of the joint account to invest in Bitcoin, which is apparently going to make us millions. As an honorary member of the fun police, I'm sceptical, but if anyone can make something from nothing – it's Dom Stringer.

Amy: '*Jacqueline, we are no longer friends. I hope you reconsider this terrible decision before you lose me forever. Peace out bitches.'*

Jac: '*Just think, the wait will be totally worth it! The ultimate girls' trip where we can leave everything else behind and just go crazy! No work, worrying about the kids, or how to make them… We're going to go all out and live our absolute BEST lives! Trust me…'*

Pulling up outside my parents impressive Cheshire country home, I fling my phone back into my handbag and exhale a long breath. I don't know what's going to feel longer – Christmas dinner at the Carmichael's, or the two-year wait until I get to let my hair down and go nuts in Ibiza.

I instruct both kids to stop showing each other their private parts, and we step out of the car and head towards the broad, stained-glass front door of the eighteenth-century property. 'Come on, the pair of you,' I say, grabbing their hands so they're unable to punch one another. 'Let's see if Nannie's still standing...'

3

No Place Like Home

I'll give it to my mother, she knows how to do Christmas... if it was still 1987, that is. Walking into the grand hallway of my childhood home, lurid red and green foil decorations hang from every inch of the ceiling as though an elf has exploded.

'Connie, darling!' Mum gushes, clearly already too far gone to recognize her eldest daughter, as she ambles her way across the black and white Minton tiles, one slender hand clutching her margarita, the other extended limply towards me as though she's a politician being forced into meeting a commoner constituent. 'It's been too long, sweetheart!' she purrs, while her brightly painted, recently filled, fuchsia lips break into as much of a smile as her botox will physically allow. To be honest, it probably hasn't been long enough. She was round at my house last week, supposedly babysitting, but actually ransacking my artisan gin collection while an unattended Nancy smeared lipstick all over my bedroom wall.

'I'm Cara, Mum,' I correct, leaning in to give her a half-hearted air hug, so as not to accidentally infiltrate her airspace with dermatologically damaging affection. I can't completely blame the booze for her mix up: it's more the fact that she rather foolishly named both daughters with similar-sounding names. Yes, Camilla, Cara and Connie Carmichael. Just call us a low-rent, *slightly* rougher round the edges version of the Kardashians. One of the many benefits of marrying my husband was that I'm now officially a 'Stringer', thank God.

'Yes, yes Cara.' She flaps a dismissive hand in my face, sloshing her drink all over the floor in the process. 'Anyway... *where* are my babies?' She slurs with the enthusiasm of a shit-faced *CBeebies* presenter.

While I'm peeling off my damp coat and hanging it over the polished oak banister, my legs are nearly taken clean out by the speeding ball of kinetic energy that is an over-excited Nancy as she torpedoes past me, her war cry of 'Nunnie!' reverberating off every wall. As Mum briefly drops her emotional forcefield, rather stiffly allowing Nancy to embrace her knee cap for all of four seconds, I debate at what point I'm going to break it to both of them that Camilla's adopted moniker is actually another word for a vagina. Mum claims it was Nancy who chose the name while trying to say 'nannie' in her younger years, but I know for a fact how much she hates any name that might identify her as being an actual pensioner and so fully jumped on board with being joyfully called a twat by a one-year-old. The irony is not lost on me.

'Look Nunnie, I'm a unicorn!' Nancy proudly announces, pointing to her X-rated forehead, a beaming smile spreading from ear to ear.

Eyeing her granddaughter with an air of wariness, Mum bends down to inspect the self-inflicted handiwork. 'Well, look at that... so you are!' She gasps in faux surprise, hands suddenly flying up to her hollow cheekbones, sending Nancy into a euphoric jumping frenzy, clearly ecstatic someone has *finally* appreciated her artistic flair. 'Do you know what a unicorn's favourite food is?' Mum gently whispers in her ear.

'SWEETIES?!' Nancy shrieks back, already twitching in anticipation of pure and refined sugar consumption.

'That's right! I've hidden LOTS around the house. On your marks... get set... fetch!' And with that, Nancy's off at the speed of light; Ben, who already has his Nintendo Switch in hand, is hot on her heels – elbow out ready to karate-chop her to the ground the minute she gets anywhere near anything that looks like a Percy Pig. I glance at my mother with suspicion: the 'fun grandmother' act is not one I've seen her attempt often, or ever, for that matter. Clocking my scepticism, she lets out a little chuckle to herself, 'Oh don't worry, darling. I haven't really hidden any, but they'll be out of the way for hours looking. Drink?' And with that she sashays off towards the kitchen, a flick of her precision-perfect platinum bob as she goes.

'Mum!' I scold, rummaging around in my handbag for a half-eaten mini pack of Tangfastic and a Bear Yoyo I can fling behind a plant pot before World War Three-year-old kicks off. She seriously has NO idea when it comes to parenting.

Walking into the traditional 'Country Living' esque kitchen, a wave of familiarity washes over me. Camilla busies herself doing what she does best, preparing something intoxicating and flammable, as I take a seat at the white shaker-style island. Inhaling the nostalgic scents of overcooked vegetables and singed poultry, I wonder whether she's even remembered to get me a gift? Probably not: it wouldn't be the first time. Two weeks after my 13th birthday, I was gifted with a kitten by means of apology, despite my allergies to cat hair. It was swiftly handed over to a tiny Connie, while I was regifted a packet of Piriton and a cheery book about puberty.

The door swings open and in scuttles Ray, weighed down by the entire contents of his car, along with Ruby who is already on the hunt for mischief and things to do that'll annoy my mum. People say dogs are often an excellent judge of character, and as she makes a beeline for Camilla's Chanel-clad leg, I would say she's got her card well and truly humped.

'DOG! CARA!' Mum shrieks. 'Eugh, I don't understand why she does this?' She shudders in disgust, batting the dog away with a tea towel. She's really not an animal person, nor, in all honesty, a people person, for that matter.

Standing up, I rescue Ruby from the most uptight shag of her life and open up one of the large, anthracite-grey bifold doors – sending her bounding out into the huge oak-tree-adorned garden to chase squirrels and harass the neighbours. Returning to the island, I see a small and neatly wrapped gift box has been positioned next to a pint glass of margarita – a handwritten golden tag displaying the message, 'Happy Birthday Cara, from Cam'. I'm thrown. The sting of one solitary tear burns at my lower lash line. Hurriedly, I blink it back before Mum catches what I know will be a very unwelcome display of emotion. After all, in this household, sentiment goes down as well as alcohol-free wine.

'What?' she says, an indignant expression on her creaseless face. 'You thought I wouldn't commemorate the day you gifted me with another orifice? Darling, you were so large I made the local news, did you know? Now open your present!'

Raising an eyebrow, because unlike her, I'm still able to, I tentatively begin to open the neat little parcel – tugging at the red silk ribbon and peeling the tape away from the glittery paper. I wonder what it could be: earrings, a bracelet, vouchers for all the gin she owes me? Opening the flaps of the box, I quickly come to realise it is none of the above. Confused, I pull out a small white pill bottle and shake it gently – listening to its ominous rattle. Trying to ignore the sound of the children murdering each other over imaginary sweets in the room above me, I look questioningly at my mother, 'Er…?'

'Tablets, darling!' She jumps in before I've had a chance to actually ask. 'For your menopause!' She honestly looks as though she's just gifted me a Gucci handbag, not a pre-emptive farewell salute to my youth. 'But, Mum,' I protest, voice cracking with the squeakiness of a pubescent boy, 'I'm only thirty-seven. I'm not going through the menopause yet!'

'Of course you are, sweetheart! I know the signs,' she says, eyeing me up and down disapprovingly. 'First the metabolism stops, then the face starts to sag… plus you're sweatier than an old cheese sandwich!'

Raising an offended hand to my apparently melty cheese face, I realise arguing my case any further will likely be as productive as a debate with Nancy about the merits of a 7pm bedtime. Ungratefully tossing the pills back into their box, I take a swig of my margarita, involuntarily grimacing at the skewwhiff spirit ratios. Shit, she makes them strong. 'Where did you even get them from?' I ask. 'I thought HRT was prescription only? These look like the dodgy diet pills you get from Amazon.'

'Excuse me! I'll have you know this is the finest and most exclusive hormone medication in the country!' She picks them out of the box and waves them in my face. 'Do you know Auntie Mollie's son?'

'What, Craig the convict?'

'That's unfair, Cara. He only did eighteen months for intention to sell. He was more of a passing guest. Anyway, he's got a new job as a security guard for some big pharmaceutical company…'

'MUM!'

'Shhh darling, let me finish before you get all Judge Moody on me. It's all totally above board. He's made friends with one of the scientists, very clever chap – he was once on *University Challenge*, imagine that? Anyway,' she continues without skipping a beat, 'they've got an arrangement where he makes special batches in the lab, and then Craig is in charge of marketing and distribution. You're very lucky, darling: there are some very hot and hormonal women out there who'd kill to get their hands on these prototypes.'

'These illegal, stolen, untested, unregulated prototypes.'

'Oh Cara, you're too sensible for your own good! Menopause is like childbirth. There's no medal at the end for doing it without drugs, you know?' Oblivious to my eye roll and unwavering respect for the medical profession over a man who used to shit in our paddling pool, 'Trust me, they're going to set your world, and your loins, on fire!' She exclaims, adding in a little hip thrust especially for the cognitive therapy folder of my brain. 'And between you and me,' she leans in closely, whispering in my ear, her hot tequila breath warm on my skin, 'they've given me the sex drive of an irresponsible twenty-year-old. Ray hasn't been able to walk right for a week! Isn't that right, darling?'

My poor red-faced father, who has walked back into the kitchen at the worst possible time, takes one look at my queasy face, turns on his slippered heel and limps back out of the door as fast as his groin strain allows.

'Ew, Mum. TMI!' The absolute horror. 'If you want to take rat poison, that's your prerogative, fill your boots – but I'm not going anywhere near them until I can get them on prescription. Anyway, I'm only sweaty because it's a million degrees in here – any chance you could turn the heating down?'

Sliding the pills back towards me, she heads back to the fridge for more limes and embalming fluid. 'Sorry darling, the only things I like to be frozen are my margaritas, and my forehead.'

4

The Con

An hour later – and with both children relegated to different ends of the house for an incident involving a fire poker and some of Dad's Rennies they wrongly assumed were a packet of Refreshers – there's still no word from Dom, and I'm fuming. In and out, that's what he said. I'm going to have to tell Mum we'll eat without him, otherwise the turkey's going to be tougher than a *Countdown* conundrum.

'Hello!' A cheery sing-song voice, indicating the arrival of my little sister, radiates from the hallway – followed immediately by a cacophony of squeals from my delighted offspring who are now so hyperactive you'd assume they were on acid, not antacids.

Standing up, I take a deep breath and mentally prepare myself to be well and truly 'Connied'. Stealing a quick peek at my reflection in the antique brass mirror above my parents' open coal fireplace, I pointlessly attempt to 'zhuzh' my now incredibly limp hair. Glancing down at the marble mantelpiece, my eyes fix on a photograph of a fresh-faced Con and me as kids, taken on holiday in France. Honestly, parents of today should be held accountable for the crimes committed against fashion back in the day. Matching fluorescent Bermuda shorts and *Ghostbusters* T-shirts: what were they thinking? Picking up the cool silver frame, the memory of that moment edges its way to the front of my mind. Connie's face is beaming, her eyes full of mischief, mouth open mid-highly-infectious cackle. She must have been only about three, four, tops. My face, on the other hand, is like chubby thunder. Chunder, if you will.

'Oh my gosh, I love that picture!' Connie squeals, sneaking up on me from behind and making me jump out of my skin. Younger sibling stealth mode is one of her many life skills. Even as a kid, she'd purposefully wait behind doors and then jump out in an attempt to scare me half to death. She'd get me every single time; I never heard her coming.

'I bet you do,' I say, more coldly than I had initially intended. 'You were mid-lifting my skirt up, thought it was hilarious. The feeling was *not* mutual.' Returning the picture to its Lladró-surrounded home, I turn to face my little sister. 'Hi Con.'

'Happy birthday, big sis! I can't believe you're still mad about that,' she guffaws, throwing open her arms and pulling me in for a suffocating hug. 'Anyway, how was I supposed to know a coach load of French high school boys would park up behind us?' The vibrations of her laughter pulsate through her recently inflated silicone implants, sending tremors of unresolved childhood issues echoing straight towards my heart. Connie's super-tactile. She's always reminded me of our (well, *her*) allergy-inducing childhood cat, Nugget: one minute, happy to wrap herself around you (mainly when wanting something), the next, unex-pectedly swiping you across the face with her claws out. Pulling away from her embrace, I hold her hands in mine and take stock of the sheer breathtaking, and highly annoying, beauty of Connie Carmichael. Raven hair so glossy you could paint a skirting board with it, olive skin that wouldn't be out of place on a

Mediterranean island, and a perfectly toned hour-glass figure that looks as though it's never seen a tub of Pringles ever. With a dazzling white smile and hazel eyes capable of captivating any room she walks into (if you can drag your gaze away from her gravity-defying rack, that is) she truly is a stark contrast to the rest of the Carmichael clan. Connie is my half-sister, but she doesn't look like any of us – not even Ray – so much so my cousin Amy and I have a longstanding wager that Mum actually shagged Mr Hernandez from next-door-but-one, which is why she's incredibly sheepish every time one of us suggests signing up to Ancestry.com.

'Well, don't you look gorgeous?' I gush, knowing full well she doesn't need the compliment, but also not really knowing what else to say to a woman who mainly communicates via the morse code clicks of the selfie shutter on her camera phone. Call it the age difference, or just a generational divide, but we really don't have that much in common – and in all honesty, we never have done. A teenager by the time she could do anything other than cry and fill her nappy, I had no interest in hanging around with a pre-schooler when there were more fun things to be doing like learning the Spice Girls' dance routines and diarising underage drinking at the park in my 'Fun-Fax' organiser. At that age, who wants an annoying little sister following you around? Spying on you, stealing your heather shimmer lipstick, and copying your double denim fashion looks? Plus, there was also that time Ray took us sledging and she shoved me head-first down an icy dog-shit-covered slope because I told her a dolphin would eat her if it was hungry enough. I broke my wrist in two places. Bitch. She was their clear favourite, so of course Ray and Mum took her side, wouldn't hear of it that their precious Connie had a violent streak. That said, much like a fine wine, I thought we'd been getting better with age but, for some reason or another, over the past six months or so there's been an awkward tension that's getting progressively worse. With most things in life, potentially, I'm overthinking it – perhaps it's just because we're at totally different stages in our lives, or maybe it's the fact she thinks Portugal is in Spain. Honestly, it boggles my mind how she managed to scrape a degree before *Love Island* came calling. 'Your dress is beautiful,' I continue, trying to find some common ground. 'Now where can I get me one of those? Please don't tell me it's some young and cool hipster shop that ironically doesn't accommodate people with hips?'

'Thanks, doll!' she giggles, twirling on the spot, in doing so sending cascades of green silk spiralling around her as though she's a swirling lily pad on an ornamental pond. 'Just a little Gucci number I picked up on a recent trip. Three grand for a dress, can you believe it? But you know me: I see something I want and I just *have* to have it!'

Three grand?! Bloody hell, no I can't believe it. The world of Instagram influencing evidently rewards well those who tread its fickle floorboards. I wonder whether I've missed my calling in life? And if it's too late for me to start an account and get a blue tick? That said, what would I talk about? My top ten tips on how to make last-minute World Book Day costumes out of sanitary towels and gaffer tape? Poor Ben never got over his DIY Hedwig get-up. Anyway, I can't even influence my children to tidy their bedrooms, so I stand little chance of making my millions 'mumfluencing'.

'Wow, nice watch too…' I say, eyeing up the incredibly blingy diamond timepiece glittering majestically on her tanned wrist. Surely, she can't be earning enough from talking about her morning makeup routine and teeth whitening gels, to be splashing that sort of cash? It looks as though it cost a small fortune. Perhaps the hunky Spanish boyfriend she supposedly met over the summer (she was very sketchy on the details) bought it for her? Or, going on the dazzling brightness of those diamonds, has she moved on to shagging a disgustingly rich Russian sugar daddy? I wouldn't put anything past her.

'Oh, thanks,' she says coyly, awkwardly dropping her arm so it's out of sight behind her back in a very non-Connie display of bashful modesty. 'Anyway, your dress is...' she attempts to distract, the whirling cogs in her mind practically audible as she searches for a plausible compliment to offer me in return, '...cute!'

'This? Oh, I saw Holly Willoughby wearing it on *This Morning*.'

'It's her M&S range from last year, isn't it?' she condescends, along with accompanying pitying head tilt.

'Maybe,' I stumble, flustered by the insinuation I'm a couture clown who can't even keep up to date with the latest trends. I mean, I am, but I don't need to be told that by a woman ten years younger and ten times cooler than me.

'I love it!' she continues, oblivious that the hole she's digging herself is about to break through to the sandy shores of Bondi Beach. 'Yeah, it reminds me of the dresses Grandma used to wear when we were little!'

'Right, thanks for that.' I cringe, adjusting the creased red and white paisley print tea dress that now, by comparison, is about as a glamorous as a very large and incredibly crumpled tea towel. Despite being the older, wiser, and more well-rounded (in more ways than one) sister, there's something about being in the company of Connie that would give even a Victoria's Secret model a crippling inferiority complex.

'MUMMMY, MUMMY, MUMMY!' I breathe a sigh of relief as Nancy explodes into the room with the whirlwind force of a tornado, interrupting our uncomfortable exchange with perfect timing. 'COME SEE! COME SEE!'

'Calm down, sweetheart.' I attempt to reason with her as she hops up and down on the spot. 'See what?'

'NUNNIE! SHE'S DANCING... WITH HER BOOBIES OUT!'

'Oh shit!' Connie and I say in unison, as Nancy begins to recreate the scene her innocent little brain has just witnessed with a series of highly inappropriate twerking motions.

'Whoa there, Miley Cyrus! How about we watch some YouTube on my phone while Mummy sorts out Nunnie?' my sister suggests, nodding towards the door with an encouraging thumbs up.

Of course it's down to me to sort her out. It's always up to me to sort everyone out. 'For fuck's sake…' I mutter as I head out of the living room and towards the blaring sound of Mariah Carey coming from the kitchen. Just one year – all I very much want for Christmas is just a normal bloody family.

Three o'clock and we're all sat round the dinner table, fully clothed and attempting to gloss over the previous hour's events. Ray, so it would seem, has not got the memo and is reading a very flippant Camilla the riot act about what is acceptable to do in the presence of her grandchildren, and what is not. To be fair to my mother, it could have been worse… By the time I got to her she'd only just started to peel back her jumper. Fortunately, getting her head and two arms stuck in its neck had prevented her from getting as far as her bra. Mum's nips, however, aren't the only ones yet to have made an appearance today: Dom is still AWOL and I'm beginning to get panicky something's happened to him.

'Is that *so-called* husband of yours ever going to grace us with his presence?' Mum slurs. Never his biggest fan, she can hardly hide the look of disdain on her face at even the mention of his name.

Maybe I should I call him? I'm conflicted though. As much as I'm worried, I also don't want to face the wrath of interrupting him while he's busy – he never takes too kindly to it and the end result is I get barked at and he eventually turns up in a foul mood, despite all my best efforts to appease him. No, I'll give him an hour; he can't be far away. God, my head is banging. Rubbing my temples in an attempt to soothe away the early morning mimosa hangover, I realise that a severe lack of hydration is going to have a knock-on effect when it comes to attempting to chew the incinerated turkey Mum has dished out. To make matters worse, a roast dinner, to my children, is a fate worse than no wifi, and the pair of them currently look as though they're being forced to partake in a bushtucker trial.

'Mummy, can't I go on my Switch?' Ben complains, attempting to spear a rock-hard potato with his fork and sending it catapulting through the air and into the middle of the decorative poinsettia table piece.

'No darling, we don't have devices while we're eating, do we?' I lie because, generally speaking, they come as a side accompaniment to most meals in our house.

'But Auntie Connie's on one!' He points a judgemental finger in the direction of my sister who, since the arrival of the very questionable prawn cocktail that I think was mostly made of frozen scampi and vodka, has been glued to her phone.

'Oh, sorry, Benjamino, I'm working. People can't influence themselves, you know!' she says chirpily, before taking a picture of her food and posting it to Instagram. Why do people do that? Who cares? If she's going to influence anyone into eating one of Norfolk's finest sand turkeys, I'd prefer she started with my kids.

'Cara, the bloody dog!' Mum holds her head in her hands at the increase of Ruby's howls coming from the kitchen, an upgrade from the garden after she destroyed twelve of Mum's pot plants. 'Please can you go and shut her up, darling? I can feel a forehead crease coming on!'

'I'll go!' Connie volunteers eagerly as her phone begins to ring. Jumping out of her seat, she excuses herself and swiftly heads out of the dining room to take the call.

After ten very stressful minutes of dealing with the catastrophic fallout of Nancy mistaking a parsnip for a roast potato, I'm ready to draw a line under the Christmas and birthday celebrations–opting to spend the next fifteen years or so in a padded cell with only a box of Quality Street for company. Also, Ruby is still going mad, pushing Camilla's hostessing capabilities to the absolute max. 'I know, I know!' I sigh, standing up from the table and pre-empting her advancing decline into matriarchal madness. 'I'll sort her out.'

Walking into the kitchen, there's no sign of Connie. Cheers Con, I think. She's probably been distracted by something shiny or her stream of Instagram likes. I locate the baying Ruby, who on seeing me immediately stands down from full scale howl mode and contentedly pads straight on over, tail wagging happily. Scooping my phone up off the island worktop, I see there's still no word from Dom. What if he's dead in a ditch somewhere? Should I call the club to see if he has left? Or even arrived in the first place? Hm, that might make me look over-bearing and nagging, though. Opting instead for a passive–aggressive message, I open up WhatsApp and type,

'Hello? Are you alive?! What happened to in and out?!'

Heavy-minded, I return my phone to the island. Picking up a forgotten-about jug of cranberry sauce from the worktop, I steady myself for the next instalment of the worst ever episode of *Come Dine with Me*. Dessert is next, and I'm scared the kids will get pissed on the trifle.

As I head back across the kitchen, a very loud and sudden crashing noise from the pantry sends Ruby into another barking frenzy and me nearly to an early grave. What the hell? Is some-one in there? Could it be an intruder? A peckish one with a penchant for dried goods and cleaning products? Heart in my mouth, I glance around the kitchen looking for signs of a forced entry. Seeing only the small window above the sink slightly ajar, I wonder whether perhaps it's a creature, maybe a squirrel? It would account for Ruby's over-excited barks, and waggy tail. I'd like to think she might be a bit more aggressive if Hannibal Lecter was lurking inside amongst the pasta and bleach. Silently creeping my way over to the pantry, I pause momentarily at its threshold and press my ear against the cool white wood – listening for any signs of a serial killer, or woodland creature. What is that? My brain tries to isolate the faint thudding noise that's audible through the swing door. With Ray in the prime of his life (for a heart attack), and Dom nowhere to be found, I'm struck by the realisation that I'm the only person equipped to deal with this right now. Pulling up my big girl pants (bloody Spanx have rolled down under the weight of too many pigs in blankets), I brandish the sauce jug above my head as though it's a baseball bat and I'm winding up for a home run. Taking a deep breath, and hoping to God it's not a rodent that's going to go straight for my throat, I stealthily push my weight against the door...

I am not prepared. Not in the slightest. The force of the impact hits me square in the chest, knocking me sideways and taking my legs from under me. Confronted by scenes straight out of a nightmare, my brain attempts to send signals to my spinal cord telling me to run, but I'm too paralysed by shock to move. I try to scream but, with lungs rapidly draining of oxygen, all I'm able to do is draw what feels like my final breath. Swathes of delicate green material I'd complimented only hours earlier are hauntingly hitched around her tiny waist... majestic, gravity-defying breasts are exposed as though she's the Venus de Milo on display in the Louvre for all to admire. With her eyes closed and head resting against a 1kg bag of Morrisons self-raising flour, for a change it is she who doesn't hear me coming – oh, but I can hear her... and him. Yes, right there, thrusting away between those long and golden legs of hers, is the biggest fucking rat I've ever seen in my life: my climaxing husband.

Funny, I think to myself just before the red mist of fury descends, in and out... just like he said.

5

Sister Sledge (hammer)

Red, viscous droplets trickle from every visible surface… Assessing the slow motion scenes of destruction before me, it's as though I've opened a gateway to another dimension and found myself in the aftermath of an IED attack. As my brain tries to compute the explosion that's just torn through my very existence, I'm vaguely aware of someone screaming: is it me? Quite possibly. One thing's for sure: it's not Connie, because she's out cold on the floor, courtesy of the surprisingly weighty and now completely empty jug that I've launched at her resulting in the very sticky cranberry sauce horror scene. Normally one to shy away from violence and any form of confrontation, my body appears to be operating entirely on spontaneous jerk reflex. Also, in my defence, I don't think I was actually aiming for her head, but one of her own ginormous jugs. Shit, how many years do you get for womanslaughter, anyway? Amongst the madness of the moment, my brain makes a quick mental note to call Jac, on a newly acquired burner phone of course (my obsession with true crime documentaries already serving me well), in order to discuss my legal options before the kids and I hop on a flight to Mexico. Maybe prison won't be so bad? Thinking about it, it's probably not too much of an adjustment of my actual life now – saggy loungewear, not being able to go the toilet without someone else watching – but with the added benefit of someone else cooking my meals for me.

Before I can plan out my plea deal, Connie groans from the floor. She's still alive, and I'm not entirely sure whether it's a blessing or a curse. Dom, dripping in cranberry back-splatter, immediately rushes to her side like a knight in shining tracksuit bottoms.

'YOU BASTARD!' I scream, lurching towards him, anger-induced autopilot mode now fully activated. In the brief second it takes for my windmilling fists to connect with the rock-solidness of his jawbone, my brain reminds me of a Roald Dahl story I read as a kid about a woman who kills her husband with a frozen leg of lamb, then cooks it up and serves it to the police officers who, without a murder weapon, are unable to prove she's to blame. The perfect crime. I wonder whether I could do the same with the overcooked turkey? Given that its density is on a par with Dwayne 'The Rock' Johnson's thigh muscles, it'd probably be more effective than a lead pipe.

A red-hot searing pain radiates through my fingers, shooting its way into my wrist and all the way up into my elbow. 'OWWW! SHIT!' I scream out, realising my unprepared fists have never actually punched someone before.

'CARA, CARA! STOP!' Dom yells, furiously shoving his treacherous hands into my chest, knocking me off balance.

Wait… what? How dare he touch me or even have the audacity to be angered by *my* actions?! Incensed by his absolute arrogance, I lunge at him again, screeching like a woman possessed, 'Don't you fucking touch me. DON'T YOU EVER TOUCH ME EVER AGAIN!'

This time, easily sidestepping my frantic advance, he manages to grab hold of my flailing arms and restrains me from inflicting any further damage to his face or my scaphoid. 'Just calm down, will you!'

Calm down! Who does he think he's talking to? I'm not a drunk girl in a nightclub who's being removed by the bouncer for having eighteen jägerbombs and bursting into the men's toilets. I've just discovered I'm married to a philandering dickhead who has a preference for sticking his wick in women I've shared a womb with, and he wants me to calm down? Blind with rage, and burning with hatred, I desperately try to wriggle free from his crushing grip.

'What the fuck are you doing?' he yells, like I'm the one in the wrong. 'Look what you've done to your sister.'

Is he actually for real? How is he not on his knees grovelling and begging for forgiveness right now? Why is he more concerned about HER? From nowhere, the crushing realisation he cares more about Connie than he does about me hits like a ton of bricks fresh from the rubble of our utterly ruined relationship. Like a toddler coming down from a sugar rush, my legs crumple beneath me. The sudden increase in weight catches Dom by surprise and he drops me like the sack of old sprouting spuds that I am. Face down on the coolness of the tiled floor, uncontrollable howls of sadness escape from within as the enormity of their betrayal hits home. From my downward – and trodden on – dog position I see a concussed-looking Connie begin to pull herself up into a sitting position. Dazed and confused, she attempts to stuff her boobs back into their cranberry-stained Gucci casing. Even in my overwhelming puddle of sadness, I take a slight moment of joy knowing that no dry cleaner will ever be able to restore the dress to its designer perfection. But then it clicks who has probably paid for the extortionately priced dress... the blingy watch... and the recently inflated knockers. Moving money around? Bitcoin my arse – more like Titcoin. Like a childhood fever the second the Calpol wears off, 40 degrees of red-hot furious heat once again tears its way through my soul and I'm up off the floor with the superhero agility of a crouching tiger, claws out and aiming straight for her jug(s)ular. Connie screams, trying to bat me away, but my extra weight, for the first time in our lives, is finally playing to my advantage. Before I know it, arms, not belonging to Dom, are around my waist and pulling me away from an uncontrollably blubbering Connie. 'No! No! No!' I bray, my outstretched hands, covered in strands of dark glossy hair, trying to claw their way back to her.

'Cara, stop! Stop! PLEASE!' Ray's voice is full of pain as I attempt to fight against the ridiculously strong arms of a seventy-year-old man as he drags me backwards out of the kitchen. Wow, I seriously need to work on my core and upper body strength. It's borderline embarrassing a pensioner is doing me this dirty.

Next on the scene is a wide-eyed and panic-stricken Camilla who has immediately started screeching, 'Connie! CONNIE!' as though she's lost a toddler in ASDA. I wonder how long it's been since I left the table. It feels like hours have passed, but in reality it's been more like minutes. Four, maybe? You get more warning of an approaching nuclear missile that you do of an imploding nuclear family, so it would seem.

The pantry door swings open, and out staggers a cranberry-covered Connie, Dom's arm tightly around her minuscule waist, those bewitching eyes of hers now puffy and connecting only for the briefest of moments with the madness of my own before glancing shamefully down towards the floor.

'Ray! Get some ice, QUICKLY!' my mother demands, taking one look at the red lump developing on my sister's forehead.

'Do not move,' he warns me sternly, as I stagger onto a kitchen stool, head in hands to reduce the waves of nausea rolling up

through my abdomen. Heading over to the freezer, muttering
something under his breath about wishing he had boys, he wraps
some ice in a tea towel and dutifully presents it to Camilla.

'No, you idiot!' she chastises. 'In my glass! I can't drink luke-
warm Chardonnay, can I?'

'Listen, Cara...' Dom begins, protectively pulling my little
sister in towards him with strong arms that once comforted me
when I needed them, that held the tiny bundles of OUR newborn
babies. 'I'm sorry that you've found out this way, ok? It wasn't
meant to happen like this—'

'DADDY!' comes the voice of Nancy who, on hearing the
commotion, has come barrelling into the kitchen to see what all
the fuss is about, shortly followed by Ben, Nintendo Switch in
hand, capitalising on the dinner-time disruptions to up his
screen time.

Oh God, the kids! How could he do this to them? To cheat on
your wife is one thing, but to cheat on your kids is next level
deceitfulness. How am I going to tell them? They idolise their
father, and he's about to rip their whole world in half. I suddenly
think about all the time he's spent away from us; the school plays
he missed, the football matches and baby ballet recitals he was
'too busy' to attend. Well, now I know why, and the fury that
brings bubbles away inside me with the intensity of molten lava
that's threatening to erupt at any second. He doesn't deserve our
beautiful children and the unwavering trust they have in him to
always protect them and have their best interests at heart. No, he
doesn't deserve any of us.

'What happen to Annie Con-Con?' Nancy questions, eyebrow
cocked and suspiciously eyeing up her bedraggled auntie who is
cowering in her father's arms. 'Did she have a bang-bang?'

'Not now, Nancy!' I bellow from my brace position. 'In fact,
both of you listen very carefully,' I instruct with a hushed threatening tone normally only reserved for week four of the school

summer holidays. 'We are going home *right* this minute. Go and get your shoes and coats on now, please—'

'What about Dad? He's only just got here. Is he coming too?' Ben interrupts, completely confuddled by the tension-wrought air.

'You're right, sweetheart,' I concur bitterly while death-staring my husband. 'Daddy has just come, so he's going to stay here for a while, and we are going to leave. GET YOUR THINGS NOW!'

For once in their lives, realising it's probably not the time to mess with Mummy, they both nod in agreement and scurry off to round up their belongings.

'You were saying...' I prompt Dom coldly, as Connie shuffles awkwardly on the spot like a five-year-old desperate for the loo.

'Listen Cara... what can I say?' he begins pathetically.

But before he can stutter out a justification for his abominable actions, my backbone suddenly clicks into place. 'WHAT CAN YOU SAY?!' I holler, with contempt as unadulterated as his adultery. 'Going out on a limb here, but maybe "Sorry I screwed your sister" would be a good place to start?'

'Cara, language!' Mum scolds while locating a wine sleeve in the freezer, presumably for her vino and not Connie's throbbing egg head.

'Oh, fuck off, Camilla!' I'm not in any sort of mood to tolerate the obvious favouritism for her youngest daughter I've been subjected to for as long as I can remember. 'How long?' I direct the question at Connie who has stayed completely mute throughout the entirety of this festive clusterfuck.

'Cara, does it matter?' Dom interjects, stepping between us.

'Yes it does matter Dominic because, after seeing your bare arse thrusting into HER, I'd like to know how long you've been bareface lying to me!' The acidity in my voice causes Connie to flinch as she cowers behind *my husband's* protective stance.

'I... I...' she stammers, staring down at the ground as though she's hoping for it to swallow her whole.

'Cat got your tongue, Con?' I press. 'Or can you not talk because your throat's sore from my husband's penis banging against it? I'm assuming this little Secret Santa wasn't the first escapade? SO HOW DAMN LONG?'

Her towering five-foot-nine frame visibly shrinks as she stumbles for a response, 'About… six…'

'Six weeks?' My fists clench at my sides. 'Are you kidding me? You pair have been sneaking around behind my back for nearly two months?' How could I not have known?

'No…' she whispers, anxiously pulling at the bangles on her wrist while Camilla takes a seat at the island and pours herself yet another stiff drink. 'Six months… actually, possibly closer to seven.'

The room begins to spin. I need to leave, and I need to leave now.

'We wanted to tell you earlier,' Dom begins weakly, 'it's just that everyone thought it better to wait until after Christmas, until after your birthday…' He trails off, sensing the temperature of the room dropping to somewhere below sub-zero.

'I'm sorry? "*Everyone*"?' I repeat the word slowly and precisely. Turning to look at my mother and stepdad, the woman who brought me into the world and the man who took on the job another had already quit, and I'm crushed by a devastating comprehension of treachery. They knew. Of course they did. Their muted reaction now made some sort of sense; why nobody else seems to be questioning what the hell is going on right now, why neither one of my parents has asked why their son-in-law is draped over the wrong sibling, and why Ray is sitting in silence instead of thrashing Dom with his Marks & Spencer slipper for betraying me. Bile rises in my throat as I bolt for the door.

'Cara, wait!' the man I used to call Dad shouts behind me, his voice bruised with anguish. 'We just want what's best for you and the kids. We thought we could make it easier for you.'

Stopping in my tracks, I spin round to face him. 'You want what's best for me? Or did you want what was best for your *real* daughter? How would you feel about a man doing this to her, hey? Would you lay a place for him at the Christmas dinner table and welcome him with open arms?'

All Ray can do is stare at me in shamed silence, mouth opening and closing like a suffocating fish out of water.

'Yeah, that's what I thought,' I conclude sadly, his lack of response cementing our family fate.

'We couldn't win either way, love. It wasn't our place to tell you. They've made their choice,' he croaks, holding back tears.

'And clearly so have you,' I say, voice cracking as my own mascara-tinted tears stream down my cheeks.

'Cara, it's not their fault,' Dom pipes up, apparently locating his own spine – hanging out of his arsehole. 'Me and Connie? It just happened and, once we knew how we felt about each other… well, we came to them for advice because we respected their opinion. We thought they could help us, you know, manage the situation.'

'Respect?' I start cackling manically, the utter ridiculousness of this bad soap opera having completely pushed me over the edge. 'Manage the *situation*? I am not a *situation*; I am your wife! The mother of your children. Where was your respect for me, hey? The woman who gave up everything so that you could live *your* life entirely the way you wanted to? More interested in the balls on the pitch and in your trousers than about me and the kids!'

'Listen, I may have not gone about this the right way… but I'm not entirely to blame here.'

'*Excuse me?*' Have I somehow misheard the utter bullshit flowing out of the mouth that once said, 'I love you', but is now a conduit for hypocrisy, and potentially herpes? 'You think that, for some reason, I'm partially to blame for the fact your moral compass points towards a stripper's pole?' I ask in disbelief.

'When was the last time we had sex, Cara?!' he swipes back angrily, the low blow of the personal attack feeling like a slap to the face. 'When was the last time you ripped my clothes off? Put on some sexy underwear and pounced on me when I got back from work? Told me how much you wanted me, needed me? What did you expect would happen? I have needs!'

If this wasn't so tragic, it'd be hilarious. Maybe this is all just a bad dream, a nightmare that will result in me being irrationally mad at him for dream-cheating on me. Yes, I conclude, it's the only logical explanation. The problem is, I don't seem to be waking up…

'NEEDS!' I explode at his gall. 'You have the needs of a sixteen-year-old boy, Dom! Welcome to being a grown-up, to being married and having children! Has it EVER occurred to you that most days, when you come home from work and are expecting to play hide the sausage, I'm already playing it? With real sausages, trying to fling them in the kids' gobs along with a portion of mashed potatoes and peas? And that, quite frankly, waiting around the house in a racy peekaboo bra just isn't practical when the Amazon man knocks?!'

'Well…' he tries to interrupt my rant, but I'm having none of it.

'Or that, after a day of tantrums, trips to the same fucking park to feed the same fucking ducks, having been pawed for hours by sticky, germy fingers, all while coordinating washing, cleaning, cooking, arse-wiping, and school runs in the pissing rain, that I might, just *might*, not feel like prancing to the door like a 1950s house wife and sucking *you* off?!'

'The pills would have helped with that, darling,' Mum chimes in.

'MOTHER, FOR ONCE CAN YOU SHUT YOUR TRAP BEFORE I RAM SO MANY OF THOSE PILLS DOWN YOUR THROAT YOUR SHITS WILL COME OUT SOUNDING LIKE MARACAS FOR WEEKS!'

'Salut,' she slurs before downing her drink and staggering out of the room to regenerate in a formaldehyde bubble bath.

'Right then, any other business?' I conclude, shakily placing hands on my hips, looking around the room at the remaining participants of the worst game of *Family Fortunes* ever.

'Yes,' Dom says stonily. 'I'm leaving you.'

'Dom,' I say, sadly looking at the complete stranger in front of me. 'No shit, Shercock.'

'Cara, I'm so sorry. Can you forgive me?' Ray begs quietly, his face ashen with regret.

'Sadly not, *Dad*,' I reply frostily, stumbling out of the kitchen without so much as a glance behind me. Uncharacteristically, both kids are waiting by the front door, coats on and bags in hand, terrified expressions on their faces as though they're waiting to be evacuated. With Ruby trotting loyally by my side, I wipe away burning tears as I scoop them into my arms and breathe in the comforting scent of bubble bath and stale dribble.

'Are you ok, Mummy?' Ben asks, the fragility of his voice completely obliterating the struggling dams of my tear ducts.

'Yes, sweetheart, Mummy is just fine. We are just fine. Who wants a service station sarnie and a ton of chocolate?!' I enthuse through my blurry veil of salty water.

'ME!' shouts Nancy excitedly, taking Ruby's lead and once more jumping up and down on the spot. Holding tightly onto the sticky little hands of the only people who truly matter to me, I take a deep breath, compose myself, and stride away from the life I once knew. You've got this, Cara, you've absolutely got this…

TWO YEARS LATER...

6

An Indecent Proposal

'You need a holiday,' Jac informs me, as I finish relaying my morning's horror story over a girly lunch at our favourite Italian restaurant The Cal Zone. Not only did I turn up late for school (in slippers, mismatching ones at that) but I arrived at the gates blissfully unaware it was 'Dress Like a Donkey Day' in aid of the local sanctuary. Needless to say, neither Ben nor Nancy were appropriately clothed and the only person who looked like an ass was me. Making them sacrifice their snack-time chocolate brioches to the charity bake sale, and giving them each a random euro I found in my purse for the collection, I threw them both in through the office doors and cried the whole way home.

'No, I don't,' I tell her, stuffing focaccia into my miserable pie hole. 'What I need is another responsible adult in my household who can co-parent my feral children while I try to hold on to my job, house, and shit.'

It's been two years since my husband ditched me and the kids in favour of a less mundane life with Connie, and in that time things have changed significantly. After granting him the quick

divorce he so desperately wanted, in exchange for me being able
to keep the house and full custody of the kids, things just got
better and better for Dom. In a feat to rival Aladdin and his
magic lamp, he somehow managed to leapfrog the lower-level
football leagues and land his absolute dream job as assistant
manager at Manchester fucking United. This, of course, I'm still
absolutely fuming about. All the years of hard service I put in
when he was at Trafford Rovers and now, after *I've* been relegated, he's playing in the big leagues – reaping the benefits of a
big fat salary, corporate hospitality and travel to places I've actually heard of. Call me a cynic, but that kind of lucky break only
happens in fantasy football. Yes, I smell a rat and I'd happily bet
it being the one between Connie's legs. She must have shagged
him all the way to the top, there's no other logical explanation.
The media, of course, had an absolute field day, especially when
they dug into his private life and discovered his success rate
while 'playing away'. But, naturally, in true Dom Stringer fashion, he won everyone over in a heartbeat, and since he joined the
coaching staff (much to my annoyance) the team has been on a
pretty unbeatable winning streak. And Connie? What comeuppance befell my sister after such heinous acts of treachery? Now
officially with her feet firmly under the WAG table, she has the
life she's always dreamed of: designer handbags, swanky restau-
rants, media attention, and a presenting job on QVC despite
being as wooden as the hand-carved jewellery boxes she's flogging to bored pensioners. As for me? Well, all the universe has
managed to manifest for Cara Carmichael is more baggage than
required to leave the house with a toddler and a part-time job
literally chatting shit for minimal wage as a telemarketer for a
company selling agricultural fertiliser. Abandoned, alone, and
fired from the PTA for getting hammered at a church fundraiser
and vomiting in the font, I'm the perfect recruit for the venge-
ance-seeking *First Wives Club*.

'Babe, come on,' Jac perseveres. 'You've been through hell. The past couple of years have been rough. I get it. But you can't carry on this way – hiding yourself away in awful activewear and drinking cheap gin while howling along to Roxette's 'Must Have Been Love' until you pass out.'

'Hey, that was one time!' I protest, wondering what's wrong with the grey maternity two-piece I'm wearing despite not being pregnant. 'And blown massively out of proportion, may I add.'

'Cara, your neighbour called the police! When they turned up, you were unconscious and propped up on the radiator with a second degree burn to your forehead.'

'I was cold.'

'Sorry I'm late!' Debs announces, rushing in with baby Harriet screaming blue murder from within the confines of her sling – a layer of cottage-cheese-sick visible on my friend's very expensive-looking V-neck cashmere jumper. Plonking herself down beside Jac in the corner booth we religiously occupy every second Thursday of the month, the 'Bitches of Eastwick', as Dom so delightfully calls us, are complete. With her normally exquisitely highlighted blonde hair haphazardly scrunched up into a mum bun, dark circles to match her roots frame exhausted and blood-shot eyes. She looks as though she hasn't slept in about three months, which coincidentally is exactly how old Harriet is.

Feeling as though now isn't a good time to remind her of how desperate she was to be in the knackered mums club, I opt for sympathy, remembering only too well the bone-aching and soul-breaking tiredness of early motherhood. 'She's still not going through the night then?' I ask, arms outstretched and ready to take a red-faced ASBO baby from her so she can wet-wipe the curdled crud from her cleavage.

'Oh, she goes through the night all right,' Debs replies bitterly, passing her over to me without a moment of hesitation. 'With ear-piercing screams that could wake the dead but not my husband, so it would seem. Do you know, he actually went to high-five me this morning on account of "*everyone*" getting a full eight hours in. "Er, no, dickhead. *You* got eight hours. I got my nips chewed off every 45 minutes while you snored so loudly I contemplated smothering you with a pillow." Anyway, what did I miss? Apart from carbs,' she says, leaning over the table to take a chunk of bread.

'Actually, perfect timing, Debs,' Jac jumps in, rubbing her hands together in glee. 'We were just about to proceed with operation—'

'HEN PARTY!' roars Amy, jumping out of her chair and whooping with delight, and gaining our party some fairly unfriendly stares from a group on the next table.

'No!' I shout at the three of them, nipping their excitement in the bud with the ferociousness of a ravenous Harriet. 'I've already told you, I can't—'

'You're right, you have already told me,' Jac confirms, signalling for Amy to sit down and for the waiter to come and take a much needed drinks order. 'But you've given me bullshit reasons that I'm, quite frankly, not accepting.'

'They aren't bullshit!' I whinge, knowing full well they 100% are. 'One: post-divorce, I can't even afford new bras, never mind a trip to one of the most expensive party islands on the planet. Two: I have no one to look after the kids, and I'm no way begging Dom to take them. I'd rather have raging thrush and knitting needles for fingers. Three: I'm just not emotionally ready yet.'

Looking at their sceptical faces, I realise this is going to be an uphill battle that, despite my fondness for activewear, I'm not sure I have the cardiovascular ability to win.

'Firstly,' Debs begins, taking a windmilling small child out of my arms and wrestling her onto a boob. 'If I can leave *this* behind for four days – getting on a plane with leaky tits and bits, know-ing that Will, of all people, is in charge of keeping her alive – then you can leave behind your arse-print on the sofa.'

To be fair, this is a semi-valid point. The last time Will was solely responsible for Harriet, he couldn't find the expressed milk Debs had left in the fridge, so instead gave her squirty cream from a can.

'Secondly,' Amy says after placing her order of an extra strong Bloody Mary. 'My mum and dad will have the kids for you at the farm, so that's your non-negotiable childcare sorted.'

Oh God. My heart drops at the mention of Uncle Geoff (mum's brother) and Aunt Sarah. Whether it was nature or nurture, there's a reason why my cousin turned out the way she did and, in all honesty, I'd feel happier booking my kids in for a long weekend at Broadmoor Hospital. That said, it's not like I can leave them with my own parents and, with that realisation, a pang of sadness catches me right in the feels. Two years after 'the incident', and the Chernobyl-esque fallout caused by my parents' complicity seems as irreparable now as it did then.

'Yeah, I'm not so sure about that, Amy,' I say, trying not to sound ungrateful. 'As much as I'm sure Nancy would love to drive a tractor unsupervised around fourteen acres AGAIN, while Ben's forced to stick his arm up a cow's arse, I think I'm going to pass.'

'I can't believe you're still mad about that.' Amy tuts in bewil-derment. 'It was character-building for Ben. And as for Nance? A total natural behind the wheel, that kid's going places.'

'Amy, she was practically on the southbound carriage of the M6. She was nearly going to Birmingham!'

'Oh shush. Dad was watching, with his good eye, it was all good. Anyway, Siri will be there and you know how much the kids love being together.' This pulls at my heart strings, because

Nancy does love Siri, Amy's six-year-old daughter, and yes, she is named after Apple's voice-controlled personal assistant, which I'm hopeful is because she's a wise and knowledgeable soul, not because Amy thinks it's a hoot to shout 'Hey Siri!' at her in public. 'Yeah, it's a shame her dad's tied up that weekend.' Amy casually runs tattooed fingers through her (currently violet) under-shaved pixie cut. 'But, you know, his schedule is crazy busy at the moment, what with filming in LA and the new movie coming out in a couple of months.'

'Ah, your international man of mystery.' Deb probes playfully. 'I see you're *still* not prepared to spill the beans on who he is?'

Leaning in across the table, Amy's face clouds with seriousness. 'You know I'm not at liberty to share that information with you,' she whispers as her eyes dart shiftily around the badly named pizza restaurant in Didsbury as though she's expecting to be silenced by a deadly assassin instead of the non-disclosure agreement she supposedly signed. Yes, the identity of Siri's father has been shrouded in secrecy ever since her conception – with Amy proclaiming she met the Hollywood megastar while he was visiting the Arlington estate where she works as gamekeeper. Initially it sounded as though it had all the hallmarks of a great romantic period drama, something on a par with *Lady Chatterley's Lover*... A rich and successful movie star meets quirky shotgun-toting girl. Judging by his previous conquests (and current wife) he seems unlikely to fall for our Angling Times subscribing heroine's charm. However, with pheromones and the smell of cow dung heavy in the air, one thing leads to another and, with the safety clearly not on his weapon, the rest is highly secretive history. Now, it's not that we don't believe Amy – it *could* have happened – it's just that my cousin is notorious for a few things in life: being able to dismantle and reassemble a hunting rifle in forty seconds, hot-wiring a tractor in thirty, and telling a great yarn. Plus Siri happens to bear a

'We're not here for kind eyes, ladies,' Amy reminds everyone. 'We're here for something phallic-shaped that doesn't require batteries. Cara, stop fixating on whether you think the kids will like him and just concentrate on whether your vag will. You've been with Dom for pretty much all of your shaggable life. Didn't you ever wonder what it might be like to bonk someone else?'

'No, not really,' I lie, not wanting to tell them about the weird sex dream I once had about Bill Clinton. 'Dom was always enough for me.'

'God, you're so vanilla,' she replies with contempt. '*But* we're about to change that because, as well as Fumble, I've also signed you up to Plenty of Dicks and snatch.com, just in case you're over mankind and are looking for a little something different in life,' she explains with a knowing wink, before stealing my phone and taking matters into her own hands.

'Seriously, Amy, I'm not ready for this!' I insist, trying to snatch it back as the mere thought of having to dip my non-manicured toes back into the dating pool fills me with stomach-curdling dread. My first, and last, attempt was about eighteen months ago when Jac convinced me to go on a blind date with her mate Graham. Completely out of my comfort zone, and totally not ready, I nervously downed five double G&Ts before-hand and was so tanked by the time he arrived I vomited on my feet then cried on the waiter to drive me home.

'Jackpot!' my cousin suddenly announces with an Ali-G-style finger flick. 'Hello David! He's forty-two, looking for love, open to kids, is a fellow dog owner, and would like someone to share his interests of gardening, fine food, and… threesomes.'

'But I don't want a threesome. I don't even want a twosome!' I shout a little too loudly, causing a group of nearby mums to huffily pack up their pots of organic green slime and put on their trendy flannel shackets. 'Give me the bloody phone!'

'Ok, ok, here you go. Don't get your flaps in a twist!' Amy says, handing it over. 'Oh, and I swiped left for him – you need a man with ambition in your life.'

'Oh my God, Amy! Is left good or bad?! Did I buy him?' I'm sweating profusely and staring down at a balding forty-odd year-old man holding a chihuahua and a riding crop. I want to be sick in my mouth. My phone suddenly vibrates in my hand. 'Ahhh, he's just messaged me!' I shout, throwing it across the table in fright. 'Did he see me?' All three of my friends are now beside themselves laughing, Debs in particular has gone a funny shade of maroon and I'm particularly worried the raucousness of her cackles might result in a pelvic prolapse, or worse, her waking up a now peacefully sleeping Harriet.

'It's not funny! I protest, hiding behind a menu just in case David is watching me with more than just his riding crop in hand.

'Cara, calm yourself.' Jac steps in before hyperventilation takes me over, passing the device back into my clammy hands. 'No, he cannot see you, and no, you have not won him in an auction. This is not eBae, ok?'

Nodding, I cautiously open David's message. 'Oh my God!' I scream again, once more sending the phone flying across the table. 'He sent me a dick pic!'

'Ooh, I wanna see!' Amy insists, grabbing the phone and scrutinising his scrotum with the thoroughness of a tax inspector. 'Huh, he needs better lighting and a filter. Rookie mistake.'

'For sure,' agrees Debs, who is now also squinting at the screen. 'It looks like those mushroom sweets you get at the cinema pick-and-mix stand.'

'Don't let that put you off though, Cara,' Amy advises, fighting back tears of laughter, 'because he might actually be a really fun-guy.'

'Amy!' Debs reproaches her. 'That joke was in such spore taste.'

This, of course, finishes both of them off completely as they titter away into their tiramisus like a pair of naughty teenagers.

'Right,' I say, turning to Jac. 'So it's NOT going to be David. Can I swipe again, do I get another turn?'

'Yes babe, you get another turn,' she says, with an encouraging squeeze of my hand, 'go for it.'

Before I get a chance, however, the ping of a news notification arriving on my phone stops my swiping finger dead in its tracks.

As all of the colour drains from my face, Jac is first to leap into action, 'Cara, are you ok? What is it? Who's dead?'

Barely able to arrange the assortment of vowels and consonants before me into a comprehendable sentence, my disbelieving eyes reread the celebrity gossip headline in a desperate bid to try and make sense of it. No, a person hasn't died, as such, just the last remaining fragment of hope I'd hidden within the remaining horcrux of my shattered soul. 'He shoots, he scores…' I mumble out loud to the girls. 'Dominic Stringer and Connie Carmichael announce surprise Parisian engagement…'

'FUCK OFF!' screams Amy, loud enough for the space station to hear.

'Oh my God,' sighs Debs, head in hands, just as Harriet wakes up and starts to wail. It occurs to me that if we weren't in public, I might very well be joining her.

'Just stay calm, Cara,' Jac instructs, reaching for her phone. 'It might not be true. Let me check her Instagram.'

One step ahead, with shaking hands, I've already opened the app and within seconds found my way onto her selfie-saturated grid. It is here that I'm faced with my worst nightmare. It wasn't lust, or a badly judged midlife crisis… it was love. There at the base of the Eiffel Tower, in the lush and grassy surrounds of the Parc du Champ de Mars, two doe-eyed lovers stare back at me in smug, overjoyed unison as Connie holds her sparkling ring finger up to the camera in delight.

'The brazenness!' Debs spits in absolute disgust while trying to battle a dummy into the mouth of what used to be a baby but has now been replaced by a furious, and furless, spitting sphynx cat.

'The audacity!' seethes Jac, wrapping her arms tightly around me, either in empathy or pre-empting my need for restraint.

'The bloody size of that ring!' gasps Amy, eyes glued to her own phone, not quite reading the mood of the room. 'It's about the same size as her left tit! Not the right one: the price you pay for bargain-basement cosmetic surgery in Turkey.'

'The hashtag…' I say, in shocked disbelief, having scrolled down to read the solitary word next to a handful of wedding-related emojis. Tears burn in my eyes, my body starts to convulse, my bladder threatens to gives way… and just before dissolving into a complete puddle of psychotic hysteria, with my last controlled breath I manage to shout out the blended moniker my sister has chosen to mark the occasion:'#CONDOM!'

There's a brief moment of stunned silence amongst my three best friends before it begins: shrieks of uncontrollable laughter so guttural, so raucous, so glorious, I don't think we're ever going to be able to stop.

7

Emotional Baggage

Perhaps this is the calm before the storm. The girls couldn't understand my calmness, or acceptance of Connie and Dom's impending nuptials, and as a result have been checking in regularly to make sure I've not got my head inside of the oven. Of course I haven't. I'd have to clean it first, and it's far too much effort. No, locking myself away with Celine Dion and a bottle Aldi own-label gin feels like a much more effective way of not dealing with my problems. The root cause of my muted reaction, I feel, lies with the fact I'm just not surprised by anything Connie and Dom do anymore – they've made me as numb on the inside as my mother's fillers have rendered her on the outside. Every night since their announcement, I've lain in bed, both children's sweaty bodies clinging to me like loving limpets, awaiting the arrival of panic attacks and waves of tears. Nothing comes. Of course, I've tried to keep as much as possible from the kids, but it's been hard to hide the fact Mummy's been a total mess. There's been lots of crying over 'onions', 'sad things on the television', 'stubbed toes' and a 'missed bin day' (they were genuine tears: it was the collection during last year's festive period and I was landed with the overflowing recycling bin for the best part of a month).

I refused to tell them about the engagement. It wasn't my job. If anyone was going to further break their hearts, it could be Dom. It went pretty much how I expected it would. Having not bothered to see them in over a month, he decided to buy their affections with an all-expenses mega trip to London – sightseeing, shopping, shows (putting my recent trip to the zoo, AKA Pets At Home to look at the rabbits, to shame) – before dropping the bombshell that Mummy was being replaced by their auntie. Talk about a mind fuck. Ben, impervious to his father's literal guilt trip, didn't take the news well. Having erupted into a ball of tweenage fury, he's refused to speak with the other 50% of his DNA ever since. Nancy, on the other hand, as fickle as a hungry cat, accepted the new arrangement on the condition of a trip to the Disney store and consumption of a Happy Meal. The air was blue when he dropped them home. A stand-off between father and son over Ben's apparent rudeness towards Connie (which I was, of course, delighted by) led to Dom's pointless threats of grounding him and taking away his Nintendo Switch, unless he apologised to her. A tricky approach to enforce when a) you don't live with said child, and b) Mummy promised him a tenner if he acted like a little git.

Out of the two kids, I was thoroughly expecting Ben to be the one who leaned more towards his father's side – lads lads lads and all that – but credit to the only reliable man now left in my life, his allegiance to the woman who shat herself in a room full of strangers while bringing him into the world has not wavered. He knows that I'm sad, and that Dom did that. In fact, Dom made us all sad, and because of that he seemingly has a rather large axe to grind.

'I hate him!' Ben had cried into my hair that evening. 'I wish he was dead!'

With a small part of me also wishing the same, I had to seriously dig deep within the realms of better parenting to try to convince him it was just his emotions talking and that one day he'd feel differently about his father. 'Oh sweetheart, no you don't!' I tried to reason. 'Sometimes grown-ups make mistakes or do things that don't make sense, but it doesn't mean Daddy loves you any less. None of this is your fault, ok?'

'Is it yours, Mum?' he asked quietly, through snot and salty tears. 'Because I heard Dad tell Auntie Connie that you were boring in bed. Did you not let him play in his room?'

'Oh darling,' I replied, with the biggest, fakest, smile plastered on my face. 'Of course I did. It's just, unfortunately, Daddy preferred playing in other people's bedrooms.'

Snapping out of the past and into the present, I realise I'm faced with a far greater challenge than adapting to a life of loneliness and unsolicited dick picks: what the heck does a thirty-nine-year-old mother of two wear to Ibiza? Sat on the floor surrounded by piles of clothes that look as though they could have come straight from the wardrobe of a deceased pensioner, I'm beginning to think my fashion sense is more tragic than my love life, which is saying something. Wondering whether googling, 'What do cool people wear to go clubbing?' automatically classifies me as chronically uncool, I flip open my laptop and log onto ASOS to see what inspiration can be gleaned from the youth of today.

A month has passed since agreeing to a vacation I'm potentially twenty years too old for, along with 20kgs too heavy for and, with our flight leaving the day after tomorrow, I'm feeling massively underprepared. Naturally, I haven't lost the two dress sizes I'd intended to – despite chugging back weight loss drinks and doing ten sit ups a day. I'm now questioning whether the two 'healthy' snacks the shake company advised eating as 'supplements' should have involved sausage rolls and pain au

chocolates? As the first part of the plan didn't quite come to frui-
tion, I also haven't got round to my much needed spray tan or
bikini wax either. Not particularly keen on the thought of getting
my wobbly hairy bits out in front of a total stranger, it looks as
though I'll be going to Ibiza pastier than an uncooked version of
my favourite snacks, complete with pubes stuck in them. On the
plus side, at least most of my gigantic bush is hidden by my still
touching thighs.

'What the fuck are they?' I question my computer as a pair of
dayglow yellow cycling shorts, minus the crotch, pop up on my
screen. Jesus wept, my growler needs caging, not liberating.
Think of all the things that could fall out? At my age it could be
anything from an ill-fitting tampon to a vital pelvic organ.
Taking a picture of the offending article, I send it to the 'Flab
Four' along with an ASOS-related SOS.

Cara: 'HELP! I don't understand fashion!'

Jac is first to reply.

Jac: Step away from the fast fashion, babe. It wasn't
designed for people like us. PS – great for incontinence
though, just sneeze and go!'

Amy is next to jump in on the action and instead of construct-
ing actual words of encouragement, has included a link for me
to click which, foolishly, I do. Finding myself surfing the six-man
tent selection at Go Outdoors, I construct an extremely polite
and intellectually superior response to the cruel jibe that only
she could get away with.

Cara: 'Fuck off, Amy!'

Tossing my phone aside, I return to mindlessly scrolling endless rows of kidney-chilling crop tops, candida-inducing hot pants, and 'Mom' jeans that ironically only look good on people who've never birthed children. Why do they have so many holes in them too? If I'm spending surplus of £50 on a pair of jeans, call me old-fashioned, but I'd like them not to be missing 50% of the material.

Returning to the task of panic packing, I'm mid-perusing a collection of sensible skirts, bingo-wing-covering blouses and midriff-covering swimming costumes when suddenly, from nowhere, I'm struck by a massive case of the 'fuck-its'. There's no way any of the blokes who keep sending me the aubergine emoji on Fumble would want to take me out for Greek food wearing Mrs Doubtfire's summer wardrobe, is there! Instructing Alexa to play Rick James' 'Superfreak', I jump to my feet, crazed determination filling my eyes, and hoof all my crappy clothes into the corner of the room. Dancing across the bedroom in my pants and bra, I locate my handbag and extract an already bursting-at-the-seams credit card from my purse. Call it anger at letting myself fall into a pit of self-destructive despair over a man who doesn't give a shit about me, or just the liberating feeling of being dangerously close the edge, but within seconds I've reopened the laptop and I'm throwing the most completely age-inappropriate, non-mumsy glittery, crotchless, and arse-skimming outfits I can find into my basket. What is it the kids say: YOLO? You only live once. Bullshit. I'm going to behave like I've lived once, died once, and have been fortunate enough to be resurrected with the sole purpose of going crazy and letting my hair down while wearing Lycra, sequins that chafe, and, in all likelihood, underwear up to my armpits. Ignited by the epiphanic realisation I'm still a fully-functioning, red-blooded woman with needs and time (kind of) on her side, I make the decision to put Connie and

Dom out of my mind, for four days at least, and concentrate purely on me. Perhaps a bit of sun, sea, and – dare I say it? – sex is exactly what I need in my life right now. Fuck it, fuck it, fuck it, I think to myself, heading into the bathroom to locate a five-year-old bottle of fake tan, what's the worst that could happen?

8

Flying the Coop

It's 4.30am, the girls will be here at any minute in the airport taxi, and it's just struck me what a monumentally bad idea this is. One: I'm so streaky I look as though you could whack me in a white roll and serve me at a truck stop. Who knew fake tan has a use-by date? Two: I've been apart from the kids for less than nine hours and I'm already fighting the urge to get back in the car and rescue them. One of the most fascinating elements of motherhood, I've discovered, is the constant internal battle between loving your kids to a point of smothering, and wanting to ditch them on a street corner if it means a weekend away and a lie in. That said, as much as I look forward to time on my own, the reality is always a completely different matter. I'm not great at leaving them, never have been. It always astounded me how Dom could flounce out of the door to go off on one of his many golfing jollies, without a care in the world, whereas I'd go to the pub for three hours with the girls and be calling home every thirty minutes, demanding to see proof of life, and bowel movements. A mother's burden, I suppose: we're natural born warriors, and worriers. Last night's conversation with Nancy is not helping my pre-jetting-away jitters either. 'But Mummy, are you coming back?' she wailed, gripping onto my leg with the ferocity of a provoked octopus.

'Oh sweetheart, why would you ask that?' I questioned, guessing the answer, as she burrowed her head into my crotch as though attempting to tunnel back into the protective safety of my womb.

'Because when Daddy left to go to work that time, he didn't come back to live with us.'

To be fair, it's a valid point, and despite my previous attempts at 'mumsplaining' the complexity of the situation, she's still understandably, like all of us, incredibly anxious about the prospect of further abandonment.

'Of course I'll come back darling!' I attempted to reassure her, bending over to give a squeezy hug so tight I was slightly worried I'd broken one of her tiny little ribs. 'Mummy will stay with you forever!'

'You can't stay with me *forever*, silly!' she giggled, removing her head from my nether regions to stare up at me with those baby seal eyes of hers. 'You're old, so you'll die soon!'

Bringing me nicely to why I'm panic-writing a post-Dom last will and testament on My Little Pony note paper at the crack of dawn while simultaneously sobbing over the thousands of baby pictures clogging up my iCloud storage. I'm not sure Rainbow Dash brings any legally binding qualities to the proceedings but at least, if I die on the plane, I'll know my collection of David Duchovony posters can be spread out evenly between my unappreciative kids. The reminder of the fact I'll imminently be hurtling through the sky at 500 miles per hour, sends my stomach lurching and my legs bolting (equally as fast) towards the sink to retch up last night's not-overly-well-thought-out pre-holiday tinned Piña Colada. My grandad always used to say, 'If God had wanted us to fly, he'd have given us wings', and I highly doubt he meant the sanitary towel kind. It'll be fine, it will be FINE, I try to convince my spiralling mind as I swill out the basin and wipe my mouth on a dodgy-smelling tea towel. Yes, I'm more likely to die in Ibiza of alcohol poisoning than at 40,000 feet, I rationalise – especially if my cousin has anything to do with it.

Strapping on my espadrilles and running through a last-minute check list of packing essentials, I still can't actually believe this day is finally here. Even long before Jac got engaged, back in a time when I still had a husband, an ability to walk in heels, and tits that didn't completely change the definition of 'ankle-grazers', we'd fantasise about what our trip to Ibiza would be like. The White Island – party capital of the world and hedonistic musical must for anyone looking to worship at the temple of electric dance music – has always been at the very top of our bucket list of things to do before we got too old. Back in our Church of England all girls' high school days, Jac and I were obsessed. Our desire to dance from dusk until dawn, in highly inappropriate fluorescent outfits, always far outweighed the importance of our religious education lessons on how to be virtuous and holy. In fact, I vividly remember us both getting a week's worth of detentions for insisting that God was not a supernatural being and source of human morality, but a DJ. The argument was further backed by an impromptu a capella version of the Faithless club classic, which nearly finished eighty-five-year-old Reverend Anne right off. It was all Jac's idea, of course… it always was. If she wasn't making DIY glowsticks in the science labs, or pole-dancing against the netball posts, she was snogging the face off Mr LaRue (the twenty-three-year-old French teacher) round the back of the bike sheds. With very little respect for rules or authority, if you'd told me back then she'd make a career out of law enforcement, I would have choked on my illegally procured bottle of Smirnoff Ice. Post-A-levels, we were all set for a Teletext £250, one-star accommodation, pilgrimage to Eivissa, when a drunken quickie in the Waterstones toilets with her on/off boyfriend Phil Harris made it very clear Jac should have taken less of an interest in extra-curricular foreign languages, and paid more attention in biology. Poor Jac went from wild child to with child and up the duff with not one, but two babies in about six seconds.

Just like that, our party dreams, much like Jac's abdominal wall, were obliterated. Sure, I could have gone without her, but it wouldn't have been the same. It was an expedition we needed to take together: the two amigos. Credit where credit is due: against all odds, Jac and Phil made it work. Phil the chilled yin to her now (disappointingly) far less crazy yang, they complement each other perfectly and are absolute couple goals. I used to wonder why they didn't get married early doors, until I realised they were both so comfortable in their relationship that they didn't need the reassurance of a metal ring or a piece of paper to make what they had official. They had love and, as The Beatles once clarified, it is indeed all you need… well that and a banging sex life. Honestly, I don't know how the pair of them find the energy, or the natural lubrication. Anyway, here we are, finally fulfilling our destiny as two nearly middle-aged women, about to head off on the trip of a lifetime, complete with Fit Flops, iron-reinforced swimmers, and an extensive first-aid kit. No, it might not be as rock-and-roll as it could have been twenty years ago, and yes there's a high probability we'll mostly spend our time complaining about the drinks being too expensive, the clubs being too loud, and consoling drunk teenagers in the toilets who've lost their shoes, but finally… it's our time. As the taxi's headlights shine through the kitchen window, I take a deep breath, grab my keys and open the door. Ok, here we go, Cara. No going back now.

'I want to go back!'

'Well we're not going back, so stop trying to get out of the bloody cab will you!' Jac yells, taking a tough love approach to Debs' existential childcare crisis.

'She's not ready to be left. I'm not ready to leave her! She's too small! What if she dies?' Sobbing, she lunges for the door handles of our taxi but is swiftly intercepted by a quick thinking Jac, who takes off her own seatbelt and sits on her.

'Debs, look at me… Harriet's not going to die, ok?' I begin, in a bid to prevent both of my friends from tumbling out onto the M56 at 70 miles per hour. 'Will has totally got this. It won't be like the time he accidentally left the dog outside Tesco for five hours. Plus, your mum's coming, isn't she?'

Debs nods in defeated resignation from somewhere beneath Jac's impressive 'mum of boys' WrestleMania body slam.

'There you go then! The baby will be safe, there's nothing to worry about. Just relax, take some deep breaths and enjoy your childfree time with a little help from the car bar – ok?'

As her fraught body visibly relaxes underneath Jac's athletically muscular physique, I fish a gin tinny out of the cool bag, crack it open, locate her mouth and force-feed it down her throat as though I'm prepping her to become foie gras.

'Dave! Can you get it up a bit more, mate? I need to feel it deep inside of me!' Oblivious to the backseat drama, Amy is leaning over the front seat of the minivan and, without the permission of the driver, is fiddling with the poor bloke's knob.

'Amy, leave the guy's radio alone. It's 4.45am in Manchester, not Manumission. Literally no one apart from you wants to listen to Pete Tong's club classics at 140 decibels,' Jac complains, now back in her own seat and helping herself to an early morning Porn Star Martini as Robert Miles' ironic rendition of 'Children' blares out.

'Cara, how are you feeling? Tummy ok?' she asks cautiously, and it's put to me in such a manner that I can't help but feel as though Jac is more concerned about her own proximity to my arse than she is about my mental health.

'Yep, I'm ok I think...' I say, wincing as another aeroplane anxiety stomach cramp twists at my insides. This will be the first time I've flown without the comfort blanket of Dom, and the sooner this is all over and done with, the better. 'Anyway,' I deflect before my own waterworks begin, 'it's probably Debs we need to be more concerned about. How are you feeling now, babes?' I give her knee a reassuring squeeze. 'Debs?'

Debs' sleeping head rolls against the window of the taxi, and a snail trail of dribble oozes from her mouth.

'Looks like she got over leaving Harriet pretty quickly,' Jac laughs, whipping out her phone and taking what I can only assume is a highly unflattering bribery picture of a comatose Debs. 'New mums. Got to get the sleep in where they can, hey?'

New and old, I think, yawning away to myself while snuggling down into my seat for a quick power nap too. Bloody hell, Ibiza isn't going to know what's hit it when us four crazy kids rock up. Talk about 'Mums on Snore'...

An hour later, including a very confusing twenty-five minutes consisting of fully grown women verbally abusing a self-check-in machine, we're now waiting in the security line of shame to see what exactly Amy has packed in her hand luggage that's resulted in her bag being searched by a very stern-faced member of airport staff. 'What the bloody hell did you leave in there, Amy? Is it liquid?' Jac accuses. 'Because if it is then I'll go berserk. It's not a new phenomenon –nothing over 100ml and everything in a plastic bag. Why do all *these* people,' she says this while wildly shaking her fist towards the crowds of irate passengers waiting for their belongings to be rifled through, 'find that so hard to understand?!'

'It's not liquid, Jacqueline,' Amy huffs back at her. 'I have been through an airport before, you know. Just take a chill pill, Bridezilla, you're going to get your full English, ok?'

'I better bloody had, Amy, and if I don't I'm holding you and your bottle of God-knows-what absolutely responsible!' And with this, she stomps off to sit on a bench next to Debs who, having temporarily regained consciousness, is now asleep on the shoulder of a confused-looking elderly man who doesn't appear to have the heart, or upper body strength, to remove her.

The security man holds up Amy's bright yellow North Face rucksack. 'This one?' he yells. 'Come forward!'

'Oh, you're up,' I say, nudging her. 'I really hope for your sake it's not a bottle of lube...'

'Of course it's not. I'm self-lubricating, babe – like a horny snail. Slip and slide!'

Lovely. Sometimes I can hardly believe I share the same DNA with anyone in my family apart from my own kids– and not even they look anything like me, thanks to the annoyingly strong cockney Viking blood that flows through Dom's mini mes. Craning my neck around the throngs of people, I try to catch a glimpse of what Amy's contraband consists of, and the minute I clap eyes on it, I immediately wish I hadn't it. 'Shit...' I mutter under my breath, bringing my hands to my face in despair.

'Oh my God!' Jac announces, appearing over my shoulder like a danger-sensing meerkat. 'What the bloody hell is that? Is it a gun? A gun in the shape of a penis?' She half whispers, half shrieks in my ear, attempting not to cause a scene but massively misjudging her volume levels – resulting in quite a few panic-stricken faces now nervously glancing in Amy's direction.

Stepping forward to get a closer look, I'm not entirely sure my response is going to provide Jac with the comforting reassurance she requires right now, because all I'm seeing, in both senses of the word, is a very large shaft.

'Lads, come on! Stand down, ok, it's not a real gun!' Amy protests, as a team of security personnel swarm around her. 'It's a just a glock cock!' she says casually, as though they've just discovered she's harbouring a kitten instead of something that could be potentially used to bring down a flight. 'It shoots out white silly string spunk, you know... for hen party bants! Someone won't do a shot or a dare, and bam! Glock cock to the face!' Amy, for dramatic effect, has her hands in the air, and is stumbling backwards, apparently re-enacting the facial expressions of someone who's just had a silly string load delivered all over their face.

'Oh, this isn't happening!' moans Jac, sinking down into a squat position on the floor. 'I'm absolutely going to get fired.'

'Yeah, potentially,' I agree, already imagining the field day the papers will have reporting on the policewoman's hen party arrested for being in possession of a deadly 'weapon'. 'Oh wait!' I say, nudging an inconsolable Jac with my foot. 'Look! She's coming back with her bag, and not in handcuffs!'

'Jeez, some people are so uptight!' Amy says, with an exasperated look on her face as she reaches us. 'I can't believe they confiscated it. What's that all about?'

'Oh, I don't know, maybe the 1982 Aviation Security Act!' Jac snaps at her, in complete disbelief.

Ignoring her fractious remark, Amy's incredulity continues, 'I mean, wow! Lighten up. Can't these guys take a joke? Maybe it's because they felt threatened by the size of it, if you know what I mean... Good job I've got another two in my checked luggage.'

As Jac, now the colour of an angry penis about to go off, opens her mouth to obliterate a blithely unaware Amy, I quickly place a calming arm around her shoulder and a shushing finger to her lips. Years of experience have taught me there's literally no point trying to rationalise with my cousin's level of crazy. Best to roll with it and hope it doesn't land you in prison.

'No harm, no foul… this time,' I say, giving Amy a cautionary 'what the fuck?' death stare, normally reserved for my children. 'How about we peel Debs off that old man's shoulder and go get this hangry bride-to-be a fry up, ok?'

'Hell to the yes!' Amy cries. 'I don't know about anyone else, but I'm ready for a sausage!'

9

Chicken Run

He made me feel safe and, with his love on my side, invincible. He calmed my erratic and occasionally neurotic side down, especially when I began to spiral. I feared nothing and lived for everything. 'I'll never let anything bad happen to you… or us', that's what he used to say. Ha! If only it were true.

'Cara, Cara, Cara! Are you still in there? Guys, it's happened, she's catatonic. Does anyone have any smelling salts? I've only got some 'penis perfume' hand sanitiser.'

The mere threat of having something cock-scented waved in the proximity of my face is enough to swiftly drag me out of my trance and back into reality. Placing my head between my knees, I see my cousin's Doc-Marten-clad feet approach the metal bench I'm slumped upon like a rag doll.

'I'm fine, I'm fine…' I mumble, flapping my hand in the direction of my advancing cousin.

'Oh, there she is!' Debs announces delightedly, relief radiating through her voice. 'Where did you go, babes? You had us all worried for a minute.'

The answer is not one I'm willing to share with the group. I don't need the sympathetic head tilts of pity as I recount my last visit to this very terminal, with Dom, waiting to board a Singapore Airlines flight to Australia for the honeymoon adventure of a lifetime. No, I need to focus on the now and the low budget flight that I'm about to be dragged on with a narcoleptic new mother, an increasingly intolerant bride-to-be, and a woman who'll now be marked as a 'person of interest' on every airport terrorism watch list in the world. Feeling my breathing once more getting away from me, I take a swig of water and try to slow my exhalations as though I'm about to birth a baby, not regurgitate a microwaved airport breakfast.

'See, she's fine! Aren't you, babe?' Jac says, in a cheery singsong voice that sounds more like she's trying to convince herself than anyone else. Sitting down beside me, she places a firm arm around my shoulders in a manner that's both protective and indicative of the fact I'm about to be dragged onto this plane whether I like it or not.

Attempting to pull myself together for the sake of my best friend who, even after years of friendship, still scares the absolute shit out of me, I put on my bravest face and agree, 'Yes I'm absolutely fine, just need a quick minute…'

'Perfect! This is nothing that a stiff on-board gin and tonic can't fix, Cara,' she insists. 'But we need to fix it now, because they're about to close our gate and I cannot miss this plane. If I end up in a Wetherspoons, while Phil lives his best life in Amsterdam's red-light district I will be FUMING. Do I make myself clear?'

'Yep, crystal…' I nod, under duress of not wanting to be placed in a police hold. Standing up from the bench, I shakily place one foot in front of the other and gradually pick up some momentum, potentially a little bit too much because before I know it I'm running at full speed – away from my friends and in the opposite direction from the gate.

'FOR FUCK'S SAKE, CARA!' Jac's furious Mancunian accent rings out around the departure hall, but I don't care – I'm off and moving faster than a nineties Pammy Anderson and Tommy Lee

Jones. Now my legs, which are operating completely independently from my brain, have neglected to realise a couple of things about this fight or no-way-I'm-getting-on-a-fucking-flight scenario. Firstly, I've not exercised in nearly five years and so possess the lung capacity of an emphysema patient; secondly, there's a very good reason why you don't see Usain Bolt legging it down the track in a pair of Aldo espadrilles. There's nothing I can do to stop myself from falling. As the oversized wicker toe of my sandal stubs against the glossy grey tiles of Terminal Two, I take off with the power of a Boeing 777 and the grace of a drunken albatross. Soaring though the air, in what feels like slow motion, gravity very quickly reminds me that I am in fact not a large sea bird, but a hen, and hens are, indeed, flightless birds. As quick as I'm up, I'm down – arse-over-tit, skirt-over-head, and lying in a crumpled heap on the unforgivingly hard and chewing-gum-covered floor. Winded, and 70% sure the fright of it all has resulted in a complete loss of bladder control, things really can't get much worse for me right now.

'Excuse me, señorita, are you ok?' A concerned, husky male voice floats from somewhere behind the perimeter of my floral upside-down skirt shroud. Frozen to the spot, I contemplate playing dead. Maybe, if I don't move, the owner of this unknown sexy Spanish voice will carry on his merry way and completely forget about the mortified woman lying in front of him, flashing a truly gigantic pair of boob-high and grey (formerly white) granny pants. 'Miss, can you hear me?' His proximity to my roadkill position shifts and, whoever he is, he is now kneeling on the floor in front of me. Oh, for fuck's sake! Just leave already, go! Through the flimsy outline of material covering my face, I see the outline of a hand coming towards me, like that of a groom preparing to unveil his wife's face at the altar. Shutting my eyes, I adopt the mentality of a dog hiding behind a table leg thinking that if it can't see the human, the human can't see it. As the fabric pulls away from my face, falling back over my hair and onto my shoulders (arse still exposed for all to see) I wonder which of my friends will speak kindly of me in my eulogy after I've died a horrific and untimely death of sheer embarrassment.

'Hola!' the voice cheerfully says, while a finger repeatedly jabs me in the forehead to check whether or not I'm unconscious.

'Hey, stop that!' I insist, reluctantly opening my eyes before he starts CPR. On seeing the face of my hunky hero, however, I immediately wish I'd left them closed and allowed him to perform the kiss of life. There, about two inches away from my nose, and looking as though he's just stepped off the cover of *GQ Magazine*, is quite possibly one of the sexiest-looking men I've ever seen in my entire life. Locks of rich dark brown floppy hair cascading loosely over caramel eyes so deep and inviting I have a sudden and overwhelming desire to try and lick them. Is that normal? Do people lick eyes? Probably not on a first encounter, lying on an airport floor with your landing flaps on display. I also wonder what moisturiser he uses because his golden and olive skin is so flawlessly smooth it's as though he's been carved, then ironed, by God himself. Realising I've been openly gawking at this rugged, bearded Adonis of a stranger for the best part of a minute without speaking, I quickly sit myself upright and start awkwardly pawing at the ground. 'Sorry, I was just… looking for my contact lens. Oh there it is!' I lie, pretending to pick an invisible piece of silicon off the floor and shoving it, along with a plethora of bacteria, into my eyeball. A grin spreads across the Spanish sexpot's face, showcasing teeth so magnificently pearly they could be classed as dentistry porn.

'Your mouth…' he says, pointing towards my lips.

'Oh yes, not as nice as yours…' I flounder, dragging myself into a standing position and brushing the dirt off my t-shirt.

'Oh, er no…' He too gets to his feet, the expression on his face sitting somewhere between baffled and amused. 'Your mouth, it's bleeding.' Retinas firmly locked onto my own, he reaches out and grazes a rough digit against my lip before lifting its crimson-coated tip to my eye level. 'Oh wow, yes I am…' I say, suddenly feeling a bit woozy, 'and, look at that, you just full on put your finger in it. What if I have a disease? Not that I do, well, that I'm aware of…'

Reaching into the pocket of his skin-tight jeans, he laughs deeply and deliciously, before presenting me with a black paisley print bandana. 'Señorita, fingering your bodily fluid was a risk I was willing to take.'

With my cheeks now as red as my haemorrhaging lip, I attempt to decline his chivalrous gesture, but my protests are in vain as the silky material is slowly and somewhat sensually wiped around the edges of my mouth. I'm not entirely sure what is happening right now, but it feels kind of sexy… and also as though I'm a toddler who's being cleaned up after eating an ice cream.

'CARA!' Jac screams as she comes hurtling towards us at breakneck speed, followed by a galloping Amy a couple of hundred metres behind, who I know for a fact hasn't sprinted that fast since the time she stole a packet of strawberry Chewitts from Woolworths when we were ten and had the audacity to slap the sixty-year-old security guard's arse on the way out. As Jac skids to a screeching halt at our feet, her attention is torn between my bleeding face and the muscular, denim-clad stranger spit-polishing my face.

'Cara, *what* the fuck was that? And who the hell is *this*?' Jac demands to know, opting to fix her ogling stare firmly on the brooding beefcake who has folded the bandana into my own hand and is now reclaiming his hastily discarded backpack, along with Pret-A-Manger chicken baguette from the floor.

Holding the material against the stickiness of my own blood, I genuinely have no idea on how to answer either of her questions. 'Erm, I don't know… and I don't know…' I weakly offer, with a casual shrug of my shoulders. Far too busy inhaling the muskiness of his manliness, and appreciating his taste in patterned fabrics, I haven't even bothered to ask for a name. In fact, the only information I've managed to glean from the man is that he's definitely not squeamish, wears black denim *incredibly* well, and isn't vegan.

'Fuck, I'm fucked!' Amy announces breathlessly as she arrives on the scene, beads of sweat from her brow trickling down her face. 'Cara, seriously NEVER make me perspire ever again, ok? I don't even put this much cardio effort in when I'm getting jiggy with it… Speaking of which, ding dong!' she enthuses, eyeing up bandana man as though he's a prime cow at a farmer's market, 'Who's the highly fuckable Hispanic hottie?!'

'Amy!' I shout in disbelief. Honestly, the woman is so unfiltered it wouldn't surprise me if she excreted limescale.

'What?! He is. Anyway, we need to go, like now.' She grabs hold of my arm and begins to shepherd me back in the direction of the plane. 'The gate's closing and I've left Debs in charge of holding up the queue, but as she can't even hold her eyelids up at the moment, I don't fancy our chances. Time to move that ass. Go! Go! Go!'

In a situation where bursting into flames, mid-air, seems highly preferable to staying one second longer in the company of the stranger who saw my embarrassing knickers (and met my even more embarrassing cousin) I pick up my handbag and coyly offer him his bloodied rag back.

'Thank you so much,' I say, holding it out to him. 'Sorry, it's a bit haemoglobiny.'

He folds it back into my hands, his fingers lingering just long enough on mine to send waves of fanny-fluttering electricity coursing through my body. 'Keep it, it's yours,' he smoulders, as my face burns brighter than combusted aviation fuel. 'Adios, Cara.'

For some reason, the only way my brain sees fit to reply to his flirty farewell is to do a weird little curtsey, followed by an even stranger royal wave. IDIOT! I scream in my mind.

Amy, seemingly wasting no time in staking a piece of tasty Spanish tap'ass, stops to rummage around in her pocket, pulls out a pen and something that looks to be a pack of Marmite-flavoured condoms. She scrawls on the back of it and tosses the box at him. 'Call me,' she instructs, as seductively as possible for a woman who apparently likes her wood to taste of Twiglets. 'Now let's roll, bitches!'

10

Trouser Snakes on a Plane

Incredibly out of breath after legging it back through the airport in the fashion of the McCallister family two days before Christmas, we're finally on board the packed flight to Ibiza.

'Thank God for that, I thought we'd never make it,' sighs Jac, sinking back into her faux leather seat in pure relief.

She, Amy, and a back to being conked out Debs are all seated/slumped in the same row, while I've managed to draw the long straw of sitting alone in the adjacent aisle seat. Fortunately, my two neighbouring passengers appear not to have not joined the flight, something I'm particularly grateful for as it will allow me to hyperventilate, tuck myself into a foetal position and nervous fart in peace. It feels weird going on holiday without the kids, and I anxiously check my phone to see if I've had any SOS texts from my auntie and uncle. Seeing no new messages, my next port of call is to head to my news app to see if there have been any major incidents involving tractors in the Cheshire area. I feel so guilty for leaving them. Ben will be fuming with me, I know he will. I'd casually 'forgotten' to tell him that there's no wifi on the farm, meaning he's more likely to be lambing right now, rather than his preferred activity of gaming.

With my overactive imagination already envisaging Nancy and Siri acting out an *Animal Farm* meets *Lord of the Flies* crossover, a distraction seriously wouldn't go amiss.

'I could use a drink,' I complain to the girls. 'What do you think my chances are of getting something alcoholic before take-off? It's for medical reasons, sedation of a highly anxious flier and all that...' Looking around the cabin, I unsuccessfully attempt to make eye contact with one of the flight attendants, despite my flapping arms and constant pushing of the bell above my head.

'Oh, don't you worry, Cara,' Amy says with a look that either means something wonderful or, knowing my cousin, something unexpected and awful is about to happen. 'You know I excelled in the Brownies, right? And that their motto is "Proper Prior Planning Prevents Piss Poor Performance"?'

'I think you'll find that's actually a military saying,' corrects Jac. 'The Brownies' is "I promise that I must do my best..."'

Amy tuts, unperturbed, and rummages around in her hand luggage before locating a pack of baby wipes and waving them around exuberantly in the air.

'Amy, I thought leaving the kids behind meant leaving behind the wipes too,' I say, closing my eyes and trying not to imagine a scenario that doesn't include us plummeting towards the ground in a ball of flames, 'but thank you anyway.'

'No, trust me' she insists, lobbing the packet at my head. 'Introducing the airport-friendly, zero-detection-by-security-personnel, gin and tonic wet wipes!'

'I'm sorry, the what now?' Jac says, leaning across the aisle and snatching them from my lap so she can examine the package and its contents. 'Amy, they're just a pack of wipes. What are you on about?'

'Oh, *are* they now?' Amy says smugly, reaching over, pulling a wipe out the pack and wafting its drippy contents in the air. 'I've even managed to get them past an officer of the law. Sometimes my genius astounds me.'

'It astounds me you credit yourself as a genius when only last week you asked why people with epilepsy don't carry EpiPens,' Jac says dismissively.

Determined to persevere with her *Dragon's Den*-worthy invention, Amy continues, 'Listen and learn, ladies. I'm going to let you in on a trade secret that's going to rock your world and make me millions. Take one pack of wet wipes; machine wash until you get all the arse-cleaning chemicals out; leave them to air until completely dry; finally, re-soak them in your alcoholic tipple of choice, repackage, et voila!' And with that she places the wipe in her mouth and starts sucking.

'Oh my God, Amy! Stop!' I say, borderline hysterical at the ridiculousness of my cousin. Say what you want about Amy, but you can never take her creativity away from her when it comes to alcohol consumption.

'Mmm, Mediterranean tonic. Just missing a slice of lemon…' she reflects critically, as though she must immediately return to her Michelin-starred test kitchen to rectify her recipe.

'Delicious. Perhaps we can ask one of the flight attendants for a hot citrus towelette chaser once we're up,' Jac suggests, pulling a sleep mask and pair of headphones out of her handbag, in an apparent attempt to block us all out.

'Cara, want one or not?' Amy says, leaning over Jac and offering me the pack.

My more sensible side is telling me to wait an hour and get trolleyed from the actual trolly. My louder, more irrational side, screams at me to take a bum-wiping beverage. 'Ok, fine, fine. Pass me one.' I glance around to make sure no one is watching – after all, desperate times, desperate gin measures.

'Cara!' Jac says, utterly disgusted by my actions, as she lifts her eye mask up just enough to witness me placing the wipe in my mouth.

'Amy…' I gasp in disbelief, '…these are actually *really* good!' I take another big suck of the fabric. 'What gin is this? It's a taste sensation!' I wax lyrical.

'Cara…' Jac says, peeling off her mask and reaching out to tap my arm, blinking weirdly and developing a bit of a neck twitch.

'Honestly, Jac, chill out. You need to try one, she's actually onto something.' So highly invested in shoving as much of the gin and tonic wipe in my mouth as possible, I completely neglect to see what she's trying to draw my attention to until it's way too late.

'Hola, Cara…'

Oh no. Oh no, no, no. With a sense of dread in my gut, and a wet wipe hanging out of my mouth, I slowly look up and straight into the gooey caramel lick pools of the man mountain from the terminal. Inhaling with a sudden gasp of shocked breath, the wipe decides it isn't sticking around to face the shame of the situation, and, as my trachea sucks it in with more power than a Dyson vacuum, panic takes over. As I start to cough and splutter, the irony of the situation isn't lost on me. I always feared my untimely end would come on a plane, but not while it was still stationary on the tarmac, and definitely not with a piece of environmentally unsound fabric blocking my airways. Honestly… what a fucking way to go. What will it say on my tombstone, I wonder? 'Cara Carmichael. Swallowed when she should have spat'. Before I have time to think too much more about how embarrassing my afterlife will be, two muscular arms drag me out of my seat, spin me round and begin to thrust against my body with the power of a jackhammer. If this wasn't a life or breath situation, it would definitely be sexy and very much on a par with something you'd see in a romantic movie – minus the part where a soggy wet wipe comes flying out of the heroine's mouth and lands on the handbag of a disgusted woman two rows in front, like a soggy hair ball.

'Oh my God!' I gasp, clutching at my throat, unable to believe I'm alive. Encased in the safety of his bulging biceps, I feel the warmth of hot and panting breath on my neck, smell the tantalising earthiness of aftershave; and either with shock, or because of the incredibly potent hit of gin, I feel myself go weak at the knees.

'Whoa there!' my life-saver says, catching me as I slump to the crumb-coated cabin carpet. Supporting my weight, and pulling me back into a vertical position, he effortlessly scoops me up and gently places me back in my seat with the care of an insect enthusiast returning a ladybird to a leaf. 'I've got you, Cara...'

I open my mouth in an attempt to say something to him in return, potentially a word of thanks or appreciation, but in doing so, all that manages to escape from my lips is a Fever Tree and full English breakfast scented burp. Still numb from the trauma, I peer round the incredibly girthy circumference of his thigh muscles, desperate for the reassuring looks of my best friends. Sadly, my counterparts appear to be the living embodiment of 'speak no evil' (Jac, whose hands are clamped over her mouth in abashed disbelief), 'hear no evil' (Amy, who has a pair of noise-cancelling head phones on and seems to be obliviously head-banging away to heavy metal), and 'see no evil' (Debs, who's still asleep). A male flight attendant, who has spotted the commotion from the rear of the plane, is now barrelling down the aisle towards us about two minutes too late and brandishing a first-aid kit in his perma-tanned hand.

'Make way! Make way! Gareth coming through!' he gesticulates wildly. 'Are you ok?' Noting the concern is being directed more at my male companion, I wonder whether there's any need for Gareth to be stroking him like a house cat too? And, more importantly, whether his kit contains anything ethanol-based that could be consumed as a shot.

'Do we need to get the pilot to call for medical assistance for your… wife?' He looks me up and down dubiously, still continuing with the stroking.

'Oh, I'm not his wife…' my voice manages to croak hoarsely, as I sink further into my seat to avoid the rubbernecking stares of practically every passenger on the plane. 'And I'm fine…'

'Fabulous!' he exclaims, clearly more delighted at our non-existent relationship status and at maintaining his departure time than at my blood oxygen levels. 'Now sir, if I could ask you to take your seat as soon as possible. We need to secure the doors and…' this he says with a wink, 'pushback.'

'Si, absolutely. May I?' My rescuer motions to the empty chair next to me.

'Oh, yes, of course.' Unsteadily, I begin to rise up out of my chair to let him by, completely unaware his intention is for me to simply move my legs out into the aisle in order for him to shuffle past. This confusion, mainly on my part, unfortunately results in me leaning forward at the exact same moment he attempts to squeeze his very large 'luggage' past my face; resulting in, quite possibly, one of the worst timed and most inappropriate head butts… straight to his crotch. 'Oh my God, I'm so sorry!' I cry out from somewhere within the denim depths of his button-down fly. This was absolutely not what I had in mind when I requested something stiff before take-off. Peeling my face away, and instinctively looking for a way to rectify the situation, I automatically reach my hand out to the affected area in an almost maternal bid to comfort it, forgetting that you *really* shouldn't be touching a stranger's penis on an aeroplane – well not in front of people, anyway.

'Cara, we're not even a mile from the check-in desk,' he says without flinching or so much as a trace of a smile. 'Don't you think we should wait until we're at least a mile high first?'

Not knowing what to do with my face, or apparently my hands, I quickly retract my fingers from his phallus and turn to face Jac so I can mouth, 'Oh my fucking God!' to her, but it's pointless: my disastrous behaviour has driven her to the point where she's now head down on the tray table (which, may I add, should be in an upright position) with what looks to be a Huggies hanging out of her mouth.

As the plane's engines roar to life and we pull away from the terminal, my heart races and my palms sweat. Closing my eyes, I say a silent prayer to any God that just so happens to be listening and is willing to overlook my foul language and blasphemous ways to allow me to have more time with my babies (and to see the inside of Pacha). Gripping onto the armrest in terror, trying not to imagine a world where my kids call Connie 'Mummy' after my horrible demise in a plane crash, I feel the warmth of a strong hand placing itself on top of my own. With shivers running down my spine, I turn to face the stranger whose name I'm yet to ask. I smile gratefully at his simple act of kindness.

'You're most welcome,' he says seductively, quickly turning my nipples from flat pieces of chorizo to very perky Manzanilla olives. 'My name is Javier, by the way,' he says, before closing his eyes and making himself comfortable in the chair.

Dropping my gaze to where his hand lays across my own, I realise this stranger has stirred something inside me that I haven't felt for another man in a very long time, and as the plane begins to soar, so does my shrivelled walnut heart. Maybe, *just* maybe, Cara, there's hope for you yet.

11

Bien*hen*ido

'Cara! Will you stop daydreaming and get a move on!' Jac's newly applied holiday nails are acting as a cattle prod to usher me out of the baggage collection hall and towards Eivissa Airport's exit. I can't believe I still haven't caught a glimpse of Javier, not even through customs, or collecting our luggage. He's like the invisible man, how has he managed to give me, a mother of two with eyes in the back of her head, the slip?

I'd spent the majority of the flight creepily staring at him as he slept, drinking in the finer details of his facial structure (along with a few gin miniatures) while simultaneously applying Polyfilla-strength under-eye concealer and lipstick to my own. Wanting him to wake up and see me looking a solid 30% better than I did when choking on a wet wipe, I was also terrified of trying to hold a conversation with the man. My first encounter with Dom couldn't have been more different, mainly because I was so different back then. Young, dumb and full of rum (it was 2for1 on cocktails at Infernos Nightclub on Clapham High Street), the moment his ego strolled in, my fearless confidence made a move and staked its claim. Whatever happened to that woman? I wished I could have her (and her great rack) back just for this long weekend – wow, she'd do some damage. Would she be the type of woman Javier would like? Could she persuade him to take her on as easily as she did Dom? Even as the plane started its final descent towards Ibiza and the girls giddily pointed out Playa d'en Bossa's golden shores, along with the famous open-air dance floor of Ushuaia, still I gazed, utterly transfixed.

The man slept like the dead; so much so that I was about to check his pulse when Jac, who'd been watching me watching him like a hawk, flicked the back of my head. 'Oi! Don't you dare!' she whispered across the aisle. 'He already thinks you're tapped. Do *not* touch him.'

Even when we'd landed, he did not move. With the girls already up and at 'em and raring to get off the plane – including Debs who apparently, after five hours of airport- and sky-snoozing, was feeling much more chipper – all I could do was take one last look at that gorgeous face of his before being dragged down the aisle away from him towards a glorious wall of heat and mini break of absolute madness.

'Amy, anything you'd like to make known?' Jac asks pointedly as we pass through a guarded green 'Nothing to Declare' exit point.

'Nope. If those sniffer dogs couldn't find it, I ain't telling them *nothing*.' She winks at the fortunately-not-fluent-in-English member of the Guardia Civil.

'Is she joking?' Debs says with a nervousness in her voice as she eyes up Amy awkwardly adjusting what we all hope is just her thong between her arse cheeks. 'Cara, I can't go to a Spanish prison on smuggling charges! I've booked in for a six-week pilates block when we're home and I'll never get my money back.'

'Along with the small matter of Harriet?' I remind her. The laid-back Ibizan vibes are evidently already working wonders for her post-natal panic attacks.

'Oh shit, the baby, I forgot about her!' And she immediately whips out her phone to check for SOS messages from Will.

'So where are we staying again?' Jac pointlessly asks Amy, knowing full well she's purposefully kept almost everything about the trip a total surprise for her. '*Please* just give me something? You're killing me here!' A natural born decision maker and control freak, handing over all the responsibility of hen party planning, especially to Amy, has crippled her. 'Is it Nobu? The W? The Hard Rock?' She wracks her brain for more of the five-star hotels she's been extensively researching and sending to the WhatsApp group at all hours of the day and night. 'I mean, retrospectively I should have prioritised the others over Hard Rock – but if it is there, I'm sure with enough margarita mix on board, it'll be fine.'

'I will tell you absolutely nothing of our plans, Jacqueline,' Amy reminds her. 'On this holiday my lips, well my facial ones anyway, will remain sealed.'

'Eugh, you're revolting,' Jac complains as we make our way towards the crowd of waiting taxi drivers and hotel transport drivers, all waving pieces of paper in the air with various names scrawled across them. 'I don't see us… Can anyone else? Amy, whose name did you give the hotel for collection?'

'Jac, just relax, will you? It's all under control. Let me message our guy to see where he is.' With a flurry of keypad clicks and WhatsApp pings, Amy points in the direction of the exit. 'Sorted. He's just arrived. Says he's standing underneath the giant 'Welcome to Ibiza' sign.'

'Nope, I don't see him,' Jac says, still scanning the arrivals hall for an elegantly dressed shuttle bus driver. 'There's only some hippy in a poncho holding a toy unicorn.'

'Branch!' Amy exclaims, heading over to the shoeless man with her arms outstretched.

'Amy!' an extremely heavy Bristolian accent replies. The hippy's ginger matted dreadlocks whirl through the air as he picks my cousin up and spins her round, recreating the Hugh Grant/Martine McCutcheon airport scene from *Love Actually*. 'My queen! So good to see you! Ah, and these must be your goddess friends,' he gushes, releasing Amy from his grip and reaching his arms out to us as though he's expecting us to also flock into his caped and, I imagine given the red-hot heat, clammy clutches. The three of us do not move a muscle. I can't be sure, but I think Jac has stopped breathing: her eyes are bulging in their sockets and her jaw has managed to dislocate itself as though she's a basking shark about to inhale krill. Seemingly unaware of the silence, he 'branches' out regardless, kissing each of us in turn on our foreheads while chanting something about heavenly blessings.

'Cara,' Jac whispers, reaching out for my arm and gripping onto it firmly to prevent herself from passing out, '*what the fuck is this?*'

'Perhaps he's from Nobu?' I suggest with unconvincing optimism. 'They're quite trendy, aren't they? Maybe new-age hipster vibes are all the rage this season?'

'What season, Cara? The Summer of Love, 1967?'

'Touché,' I admit, tactfully trying to catch Amy's attention as she's taking selfies under the cherry-emblazoned Pacha signage. 'Amy… Amy… AMY!' I eventually yell, opting to switch subtlety for shouty. Strolling coolly over, with a wide smile beaming across her very-pleased-with-herself face, 'Isn't he just *amazing*?' she swoons.

'He's certainly something,' I agree, waving to Branch who is gesturing for me to come and join him as he dances on his own in the middle of the arrivals hall, presumably to the music of the LSD-induced fairies in his head.

'Listen, I know what you're probably thinking, Jac...' begins Amy.

'Oh, are you also thinking of homicide crime scenes you've attended over the years and what you'd do differently to make sure you got away with it?' Jac hisses back at her.

'Jacqueline, we're in Ibiza, home of spirituality and wellness...' Amy begins again.

But Bridezilla has well and truly arrived and is having absolutely none of her bohemian bullshit. 'No Amy, we're in Ibiza, home of five-star hotels, glorious day bars and some of the most pretentious night spots in the whole world – all of which I WANT TO BE IN!'

'And you will be,' Amy reassures her. 'Branch is a trailblazer, Jac. He runs one of the most sought-after holistic retreats in the whole of Europe. Bella and Ken have just been here! Trust me, if it's good enough for those two famous faces, it's good enough for us.'

'Ladies!' Branch calls over to us. 'Come please, your chariot awaits.'

'Bella and Ken, really?' Jac asks, still resistant but now a lot more intrigued, as Amy guides her by the shoulders through the sliding glass doors of d'Eivissa Aeropuerto and into the blazing hot heat of the June sun. 'Just you wait, your mind is going to be blown.'

Bouncing along the pine-tree-lined highway leading away from the airport and towards God knows where, I wonder whether Bella Hadid and Kendall Jenner were also treated to the spine-crumbling, open-air luxury transportation of a 1994 Nissan pickup truck. Looking at Jac, I think she might be sick. She's gone a funny shade of grey while Instagram-stalking the Kardashian sister's Instagram page for signs of Egyptian cotton and an infinity pool. Talking of 'let down', things aren't looking much better for Debs; the lack of suspension in the back of the truck is making it increasingly difficult to attach a battery-operated breast pump to her now engorged boobs, and tears are flowing as fast her spurting milk supply.

Amy on the other hand is loving life, very much like a dog who's been allowed to stick its head out of the window. 'Isn't this incredible!' she hoots above the deafening roar of wind passing over our heads at 120 km/h and the rhythmic mooing of Debs' pump.

I have to say – although I'd be furious to have survived childbirth twice, a cheating husband and a backstabbing family just to be decapitated in a rusting, roofless death trap – I can't help but take a moment to admire the panoramic views of Ibiza's breathtakingly beautiful countryside. It's vibrancy and greenery has surprised me. I'm not sure what I was expecting (glow sticks and drugged-up ravers on every street corner, perhaps) but it wasn't this. Nestled in lush vegetation, white rustic farmhouses built on dry and sandy earth gleam in the brightness of the early afternoon Mediterranean sun. Despite our speed as we hurtle past picturesque roadside cafés, there's a calming sense of stillness to my new surroundings. I catch blurry glimpses of elderly locals taking refuge from the harsh heat underneath large green parasols (accompanied by nearly as large pitchers of ice cold beer). It looks like the only problem they have in the world is who's going to buy the next round of San Miguel. Speaking of which, I'm about ready for one of those myself.

I wonder how much longer until we arrive at our final destination. Branch wasn't overly forthcoming as he bundled us into the back of his wagon. Thinking about it, for all we know, he could be driving us to our deaths, or worse… a one-star hotel. Wondering if we're all about to be sex-trafficked, I can't help but feel that any recipient of this particular cargo would refuse to take delivery of our misfit mum crew. Looking up at the postcard perfect blue sky with not one trace of a fluffy white cloud to mar its beauty, I wonder what the kids are doing and if they're ok. I make a mental note to call them as soon as we arrive… after I've had a cold beer or two, of course. Priorities.

In this moment, I also briefly allow my mind to flitter to Dom. He was very cagey with his exact whereabouts when I offered him the opportunity to spend some quality time with 50% of his gametes, despite it not being his allocated weekend. Most fathers would have leapt at the opportunity, but not him. You see, nowadays he's far too busy and far too important to want to associate with unruly reminders of how boring his life used to be. I often wonder why he was so keen to have kids when in reality he didn't have the time or patience required to be a father. In the early days, he was totally useless. Nappy changes weren't really 'his thing'. I mean, honestly? Are they actually *anyone's* 'thing' (weird blokes with fetishes aside)? He'd joke that they were 'women's work' but, much like the nappy, the quip was always fully loaded. Quality time with us was shunned in favour of spending time with the 'lads' down on the golf course, in the pub and, by the smell of him when he eventually rolled home at 2am, strip joints and kebab shops. The sun, however, always reminds me of him, along with sandy toes and the salty sea breeze, because for just one short week of June he was officially ours. Summer holidays, at his insistence, were always spent at the best resorts, the most exclusive hotels – regardless of whether or not we could afford them. It was a chance for him to show off, walk the walk and flaunt his superiority. Yes, Dom Stringer liked to be seen to be living his best life, even if, underneath the surface, the family and existence he'd created for himself were never enough. He is evidently far happier in the glitzy materialistic world he now occupies, but I take some level of comfort knowing that one day he'll get his comeuppance. He'll realise what he's missed out on, what he threw away and dumped on the side of the road. But by then it'll be too late. The ship will have sailed, and he will be in our children's lives mainly as an example of what not to do when it comes to marriage and parenting – just like my own dad.

Anyway, enough about Dom, I think, taking a deep and re-centring breath. This is my time to rediscover myself and my future. This weekend has absolutely nothing to do with *him*. Closing my eyes, I drink in the warmth and calming energy of the sun. Although I know they are ageing and carcinogenic, the rays feel comforting and empowering. Now that I'm here, I have a good feeling about Ibiza, as though this island of hedonism and dreams might just prove to be the answer to all of my problems.

As the UVA rays begin to tingle on my skin, I ponder whether this new and slightly more positive side of me has come to light as a result of letting myself daydream about a certain tall, dark and handsome stranger. What is it they say about manifestation? Build it and they will come... Or is that from a 1980s Kevin Costner film about a man who builds a baseball pitch in his back garden? Regardless, I do know that when I saw Javier a part of me presumed dead was, if only for a second, resuscitated – despite my very insistent request for a DNR. Could it be that desire isn't the dangerously treacherous thing I've feared it would be? Maybe I could let myself live, and lust, just a little.

It might not be exactly what Jac had imagined, but a wellness resort might be exactly what I need right now – out with the negativity and in with the positivity, and all that. You never know, I might learn how to turn my bitter and twisted thoughts of 'beat, slay, shove' into the somewhat less homicidal mantra of 'eat, pray, love.'

Yes, the world works in mysterious ways and perhaps, especially on this trip, I should learn to go where the universe (and this neck-breaking 4x4) take me.

12

Goddess on a Mountain Top

As the four of us, all at a complete loss for words, stand in front of the dilapidated countryside finca – its crumbling stone walls covered in ivy, an oxidising corrugated iron roof hanging on (much like Jac's sanity) by a thread – I can't help but think the universe needs to have an immediate fucking word with its malfunctioning sat nav.

'Ladies, welcome to Unicorn Utopia!' Branch says proudly, as though he's introducing us to Jurassic Park – but after the dinosaurs broke out of confinement, ate everyone, then got pissed at the hotel bar and trashed the place. Assessing the highly questionable collection of rickety raised wooden shacks interwoven with overgrown weeds and olive trees, it's a given that Jac can forget about her infinity pool fantasy – or any kind of running water, for that matter. This has to be a joke, surely? Amy has got us all good. I'm absolutely convinced Ant and Dec are about to jump out with a camera and tell us we're part of an elaborate prank for their new TV series *Saturday Night Rave Away*. Jac, in a state of shock, hasn't moved or spoken in the three minutes since our chariot of dire rumbled down the dusty dirt track towards the 'rustic retreat'. As her eyes dart around the sandy, chicken-covered, ground, I wonder if she's contemplating where it might be easiest to bury my cousin's body. No, this most certainly is not the bouji wellness experience I had in mind and, looking at Amy's awkward face, I'm guessing it's a little left field (and in the middle of an actual one) of what she was expecting too. There's being at one with nature, and then there's finding yourself as an unwilling contestant on *The (Party) Island With Bear Grylls*.

'Now, we have a few ground rules for all goddesses staying here at our sacred spiritual sanctuary,' Branch, with his hands clasped together as though he's about to deliver the Lord's Prayer, begins to lecture, oblivious to our ashen faces. 'During our time together, we expect you to commit yourselves fully to the experience and embrace Mother Nature along with the beauty she offers us.'

Scanning an outbuilding that, instead of sporting the words 'communal shower', looks like it should be surrounded by crime scene tape, I wonder whether Mother Nature will also be providing hand sanitiser and a self-defence weapon of our choice. Deliriously smiling at us as though he's just smoked eight joints (highly likely) and is listening to a voice in his head telling him to make tambourines out of our skins, he signals to a half-naked bearded Jesusy fellow who's magically appeared from behind a giant bush. 'This is Guthrie,' Branch introduces. 'He'll take your luggage for you as we head down to your love lodgings.'

Love lodgings? I don't like the sound of this, not one bit. Pretty sure there's a brothel adjacent to a truck stop on the A1 with a similar name.

'My beautiful queens!' gushes the Cornish Christ. Putting down an acoustic guitar, he flicks perfectly styled surfer-dude beachy waves away from his face. Why can I never get my hair to do that? How does he get those waves to hold? If we haven't all succumbed to a group sacrifice by the end of this trip, maybe I'll ask him for a tutorial. Taking my hand in his, Guthrie raises it to his mouth and kisses it gently before working his way down the rest of our highly standoffish line – all of us frozen in fear of either an unprovoked poultry attack or receiving a poorly executed tribal tattoo. Reaching Debs, he takes one look at her postpartum midriff and falls to the ground in front of her as though he's been shot.

'Jesus!' she shouts out in shock, clearly also confused by his parentage. 'Are you ok? Are you hurt?'

'Oh celestial giver of life,' he moans from her feet, 'I am truly humbled to be in the presence of your divine fertility. Myself and the universe are eternally grateful for the gift you are growing for us.'

Realising Guthrie thinks she's still pregnant, all super-polite Debs can do about the strange man rolling around at her platform Converse is apprehensively pat him on the head as though he's a stray dog that might have rabies, and sniff back a confidence-dented tear.

'Leave it out, mate,' Amy jumps in gallantly, never afraid to point out a non-feathered cock when she sees one. 'She's already had the baby, so the only thing my friend is growing right now is the desire to throw a right hook. If you know what's good for you, I'd move away from support Tights-on Fury over here before she knocks you straight back to Bethlehem.'

As a clearly embarrassed Guthrie scrambles to his feet and begins to apologise profusely to Debs, Branch signals for us to follow him. 'This way ladies, your accommodation awaits.'

Narrowly avoiding ripping my calf muscle open on a piece of tetanus-coated metal poking out of the ground, I attempt to pull Amy to one side so I can read her the riot act before there's an actual real life riot.

'Isn't this wild?' she over-enthuses, sensing what's coming and quickly sidestepping my angry advance. 'I'm just going to go and ask Branch where the pool and bar area are.' And with that, she quickly scurries off to catch up with the man who has seemingly named himself after one of the characters in the *Trolls* movie.

'Here at Unicorn Utopia, we are a community powered by love and spirituality only,' Branch explains as we pass under the welcoming shade of olive trees and shredded boat sail canopies. 'Now you have stepped foot over the retreat's entrance we ask you to leave your normal life and traditional values behind. You will stay on site for the entirety of your stay, relishing the opportunity to redefine your lives through positivity, plant power and sobriety.'

'Sobriety?!' Jac shrieks so loudly poor Guthrie drops Debs' extremely heavy Louis Vuitton suitcase on his unprotected bare foot in fright.

Branch chuckles knowingly. 'Yes goddess, no alcohol is to be consumed on the sacred grounds of the retreat. Here we aspire to raise the health of all our visitors through meditation, happiness and the awakening of our pure truth. Only then can we contribute to inner and world peace.'

I can't help but feel Branch's aspirations for world peace may come a cropper once it comes to light that the majority of our party's 'pure truth' is focused around the clarity of the alcohol we plan to drink.

'But this is Ibiza!' Jac objects, dumbfounded, and now also on the brink of tears because her glittery silver Aquazzura platform sandals have just had a fight, and lost, with a pile of chicken shit. 'It's the home of letting loose, partying, and making bad life choices.'

'That may be the case for some, my divine being, but here we are conscious clubbers. We feel and move to the rhythm of

Mother Nature and all her creatures, not to alcohol and its nega-
tive energy. We party through yoga, high vibrations and the
most deliciously fulfilling elixir of the gods… cacao and kale
smoothies. Now,' he says as we arrive at two non-building-
regs-compliant wooden huts with our names drawn on the doors
in chalk. 'Here we are. Your home for the next three nights. I'll leave
you to settle in. Perhaps, once you are feeling refreshed, you'll
join the rest of the community and me on the moon deck for a
late afternoon chickpea mezze before our evening star worship?'

'Oh, we wouldn't miss it for the wondrous world, would we,
ladies?' Amy nods, attempting to coerce us all into agreement,
but in return receives three icy stares as cold as the frozen
margaritas currently not in our hands. As Guthrie opens the
door to mine and Jac's cabin, any last hopes of a five-star
freshen-up and a Lindt chocolate on the pillow fade faster than
a cheap box-dye hair colour. There in front of us, instead of two
luxury queen-sized beds are two grotty single camping beds
complete with sleeping bags that look as though they'd be able to
enlist the power of all the bedbugs living inside them to stand up
and crawl their way to safety. As Jac lets out a stifled scream of
anguish, it strikes me that our bleak and basic surroundings are
much more reminiscent of a crack chalet than a love lodge.

'Namaste!' Branch smiles gleefully, before he and Guthrie
walk away, arm in arm, to presumably milk some aloe vera
leaves and dry-hump a conifer.

'Nah mate, I want to leave!' Jac desperately calls after them.
'I WANT TO LEAVE!'

'I mean, it's not *that* bad,' Amy says, sticking her head in
through the doorway of our cabin before whipping out her
phone so she can take a selfie next to an empty oil drum
masquerading as a washbasin. 'Come on, where's your sense of
adventure?'

'My sense of adventure? I'M GOING TO FUCKING KILL YOU!' Jac roars, storming towards Amy as though she's the bad cop from *Terminator 2*, and sending Debs and five chickens scurrying for cover.

'Whoa, whoa!' I shout, grabbing hold of her and pulling her back from my cousin, who has her hands in the air as if she's a completely innocent bystander accused of a great injustice.

'Amy, what were you thinking?' I bark, still wrestling with a seething T-1000. 'Why on earth would you book us into a teetotal beardy-weirdy woman-worshipping wellness cult?'

'Ok, in my defence,' Amy says semi-apologetically, as Jac shrugs me off and heads to her handbag for a discarded Hendricks Huggies to suck on. 'It's not *quite* what I thought it was going to be like, either.'

'Not *quite*!' Jac's voice is so shrill she's kicked off the donkeys in the next field. 'It's called Trip Advisor, Amy! You type the name of the hotel you want to stay at in the search box and then read to see how many people were either killed in their sleep there or died of a 13th Century illness. And for the love of God, what is *that smell*?'

'I think we're downwind of the long-drop loo.' Debs scrunches her nose up at the putrid aroma of digested plant power wafting its way over our heads.

'Branch and I go way back, you see,' Amy dreamily reminisces. 'It was the early noughties, a time when the skirts were denim, belts were plentiful and I was working a summer season out here on the doors. He was totally different vibe back then, a club promoter who went by the name of Kev.'

At this, I can't help but let out a proper belly LOL, much to Jac's annoyance. Kev to Branch is *quite* a transformation.

'I had a particular penchant for skinny ginger dudes who wore Von Dutch caps and Singha Beer vests, back then.'

Some things never change, I think, recalling the looks of the man boy who works behind the counter at Greggs.

'He used to run some of the mega big nights over here. Honestly, Jac, he was proper 'Mr VIP', knew everyone, could get you on all the guest lists, the best hotels, the proper good drugs. He was THE man to know. So when you said about coming to Ibiza I thought I'd get in touch with him to see if he could fix us up. And he did, of sorts…' She trails off as a rat the size of Ruby runs across our feet, sending a quaking Debs clambering up Jac's body in revulsion.

'He told me it was an A-list bouji retreat. The only place to be seen on the island. In retrospect, I may have misunderstood some of his descriptions.'

'You had one job, Amy.' Jac scrapes Debs off and sources a tree stump hygienic enough to perch an inch of her arse cheek on. 'All you had to do was click one of the many, *many* links I sent you – that was it! No intuition needed. I was very clear I wanted luxury, pocket-sprung mattresses, to be waited on hand and foot by hotel staff who offer to spray your face when you get too hot.'

'Pretty sure Guthrie would spray something in your face if you asked. He seemed pretty eager to please,' Amy says.

'Right, it's fine, Jac. Don't worry, we won't stay here.' I jump in, trying to de-escalate the situation. 'We'll make a reservation at another hotel.' It's a suggestion my mind knows makes sense, but at the same time reminds me of an already pushed-to-the-brink credit card limitation. 'Debs, Amy? Do you agree?'

Debs nods her head in agreement so quickly I worry she may actually be fitting.

'Ok, that's sorted then. I'll make some calls.' I dig my phone out of my handbag. 'Just need to get some signal… Wait, why's there no signal?'

'We're in the hills above San Antoni, literally miles from anywhere,' Amy reminds us. 'You ain't going to get a signal here, cuz. That's why it's the perfect location for a spiritual retreat – no interruptions from the outside world. Even if you could get through to anyone, June is peak season in club land, plus David

Guetta's on this weekend – so unless you've got money to burn, we ain't getting in anywhere.'

'FUCK!' Jac yells again, throwing her head into her hands. 'I'm not being held hostage at a hippy retreat on my hen party! He can't keep us here, it's birdnap! There *must* be somewhere? I say we get changed, walk up to the road, flag a cab or hitchhike our way into town and ask around – then we go to Café Mambos and get shit-faced. Who's in?'

'Yaaas!' roars Debs, standing up and enthusiastically beating her chest. Jeez, I haven't seen her this passionate about something since Farrow and Ball released five new paint colours.

'Hippy prison retreat breakout, I'm in!' Amy rejoices, holding out a wipe for a poorly judged celebratory toast that's left hanging, literally and figuratively.

'So,' I announce with determination in my voice and a passion for drunken, reckless abandonment in my heart. 'We have a plan. Get our glam on, give Branch the slip, try not to get run over and/or murdered by the side of a country road, find a hotel with flushing toilets and down some margs? Sounds like the delayed but perfect start to the perfect girls' trip.'

'Seriously,' says Jac, looking around the retreat in complete disbelief. 'I still can't believe Bella Hadid and Kendall Jenner stayed here.'

'Oh wow, have they?' Amy slaps a mosquito off her face.

'You told us they did!'

'No, I said Bella and Ken. You know, my weird neighbours in the flat below who went viral for stealing a penguin from the zoo.'

'FOR FUCK'S SAKE, AMY!' we all scream at her.

The sooner we make our escape from here, the better.

13

Dodge Balls

Less than thirty minutes – and a lot of screaming at six-legged creatures who were most definitely not more scared of us than we were of them – later, we're ready to implement operation 'Run The Fuck Away'. Having left our luggage behind, under Amy's reassurance of 'some dude' she knows being able to collect it in the morning, we resemble four glamourous, high-heeled mountain goats trying to clamber our way through dimly lit terrain towards freedom. After much hysteria at something we initially feared to be a panther, only to discover it was in fact a very large stray cat, we have so far made it through the slalom of shitty shacks uninjured and undetected.

'Head for the main road we came in along,' Debs whispers as we stagger along the dusty path leading to the main house, cautious of who might be listening and not wanting to alert the roaming 'Poultry Patrol' who I'm convinced are an organically powered elite unit of anti-escape operatives.

'No, we'll be seen,' Jac whispers back. 'We need to cut through the woods and bypass that bit of the road. Trust me, I did the Duke of Edinburgh.'

'Christ!' gasps Amy. 'When he was how old? Not much meat on that bone. Must have been like shagging a chicken wing.'

'What? No, you idiot. As in the orienteering award. Shut up and trust me, it's this way.'

'Actually goddesses, I think you'll find the moon deck is this way.' Branch's Bristolian voice booms from the depths of darkness, causing our bleating herd to jump out of our hides. I'm not sure what's worse, the fact we've been caught, or we've been rumbled by a man wearing a hemp thong and a palm leaf crop top Sinitta would be proud of. 'May I say you're all looking glorious this evening, albeit perhaps a little overdressed for star worship. Regardless, you ladies must be famished. Please follow me and I'll get you some much needed soul-strengthening sustenance.'

'Oh no, honestly, it's fine, thank you. We're still full from the dish of complimentary cacao nibs you left in our rooms,' I insist, desperately hoping he's not about to tell me they were rat shit, and that he'll take the hint and leave us to continue with our great escape.

'Yeah, we're off for a sunset stroll,' Amy says, as we try to inch our way away from Branch and towards the trees. 'To er… re-energise our… chi… chi… spots.'

'Trust me, goddesses, the community will be more than pleased to accommodate all your chi spot needs.' He laughs exuberantly. 'Now, come, come!'

Flashing nervous looks at one another in the diminishing light, we begrudgingly follow our foliage-clad, 'So Macho' self-appointed leader towards the candlelit finca. To be fair, by nightfall, it actually looks rather pretty… if you pay no attention to the structural damage, bat droppings and rickety windows with what I can only assume is Spanish for 'SEND HELP' etched into their grime. As we approach the moon deck, I can just make out the silhouettes of people lying on the ground rhythmically moving their bodies to the sound of chilled out electronic dance music.

'What are they doing? Is that yoga?' I ask Jac, squinting through the gloom to get a better look at the mass of writhing people on the floor.

'Of sorts,' answers Branch, despite not being asked. 'It's part of our star-worshipping ceremony – something we like to call Sensual Ascension. As the stars rise in the sky, we allow their power to infiltrate our bodies – freeing them of tensions and allowing us to return our souls to their most basic state of desire. Now that our four newest unicorns are here, the ceremony can truly transcend into new and dazzling heights.'

Grinning, he takes Amy and Debs by the hand and leads them towards the music. I exchange nervous glances with Jac as we walk. 'What do you think he means?' I whisper, as we slow our pace to drop out of Branch's ear shot.

'I'm not sure, but I think there's something about being called a unicorn, isn't there? Some kind of urban slang, but I can't remember what it is.'

'Well, I don't have a bloody clue. The most "street" I've ever been was the time I accidentally went into Urban Outfitters looking for shelf brackets because I thought it was a hardware store. Maybe it's some spiritual terminology for lovely ladies who are rare and beautiful.'

Up ahead, Amy and Debs have stopped dead in their tracks and have turned to face Jac and me with their jaws wide open.

Amy has a look of delighted astonishment. 'Ladies, I think I know why it's called the moon deck.'

'Why?' I head up to where they're standing to get a better look at the weird entanglement of yogi star worshippers.

'Because I can see lots of arses.' She's jumping giddily up and down on the spot, and pointing towards a group of what must be over twenty people all stark bollock naked and adopting positions more likely to be seen in a porno than a David Lloyd exercise studio.

'Oh my God! My eyes, my eyes!' Debs thrusts her hands in front of her face in a bid to protect her retinas from the X-rated scenes.

'Ladies, please, come!' Branch grins, guiding the four of us towards the labyrinth of groaning bodies.

'I don't want to come,' Jac whispers to me, as we slowly shuffle along like we're being led to our execution. 'I *really* don't want to…'

'Please take a seat.' He gestures as we reach a collection of Thai triangle pillows in the centre of the decking, directly next to two women playing a non-PG version of Twister.

'What can I get you ladies? A smoothie perhaps?' Branch casually asks, as though he's taking our order in Starbucks.

Not feeling like kale's going to be able to block out the graphic exploits happening before us, I ask, optimistically, 'Anything harder?'

'Yeah, that 300lb hairy biker dude in the corner.' Amy joyfully returns the wave of an extremely-pleased-to-see-us elderly gentleman propped up on a beanbag.

Trying to make as little eye contact with any of the people surrounding us as humanly possible, I politely decline Branch's hospitality on behalf of us all.

'Oh nonsense, you must try Guthrie's world-famous courgette fritter. They're pretty spectacular, are they not, my friend?'

As if by magic, up pops Guthrie from behind yet another bush – this time female in origin.

'That they are, my goddesses!' He happily removes himself from between the legs of his lady friend, his Cornish pasty on show for all to see. 'And, of course, I'm more than happy to serve all of your needs…'

'NO! Really Guthrie…' I most definitely do not want his courgette fritter anywhere near my mouth. 'I wouldn't want to
interrupt you when you're… er… busy. Great job by the way,
excellent technique, well done you.' And with no idea of how to
conduct myself socially in this sort of situation, I thrust my
palm towards him for a congratulatory high five.

'Cara!' Jac shouts, utterly horrified as she slaps my hand
away.

'Oh my God, thank you so much,' I whisper to her. 'That was
so awkward. I don't know what came over me.'

'Well fortunately it wasn't Guthrie, so you're welcome.'

Guthrie's partner, now evidently bored of her long-haired
lover, rolls away from him and sits up to drape her arms around
mine and Jac's shoulders. 'He's all yours, mes chéries,' she says in
a breathy French accent. 'He has already fulfilled the needs of my
internal galaxy with eleven climactic starbursts.'

'Do you think she means the sweets?' Debs asks as we watch
in quiet amazement as the curvaceous continental beauty stands
up, pads her way over to the elderly chap on the beanbag and
starts getting to work on her twelfth.

'Ok then!' the Cornish Casanova pipes up. 'Fritters for four it
is.' And before we have time to protest any further, he's bounding
off in the direction of the house, white bum cheeks glowing in
the moonlight.

While Guthrie is off risking life and limb limb over a deep fat
fryer, and Branch is making us detoxifying pond sludge I very
much hope doesn't come with the additional ingredient of
Rohypnol, we hatch a plan to remove ourselves from this low
budget production of *Hippy Hippy Gang Bang*.

'I have a baby, I have a baby, I have a baby,' Debs chants to
herself, while rocking and trying to send an SOS message to Will.

'Let's make a run for it.' Jac is already undoing her shoes for a
speedy get away. 'We'll pretend we're going to the loo, safety in

numbers and all that, and then, when no is looking, we make a break for it. It's subtle, believable and, if we say one of us is constipated, it buys us time.'

'We're fully grown women. We don't need to run, or make excuses. Why can't we simply thank them for the opportunity, grab our things and leave?' I ask, as my eyes continually dart between the house and the bar area to make sure our holistic hosts aren't yet on their way back to us.

'Because we have not been fired by Lord Sugar, Cara,' Amy says. 'Plus, I'd feel a bit awkward explaining we're not staying…'

'Awkward? Are you joking? Amy, I think I've just seen a man stick a telescope up another man's arse. I think us politely leaving is probably going to be the least awkward part of this entire evening.'

'But it's a bit rude isn't it? We've led them on. We can't simply tell them we're off before it's our turn.'

'Sorry, before it's our turn?' My eyebrows are raised so high they're now stratospheric and probably only visible via said shitty telescope. 'We haven't led them on and it's not going to be our turn. Why on earth would they think that?'

'Because we're their unicorns,' Amy says condescendingly, as though the three of us are as thick as the wooden planks we're sitting on. 'You know, single females at sex parties?'

'Oh! I knew I'd heard it somewhere!' Jac suddenly remembers in a moment of delighted clarity, as if she's finally cottoned on that the annoying theme tune in her head is actually from *Grange Hill*.

'Oh. My. God. Are you joking?' I gasp in horror. This now makes a LOT more sense, and also raises the question of how I'll ever be able to look at Nancy's wallpaper in the same way again.

'That's it, and we're done!' Debs stands up, holding her Valentino sandals in her hand, ready to run faster than Seabiscuit. 'I'm not even my husband's sexual partner so I'm sure as shit not hanging around here to be approached by that creepy dude who keeps winking at me while flicking his nipples. Girls, I'm going to the toilet – I'm more backed up than Royal Mail at Christmas, so I may be some time!' She announces this loudly as she backs away from the circle.

'Me too.' Jac immediately understands the assignment and jumps up to join her. 'Cara, hope you brought the Senokot!'

Nodding, I grab hold of Amy and drag her up to a standing position.

'Just a minute!' she says, swatting me off so she can retrieve a pen out of her 1990s-style mini rucksack. 'Just leaving my number for Guthrie… that man's got some serious skills.'

'Amy.' I growl at her, trying not to draw attention to ourselves, but in the same instance also noticing Debs who, in her haste to escape, has stacked it over the leg of the nipple-flicking dude and fallen backwards into a table of lit candles. As a cascade of molten wax is catapulted through the air, meteorites of hell fire begin to rain down on the unprotected (in more ways than one) pubic regions of sex-mad stargazers – turning moans of pleasure into howls of pain. Chaos ensues, as wobbly bits and flabby arses scramble for cover, sending even more candle-containing tables scattering across the alfresco deck. 'This is not good…' I duck, dive and dip my way through a stampede of swinging scrotums as though I'm playing a game of dodge… balls. As a whiff of smoke tingles at my nostrils, I turn around in time to see an upturned plate of tea lights ignite a pool of highly combustible massage oil. Uh-oh. 'Amy, we need to go NOW!' I scream, as the orange flames dance their way across the dry and flaking wood of the finca's outdoor area. Quickly scrawling her number, along with the words, 'I'll eat your courgette, call me!' on a soon-to-be incinerated timber beam, Amy legs it towards a shell-shocked Debs, grabs her by the elbow and drags her towards the dirt track.

Coughing and spluttering, we waste no time in sprinting after Jac who's already half way to the main road and shouting something about us all going down for arson. A prison sentence would not be ideal, granted, but I'm also highly optimistic an Ibizan jail cell might be a step up from the rat-infested lodgings of a now smouldering 'Unicorn Utopia'.

'Oh my God, are they all dead?!' Debs wails, as we breathlessly make our getaway along the dusty road. 'Am I a murderer? Is someone going to make a Netflix documentary out of me?'

Turning round to assess the carnage we've left in our wake, I see the dark outlines of revellers safely gathered in the surrounding grounds of the farmhouse as a considerably angry-looking Branch extinguishes the majority of the flames with, what looks to be, a giant pitcher of kale and cacao smoothie. 'They're all fine, babes. Relax, you didn't kill anyone.'

The acrid smell of singed lavender oil, wood, and body hair floats through the air. Stopping to catch her breath, and work out a stitch, Amy erupts in raucously deep, raspy, laughter.

'It's not funny, Amy!' Debs pants tearfully, as the adrenaline begins to wears off and the post-traumatic shakes of 'what could have been' set in.

'No, I know,' Amy agrees, trying to breathe deeply in through her nose and out through her mouth. 'But it's occurred to me…' she's biting her bottom lip to prevent her hysterical laughter from escaping, 'I hope Branch has excellent *pubic* liability insurance…'

I roll my eyes, and push her convulsing body up the road. 'Too soon, Amy. Too bloody soon.'

14

First Shots Fired

Having trekked in the dark for an hour and fifteen minutes, most of which was spent calming down Debs, shouting at Amy to stop humming The Prodigy's 'Fire Starter', and trying to convince taxi drivers we weren't mad, we're standing in the heavenly scented and air-conditioned lobby of St Eulalia's M Hotel.

'I'm sorry, if you could repeat that... how much a night?' I ask again, assuming I've misheard the impeccably dressed and gorgeous reception lady who, instead of a poncho or a hemp thong, is wearing a much more professional-looking white pressed linen suit. Looking like she's just stepped off the front cover of *Spanish Vogue*, she's a far cry from Branch. In fact, the closest we are to any kind of wood-based objects is the minimalist twig art installation hanging from the hotel's impressively grand ceiling.

'Si madam, it's 1,663 euro per night per room. Would you like me to make the reservation for you all?' She smiles with a luminous set of white teeth, as two twenty-something tanned and toned bell boys arrive with a tray of iced complimentary cocktails. I turn to look at Jac who has the same pleading expression my children used to convince Dom and me to buy a cocker spaniel puppy when we were absolutely adamant we were never going to be dog people.

'Sure thing.' I grimace, pulling out my credit card and praying to the Mastercard gods that my limit can take it. Despite the girls' kind offer to pay my way when we were back in Blighty, I can't help notice there's a distinct lack of enthusiasm for extending the budget to cover a last-minute five-star luxury upgrade. I know they'll all pay me back, I'm just hoping it's before my kids need new clothes, or food…

'Perfecta!' The receptionist takes my card. 'We're going to give you two of our best rooms here at the hotel.'

'I should fucking think so,' Amy pipes up. 'At that price I'm expecting one of these cocktail boys and a bag of coke to be included.'

'She's joking! Of course, she's joking…' I laugh nervously, as the receptionist suspiciously swipes my card through the reader.

'And your luggage? Do you need help taking that to your room?' she asks, peering round the desk in confusion.

'Ah yes, about that…' Amy butts in, casually lounging over the cool white marble desk. 'Don't suppose you have a taser and a bottle of pepper spray we can borrow, do you?'

'Oh my gosh, this is HEAVEN!' gushes Jac, collapsing onto the cloud-like mattress of our new lodgings. 'Babes, the sheets have an actual thread count, and what *is* that smell? This time in a good way!'

She's right: a perfect blend of bergamot oil and lavender gives our minimalist designer-curated Insta-worthy room some serious day spa vibes – a far cry from the retreat's nasal ambience of eau de rancid toilette.

'Right, plan of attack, ladies!' Amy announces, barging into our room with a bottle of Prosecco in hand, having apparently blagged herself an extra key from reception. 'Bits and pits wash – no time for full showers – drinks in the room and then we're hitting the West End! Waiting for Debs to finish crying on the phone to her mum while milking herself then we're good to go. I've been to the bar, ridiculous prices, so this will be the first and last drink you'll get from me here – don't waste it. You've got twenty minutes and then we're going to go and fuck shit up!' And with that she turns on her heel and slams the door.

'Right then, looks like we're getting drunk and going dancing,' I say to Jac as she fishes two tumblers out of the bathroom.

'I'll drink to that!' she rejoices as I tip fizz we'll no doubt later regret into our glasses.

'Salut!' I raise my drink in the air. 'Here's to mums on tour!'

'Absofuckinglutely! And remember: what happens on mum tour...'

'Stays on mum tour!' I finish, before we clink and sink the deliciously ice cold bubbles. Sitting down on the edge of the bed, and allowing the relaxing warmth of the alcohol to filter through my veins, I send an obligatory 'All ok?' message to my aunt and uncle, before closing my eyes and soaking in the welcoming bliss of pure silence. Yes, now that we're safely away from swinging holidays from hell, this was most definitely a good idea. I can feel it in my bones.

Stepping out of the taxi and into the warm Ibiza evening air, I realise, for the second time today, that Amy being left to organize everything on her own wasn't only not very fair, it wasn't particularly wise. 'Amy, are you sure this is the right place?' I eye up the long, narrow and incredibly seedy-looking strip brimming with open-shirted and mini-skirt-clad teens.

'Sure am. Welcome to the West End!' she declares, spinning on the spot with her arms outstretched as though she's Julie Andrews.

But in this adaptation of *The Sound of Music* it isn't the hills that are alive, it's the copious number of squalid, throbbing nightspots with flickering neon signs outside. Where the heck are we? Where are the classy beach-front bars with exquisite sea views for watching world-famous Balearic sunsets melt into picturesque oceanic horizons? Also missing are the beautiful people in extravagant designer outfits sipping champagne while dancing to chilled out classics. They've been replaced by throngs of raucous, predominantly male, youths with daft haircuts, either being sick into drains or sucking air out of balloons.

'What *are* they doing?' Debs asks, digging in her clutch bag for her hand sanitiser. 'Trying to change their voices on helium?'

'Not quite, no,' Jac says, patting our sweetly naive friend on the head. 'Listen, I'm not sure about this, Ames, it looks dodgy as fuck and I reckon we're a solid twenty years too old to even be contemplating this madness. Plus Debs is still wearing her Valentinos and it's sacrilegious to make them walk down that urine and puke-covered street.'

'Also, why does it smell like feet even though we're outside?' I ponder, further adding to our hesitancy to take even half a step further.

'Girls, come on! This is an Ibizan rite of passage. Everyone who comes here, especially on a hen party, has to experience one night in the West End – it'll be a scream, trust me!'

'But where are all the theatres?' Debs strains her neck to see past the masses of youngsters grinding their way along the thoroughfare, apparently hoping to see an advertisement for *My Fair Lady* or *The Lion King* – although *Les Misérables* would be more fitting.

'Ok, fine…' I reluctantly agree 'A few drinks, but then we move on, promise?'

'Promise!' Amy agrees, as we follow a ridiculously over-excited Maria Von Crap into the bristling flow of utter pandemonium.

Making our way through the hustle and bustle of the strip in riot police style formation (for safety), it feels as though we've stepped back in time to our trashy 18-30 holidays of yonder years. However, this time round we're living it through the horrified eyes of our parents. Watching a group inebriated girls having a cat fight outside of a kebab shop while sunburnt pervy blokes in beer slogan sleeveless vests cheer at them from the side-lines is enough to make me consider enlisting my own children in a strict underground religious cult for the foreseeable.

As we walk, young 'cheeky chappy' lads from all corners of the UK attempt to stop us every 500m or so, with varying offers of cheap shots, fishbowls and half price vodka Redbulls – all desperate to drag a bunch of nearly middle-aged mums into their dingy dark holes.

'No thanks, dickhead!' Amy yells, storming past the latest overly tactile toy boy wannabe vying for our attention by using the term 'sexy mamas', and directing us into the relative safety of a questionable Irish bar named 'The Leprechaun With the Horn'.

'Ok.' Amy assesses the sticky laminated menu welded to the empty Guinness barrel we're now huddled round. 'Shots?'

Despite our best protests, moments later a tray of highly questionable clear liquid, limes and salt sachets arrives at our makeshift table. 'Bottoms up, ladies!' She grins, dishing us out a double portion of something I sense we'll all be seeing again later.

'Is this Patron?' Debs asks, dubiously sniffing the contents of the plastic containers. In all honestly, she's going to be hard pushed to smell anything other than the pungent aroma of cannabis lingering heavily in the air.

'Will you drink it if it's Patron?' Amy says.

'Yes, because it's the only tequila that doesn't make me sick,' Debs reminds her, as though this is a question that, after eighteen years of friendship, she should really know the answer to.

'Amazing. It's your lucky day, babe, because Patron is all they had! Ready? Lick, shoot, suck!'

Fifteen seconds later and Debs is running as fast as her heels can allow, hands over her mouth, towards the toilets and Amy is creased on her bar stool. 'Man, she's too easy!' She cackles into her next shot. 'Of course it was going to be shit cheap bar tequila! Knowing what most of these places are like, she's lucky it wasn't on a par with that hand sanitiser she's always carrying round.'

'Amy, she's just had a baby! She's sensitive at the best of times, but even more so after being on a forced journey of sobriety for the past twelve months. Can we go easy on her? I don't have the upper body strength to be carrying her home later,' I plead.

'Agreed,' Jac says. 'I've seen enough bodily fluids today to last me a lifetime.'

'On the plus, though, ladies…' I change the course of the conversation away from one unsavoury topic towards another, 'it's been a solid ten hours since I last had a vindictive and murderous thought about my ex-husband and sister. So, as comically awful as this first day in Ibiza has been, I feel I may be turning a corner.'

'I'll drink to that!' Amy rejoices, offering me another shot.

'Not with that, thanks. I'd rather drink cat piss,' I say, slapping Amy's hand out of my face.

'Ok, as much as I'm loving the Dublin vibes of this place,' Jac says, 'they've played Ed Sheeran's "Galway Girl" six times – I think it's time to move on. We just need Debs and then let's bounce.'

'There she is,' I say, pointing as she attempts to swerve past a group of fifty-year-old women flipping about drunkenly like rebelling Sea World dolphins and most definitely not profession-ally trained in the art of *River Dance*.

'What the hell has she got on her head?' Amy asks, hoovering up the rest of our unwanted shots.

'It's an LED light-up crown I was coerced into buying by a rather relentless man with sunglasses sewn into his jacket lining,' Debs answers huffily, as she plonks herself unsteadily at the table. 'He was waiting for me outside the toilet. Thanks for coming to look for me, by the way. This piece of crap cost me eight euros!'

Laughing at Debs' typical British over-politeness, I'm actually surprised she managed to escape with only the headband and not a knock-off pair of 'Tommy Hollflogger' sunnies to boot. 'Babe, you could have said no – like everyone else does – and then walked away. Those guys are used to it, believe me.' I tell her, admiring the flashing multicoloured headdress that Nancy would absolutely adore.

'I didn't want to be rude –he was actually very complimentary and sweet. He told me I was the most beautiful woman he'd ever seen in his entire life, which is more attention than I've got from Will of late. Anyway, he had some lovely necklaces I thought were *super* cute so I took the liberty of buying us all one as a little keepsake of our trip. Here…' She hands the silver chains out to each of us, one-by-one. 'They have little spoons on the end of them!' She claps her hands together in joy. 'Who knew kitchen-themed jewellery was such a big thing in Ibiza! His English wasn't great but I asked if he had anything special to go with them and I think he got the gist because he tapped his nose and told me he'd be right back. So… hopefully we'll all have some little knives and forks to match!'

'Er, Debs…' Jac says, suspiciously eyeing up the spoon neck-lace she's rotating between her fingertips, 'I don't think you've ordered us more miniature tableware… I think you've solicited us some cocaine!'

'What?' Debs screams, dropping her necklace on the table. 'No, I asked for something to go with the little spoons!'

'Yes, and these teeny tiny little spoons are for scooping up teeny tiny portions of coke and then shoving them up your blower.' Amy hangs the chain around her neck. 'Might come in useful...'

'Oh my God, oh my God, oh my God!' Debs starts to spiral. 'What do we do?'

'I suggest we get the hell out here before he comes back with his dealer and they realise we have no intention of securing illegal narcotics from them.' Jac says, standing up hastily and beginning to gather our handbags off the table.

'Jeez, going on a copper's hen party is about as much fun as, well... going on a copper's hen party, I suppose.' Amy looks disappointed. 'Ok bitches, you heard the fun police – time to roll out!'

As we speedily make our way out of the Irish bar, I throw a quick glance back over my shoulder in time to see a confused man with twelve pairs of sunglasses on his head arrive at our table – accompanied by a significantly angrier-looking bloke with facial tattoos and nearly as much gold in his teeth as the heavy chains (minus spoons) he's wearing around his neck. Ushering the girls past the inebriated Irish jiggers and towards the doors, the more intimidating of the two men furiously scours the crowd for his escapee punters and briefly locks eyes with my own gawping stare.

'Shit!' I shout to the girls as we bundle ourselves out of the exit and back into the chaos of the strip. 'GO, GO, GO!'

15

A Man After Midnight

Back out in the buzzing hive of the strip, ignoring the cat calls from shit-faced rugby players, we keep our heads firmly down as we weave our way quickly through the crowds of bucket-hat-adorned, crop-top-wearing revellers drunkenly falling over each other as they move from one dive bar to the next. The constant movement of groaning and shuffling bodies reminds me of something you'd see in a scene from *The Walking Dead*: mindless, jaw-swinging zombies all after their next fix of human flesh.

'In here!' Amy calls out from ahead of us, signalling to a small doorway with a luminous blue sign above it.

'Hooters & Shooters,' I read out. 'Sounds classy…'

'This was one of my old doors – banging tunes and fishbowls as big as your sister's tits. Come on!'

'Perfect, sounds right up my street.' I eye-roll, stepping foot over the sordid threshold and following Amy down a precarious flight of stairs. What is it about this part of Ibiza that makes me constantly want to whip out a pair of Marigolds and bottle of Dettol?

Inside, the heat is stifling, and I wonder whether we've actually descended into a sweaty and UVA-lit hell. In the oppressive humidity of the purple dungeon, I immediately curse my fast-fashion impulsiveness for the baby-pink, very clingy and glittery dress that's now welded to my perspiring body. A badly chosen white thong and strapless bra glow brightly from underneath it.

'Jeez, Cara, put it away!' Jac jests as I try to cover my foo with my hand and tits with a tiny clutch bag. I feel like I'm having one of those naked-in-public anxiety dreams.

Leaving Debs on a lilac crushed velvet sofa to wonder what the stains are and dutifully check her phone for baby updates, we make our away across the buzzing dance floor in search of a much needed cocktail, or seven.

'Oh my God, look what the cat dragged in!' The voice of an extremely Scouse, six-foot-plus, drag queen with eye makeup as fierce as her bondage outfit, thunders from behind the bar as we make our approach.

'Betty? No fucking way you're still here!' Amy cries, running round the back of the black glossy counter to hug who I presume to be an estranged friend and not an old flame, but, with Amy, one can never be too sure.

'Of course I am! Where the bloody hell else would I be? Back in Liverpool wiping old dears' arses in that god-awful nursing home? No fucking thank you. I've seen the future – it's wrinkly and smells of shite! Anyway, more to the point – what are you doing back here? I thought you'd run away to Sydney with that hot psychic medium you met in Amnesia?'

'Sadly not,' Amy says with a dejected sigh. 'Turns out he was a fan of amnesia alright –completely forgot to tell me about his wife and three kids. Kicked his ass to the kerb.'

'Savage!' the drag queen gasps, with a disapproving shake of her head which jolts her sensationally glittery bin-lid millinery off at even more of a wonky tangent. 'You'd have thought he'd have seen it coming, given his 'sight' – that said he did have that lazy eye going on too, which, in retrospect, might explain its wandering nature. Anyway, who are *these* beautiful bitches?' she says, specifically turning her attention to my glowing orbs. 'Alright, sparkle tits, no need to bring your headlights, love. It's an underground nightclub not a coal mine.'

Blushing, I fold my arms over my chest and wait for the ground to swallow me whole.

Amy introduces us. 'Girls, this is Betty... Betty Swallows.'

Betty bends into a pretty impressive curtsey, given the height of her PVC thigh-high boots. Between her leather dominatrix dress and floor-length cape, I'm amazed that, in this heat, she hasn't collapsed into a puddle of perspiration and eight inches' worth of full matte foundation.

'What's wrong with that one?' Betty asks, pointing to Debs who, left to her own devices for more than three minutes, is now fast asleep on the sofa, phone in hand.

'Oh she's fine. New mum – due a quick disco nap,' Amy explains. 'Right, Betty my woman, a round of your finest fish-bowls, and don't scrimp on the blue curaçao. If my shit doesn't resemble antifreeze in the morning I'll be furious.'

'You know me, darling, I specialise in stomach pumps and blue dumps.' Betty winks ominously. 'Take a seat, gals, and I'll bring it over.'

As we head back over to a snoozing Debs, the familiar opening chords of Abba's 'Gimme Gimme' blare out from the DJ booth. 'I love this song!' squeals Jac, jumping up and down on the spot. 'Can we dance? Pretty please?'

Laughing, I allow her to lead me by the hand onto the tacky (in more ways than one), flashing disco-style floor. It's been so long since I last danced, I'm unsure my body even knows how to move in time to music... but sure enough, as the beat ramps up, so do our moves and before I know it the three of us are shaking our bootays and strutting our stuff as though we're in the semi-finals of *Strictly Mum Dancing*.

'Oh Amy… can you hear my prayer?!' I holler at my cousin as she gyrates against a muscly shirtless man in a pair of gold Speedos.

'I can feel something!' she shouts back, gripping his giant thighs, before slut-dropping on the ground with the ease of someone in her twenties but forgetting how much harder it is to return to a vertical position when you're actually in your late thirties.

Maybe it's the cheap tequila talking, but watching the clenching arse cheeks of Speedo Man trying to heave her off the ground but losing his balance and falling on top of her is quite possibly one of the most hilarious things I've ever borne witness to. Tears of laughter fall down my face. Wait, is this fun? Am I actually enjoying myself? It's been so long I can hardly remember but, as I watch Amy and the male equivalent of Kylie Minogue thrusting against one another on the floor, my mind reasons that I am and it's bloody wonderful.

As our very loud, and very out of key, singing reaches its crescendo, Jac thinks it's a marvellous idea to act like a drunk uncle at a wedding, taking me by the hand and spinning me energetically across the room. Sadly for anyone in direct proximity to my runaway tornado, velocity is quick to take hold and I'm propelled across the room with the finesse of a pirouetting elephant – straight into a very large human equivalent of a brick wall. Whirling round to extend a grovelling apology to the poor soul I've just collided with, I realise that by screeching for the universe to 'give me a man after midnight', the universe has indeed made good on the request and delivered…

'Hola, Cara…' he smoulders, as my mouth drops open in complete and utter disbelief.

'Oh shit!' I word-vomit as, for the third time today, I'm faced with the all-encompassing beauty of 'Javier the Handsome'.

'Well, it's nice to see you again, too…' he muses, looking as hot as a non-air-conditioned Ibizan nightclub. 'You look…' he says, taking a minute to slowly let those irresistible brown infinity pools of his lazily roll their way over my glowing body, 'radiant.'

My face is now beaming brighter than the collective efforts of my tits and bits. 'Oh, th-th-thanks…' I stutter, awkwardly trying to cover my not-so-private parts with shaky arms. 'Anyway, what are you doing here?' I ask, as if I've just found him standing in my kitchen helping himself to a packet of chocolate digestives.

'I'm here for the same reasons as you, Cara,' he answers smoothly.

'Oh really?' I feel brave and – quite possibly – a little flirtatious. 'You're here to escape a poisonous ex, treacherous family, perverted sex cult, counterfeit cutlery seller, and metal-mouthed cocaine dealer too?'

A wry smile spreads across his snoggable face and, as he nods his head in mock contemplation, strokable locks of floppy boy-band hair glisten majestically in smoky beams of school-disco strobe lighting.

'Ah, no. I thought you were going to say you're here for the coolest floor-filling hits from 1983…' He trails off, gesturing to the jam-packed dance floor filled with sweaty bodies, those of my friends included, busting their best moves to The Weather Girls' 'It's Raining Men'. Seeing Javier, Jac and Amy stop dead in their uncoordinated tracks and simultaneously mouth 'NO FUCKING WAY' at me before Amy bends Jac over and hip-thrusts into her bum cheeks, all while giving me an encouraging thumbs up.

'Drink?' I pivot quickly, hoping to distract him from my friends' anal antics. 'I'm so sorry, I've obviously just spilt yours,' I say, alluding to his empty glass and the giant wet patch spreading down his T-shirt – showcasing bulging muscles of what must be at least a sixteen pack. Honestly, not even a 1990s Peter Andre can compete with this man.

'Come on,' I say boldly, and as nonchalantly as possible in his presence, 'my way of saying thank you for coming to my rescue, not once but twice today.' Wow, thinking about it, a LOT has happened since the early hours of this morning. In the past fifteen hours, this trip to Ibiza has provided me with more excitement than I've experienced in the past fifteen years of my life.

'Cara, please, let me be the one who buys you a drink – if nothing else so that I can save you one more time today, from that…' Javier says, nodding towards Betty heading over to Jac and Amy with a tray of something bright blue that looks as though it'd be better served cleaning a toilet.

'Wow,' I say, assessing the hideous vibrancy of the cocktail. 'Do you know what? That would be lovely. Thank you.' Cara Carmichael, I think, who even are you? Accepting a drink from a tall, dark and handsome man in a shady nightspot. Having not been in this position for an extremely long time, and unable to contain my awkwardness at not knowing how to conduct myself socially, my nerves get the better of me and I fall to my default defence mode of making a poorly executed pun: 'Don't suppose you Havier any tequila do you?'

The joke lands as well as a hijacked plane as he cocks a confused eyebrow at me. 'Let's ask, shall we?'

My skin tingles with anticipation as he places a strong hand on the small of my back and guides me towards the glistening fairy lights and pleather stools surrounding the bar.

Easing myself down next to him, it occurs to me that I have no idea what I'm going to say to this fine specimen of a man. The last time I attempted heavy-duty flirting, Christina Aguilera's 'Dirrty' was number one in the charts. To say I'm a little rusty would be more than an understatement. Deciding it's safer for me to talk as little as possible, I call on a female seduction tactic as old as time in the form of a bit of reliable eyelash fluttering.

'Cara, are you ok?' Javier asks, clearly concerned for my well-being. 'Is there something in your eye? Are your contact lenses giving you more problems?' And with that he reaches out and tilts my chin up for a closer inspection. 'You should really think about glasses, or actually laser surgery. Those eyes of yours are too beautiful to be hidden away.' He traces his fingertips up my cheek letting them rest next to my lashes. Desire stabs at my groin and I'm amazed at how quickly my libido has woken from its enforced hibernation – like a ravenous snuffling hedgehog.

'Señorita, two of your finest tequilas, por favor!' He retracts his hand from my face to pull out his wallet – which I can't help but notice, is bursting at the seams with a thick wedge of euro notes.

'Sorry, Ricky Martin, no living your vida loco here. I've only got the stuff that comes in a bottle with a little red hat,' Betty replies haughtily, before sashaying off to fetch her liquid poison.

Still in his same all black, mostly denim, outfit he was sporting on the plane, the pared-back effortless coolness of his aura, combined with his apparent financial prosperity, makes him seem so out of place in a spangled, camp pleasure dome like this – making me wonder why he is really here. It's definitely not the kind of bar you'd come to for a quiet sundowner on your own. I can't see any angry-looking female acquaintances giving me the evil eye for whisking away their bloke, nor can I see any abandoned-looking friends in search of their considerably more good-looking wing man. Then it dawns on me... maybe he's gay. Men that look like him were never designed for women like me, or women in general: absolute facts. Handing me the cool shot glass of inhibition-lowering elixir, his fingers brush against my own, sending my stomach lurching with sexual tension. But still, I stand by the fact that people like me do not have flings with people like him. *Or do we? No Cara, don't be daft!* Knocking back the tequila, I tell myself how ludicrous I'm being. Realistically, what would I even do, should the opportunity arise? A new penis to deal with? I reckon I'd scream and run away. What if it had too much foreskin, or not enough? I've never operated a circumcised one before. Dom's was always dressed for cold weather, in a turtleneck sweater.

'Suck?' Javier suddenly asks, as though he's penetrated my mucky mind.

'I beg your pardon?' I protest, as though I'm Elizabeth Bennet warding off an unwarranted approach by an inappropriate suitor.

'Lime, do you want to suck?' he asks again, holding the fruit up to my face.

'Oh… Yes please, thanks.' I blush, taking it from him and cramming it in my mouth. 'So you're here – gah, that's sharp – sorry – in Ibiza on your own?' I'm eager to find out more about this international man of mystery as my mouth waters with the acidity and with eagerness to devour him whole.

'You're never really on your own, Cara,' he says, wisely. 'You may travel through life without a designated companion, but am I alone in this instance, sitting at this bar, drinking these drinks with you?'

This is very true but, in all honesty, I was after somewhat less of a philosophical answer and more a determining factor as to whether or not there's a Mrs – or Mr – Javier waiting for him back at his hotel.

'Deep…' I acknowledge. Recircling, I attempt another extraction of information. 'So, what brings you here – not on your own, maybe on your own – to the White Island? Business or… *pleasure*?' Despite the cringiness of my words making my insides fold in on themselves, oh how desperately I want him to reply 'pleasure', and to then follow those words up by saying, 'with you…'

'I guess you could say a bit of both,' he answers coolly. 'You see, Cara, my work is all-consuming. It's hard to separate the personal from the professional – they are very much… entwined.' As he says this, his hand falls purposely to my lap, resting against my inner thigh. All I can think of, in this moment, is how very much I'd like to be entwined… around his face. Batting away my now fully awake spiked bush-dwelling creature, I try to block all images of what I want to do to him from my mind and attempt to sound composed, interested, but not too keen.

'What is it that you do?' I ask, guessing maybe an actor, war reporter, or stripper.

'Waste management.'

'Oh! Ok…' I say, trying not to sound disappointed by the least sexy job ever. 'I love a man who's not afraid to get his hands dirty.'

He throws his head back and laughs. 'I'm joking, Cara, of course.'

God, I love the way he says my name, rolling the Rs as if he's gargling Listerine. It's so bloody seductive.

'No, I'm in, shall we say, international investigations,' he continues, rather seriously. 'My job is to find people, Cara,' he continues, his fingers upping their thigh game from grazing to caressing, 'wherever they might be, even when they try to hide themselves from the world.'

'Like Interpol?'

Hesitating for the briefest of moments, 'Yes,' he answers. 'Perhaps that is why our paths have crossed, Cara Carmichael. Maybe you are a wanted woman?'

'Me? Oh no…' I protest, hoping he hasn't noticed the increasing sweatiness of my ham hocks and also wondering when I told him my surname. 'The most criminal act I've committed is not telling the woman in Zara that she'd only scanned one pair of jeans when I'd actually given her two. Unless that makes me the terrible kind of person you go after?'

'Cara,' he says, leaning in so closely to my face that he's in inhaling distance, 'believe me when I say you are *exactly* the kind of woman I would go after.'

I feel the heat of his breath on my face, I see the wanting in his eyes, and as he goes in for the kill I hear—

'CARA! Time to bounce, let's go!'

'Amy, what the…?!' I growl, snapping my head around to see my cousin and Debs, now back in the world of the living, holding Jac up between them. She is absolutely off her skull and mumbling something about a doner kebab.

'She got a bit carried away with the fishbowl – strawpedo'd the whole thing in one – went from 0 to 100 on the drunk scale in about thirty seconds. Now she's about to blow and I, for one, do not want to see that cocktail in reverse.'

'Man from the plane,' Debs says, like a toddler who has spotted a duck, as she enthusiastically points at him with the free hand that's not holding Jac up.

Clambering off my sweaty barstool, leaving half of my thigh skin behind and cursing my friends, I weakly offer Javier an apology. 'I'm so sorry. A hen's gotta do what a hen's gotta do… Thank you for the drink, and of course the Heimlich manoeuvre…'

'Entiendo…' he says, taking my hand and gently kissing my fingers. 'Adios Cara, I'll be seeing you soon.'

Waving, I shuffle away from one of the most electric connections with another human being I've ever felt. There's something about him that sends my senses into overdrive. He feels different… dangerous almost. I'm not sure how to describe it, but there's a darkness to him I'm drawn to that's both intriguing and terrifying in equal measure. What I do know for sure is that, without a shadow of a doubt, he's unlike any man I've ever met before. Conflicted, I stop in my tracks. Should I go back and give him my number and snog the face off him? Or do I leave it in the hands of fate? Sod it, I think, remembering my pre-departure promise to live my life to the fullest. Spinning on my heel to run straight back to him, I'm surprised to see the decision has been made for me by the cock-blocking cosmos. There, where the pair of us sat only moments ago, stand two empty seats. My eyes dart around the dimly lit room. I scan the dance floor for signs of Javier, but as Simple Minds' 'Don't You' reverberates ironically around the club, it seems he's forgotten about me exceptionally quickly, walking away without so much as calling my name. I've not got long to wallow in how I should have seductively scrawled my number up his arm in lipstick, as my disappointment is quickly interrupted by Amy's panicked voice.

'FIRE IN THE HOLE!' she yells as a torrent of blue vomit erupts from Jac's mouth all over the nightclub stairs. Wonderful, I think, sidestepping what looks like exploded Smurf entrails. The perfect end to the perfect first night.

Having had to stop the cab every five minutes for Jac to empty her guts at the side of the road, we're safely back outside the M Hotel.

'Jac, can you please hold yourself together, ok?' I plead, as she stops about two feet away from the glitzy entrance to pee in a bush. 'For God's sake!' I despair, as she promptly gets her foot caught in her knickers and falls fanny-first onto the ground. Seeing two white-polo-shirt-clad bell boys rushing towards to the door, I scoop her up off the ground and pull her knickers back up into their rightful position before they get a right eyeful.

'Behave...' I warn her as Amy and I bundle her though the open door.

'Muchio grassy arse, me not you!' Jac shouts at the poor lads as we drag her through the lobby under the disapproving eye of the snooty evening receptionist. As we head towards the lifts, I say a silent prayer that all of our hen's bodily fluids are now safely expelled from her body and that she doesn't get us all thrown out for throwing up. I'm sure as shit not going back to that retreat. I'd rather go on a spa day with my mother and sister.

'Great night, hey?' A refreshed Debs grins, giving Amy and me a thumbs up. 'Mission accomplished.'

'And what was that mission, Tom Snooze? For half the hen party to puke and then to be back at the hotel for 11.35pm? This is Ibiza: all the young and trendy people are only heading out now and we're off to bed!'

'Valid point,' she agrees reluctantly. 'We could put Jac to bed and watch something on Netflix with some snacks? There's a shop round the corner that's still open. I could get some Jamon Ruffles?'

I do love a bag of Jamon Ruffles… but no, it's probably best to draw a line under today and wake up bright-eyed and bushy-tailed ready to start again tomorrow. Hitting the 'up' button on the lift, I reflect on the evening's shenanigans and wonder how the rest of our trip is going to shape up in comparison. Surely that's the worst of it now: it'll all be plain sailing from here on in. At least I got to see Javier again and had a near-kiss with a total stranger – that's a definite improvement on my normal state of self-pity. Maybe, just maybe, I'm beginning to get to a better place in life. Maybe I'm doing what everyone wants me to do by finally putting the past behind me. Hitting the button again, my mind drifts to Javier and what might have happened if we hadn't been interrupted… As the lift finally begins to approach, I hoist Jac up onto my hip, ready to throw her inside. But, as the doors slowly slide open and I see who's standing inside, my stomach falls to the floor with the ferociousness and speed of Jac's projectile Blue Lagoon.

'Hello Cara…'

'Hello Connie.' I reply shakily. 'Hello Mum…'

16

Family (mis)Fortunes

'I cannot believe this!' Amy fumes. 'It's an outrage! The affront, the audacity, the pure brazenness! Are they taking the piss? Twelve euros for freshly pulped orange juice?!'

Breakfast, the morning after the night before, and the four of us are conspicuously crammed into a corner of the hotel's poolside restaurant – still wearing last night's clothes since all our luggage is still being held hostage at the retreat – heads down, sunglasses on and deep in mutinous conversation.

'Amy, focus!' I hiss at her. 'Is it not more atrocious that my sister is here on her hen party? Celebrating her last hurrah of freedom in the same place as us before marrying my husband!' Absolutely seething, I slam my fists down on the table with such exertion it causes an elderly man next to us to spill coffee all down his Hawaiian shirt.

'Well, ex-husband, for one,' she unhelpfully corrects, 'and two, what are the bloody odds? Crazy! It's almost as though the universe wanted you both to collide. Don't you think? Like it wants to repair broken bonds.'

'I most certainly do not. When it comes to having to spend time with the female members of my family, the universe would be better served busying itself in the art of how to repair broken bones. Who gets married that quickly after getting engaged anyway? It's weird, don't you think?' I ask, angrily jabbing at a plate of Serrano ham and melon with my fork as though it's a voodoo doll of Connie.

'Unless it's a shotgun wedding?' Jac suggests from her hungover head-down position on the table, gracing us with her first words of the day that haven't consisted of 'I'm never drinking ever again.'

'No, no way she's pregnant. Did you see how skimpy her outfit was last night? We Carmichael women are plagued by pregnancy bloat – both Camilla and I resembled sea-going mammals from the minute our positive test results came up. Plus, she had a bottle of Veuve Clicquot in her hand. She's an airhead, sure, but surely not stupid enough to inflict foetal alcohol syndrome.'

Staring out of the hotel's open-fronted restaurant and onto the serene waters of the adults-only pool, ripples of nausea swell in my stomach – possibly down to the toxic tequila, possibly down to the toxic sister. Am I a bad person? Is this why I keep getting karmically punished by the powers that be? Maybe I'm being punished for sins committed in a previous existence… All I wanted was one weekend away with my friends, free from the constant mind-bending realities of my normal existence. But no: here I am again, trapped in an enveloping never-ending nightmare.

'Can you believe she invited us out to dinner tomorrow night? The absolute gall of it!' I continue to rant. 'And the hugging? Really? Like we were long-lost sisters separated by natural disaster or adversity not her and Dom's deep-seated perversity.' Just thinking about the way she flung her arms around me as those lift doors pinged open, gushing about how lovely it was we were here together, makes me want to Hulk-tear my clothes off and scream into a pillow – and then smother her with it. Did I hug her back? Did I heck. I stood there like a mute statue as she rambled on about all the fun things she and her hens had planned and about how it would be 'super' lovely to catch up. What were we doing? Going to bed? How funny! They had VIP tickets to a 'super' cool nightclub that was opening in a few hours so they were about to head out for a 'super' fun pre-drinks and dinner... at nearly midnight.

'Super,' I eventually managed to mutter, biting back the rest of what I was tempted to say as I pushed a belching Jac into the lift.

My mother was just as bad, of course she was. Wouldn't be a show without Punch, would it? A punch to the self-esteem, that is. 'Oh Cara, darling, don't you look... well?' she'd slurred, which is always Camilla code for 'lay off the pies, thunder thighs'.

'Cara, don't worry about it,' Amy attempts to reassure me. 'Ibiza is a big island, lots of bars, lots of nightclubs. We're probably not even going to see them again, ok? Oh wait, I retract that statement: they've just walked into the restaurant. Connie, Auntie Cam!' She stands up to wave at them.

'*What are you doing?*' I furiously mouth at her while sinking down into my chair and hiding behind the menu.

'I'm sorry,' she whispers out of the side of her mouth, 'but your mother ages like Benjamin fucking Button and I want her surgeon's number. Plus, she still sends me £20 in a card for my birthday. I feel rude ignoring her...'

'She does *what*?!' I boil, thinking of the empty, soulless birthday cards I've received over the past couple of years, weeks after the actual event and still with their 99p Card Factory stickers on them.

'Cara, Amy! How are you, my darlings?' My mother's loud and pompous voice booms across the restaurant. Now, Camilla's accent may sound like it wouldn't be out of place in the ballroom of Downton Abbey, but her current attire of choice makes her look like she'd be more at home hanging out on the street corners of Downtown LA with Vivian Ward.

'What *is* your mother wearing?' asks Jac who, hearing the commotion, has finally lifted her head above her shoulders and is squinting, albeit with her eyes still pointing in different directions, across the room at my mother sashaying over to us in a pair of white camel-toe-emphasising hot pants and an orange sequined bandeau top that seems to be held up only by the wishes of my queasy disposition.

'Cara, is that you? Oh and Amy, how wonderful!' This is my Aunt Mollie about two feet behind Camilla, dressed in a skin-tight lilac Lycra onesie that was mostly definitely not designed to be worn by a seventy-year-old woman, especially one who refuses to wear a bra. As the two pimped-up pensioners totter over to our table, arms outstretched as though they're trying to pet a litter of puppies, I keep my eyes firmly locked on the menu – busying myself with the detailed intricacies of how one would go about making an extortionately priced avocado and wheatgerm smoothie. Amy, on the other hand, the treacherous wench, is offering out warm hugs as though she's Olaf.

'Jacqueline, Deborah! How lovely to see you girls too!' my mother gushes. 'Gosh, it feels like only yesterday you were all staying round at the house and getting tiddly on bottles of Hooch. But wow, here you all are – looking fabulous and not a day over forty-five!'

Opening her mouth to protest that none of us are actually in our forties quite yet, Jac gives in to dehydrated defeat and slumps back down on the table with a groan. As if we are a bunch of ageing aunties at a wedding who everyone feels the needs to briefly say hello to, Connie is next to make an appearance, her silver iridescent bikini glistening under a white crochet beach cover-up (that's not covering much) as she saunters over.

'Good morning, ladies. How are we all?' she purrs, eyeing up our previous night's ensembles with interest. 'I thought you lot were all going to bed. What an absolute bunch of dirty stop-outs!'

Holding onto the menu with increasingly whitening knuckles, I find it laughable my sister feels safe to throw stones from her glasshouse of moral righteousness.

'OMG babe, have you seen the smoked salmon and dairy-free milk selection?' a rake-like woman with blonde hair down to her arse cheeks enthuses, bounding up to Connie so she can take a selfie of the pair of them brandishing the peace sign and a miniature bottle of Alpro.

'This is my friend, and maid of honour, Jennie,' Connie introduces, lovingly hugging the gold-kaftan-wearing woman whose cheekbones could easily be interchanged with cheese wire. 'We do online stuff together. You've probably seen us doing our 'two girls one cup' videos?'

I immediately regret choosing that precise moment to take a swig of my freshly pulped orange juice: burning pieces of citrus fibre are sucked into my nasal cavity with the intensity of a Dyson vacuum and then sprayed out across the table into a disgusted Debs' hair.

'Yeah, our new coffee-tasting podcast has been getting *so* much attention online,' Connie brags, only pausing for the briefest of moments to side-eye my reaction. 'I mean, who knew men were such caffeine freaks?'

'Sorry,' I whisper to Debs while attempting to mop up nose juice with a soggy napkin.

'Oh my gosh, I've just realised… *you're* the sister!' Jennie suddenly interrupts, her hands flying into the air in gossip-mongering delight. 'Wow. Wow. Wow. Let me say, I've heard *so* many things about you.'

Wiping the dregs of juice from my nose, I calmly place the napkin back down on the table and face Jennie, whose fillered mouth is agape in awe as if she's spotted a silverback gorilla in the wild.

Coldly returning the duck-billed platypussy's stare, I say, 'Sure am, but I also go by the aliases "ex-wife", "mother of *his* children", and "potentially a direct match if ever she needs a kidney", not that I'd ever give *her* one.'

Swiftly returning to the drink menu, I waste no time in choosing spirits over spirulina.

Jennie, deciding to take one last parting shot, before I've had a chance to order mine gushes, 'It's seriously so cool you're all here,' with sincerity as fake as 80% of her hair. 'Honestly, you lot are absolute goals. I really hope that when I'm as old as you I'm still coming out to Ibiza and trying to keep up with the young and beautiful. Come on, Con, let's go. I'm starving.'

With a flick of her hair, and stopping briefly to Snapchat a *pain au chocolate* she has no intention of eating, Jennie heads over to where an army of slinky, long-haired beautiful women have convened like they're waiting for the Miss World heats to begin. I notice one stunner in particular is doing her very best to ignore my presence in the room. Gemma, Dom's turncoat of a sister. I make a point of waving at the defector, and she speedily ducks out of sight behind a carafe of lemon water – evidently spying something fascinating on the floor.

'I'd better go and order, but hopefully we'll catch you guys later?' Connie says optimistically, almost pleadingly. 'Maybe for a few drinks around the pool?'

'Yeah, probably not. Old people shit to do, you know… sleeping, pissing ourselves, complaining…' I answer swiftly, before Amy has the chance to agree.

'Oh… sure, no worries…' Connie says, her voice laced with sadness.

Honestly, what was she expecting? That we'd have a lovely girly day lounging around, drinking mai tais while exchanging hilarious 'cock tales' about Dom?

'Bye, darlings!' Camilla waves, swiftly grabbing her youngest daughter by the shoulders, steering her away from our table of hungover trolls and towards her much more glamourous friends. 'Oh and Cara…' she calls behind her as she totters away in heels five inches too high for her, 'stay away from the pastries. You know what butter does to your face. Adios!'

Picking up a croissant and aggressively slathering it in an inch of full fat, full salt dairy goodness, I shove it into my mouth in one, flipping my mother the 'V's.

'Wow…' a normally polite-as-the-queen and seldom sweary Debs exclaims, fishing a bag of Jamon Ruffles out of her bag so that she can emotionally eat away her hurt feelings, 'what an absolute bunch of cunts.'

A quick call with my highly unimpressed wifi-less kids, some guided meditation with Matthew McConaughey, and several YouTube videos of kittens later, I'm feeling 10% calmer than I did an hour previously. Even better, our luggage has been safely retrieved from the clutches of Unicorn Utopia. I don't know what (or who) Amy did, or how much she paid, but I've never been so happy to see oversized underwear and panty liners in my entire life. Showered, makeup trowelled on, and dressed in my steel-reinforced control wear swimming costume, I'm ready to put this morning's unpleasantries firmly behind me.

'Fucking hell!' Amy bellows, again marching into mine and Jac's room unannounced. 'Are you able to take a bullet in that thing? I didn't know M&S sold military grade kevlar…'

'Hey, I have diastasis recti!' I whinge defensively. 'My stomach muscles gave up holding anything in, apart from carbs and trapped wind, a long time ago. It was either this floral monstrosity or a cold-water wetsuit.'

Honestly, as a mum, shopping for swimwear has to be right at the top of all soul-destroying tasks, even above a child asking you to smell their finger. All I wanted was something flattering, fashionable, and (in a feat of mechanical engineering worthy of a Nobel prize) possessed the capability to shave off two stone. But no, all that was available to me was a blue and yellow low-rise eyesore that my grandmother would have worn on a cruise thirty years ago.

'Where's Debs?' I ask, eyeing myself up in an antique copper full-length mirror I'm hoping is tilted at a very unflattering angle. 'Don't tell me she's asleep again?' The woman has only been awake for approximately 43% of our trip so far. If she sleeps any more, I'm concerned she may be certifiably classed as being in a coma.

'She's bollocking Will for not wiping Harriet's bits properly – something about front to back and crotch rot?' Amy casually mentions while rummaging through my suitcase in a bid to find me something else to wear. 'Ah-ha, what about this?' she says, pulling out a lacy black bra-and-thong set.

'Amy, that's *actual* underwear, for use under *actual* clothing,' I inform her, snatching it away and stashing it in a drawer. Why I bothered bringing it, I have no clue. Who did I think I was going to impress?

'All I'm saying is you can't go to Passion Beach wearing whatever the fuck that is.' Amy points at my costume accusingly. 'That, combined with Debs' hand sanitiser and the picnic Jac stole from the breakfast buffet, and we'll look like a right bunch of… well, mums,' she finishes, wrinkling her nose in disgust.

'I hate to break it to you, babe,' replies Jac, mid-unpacking bread rolls and slices of Serrano ham from a napkin and placing them into Tupperware containers, 'but we *are* a bunch of mums. Oh, and it's not stealing. We paid for the breakfast buffet – they always expect you take extra.'

'Anyway, what does it matter what we look like? We're only going to the beach, right?' I naively add. It's bad enough I'm wearing mascara I know will be sweated off the minute I step foot outside; attempting to dress nicely as well seems positively unbearable. 'And maybe one of us should check on Debs. I'd be losing my head too if I'd left a small baby at home, especially with Will. I know we're all trying to convince her it'll be fine, but he is a bloody liability, isn't he?' A shudder runs up the length of my spine as I remember the time he didn't know how to attach the car seat to the ISOFIX base – and so opted to use an Amazon box in the footwell instead.

'Don't go in there, trust me, it's not pretty. I'll get her when you're all ready – she's too light to fend me off. Also, Cara, we are not *only* going to the beach, thank you very much. We're talking about Passion Beach! Only the hottest day club on the whole island, with the best DJs and coolest people. It's *THE* place to be seen.'

'Er, didn't you say the crazy unicorn sex cult was *THE* only place to be seen?' I'm quick to remind her.

'Without your clothes on, maybe…' she reflects wistfully. 'Anyway, guess who pulled some strings and got us VIP entry, bitches?! So take off your Lycra tablecloth and crack out your high-heeled drinking boots because there's an 800 euro minimum table spend. We roll in ten. I'm off to body slam Debs. Ciao!'

Jac and I look at each other apprehensively: an 800 euro minimum spend? I'm beginning to wonder whether 'VIP' in Ibiza stands for 'Very Inebriated Parents' because, with nearly a grand's worth of booze under our belts, that's most certainly what we'll be.

17

Club 18-75

'What do you mean my name isn't on the list?' Amy snaps, towering over Marco, the impassive Passion Beach host, as though she's about to lamp him. While he lazily flicks between various sheets of paper on his clipboard, I peer beyond his sacred wooden altar, as though he's the gatekeeper to Narnia, and gaze longingly at the world located just beyond my reach. This place is beautiful, and to be fair, I can see why the whole of the island in-crowd, their tiny dogs, and TikTok profiles would want to be seen here. Nautically themed upholstered rattan furniture adorns the lime-washed wooden decking of the club's sprawling outdoor patio, where immaculately dressed waiters rush around serving over-priced bottles of Tattinger and Vos water to beautiful people with even more beautiful bank accounts. Behind the heavenly-looking infinity pool, where dozens of sun-kissed bodies bask in patches of sun – a mix of pine and palm trees idyllically frame the heavenly white sandy shores of Santa Eulalia's spectacularly glistening Mediterranean coastline.

'There is no reservation under that name...' Marco explains, without a jot of sympathy to our current predicament, 'and I'm afraid we're fully booked so there's no way we'll be able to accommodate you. Perhaps you'd like to make a booking now for...' and with this he takes a couple of seconds to scroll through the calendar of his iPad Air, '... for July.'

'July? Are you joking, mate?' Amy erupts. 'Yeah, I'll tell you what... we'll fly all the way back to England, re-mortgage our homes and come back next month, shall we?'

'No, of course not,' he says, now with a faint trace of a smile. 'I'm sorry for the misunderstanding... I meant July, next year.'

'DO YOU KNOW WHO I AM?!' Amy roars at him in livid disbelief.

'Sorry madam, I don't believe I do,' he says without flinching. Evidently not his first rodeo of dealing with unsavoury chancers he has no intention of letting in.

'Great, that makes four of us,' I say, pretending we're not with the crazy diva lady causing a scene, and dragging Jac by the arm onto the baking hot street outside.

'Well, that's it!' I hear Amy yell behind me. 'My seven million social media followers and I are leaving!'

'Wait!' he calls after her, as she haughtily walks down the steps towards us.

'See...' Amy mouths to me, with a knowing wink. 'Works every time. They can never resist the lure of the hashtag. Yes, Marco?'

'Your friend,' he says, pointing at Debs who's comatose on a white leather chaise lounge next to the toilets. 'Please can you take her with you?'

Having scaled a small wall on Passion Beach's remarkably lax perimeters, the four of us are inconspicuously perched on two broken sun loungers in the far corner of the club – firmly out of Marco and his judgemental clipboard's sight. I'm not entirely sure what's come over me. Once upon a time, being rejected from somewhere like this would have made me run a mile and accept my place on the wrong side of the velvet rope – but the minute Amy suggested a reverse jail break, I was game. As a completely risk averse individual, was I convinced we were going to get caught? Absolutely. Did I think we were going to be made examples of and frog marched out with bells of shame tolling loud enough to be heard in neighbouring Majorca? 100%. Here's the thing, though: for once in my sensible life, I didn't care. Why shouldn't I be allowed to take a little bit of what I wanted, for once? Playing by the rules has done me no favours in the past, and having had a glimpse of the luxury – men with chilled towelettes on hand to mop sweaty brows, and exotic fruit platters – I wanted in. Yes, that's right: today's the day that I, Cara Carmichael, have had enough of not being good enough, beautiful enough, or rich enough. Screw the elitist establishment telling me I can't come in here. I don't give a fuck what they say. I'm not scared of them. This is my time to feel like a someone, to have fun, enjoy the finer things in life and…

'Oh shit, is that security coming for us?' I shriek, throwing an exquisitely smelling beach towel over my head in fear. What is that scent? Nectarines and honey? Why is it that my towels at home all have the funky sourness of dishcloths that have been left screwed up on the sink for a week?

'Cara, seriously, you need to chill,' Amy instructs. 'I knew you'd do this, act like "Billy Big Bollocks" while breaking and entering, then have a complete goody-two-shoes breakdown once inside. You are not going to go to prison for this. It's a beach club, not the vault of a casino, ok?'

Nodding my head, and reluctantly letting her pull the towel off my face, I take a drinks menu from her outstretched hand and peruse the options. Bloody hell, eighteen euros for a gin and tonic! We might not have broken into a casino vault, but we'll certainly need to if we're to stay here any longer than half an hour. At least it's not going to take long to get through the 800 euro minimum spend. Never mind mother's ruin, we'll be well on our way to financial ruin.

'I'm starving,' complains Jac, looking as enthused to be here as Marco was to let us in. 'I feel like I've thrown up every trace of food I've ever consumed in my life.'

'You'll be glad you came prepared then, babe,' I say, chucking the menu at her. 'I'd whip out the stolen sarnies if you don't fancy spending about forty quid on a spicy bean burger.' One can only assume the food prices are so high because hardly anyone who comes to places like this actually eats, so they have to make their money back somehow.

'Who fancies a dip?' Amy asks, after ordering a round of drinks for us all that would pay for a term of college tuition.

'Absolutely not,' Debs says, miserably shrouding herself in a pool towel tent, despite it being 30 degrees.'Unless Jac managed to smuggle in some humous… Have you seen these women? My veiny feeding knockers, much like my still enlarged labia, will never see the light of day in a place like this.'

'Debs, don't be daft,' I laugh, giving her an encouraging squeeze, 'your big hard tits are positively on point somewhere like this. All these women will be desperate to know where you had them done!'

'No, go on without me. I'll only hold you back,' she sniffs. 'I'm going to sit here with a jamon croissant and FaceTime Will to talk him through how to use the microwave again – he's been living on cold beans and white bread for twenty-four hours. His IBS will be crippling him.'

Sitting on the edge of the world's most pretentious swimming pool, having left Debs angrily shouting, 'P for power, dickhead!' into her phone, I'm beginning to wish I'd listened to Amy's advice on my choice of swimwear. Assessing the skimpy-thonged bum cheeks cavorting around in front of me, I'm feeling super self-conscious in my, by comparison, nun's habit. 'Why are their cleavages in reverse?' asks Jac, unashamedly staring at the masses of twenty-something women with their boobs hanging out the bottom of their bikini tops.

'Under-boob, innit,' explains Amy. 'All the rage.'

'I guess they should enjoy it while they can,' Jac shrugs bitterly. 'I give them twenty years before their under-boobs are under their knee caps.'

As the DJ booth pumps out throbbing electronic beats more akin to sounds you'd hear at the dentist than club classics of yonder years, I wonder whether it would be considered highly uncool to offer to rub sunscreen into the sizzling back of a teen-age girl developing a deep tissue burn before my very eyes. You can take the mum out of suburbia… but she'll always be carrying SPF and a pack of (alcoholic) wet wipes – just in case. 'Jesus, any chance of them playing something we know?' I shout loudly above the pulsating din.

'Oi mate, you got any Darude for my cousin here? She's trav-elled a long way for this… all the way from 1999!' Amy yells over my head to the balding man in a white leather shirt who, fortu-nately, is too busy whipping the crowd up into a frenzy to pay us any attention.

'Cara…' Jac says, grabbing my arm and shaking it like a small child desperate to show a parent something green they've pulled out of their nose. 'Babe, don't freak out, but…'

And as my head follows the line of her pointing finger, I engage my default mode of… freaking out. There, on the other side of the pool, having flounced through the entrance as though she's sodding Beyoncé complete with her entourage of beautiful backing dancers (and two token pensioners who look like they're on the game) is Connie.

'Oh, for fuck's sake!' I despair, hauling myself out of the pool before she has a chance to see me. Is it beyond the capabilities of the universe to allow me just one day where I don't have to think about, hear about, or lay my eyes upon Connie bloody Carmichael? It's beyond ridiculous, and I've 100 % reached my toxicity tolerance levels. Taking decisive action, I storm back towards Debs, vowing under my breath to no longer allow *that* woman to dictate my life for one moment longer than she already has.

'At least we're no longer the oldest ones here!' Amy revels, nodding towards a twerking Mum and Aunt Mollie. 'Who wants another?'

'ME, and I don't care how much it costs,' I tell her, draining my own cup, mid-epiphany, while looking at the pretty miserable faces (bar Amy, who always reminds me of an over-excited Labrador) of our party. 'Right, you lot. Mums assemble and listen up,' I declare decisively. 'I'll be the first to admit I've not been much fun of late—'

'Slight understatement,' Amy interjects, signalling to a pool boy for an immediate refill of our drinks.

'But I promise, I'm not going to let *this*…' I say, flapping my arms behind me in the direction of Connie, 'impact our time here together any more than it already has. This weekend is about you, Jac, and it's also about all of us – The Flab Four on Tour! We'll never get this opportunity again – to leave our normal lives, inhibitions, anxieties, and kids behind for an actual justifiable reason. Look at us all, though. We've travelled over a thousand miles and, Amy aside, we've all got faces like slapped arses. We need to embrace Ibiza to the max! Debs, you've done brilliantly leaving Harriet at home. But that's the hard part done – may as well let go and enjoy yourself, because the minute you get home it'll be months of zero sleep, weaning, and wishing you were here instead of at a baby group in a crappy church hall. Whip off the towel, get out those cracking bangers and show these twenty-year-olds how us mums rave when we know our next night out won't be for at least another fifteen years.'

Evidently inspired by my TED talk, Debs confidently flings off her towel and downs her Prosecco. 'I bloody hate baby groups! Awful coffee and stale biscuits – like, put them in a sealed tin, Janet! You're right, Cara, I don't know when this might happen to me again… I need to live it, love it, and really relish wearing bras that don't have clippy bits on for breastfeeding. So, yeah, let's do this!' she yells, enthusiastically throwing her arms into the air – in the process dislodging a circular version of a sanitary pad from her bikini top, which she quickly shoves back in before anyone cooler than us sees.

'Jac,' I continue, turning my attentions to the bride-to-be. 'I know it was a bumpy start, you're currently hungover and never want to drink again – but it's your hen party! You'll only ever do this once, hopefully, so it's time to turn that frown upside down, have a hair of the dog and crack on. I'm sorry I wasn't emotionally available to help get everything sorted, but I'm here now and I'm ready to do whatever it takes to make this a weekend you'll never forget. You're my best friend, you deserve the world, and I love you to pieces.'

'Oh babe.' Jac wells up, standing to hug me. 'I love you too.'

'And Amy…' I address my cousin, who is brazenly readjusting her tampon string in the crotch of her bikini bottoms. 'Er, you carry on as you are. No room for improvement. Girls, we're not just doing this for us, but for every mum who thought she couldn't. We power on, drink through it, and party like it's 2002! Who's with me?'

'Yes, ma'am!' My cousin whoops with glee, snapping her fingers at the other hens to get off their arses and start enjoying themselves. 'Come on… you lot heard the woman: time to fuck this shit up!'

Several rounds of shots, three pitchers of cocktails and with all of Jac's stolen breakfast buffet rolls demolished, the party is finally in full flow. As Debs mum-dances on a sun lounger, off her engorged tits on a concoction of alcohol and liberation, Amy is trying her luck with the eighteen-year-old (at best) pool boy, and Jac is life-coaching two student nurses about why they need to leave their moronic-sounding boyfriends. Watching over the proceedings like a proud mother, I too am very much trying to live by my own rallying cry of 'seize the day' and 'live for the moment', but it's proving tricky. With Connie still unaware of the fact we're sharing the same airspace, for her I'm clearly out of sight out of mind. But from where I'm sitting – only a hundred feet away – she's very much at the forefront of mine. I can see that curvaceous booty of hers shaking away, hear her smug shrill laughter, and smell the scent of betrayal still lingering heavily in the air.

Having suppressed my rage, and desire for a wee, for the best part of an hour, with my sunglasses on and head down, I slip away from the others and head off in search of the loos to officially break the seal. Wary of being an easy-to-identify illegal immigrant in this land of sex appeal and bare bottoms, I move stealthily through the crowd, keeping one slightly drunken eye out for Marco and his cock of a clipboard. I'm about to enter the main building when I see a sight more terrifying than an A4 piece of plywood with paper attached to it; one that sends me leaping for cover behind the relative safety of an outdoor tiki bar. There, only a few metres in front of me, along with two muscle-head henchmen, is the shady-looking drug dealer from the Irish bar. Shit! Did he see me?

Peeping out from behind a storage fridge, I watch with intrigue as the three men work their way speedily through the party-goers. As they stop for a hushed tete-a-tete, I can't help but wonder what they're doing here... apart from selling illegal narcotics to a perfectively captive audience, of course. I imagine in places such as this, it's like shooting up fish in a barrel. As they turn their attention back to scouring the masses, it occurs to me they appear to be looking for someone in particular. A jolt of fear strikes my heart: could it be us? Surely not. How would they even know we were here? It also seems a bit extreme to come after four women who accidentally put in a pre-order for a few lines of cocaine when they could be off supplying blow to half the tourists on the island.

Making their way through large groups of gyrating day-clubbers, it doesn't take them, or me, long to spot the object of their interests. Strolling over to a cornered-off VIP area, scary dealer man signals for the bouncer to lift the rope – allowing him and his band of not so merry men to effortlessly skulk, like a pack of foxes, straight into the middle of Connie's hen-house. If the three men were expecting a warm response to their entrance, their egos must be feeling pretty bruised by my sister's less than impressed reaction. Rooted to the spot, and looking as though she's seen a ghost, I can immediately tell this is an unexpected and highly unwelcomed visit. Regaining her composure, after briefly allowing her mask to slip, she greets the men with a forced smile – a façade that isn't fooling anyone, and one I've seen twice before: the first when Mum caught her topping up with water the household vodka supplies she'd been syphoning off; the second when I caught her humping my husband.

Oh Connie, what *are* you up to? Is she buying coke from him? Did she too get done over by the mini spoon man with enough sunglasses to keep Bono appeased? Signalling once more for the bouncer to lift the rope, scary drug dealer man leads an extremely uneasy Connie by the arm away from her friends and towards the beach. With none of her hens seemingly phased by the abduction of their high priestess happening right in front of their faces, curiosity more than concern tells me to follow. Standing up, I'm about to stealthily pursue the foursome when a heavy tap on my shoulder stops me in my tracks.

'Excuse me, miss, but should you be here?' Spinning round and squinting into the sun, I see it's none other than Marco. 'Do I know you?' he says, trying to recall where he's seen my face, while eyeing up my bulletproof swimming costume with great suspicion.

'Er… Er…' I stumble, trying to think of a way out of this that doesn't result in our immediate extraction from the club. Spotting an electric instrument lying on the wooden strip of bar beside me, 'Yes you do,' I tell him, matter-of-factly. 'I'm the, erm, violinist.'

'You're the violinist?' he says. 'What happened to Frankie?'

'Well, he…' I begin.

'She?' he corrects, now observing me with even more distrust.

'Sorry, she! Of course… *She* had to go, bad tummy. Said something about the spicy bean burger tasting funny? Never mind Vivaldi, the poor love had four seasonings, one of which was cayenne, coming out of her. So here I am!' Jesus, Nancy would be doing a better job of lying. If this man believes me then he's more gullible than Debs when we told her childbirth was like a really bad episode of period pain.

'Oh God…' he says anxiously, reaching into his pocket for a walkie talkie. 'Kitchen, this is Marco. Pull the burger – it's happened again!'

While he's distracted by the prospect of another food-poisoning scandal, and with Connie and her entourage now with a head start, I try to sneak past him so I can catch up to them.

'Hey, you forgot your violin!' Marco shouts, running after me as I'm midway through the world's slowest getaway, severely hampered by the weight of my Fit Flops. 'DJ Harv'esther is ready for you NOW, let's go!' he says, poking me in the back with his clipboard, thrusting the white instrument into my hands and chivvying me towards a giant fibreglass swan next to where the carvery king is spinning his tracks.

'Get in,' he instructs, opening a hatch to the rear of the feathered beast. 'Quickly! It's nearly time for your part.'

'What? Now?!' I panic, trying to head back in the direction of the tiki hut and away from what feels like a bizarre bird-orientated kidnap scenario. 'I've not warmed up! No one enjoys a stiff finger, trust me – it's very unpleasant.'

'It's 32 degrees today.' He shepherds me back towards the swan with his clipboard. 'I'm sure they're warm enough.' And with that, he shoves me inside and closes the door.

Locked in the stuffy darkness of its feathery arse, and with claustrophobia setting in, an upwards jerk sends me hurtling to my knees with a thud. As I'm winched towards the heavens, the swelling cheers and whoops of the crowd below send my blood pressure skyrocketing. Oh shit, oh shit, oh shit. What do I do? While I'm trying to think of an escape plan that doesn't involve the breaking of leg bones, Newton's Third Law of Motion comes into play: what goes up, must come down. The force of the bird's dodgy landing in, what I presume to be, the middle of the swimming pool, sends me from my knees and onto my back – legs over the head and totally disorientated. Lying there, listening to people chanting my name, well Frankie's, as bright cracks of light appear in the darkness above me, I wonder if I'm dead. Realising I'm not that lucky, I clamber to my feet as the swan unfolds around me like origami. Shielding my eyes from the sun, I scramble out of the bird's insides, just in time to hear DJ Harv'esther introducing me (and my mum cossie) as the sexiest thing to ever happen to strings.

With no obvious escape route in sight, I'm like a drunk deer in the headlights… Amongst the cheering crowd, I see the mortified faces of my friends (who have already started to hurriedly pack our things away) and, as the floor-filling beat of Eric Prydz's 'Pjanoo' begins to build to its classical crescendo, sensing no other option, I locate the violin, raise it to my chin and say a prayer that I can still remember something of the lessons Camilla forced me to take when I was seven. Finding some solace in the fact I at least know the tune, I lift the bow to the strings and start to play… 'Twinkle Twinkle Little Star'. I don't know who's more surprised: the pissed-up clubbers, me at actually kind of remembering the notes (well, some of them), or a furious Marco and a woman I assume is Frankie standing at the side of the pool. Shocked silence soon gives way to jeering boos and, aware the not particularly tuneful jig is up, I scan my surroundings for a speedy exit strategy before the five burly bouncers charging their way towards me get any closer.

'CARA!' I hear my cousin bellow as she barrels her way through the crowd, sending unsuspecting clubbers scattering in all directions like bowling skittles. 'RUUUN!'

Unsure if she's sober enough to realise I'm marooned on a giant swan in an open body of water, I throw my hands in the air as if to say, 'Er, how?!' Then immediately wish I hadn't. As her velocity increases, and feet take off from the ground, she flips the bouncers a completely different sort of bird before embodying the spirit of *Braveheart* and roaring, 'You make take our day bed and freshly laundered towels, but you will never take our freedom! Come and get me, motherfuckers!' Then she cannonballs into the middle of the pool.

Credit where credit is due: it's a spectacular effort. The impact of her mum-missile causes a tidal wave so vast it takes out the false eye lashes of about thirty Instagram models, as well as pushing my feathered flotilla to the side of the pool. Scrambling to solid ground, I peg it towards a waiting Jac and Debs. Amidst the screams of chlorinated retinas and ruined hair extensions, I fling the violin to one side, and with the new-found agility of tipsy ninjas, the four of us hurdle over sun loungers and champagne buckets, away from the bouncers and towards the beach. Weighed down by a Morrisons cool bag, a platter of spicy bean burgers Jac's acquired from somewhere (which I quickly slap out of her hand), and three bottles of Prosecco Debs has pinched on the way out, we leg it across the sand as fast as we can.

As we sprint, I'm distracted from the lactic acid gathering in my calf muscles by the whirling motor of an inflatable RIB making its way out towards a ginormous superyacht anchored in the rolling waves. Slowing to get a better look, from thirty or forty feet away, I can just about identify the outline of my sister, her hands waving about madly in the air as she appears to be knee deep in a heated argument with scary dealer man. Shit Connie, I think, propelling myself forwards to catch up with the girls before five hairy bouncers catch up with me, what the hell have you got yourself into this time?

18

Undercover(s)

'Maybe she's having an affair?' Jac suggests, once we're all safely back at the hotel bar and digesting the events of the past few hours. My muscles are already cramping after our impromptu cardio session, and Amy's on her sixth retelling of a (by all accounts) pretty astounding Houdini-esque escape from Passion Beach.

Ignoring my cousin, I cast my mind back to Connie on that boat. Perhaps she is having an affair? It certainly looked like she and scary drug dealer man had some kind of history together: I know an argument born of passion when I see one. Plus, it's not like it's out of the realms of possibility. We're not exactly talking about someone with impeccable moral fibre here, are we? I can't help but feel it would be poetic justice for Dom to be cheated on and get a taste of his own toxic medicine for once. Speaking of the devil, it's just dawned on me the reason why the fucker was being so elusive when I asked him if he wanted the kids this weekend. I'd put all the money in my bank account (admittedly, not much) on it being because he's on his stag do. It's a realisation that causes my stomach to churn with rejection all over again.

'It's probably just a good old-fashioned coke habit,' Debs reflects, trying to quash my overactive imagination before it gets well and truly out of hand. 'They all do it nowadays, don't they? Young people. They'd much prefer to shove chemicals up their nose than drink a vodka and Diet Coke.'

This is true, and something I also wouldn't put past Connie. After all, she's her mother's daughter – happy to turn a blind nostril to hard drugs in the interests of an increased metabolism. Yes, that was probably it. She was probably securing a few lines. But why did she look so panicked? Dare I say, scared? And why the outing to the middle of the ocean? Surely the shady slipping of some euro notes into his hand under a table would have sufficed? Unable to let it rest, I can't shake the feeling there's more to this than meets the eye.

'No, she's up to something.' I'm absolutely revelling in the prospective collapse of their egocentric empire. 'I'm going to find out what and then I'm going to expose her dirty little secret. If nothing else, so I can flaunt it in Dom's smug face. He's about to find out karma's a bitch named Cara.'

'Ok, enough,' Jac snaps. 'What happened to not letting *her* impact *our* weekend? To us making the most of Ibiza and living life to the max? You're spiralling, Cara, and you need to let it go. Whatever it is, it doesn't concern us. We're here for *my* hen party, not to fulfil your constant and unwavering desire for revenge, ok?'

Completely taken aback, and feeling personally attacked by Jac's sudden outburst, I allow my emotions to get the better of me. 'Well, it's easy for you to say, isn't it? With your perfect fiancé, successful career, and general shit all held nicely together. You didn't give up your independence, financial security, and self-esteem for a man who you thought loved you, did you? Were you cheated on, humiliated, abandoned, fired from the PTA, AND made into a complete national laughing-stock? No? So don't tell me I need to move on when you have absolutely ZERO idea of what I'm going through!' Blinking back burning hot tears, I refuse to meet her eye as I look out across the pool at a group of Spanish women drinking rosé and laughing as they frolic together at the water's edge – evidently having much more of a successful girls' trip than we are right now.

'Cara, look at me,' Jac instructs with her most serious mum voice – which is much more terrifying than her police officer voice. 'You're right, I don't know what you're going through, but it's not like I haven't had my own shit to deal with over the years – we all have.' She gestures to the rest of the emergency intervention group, who are all nodding along in agreement. 'There comes a times, however, when you have to accept the hand you've been dealt and move past it. They may have fucked up a small proportion of your life, Cara, but it's you who's in charge of either pushing through and turning things around, or pushing the self-destruct button. So what are you going to choose?'

Deep down, I know she's right. Guilt begins to nibble away at my insides: I've made a weekend that should be about my best friend into something that's all about me. Cataclysmic grief, so it would seem, has a certain knack for turning ordinary folk into narcissistic dickheads.

'I'm sorry,' I start, with tears dripping down my face. 'I only wanted to prove she's the bad apple, not me. She's been getting away with murder, always has, since we were kids. If Dom were to see what she's really like… maybe he might come back to me.'

'Oh Cara,' Jac sighs, taking my hand. 'You know he's not coming back, though, right? Regardless of what's happening with Connie. You also know that revenge seldom has the desired effect the person seeking it expects. Seriously, take it from some-one who has seen the nastier side of a LOT of relationship retaliation in her time. Generally speaking, you end up either just as miserable as before, or in jail. I know you think you want him back, but, babe – there's too much water under the bridge now. It'd never be the same. Believe me when I say, and this comes from a place of love, but you *need* to move on.'

Blubbering into my piña colada, I shake my head in acknowledgement. She's right, on all levels. This I know deep down, but oh how I'd love to feel like I have some control back – to feel the power of knowing I have something to lord over the pair of them before delivering my payback, or at the very least, a self-respecting middle finger.

Whether it's guilt, or an inability to deal with seeing her best friend shattered into a thousand pieces, Jac relents. Sighing, she reluctantly cuts me a deal. 'Ok, fine. FINE! I can't stand to see you dilute that cocktail with your tears. It was my round and it cost twenty euros. Listen, this morning, at the omelette station, I overheard one of Connie's scrawny hens saying they were going to Smiths tonight… Amy, do you know it?'

Amy's face lights up with excitement. 'Sure as shit I know it! Smiths Hotel? You're talking about the most rock-and-roll legendary establishment on the whole island! Drugs, sex, and rock-and-roll! It's also where George Michael and that other bloke filmed Club Tropicana.'

'I love that song,' Debs pipes up, starting to sing the chorus, with Amy joining in for an out of key rendition/murder of the eighties classic.

'Ok…' Jac ignores the high-pitched mating calls of the two sunburnt foxes sitting beside us. 'So why don't we swing by Smiths tonight, after we've done sunset at Café Mambo, and see what we can see? If there's something shifty going down with dealer man, we'll assess next steps accordingly. But that's a BIG "if". If we don't, we move on, you let it go and we carry on our trip without any more talk of revenge or payback. Do I make myself clear?'

'Crystal!' I rejoice, leaping up to hug her.

'Don't make me regret this, Cara Carmichael. Last thing I want is for my hen party to take a further turn for the tits-up. We've already had swingers, drug dealers, violin recitals, and cannon balls. Trust me when I say I do not need to add espionage and sabotage to the list as well. Ok?'

'Ok, ok! Just a super low-key recce with binoculars... maybe night-vision goggles, audio equipment, and a button-hole camera? Jokes! Just an iPhone camera and some rope. Promise!'

'I knew we should have gone to a spa hotel in York,' Jac grumbles before downing her drink in one.

'I'm not saying it was rubbish,' Debs protests, en route to Smiths in a taxi. 'All I'm saying is it was just a café... a very expensive one, with a DJ and cheap bistro furniture.'

'You can't say that. It's a fucking Ibiza institution!' Amy declares, absolutely disgusted by Debs slagging off Café Mambo. 'It's not like you've only popped down to your local Starbucks for a cheese and ham panini and a caramel latte, is it!'

'Tell me about it! I don't have to spend the best part of eighty quid just to leave my local Starbucks! Why is there a minimum spend for everything on this island? I went for a wee and was half expecting someone to charge me £45 for the pleasure. Is it not possible to have a jug of sangria and a bowl of dry roasted peanuts round here?'

As our taxi winds through the darkness of the Ibizan countryside, my phone starts buzzing in my hand. Looking down, I'm surprised to see it's an incoming FaceTime from Uncle Geoff. The kids must have drugged him with an animal sedative, pinched his phone and discovered the poor guy's mobile data allowance.

'Hello, sweethearts!' I answer the video call, despite being sat in the pitch black.

'MUMMY!' comes Nancy's angry voice and, as the signal improves, even angrier face. 'WHEN ARE YOU COMING

HOME?' she demands, arms crossed over chest in fury, her knotted and tatty hair looking as though it hasn't seen a hairbrush since the day I dropped her off at the farm.

'Well it's nice to see you too, darling, Mummy's missed you so much!' This is a half truth. Of course I love my kids, but the freedom of being able to go where I want when I want, with a handbag big enough only to contain my lipstick, debit card, and emergency tampon is amazingly liberating. No soggy rice cakes, no half worn down pack of Pizza Express crayons, no dubious crumb layer studded with the odd fur-coated raisin or stray particles of glitter. It's perfectly sized for just me. Also, the prospect of tomorrow morning's hangover without having to contend with two small scrappy people yelling in my ear about Coco Pops and Youtube at 7am is wildly appealing.

'We want you now!' she insists, swinging the camera round as though we're participating in a live *Blair Witch* murder-along.

'Nancy!' I yell, trying to get her attention. 'The camera is making Mummy feel a bit sick, sweetheart. Is Ben there?' Cue Ben's turn to strop into shot as though he's been abducted by a terrorist group and is being held against his will. I'm half expecting him to hold a newspaper up with today's date on.

'Mum, it's awful here. I can't do any online gaming and Aunt Sarah keeps making us eat food made out of animals we've been stroking!' He shudders, either with wifi withdrawal or at the memory of eating Shaun the Sheep.

'Well, Mummy will be home in a couple of days, darling. Not long now, promise!'

'Have you bought me a present?' Ben probes, changing the conversation with the ease of a swallow darting through the air. 'Dad says he's bringing us something *really* good back from America—'

'Wait! You've spoken to Daddy? Did you call him?'

'Yes, I wanted him to come and pick us up, but he said he was away and he'd get me something cool to make up for it. I reckon it's probably going to be something really expensive. What kind of things do they sell in Ibiza?' he enquires, a little too obnoxiously for my liking: something, of course, I blame my ex-husband for.

'Mainly MDMA, coke, and ecstasy, Benny boy,' Amy jumps in. 'Oh and the acid, never forget the acid.'

'Is that Cousin Amy?' Ben asks. 'Does she want to talk to Siri? Hey, Siri!' he yells, sending all of our Apple devices into overdrive.

'Whoa there Ben,' Amy interrupts. 'Is she breathing and does she have a pulse?'

'Erm, yes… I think so?' he answers unconvincingly, as I cross 'doctor' off his list of potential future careers.

'Then I'm good. See ya buddy!' she says, turning her attentions back to petty squabbling with Debs. Next thing I know, three beeps of my phone tells me my signal, and children, have gone. I feel guilty. I've effectively abandoned them with the people responsible for making Amy the way she is. What kind of mother does that make me? Maybe I should try and fly back a day early to rescue them? No, after the drama I've caused thus far on Jac's special weekend, she'd go absolutely barmy. Key takeaways from that call, however: one, at least I know Dom is definitely out of the country, and two, he's in America. Even though I assumed he was on his stag do, the confirmation of it by our child feels like a stab to the guts. The thought of him being out on the lash with all his middle-aged dad lad friends, celebrating his soon-to-be nuptials to someone who isn't me makes my skin crawl. It feels weird and wrong. Will they all be congratulating him on how he definitely got the better sister this time? How he landed himself a cheeky little upgrade on his old banger, now with better rims and better off-road handling? My chest tightens as I allow myself to think of what their wedding might be like – where will it be? Who of our friends have they invited? I need to know so I can ceremoniously Marie Kondo them from my life. I wonder whether he's planning for the children to attend? I assume they know nothing of it thus far. Nancy literally can't hold her own water: there's no way she wouldn't have let it slip by now.

'Right, squad. We're here,' Amy announces, as the wheels of our taxi slowly crunch their way down an eerie and isolated drive.

'Why am I getting serious hippie sex retreat vibes from this?' I say, peering out of the car windows into blackness, attempting to suss out where we might be heading and praying it's not back to Branch and Guthrie. Even under the bright and twinkling stars of the clear night sky, all I can make out are the tall looming shadows of surrounding trees and foliage. It doesn't feel like we're heading to a hedonistic rock-and-roll establishment, more that we're en route to an axe murderer in the woods. After a couple of minutes, we rumble up to what looks to be a very small carpark located next to a crumbling whitewashed outhouse with the words '*Escape is not only futile, but a state of mind*' painted in black cursive italics.

'Ominous…' I observe, paying the driver and clambering out of the cab, 'Maybe we should ask the driver to wait a minu—' I haven't even managed to finish my sentence before the car speeds off in a cloud of dust leaving the four of us spluttering outside the somewhat shady-looking gated entrance. As I'm about to suggest a mad dash sprint after the taxi, a tall and catwalk-esque woman in a psychedelic print mini dress and platform shoes higher than the person who designed them struts towards us brandishing the second clipboard of the day. This time, however, Amy is prepared. 'Karin? It's Amy, we spoke on the phone?'

'Amy, welcome! And these must be your friends from *Good Housekeeping* magazine?' My eyes flit to Jac and Debs, and then to Amy, who is standing nodding her head in complete agreement. 'They sure are. Thank you so much for fitting us in. I know you guys must have been fully booked.'

I wonder what the hell has come over Amy's accent, she sounds like a member of the Royal Family after having a few too many sherries, watching an episode of *Coronation Street* and then thinking they can do a Mancunian accent.

'Well, yes we are, but we always like to make a special exception for members of the press,' she purrs. 'Although, I have to say, I was surprised when you said the magazine were looking to run an article on us... Can I ask what the theme of the story will be? We are home to some very, let's say high profile guests and wouldn't want their privacy to be compromised...'

'Oh absolutely, don't you worry. What happens in Smiths, stays in Smiths and all that... Cara, maybe you could fill Karin in on your angle?' Amy suggests, gesturing to me expectantly.

'Absolutely...' I flounder, my ability to think quickly on my feet, sadly much like my pelvic floor, sabotaged by my two children. 'It's about, how... how... good your housekeeping is...?' Amy shoots me a withering look, as I continue to grasp at straws. 'So... your bed linen, towels... what shampoos you leave in the showers, chocolates on the pillow – that sort of thing really.'

'Right... ok...' Karin says with an air of dubiousness in her anglicised Swedish voice. 'Well, that seems fine. Why don't you ladies follow me and I'll take you on up to the main house?'

'Perfect, thanks so much Karin,' Amy gushes. 'I know this is going to be an amazing story... about what happens between your sheets.'

Ignoring Amy's innuendo, our glamorous hostess beckons for us to follow her through the wooden gated doorway. 'Oh just one thing, ladies. While you're with us, we need you to follow a few house rules…'

She points to a black peg board on the floor that reads:

Smiths' Code
No Sliders
No Glow Sticks
No Influencers
No Camera Phones
No Under 18s
No Twats

A little bit gutted she hasn't asked us for proof of age, we dutifully agree and follow the endless legs of Karin up the treacherously steep terrain of a terracotta tiled staircase. Giving Amy a dig in the ribs, I mutter, 'You could have said we were from somewhere trendy like *Vogue* or *Harper's Bazaar.*'

'Babe,' she whispers back condescendingly, 'I had to make it realistic.'

Having ditched my IBS-inducing fast-fashion purchases for tonight's outing, I glance down at my sensible mum espadrilles, Boden maxi skirt and palm leaf print shirt co-ord, and realise she raises a valid point.

'Anyway, I'm surprised Connie would be coming to a place like this,' I speculate breathlessly, clapping eyes on a traditional yellow-rendered Ibizan finca as we approach the summit of the Balearic Islands' answer to Mount Everest.

'Why's that?' Amy bends over with yet another stitch while I soak in the quirky, stone-clad buildings in front of us – complete with neon signs and contemporary Rory Dobner illustrations etched onto its walls. 'This place is cool as fuck, absolutely legendary!'

'Oh Amy, did you not see the sign?' I remind her breezily. 'No twats allowed.'

19

Dirty Laundry

After a lengthy and highly informative tour of Smiths' laundry facilities and linen closets, we're sitting awkwardly around the famous Wham swimming pool on a circular sun bed that feels as though, if a black light was shone on it, it'd be visible from outer space. Surrounding us, an eclectic mix of the young and beautiful, music lovers, oddballs and elderly have convened by the Club Tropicana Pool Bar to drink ironic piña coladas and soak in the relaxed rock-and-roll vibes.

'Look at that lot, they aren't even talking to one another,' Amy observes, clearly fascinated by a group of rule-flaunting selfie-takers striking their best Instagram poses underneath a fringed palm leaf parasol. 'Mike Smith was an icon,' she continues, a little misty-eyed, as Jac, Debs and I are silently heads down on our own devices, checking for SOS messages from respective children. 'Total top shagger, bedded thousands! I bet if you DNA-tested half of this island, they'd stem from him. Wow, if these walls could talk...'

'I'm more concerned about what this bed would say.' I shift uncomfortably to its outer edges.

'See the tennis courts down there?' Amy says, pointing just beyond my shoulder. 'That's where Freddie Mercury used to play with his balls: Slazenger ones, of course. How mad is that?'

I nod enthusiastically, not fully paying attention to Amy's historical guide – I'm too busy keeping an eye out for signs of Connie.

'Do you see anything yet?' I ask Amy.

'Yeah, a hot guy in a pair of white skinny jeans giving me the eye. You girls want another drink? He's paying.' She levers herself off the bed and walks seductively over to the bar where a grinning slime ball sporting loafers, minus socks, is perched.

'God, I wish I had her confidence,' I complain, watching Amy work her magic on the man whose teeth are more dazzling than his choice of denim.

'Not even Naomi Campbell has the confidence of Amy,' Debs says, with a commiserating pat on my back. 'Anyway, I bet his feet absolutely stink.' She grimaces, clocking his shoe selection. 'Oh Cara, but look!' she announces with the discreetness of a fog horn, waving wildly towards a first-floor balcony about twenty feet away from us. 'Isn't that the nice man from the plane?'

Turning my head so quickly I'm astonished not to get whiplash, I see the familiar outline of a dark-clothed hunky man, seemingly in deep conversation with a petite blonde-haired woman, her face obscured by the wingspan of his broad shoulders.

'SHIT!' I yell, a little louder than intended, because, not only does Amy look over at me in surprise, but so does Javier. 'Oh shit!' I shout again, realising I've been seen. Panic-laden instinct takes over and I'm left with only one practical option: to rather unstealthily roll off the back of the totally impractical sun lounger and out of sight. Very much forgetting that I'm a mum of two and not the hero of an action film, the resulting manoeuvre is much less Chuck Norris, and much more slow loris...

falling off a branch. On my hands and knees, hair in front of my face, I start to crawl away to the safety of a neighbouring sun lounger which, unfortunately for me, is home to bunch of lairy Essex boys who all take out their phones and start filming the crazy middle-aged woman dragging herself across the ground like she's the girl from *The Ring*. As I reach them, a stampede of incoming flawless pins march their way towards me, the booming voice of my Aunt Mollie bragging about the time she and my mother met Mike Smith and gave him a hand job audible above the clatter of their stilettos.

'Cara, darling! What on earth are you doing down there?' my fake aunt asks, staring down at me. Next to her stands Connie, dressed in an immaculate white blazer dress. A pearly sergeant major's hat with the word 'Bride' emblazoned across it in diamanté lettering sits on top of her glossy, perfectly coiffured, mane like a crowning jewel.

'Oh, you know, getting a closer look at the tiling… I'm thinking of having the garden landscaped,' I blag, righting myself and brushing off my skirt as a contemptuous shoal of dazzling pageant beauties line up in protective formation behind my sister, trout pouts pursed in unimpressed smirks.

'Cara dear, don't you look… your age,' my mother announces gleefully, shimmying towards me from behind Connie's friends, and air-kissing twelve inches to the left of my cheek.

'Oh, thank you. And can I say how absolutely incredible you look in skin-tight mesh…' I stand back so I can fully appreciate the see-through neon green outfit, through which practically every nook and fanny is visible. 'Well, this was nice,' I announce, clapping my hands together in an attempt to draw the conversation to an end before anyone else has a chance to flash me their labia.

'Do you want to join us for dinner?' Connie pipes up, her voice hopeful as she smiles awkwardly at me.

'Babe, the table is tight…' Maid of Honour Jennie steps in, placing an arm protectively round my sister's shoulders. The table may be tight, but it won't have anything on her pleather catsuit – a bold move in a still sweltering 28 degrees of evening heat.

'No, we'll have enough space for you all,' Connie reassures me, reaching out and taking my hand, the metal of her engagement ring burning into my skin despite the coolness of the platinum. 'It'd be *so* lovely to catch up, don't you think, Mum?'

Mum's not listening, she's located a bar menu and is busily lining up her liquid starter, main, and desert.

'Sorry…' I say, instinctively pulling my hand away and shooting her a withering look. Is she for real? 'Can't… already have plans. *Catch* you later, Connie,' I warn, turning my back on them and hurrying towards the safety of my mother hens as a fast as my flat-formed heels allow. Arriving back at the sun lounger where Debs, Jac and now Amy, are all sat, I nestle down between them, my head in hands with embarrassment. 'Do you think he saw?' I ask, from the depths of my palms.

'Noo, not at all,' Jac lies, picking a leaf out of my hair. 'You were *very* inconspicuous.'

Somehow bringing myself to look up once more to where Javier and the mystery blonde lady had been only minutes earlier, I see now that the table is completely empty. Only a candle remains, along with an empty cocktail glass. 'Probably gone off for a shag, haven't they?' I speculate with defeatism.

'Absolutely not,' bluffs Debs. 'I think they've probably gone for a nice evening stroll and a crêpe. Speaking of which, I'm starving. Shall we go and get some dinner? The restaurant is meant to be amazing here.'

'What happened to white trouser man?' I ask Amy, wondering if she's finally lost her touch with the opposite sex.

'Non-starter. He was into weird shit… honestly, blokes nowadays. Disgusting. Talking all sorts of filth about his "desires"…

marriage and children. No thanks, Bobby, I'm here for a one-night stand so impressive that, afterwards, I can't stand. Never mind, plenty more fishing rods in the sea. Vamos, my pequeño pollos – an evening of debauchery awaits!'

Sat in Smith's brilliant bright-pink, semi-alfresco Peggy's restaurant, I've just inhaled a deliciously light tuna tartare, while everyone else tucks into meat-sweat-inducing fillets of beef.

'Oh, I regret my life choices…' Jac surrenders, throwing her napkin across the table in defeat, and undoing the top button of her skirt to try and alleviate some of her bloat.

Fully embroiled in a steak-out of my own, of my shifty little sister, our elevated balcony table is providing me with the perfect vantage point to keep both eyes firmly on her at all times. Sadly, thus far, the only point of interest has been one of the hen party setting her feather boa on fire after leaning over a table candle. Where is scary dealer man when you need him? And Javier, for that matter? I could do with both of them turning up before our night out is foiled by having to leave early in search of Gaviscon. As I continue to scour the crowds for signs of them, I'm vaguely aware of the sound of news notifications pinging around the table. 'Who died?' I ask my girlfriends, without taking my eyes off the pulsing restaurant floor.

'Er, Cara…' Jac says slowly, her tone indicating a problem she's not entirely sure she should tell me about, but knows she going to regardless. 'I think *you're* about to—'

'Eh?' I mutter, turning my attentions away from the table below and back to the floored expressions of my two amigos. (the third amigo is asleep in her panna cotta) phones in hand.

'You're going to want to see this,' Jac says, handing hers to me, a hint of a smile now creeping onto her face. 'Brace yourself…'

Super-anxious as to what I'm about to see, I cast my eyes down to the white glow of the screen. The second I clap eyes on it, I throw my hands to my mouth in a pointless endeavour to muffle the flow of obscenities. 'FUCK OFF, NO WAY,' I gasp in disbelief through my fingers. 'Is this for real? Could it be fake news?'

'I don't know about fake news,' Amy says, holding her own phone an inch away from her nose and visually dissecting the imagine in front of her. 'But the boobs being motorboated most definitely are!'

Unable to quite believe what I'm seeing, I read aloud the tabloid caption: 'Red Devil Dominic Stringer Scores Hat-trick in Las Vegas Threesome.'

'To be fair, great headline,' commends Amy. 'Bravo.'

Choosing to ignore her, I read on: 'The assistant coach, who is believed to be celebrating his stag party ahead of upcoming nuptials to fiancée Connie Carmichael, was caught breaking a little more than the no touching rule at exclusive Las Vegas strip club 'The Sapphire Rooms' on Friday evening. The Manchester United coach, notoriously known for his questionable conduct both on and off the pitch, partied with friends and fellow staff members before enticing two scantily clad employees into the club's infamous 'back entrance' rooms. Video footage, believed to have been taken by one of the ladies in question, has emerged of the tryst, appearing to show the one-time defender in a comprising sexual position that he's going to find very difficult to defend to his future wife, who happens to be the sister of his ex-wife.'

Scanning down the article, I see the same unflattering picture of myself they always drag out of the archives at any mention of Dom and Connie. Clicked by a lurking paparazzo as I was taking six empty bottles of Blossom Hill out to the recycling bin with my mismatched pyjamas, puffy face, and unwashed hair (by a solid fourteen days), the snap is most definitely not one for the Fumble profile.

'For fuck's sake!' Enraged, I throw the phone back across the table. There's just no need.

'Bloated wino picture?' Jac guesses. 'But Cara... Wow. This is huge...' She presses her hands to her face like eight-year-old Kevin McCallister trying aftershave for the first time. 'Nearly as big as your face in that picture huge...'

'Do you think Connie knows?' asks Amy.

All three of us jump up out of our seats and rush to the balcony railing to look down at their table. Every hen, apart from my mother and Aunt Mollie – who appear to be sexually harassing a young and terrified waiter – has her phone in her hand. They all have the same expression of disbelief as we do. My head spins round to where Connie was sitting only moments ago, but all that remains of her presence is a discarded bridal hat, its shiny man-made fibres stained with the bright blood-like splatters of a knocked-over glass of sangria.

'Yep...' I say, my heart pounding out of my chest. 'She knows.'

'Well ladies, things just got a LOT more interesting,' Amy declares, rubbing her hands together gleefully.

'What did I miss?' A sleepy Debs, with a blob of panna cotta on her nose, yawns while lazily sauntering up to join us at the balcony. Peering over its edge and taking one look at Connie's claret-stained headwear, she immediately fears the worst. 'Oh my God! Who shot Connie?' she shrills, gripping my arm with fear.

'Karma,' I reply, coldly.

20

Even Dirtier Dom

Leaving the girls at the table to obsess over what the Twitter trolls are saying about Dom's Las Vegas antics, I slope away from the restaurant and into Smiths' impressively manicured grounds. Connie always liked nature, even as a kid. Whenever she had a falling out with Mum and Dad, which, granted, wasn't all that often given the fact she was the favourite, she'd head straight outside and hide behind the large oak tree at the bottom of the garden.

Under the brightly glowing moon, the white of her ill-fated faux bridal outfit shines out luminously. Head slung low, her shoulders shudder with sadness as she battles to control the seismic sobs wracking her body.

Why am I even here? Perhaps it's down to a misplaced and subconscious sense of sisterly solidarity, or maybe I'm simply seeking an opportunity to gleefully rub tequila salt into her wounds. My money's on the latter. Slowly and silently, I sidle down next to her and plonk myself onto the cool terracotta step. She doesn't speak, but instead rifles through her clutch bag in search of a much needed fag. Having located one, she lights its tip and inhales deeply before shakily exhaling its woody, acrid smoke into the close warm night air.

'I bet you're loving this, aren't you?' she sniffs, offering me the pack as streaks of snot and mascara freely flow down her blotchy face.

Pulling a Marlborough Light from the carton and placing its dry filter to my lips, I lean into the open flame of the flickering lighter she's brandishing about an inch away from my face.

'Do you know what?' I stop briefly to allow my bummed smoke to ignite in a mesmerising glow of orange embers. 'In all honesty, I thought I would.' And wow, isn't that the truth. I've spent two years dreaming about the demise of my sister and Dom, of all the things I could do to unravel them, destroy their relationship, and to inflict the crushing blow of payback. But now it's actually happened, and the #CONDOM has officially burst, the victory feels a little flat – anticlimactic, even – very much on a par with begging your parents for a Mr Frosty as a kid, then finally getting one on Christmas Day only to discover it's not as good as you thought it'd be. Taking a half-hearted drag of the cigarette, I immediately remember the reason why I'm not a smoker. Violently coughing on the brink on an asthma attack, I flick the offending cancer stick away and stomp it out with my foot.

'Shit, they always make that look so much cooler in the movies, don't they?' I observe, wishing I'd brought my drink with me to wash away the bitter-sweet taste in my mouth – from the tobacco, or the strippers, I can't decide.

'I didn't plan for any of this, Cara, you know that, right? I didn't set out to hurt you,' Connie says, her voice quiet and remarkably remorseful. 'I've spent every day of my life since feeling awful, and trying to think of ways to make it up to you.'

'Not agreeing to marry him would have been a start,' I point out, as a fresh batch of clumpy black tears streams down her face.

It's so very typical of Connie that this revelation has come too little too late. I wonder whether it's only now that the high-heeled shoe is on the other foot she finally realises 'empathy' isn't the name of Christian Dior's latest perfume.

'I know I'm to blame, too,' she whimpers, her puffy face now turned to me, 'but he was just so, so...'

'Charismatic? Addictive?' I answer for her, knowing exactly my ex-husband's modus operandi when it comes to bending the wills of members of the opposite sex. After all, I'd fallen for his pant-dropping charms myself. 'Yes he was, and still is, all of those things. I mean, just ask those strippers in Vegas. But he was also mine, Con, and you took him away from me. You took him away from the kids! You steamrolled in like a busty weapon of mass destruction, thinking you had a God-given right to have whatever the hell you wanted, annihilating everything and everyone in your path.'

'Hey, that's not true!' she protests, raising her hand to her chest as though she's been fatally wounded by my sniper-precision character assassination.

'Oh, really? I believe the first man you ever stole from me was Sun Sensation Ken, shortly followed by my Take That Mark Owen doll. If memory serves, you didn't actually want to play with either. You snapped off their limbs and attempted to flush their amputated torsos down the toilet. Then there was Ian from next door, do you remember him? I'd fancied him for years, and you were very jealous of that – despite him being twelve years your senior. That didn't deter you though, oh no... You decided to sabotage our budding teenage romance by show-ing him a pack of my tampons and telling him they were butt plugs for my chronic diarrhoea. The lad never spoke to me again and, to make matters worse, the local boys called me Cara Crapmichael for years! Should I continue? Because believe me, there's more...'

'No, fair enough,' she grumbles, taking a long puff of her cigarette.

'The point I'm trying to make here is that you never wanted Ken, Mark, Ian, or possibly even Dom. You just didn't want me to have them.'

'Ian turned out to be a right weirdo, though A Crocs-and-socks-wearer who hangs out around primary schools – so, in a way, I kind of did you a favour there… Listen, I know you're never going to forgive me, ok? I wouldn't forgive me either, but I want you to know it's not quite as it seems, ok? There's more to it that I can't explain right now. I tried to do the right thing and stay away, but he's, well… incredibly persuasive.'

This pathetic excuse to portray herself as an angelic defender of my honour does nothing to appeal to my better nature. All she has done is add fuel to the funeral pyre of my marriage.

'What you're telling me here, Connie, is that the only reason you stole my husband is because he had the tenacity of a double-glazing salesman and the stubbornness of a verruca? Shit, is it even love? Or like when someone cold-calls you about life insurance and you feel you can't say no?'

'Like I said, it's complicated. Also, can you stop with your scorned wife bleeding heart routine? I didn't pilfer him from you – he was there for the taking. Why do women always blame each other? It's not like he was some weak-minded victim I manipulated into leaving you. He's a fully grown man who was a more than willing participant, believe me. Cara, the man checked out faster than an Aldi cashier – you were just too busy trying to be Supermum to realise.'

This assault on my very purpose in life – motherhood – kicks me right in the crotch, the one that birthed the kids responsible for supposedly turning me into the world's most boring and undesirable wife. Honestly, what do men expect? That all child-bearing women are going to stay sexually ravenous twenty-year-olds with unwavering sex drives forever? Why is it they can't get their heads around the fact that living with people more high-maintenance than Mariah Carey has a knock-on effect on life, lust, and libidos? Also, sorry lads, places to go, shit to do, and I'm afraid the Tesco big shop comes before you do.

'When it happened, I'd been going through a really difficult time… it was almost as though he'd been sent to rescue me, to take me away from the awfulness of it all… Rightly or wrongly, at that moment in time, it kind of felt destined…'

I roll my eyes at Dom's knight-worthy heroics in rescuing my sister from, presumably, 1kg of weight gain or a broken nail. 'Well, for one – wrongly. For two – I hope it was worth destroying your whole family over.'

Picking up her half-drunk glass of fizz, she suddenly screams and launches it overarm at a whitewashed wall, sending shards of glass ricocheting onto the tiled ground below. 'God, I HATE him! How could I not see this coming?!'

Chuckling to myself. 'That's the problem with Dom,' I inform her bitterly. 'You never see him coming… you just read about it in the newspaper. Anyway, if you're stupid, then so am I. Granted, your little liaison was an initial shock to the system, but I knew something was off. You weren't his first away game. I knew the signs but, in typical Cara fashion, I chose to ignore them. Thought he'd changed, didn't I. That he'd at least be able to put the kids before his cock. Clearly, I was wrong.'

'When was the first time? You know, that he cheated?' Connie asks solemnly, as she turns her attentions to flicking away a startled cricket who's picked the wrong moment to stick his head out of a bush to see what all the commotion is about. 'Because I know this isn't the first time he's done it to me.'

This comes as a semi-surprise. I'm shocked, but then I'm also not, in equal measure. Sure, I always assumed at some point this is how things would go down between them, but not before he'd even walked her up the aisle. I'm especially bewildered at the fact that she knew, but yet here she is… on her hen party, still intending for their marriage to go ahead. I'd already committed to an eternity of togetherness at the point I discovered Dom's philandering ways, but Connie? She has an out, an opportunity to walk away, a 'try before you buy' no qualms, money back, guarantee. Why would a ten-out-of-ten, strong-minded stunner like her – who could take her pick of skinny-jean-wearing womanisers – choose to stay with this one? It seems so very unlike her.

The deafening silence between us is so profound, it practically drowns out the rhythmic thud of Spiller's 'Groovejet' radiating from the dance floor beyond the pool bar. Conflicted, I contemplate my response. Do I confide in Connie, of all people? Maybe, after all these years, it's finally time to unlock pandora's box and unleash the beast held captive within. At this point, what's the worst that can happen? The admission that Dom has more than likely never had a monogamous relationship in his entire life is hardly going to be a shock to anyone's system, especially after tonight's revelations. It would come as no surprise to either Connie or me if the next news story to break was that, as a baby, he'd traded his own mother in for a woman with bigger jugs.

'I'm not exactly sure of the timelines, or who the first was, but things came to light pretty soon after the wedding…' I begin, opening both my mouth and heart. 'We were still on cloud nine, right in the midst of our newlywed bubble – untouchable, inseparable and unstoppable. Life was wonderful – well, so I thought – made even better by the fact I'd just found out I was pregnant.'

Connie gasps at the audacity of Dom's adulterous gall, horrified he'd be callous enough to cheat while I was up the duff – her skewwhiff morals seemingly indifferent to homewrecking once children have been evicted from the womb.

'But, there were problems.' The pain of what could have been stabs at my heart – still as soul-achingly torturous today as it was back then. 'I'd had some stomach-cramping, a couple of little bleeds. The hospital decided to run some tests, and what do you know? Chlamydia, apparently.'

As this bombshell hangs in the denseness of the taut air between us, I continue to relive the heart-stopping awfulness of discovering the wonderful man I'd just committed my heart, soul, and entire life to really wasn't all that wonderful. 'It couldn't be right, there was no way… I'd had a smear test about six months before the wedding and, while they were down there, I thought, "Sod it, I'd get the full check", just to be on the safe side. Those results had come back all clear. I told them it was impossible, that I was a married woman, someone must have made a mistake… little did I know, that person was me. Sadly, I learnt far too late that, when it comes to being married to Dominic Stringer, nothing is beyond the bounds of possibility.'

Connie's face is ashen, her mouth agape in disbelief. 'Shit, Cara, that's awful,' she whispers. 'What did you do?'

'I did the worst thing in the world,' I answer, my face now in my hands, still to this day absolutely mortified by my weakness of resolve. 'I let him gaslight me into believing it was my fault.'

'WHAT?!' she splutters. 'How on earth did he manage to spin that? I reckon nuns are more sexually promiscuous than you!'

Annoyingly, she's right. 'Here's the thing about pathological liars, Connie,' I explain condescendingly, 'they're natural performers. It's effortless for them, second nature. When I confronted him, oh, he didn't skip a beat. It was down to my own negligence, you see, of course it was. I'd been to a music festival that summer – I must have picked it up from a contaminated toilet seat. He questioned how I could be so irresponsible. Can you believe it? I mean, really? I wasn't a naive teenager who didn't know how the world, or venereal diseases, worked. Also, he forgot to take into consideration the number one rule passed down to all members of the female species from birth…'

'Never sit on a portaloo seat.'

'Exactly. God, the anger from him, though. He raged at me for days that I'd potentially given him fifteenth-century pussy plague, too.'

'Fucker…' Connie whispers. 'But everything was obviously ok with Ben?'

'It wasn't Ben…' I wipe away a lone tear that's begun its descent down my cheek. 'We lost that baby. No heartbeat at the twelve-week scan. One of those things, they said. Nothing anyone could have done. Not necessarily the STI, either… oh, but I blamed him, naturally. Never out loud, or to his face, but internally… my betrayed blood boiled.'

'Oh…' she whispers, her eyes tearing up once more as she reaches for my hand. This time I'm not so quick to retract it. 'Why didn't you tell anyone, about the baby, about the cheating? Why did you stay?'

'You know, the normal reasons. I felt ashamed, like it was my fault, that I was a failure as a wife and a mother. Also, I had no solid proof of an affair – it was his word against mine – and at that point, he had me questioning my own sanity. Plus, what would I do without him? Who'd have little old divorced me? So, I did what I needed to do to survive – and that was to push it completely to the back of my mind, locking it away forever. I loved him, plain and simple, Connie. All I could do was cling onto the hope that, one day, I'd be enough for him, and move on with the rest of my life – praying he wouldn't move on to another woman.'

'Wow, you must hate him, too.' Connie stares up at the glittering heavens with what looks to be the weight of the world on her heavily padded shoulders.

'Yeah, I guess I kind of do,' I conclude before we both return to our default silent setting, and I wonder how a man as fucked-up as Dom continues to live a life so charmed and blessed. Nothing is sacred to him; no line is uncrossable, and there's certainly no space in his cold, dead excuse for a heart for anything that even vaguely resembles love or loyalty. If I'm being honest with myself, as pathetic as it sounds, I'd been fixated on breaking the pair of them up in the vain hope he'd come running back into my open arms. Now, in a moment of awe-inspiring clarity, I realise it should be me doing the running – as far away from him as humanly possible – head held high and dignity firmly intact.

'Do you hate me, too?' Connie asks, with a snivel.

Answering possibly a little too quickly, and incredibly honestly, 'I did. But now? I kind of pity you. I've been there, done that, several times, and got his Armarni t-shirt that smells of another woman's perfume.'

'I feel like you've always hated me,' Connie says, as if we're suddenly participating in a group therapy session. 'Right from the moment I was born, I couldn't do anything right in your eyes.'

'Are you joking?' I say, gobsmacked, her left-field childhood guilt trip coming as breaking news to me. '*I* hated *you*? You constantly snitched on me to Mum and Ray, broke my actual bones, and thought it was hilarious to put the cat on my face while I was sleeping – knowing full well I was allergic! You were like one of the kids from *The Shining*, appearing from nowhere and trying to drag me down into hell!'

'*You* never gave me a chance!' she squawks back at me. 'It wouldn't have mattered if I was the best sister in the whole world, never putting a foot wrong and constantly kissing your arse, I was damned from the get-go. *You* hated the fact Mum found a new man to love, and a new daughter to dote on. Jealousy turned *you* sour. I was never wanted by you, never given the time of day. I was a complete inconvenience in your life. Heaven forbid that Cara Carmichael could find room in her heart to love and accept a little sister who took some of the attention off her, the sacred pure-blood. I've never been anything other than a muggle to you.'

'A fucking muggle?! Oh, ok, if we're throwing Harry Potter analogies around – who was the one forced to practically live under the stairs while you got the master bedroom, an ensuite, and all the undivided attention you could ask for? Once you arrived, I didn't get a look in. Did you know I was hospitalised with mumps after Mum cancelled my booster jab because it clashed with one of your stupid 'Bonnie Baby' competitions?'

'Hey, the way they treated me wasn't my fault!' she argues, the rawness of her repressed pain and rejection flowing as freely as the drinks at the pool bar. 'But you made me constantly feel as though it was. All I wanted to do was be like you. I thought you were so fucking cool. Being able to go to friends' houses for sleepovers, being allowed to ride your bike out on the country lane, wearing clothes you wanted to wear and not the pink frilly shit Mum used to wrestle me into.'

'Don't you get it?' I shout at her, furious she's unable to see things from my perspective. 'I wasn't cool, they just didn't love me as much! They let me do all of those things because they didn't care where I was, who I was with, or what I was wearing. Ray, I understood – I wasn't fully his – but Mum? She wasn't arsed, Connie.' Years of my own pent-up emotions are now bubbling to the surface, threatening to overspill and break me in half. I really can't be dealing with this right now. I should be in a nightclub dancing my heart out, not having it emotionally trampled on by my sister, *again*. 'Well, here you are, Con. You always wanted to be me,' I announce triumphantly. 'Congrats, you finally are! Welcome to the shit show that is my life. I hope it lives up to the expectation.'

Wounded, drained, and absolutely not living our best hedonistic lives, neither of us quite knows what to do or say next. While I'm waiting for divine intervention, or an alien abduction, to resolve our sisterly situation, an unnerving sensation brews inside me – one not normally associated with any matters relating to Connie. Struggling to put my finger on exactly what I'm experiencing, it dawns on me it could actually be a multitude of emotions… guilt, regret, sadness. Maybe she's right: over the years, I haven't exactly been the poster child for 'Big Sister of the Year'. There's probably some truth in her claim I've always kept her at arm's length – purposely making her feel unworthy of my attention and affection. I've always been jealous of her; this I know. Have my own insecurities and feelings of inadequacy pushed her away? Quite possibly. Does it make what she did excusable, or forgivable, in any way? Absolutely not. I am, however, able to see a little more clearly how it was possible for her to reach that awful decision. After all, why show a person respect and love when they've never shown it to you?

'So now what?' I ask her. 'Are you going to make the same mistakes as I did? Are you going to stay, or are you going to cut and run?'

'Maybe it was his last time… One last final blow-out before the big day.'

The blindness of her optimism causes me to ugly-snort in amusement. 'Well, something's most definitely been blown. Connie, wake up and smell the stripper's crotch, will you? The only thing that man has changed is a twenty-dollar bill into smaller thong-appropriate notes. He is Satan in a silk shirt. He'll never change, not for me, not for you, not even for the kids. The only self-growth Dominic Stringer's interested in is his erection. He's a total lost cause.'

Nodding in resigned agreement, she stubs out the last of her chain-smoked cigarettes into a nearby plant pot. 'You're right. He does need stopping, putting in his place, taking down a peg or two – but how?'

'We could kill him off,' I joke. 'Marry him first, then we can split the life insurance. I'm sure I could explain it away to the kids with a trip to Disneyland – the amount he sees them, they probably won't even notice he's gone.'

'Sounds like an excellent plan,' Connie chuckles wickedly, picking up her handbag and sifting through a department store's worth of makeup inside it. 'Anyway, for what it's worth, I'm sorry I stole your creepy man-dolls, and your sleazy husband.'

Wow. Stone the bloody crows, is this an *apology*, from my sister, at long last?

'Er, thank you,' I reply, hugely sceptical of her apologetic agenda. 'But the words 'I'm sorry' are just that, you know: words. On their own, they go no way towards repairing the damage you've done. Let me make something very clear to you: hair braiding, slumber parties, and shopping trips are not on the agenda. I do not forgive, nor do I forget. You crossed a non-returnable line, Connie. There's no coming back from that for us, but I appreciate the gesture. From my side of things, I'm sorry I *supposedly* made you feel like shit throughout your entire childhood.' This, I feel, is very big of me, all things considered.

'You know your apology means nothing if you say *supposedly*,' she says, reminding me a little too much of myself when I'm trying to broker peace deals with the kids.

'Well, it's as close as you're going to get. I'd be grateful this conversation hasn't ended in me ripping out your Brazilian weave.'

'Touché. At least this was cheaper and more time-effective than family therapy,' Connie proclaims, finally finding what she's been looking for in the neverending depths of her Mary Poppins purse. Pulling out two small white pills and placing them in the palm of her hand, she extends her arm towards me. 'Care to join me in a spot of much needed anxiety medication? I have a spare...'

Whether it's alcohol immobilising my inhibitions, or the liberating feeling of lightening my mental load, for once in my sensible life, I decide to throw my normal caution completely to the wind.

'Sod it,' I say, taking the tiny tablet from her hand and tossing it into my mouth. 'We could both do with a bit of a stress reliever after that emotional clusterfuck.' It's only a bit of valium, I reason, gulping it down with my saliva, it might just help to take the edge off everything.

Holding the other pill up to the moonlight, Connie studies it for a moment before doing the same. 'Hopefully we'll both be feeling like how the tablet looks,' she giggles, once she too has swallowed.

'What?'

'The little smiley face on the tablet? Maybe it means we'll be filled with feelings of blissful euphoria for once, instead of bitter resentment. In twenty minutes we'll be like "Dominic Stringer who?"'

'Connie...' I say, a feeling of dread, but sadly not the tablet, rising in my throat. 'Where did you get those tablets?'

'Mum gave them to me just before I came outside. Said something about Aunt Mollie's son Craig giving them to her, and them helping to reduce my "heightened" emotions. Why?'

'For fuck's sake, Connie!' I say, trying to dry heave the pill back up. 'We're not going to be in euphoria, we're going to be in sodding ecstasy!'

21

H2Hoe

Water covers my head, I can't breathe, and – much like my normal life – I have no sense of which way is up and which way is down. The darkness of the deep blue calls to me, and I willingly follow its voice into an inky abyss. Am I dying? Or, for the first time, am I truly living? It's hard to tell, but this much I know: no longer do I feel trapped by the confines of my worldly problems, only the weight of the water holds me down now. I have a sense of freedom at my webbed fingertips, and Atlantica beckons as though I'm Ariel returning home after a busy day scavenging through a Diet-Coke-bottle-and-sanitary-towel-laden ocean for whosits and whatsits galore. Furious, I'm unable to locate my giant conch-shell chariot or golden dolphins – were they not alerted to my arrival? Perhaps they caught wind of my preference for a tuna tartare? Awkward. Unable to go on any further, my body floats motionless in the water. I'm about to succumb to the voices in my head telling me to close my eyes and take a little nap when I feel the strong arms of Aquaman himself enveloping my limp body, hauling me up towards the surface with the power of a recoiling bungee cord. As our heads break through the choppiness of the chlorinated waves, Jason Momoa's hot and desperate lips press against my own, and I am 100% there for it. Flinging my arms around the girth of his strong, gilled neck, I wrap my legs against his rock-hard body and thrust my tongue into his mouth with the red-hot urgency of a teenager at the school disco.

'Will you stop? I'm trying to get oxygen into you!' my life guard yells, mid-resuscitation, as he attempts to peel me, a suffo-cating giant pacific octopus, off his face. Staring into those gooey lick pools of his, as deep as the water we're treading, I'm all of a sudden overcome with shrieks of laughter. I can't seem to control myself. Deep, hearty cackles escape from inside me and I'm thankful we're in water because at least, if I lose control of my bladder, no one will know.

Completely bemused, and unsure what else to do in this bizarre situation, he places his hands on my cheeks and pulls my face towards his – this time not with the intention of increasing my blood oxygen levels, but my sexual appetite.

Very quickly, things are not quite so funny. The tryst is primal, passionate, and, above all, sexy as hell. Hot breath, frenzied hands, and the ripping off of skin-tight, soaking wet clothes quickly follows – jeez, Sebastian wasn't kidding when he sung about it being better down where it was wetter. Flickering tongues, guttural groans, pulling down of trousers and… oh my God, hello Moby Dick! Fear quickly tugs at my confidence. What if his giant sperm whale doesn't like me? What if, going off size alone, it completely destroys my ship? As his expert hands begin to roll my support pants seductively down my thighs, I rapidly lose enthusiasm for my very rash idea of telling him to stop. Absolute madness, Cara. Get a grip of yourself, and then get a grip of him before he changes his mind.

Now out of the pool, we burst through the door of his hotel room. Kissing my neck, he slowly traces his tongue to my clavicle, before ripping my bra off with his teeth. Yes, I very much want him to continue. VERY MUCH. He feels incredible, I feel incredible, there are bursts of colour everywhere – along with a weird four-headed purple devil-cat that's giving me an evil look with all of its eight shady eyes… Most of all, I feel hedonism, escapism, and pleasure like I've *never* experienced before. Gasping in delight as his rippling biceps effortlessly lift me up and onto him, my phobias and feelings of insecurity fall by the wayside. With my thighs wrapped around him with the ferocity of a murderous Bond girl assassin, I marvel at the sheer strength of his core as he thrusts me passionately up against the wall. My body, delighted the drought is finally over, can't get enough of him. He's the perfect hydration to my withered libido and, like ice cold water on a scorching hot day, I drink him in. As every thrust pushes me closer and closer to a euphoric ledge, I congratulate myself on this being the best decision I've ever made. Yes, Cara… yes… yes, yes, yes, yes, YES!

There's a banging, oh dear God, there's a banging… is that in my head? Or is it the door? I try to open my mouth to shout for the noise to stop, but my mouth is as dry as if I've spent the past four hours snogging the face off an air dehumidifier. Even with my eyes clenched firmly shut, I can sense the rays of light streaming into the room and I curse both myself and Jac for not closing the blackout blinds last night.

'Jac!' I croak, groggily. 'Jac, can you get the door?'

She doesn't answer. Damn her, and her ability to sleep like the dead. The banging stops, and breathing a sigh of relief, I snuggle back down and try to get back to the precise moment in my peculiar, nautical but nice, sex dream where Javier's magic manhood is putting Meg Ryan's *When Harry Met Sally* scene to shame. As our dream banging resumes, so does the person on the other side of the door.

'Uuugghh!' I sit up in bed, wincing at the brightness of the room as my hungover pupils try to focus in unison. 'I'm coming!' I yell. Well, not anymore – thanks to whoever this is.

Swinging my legs over the side of the bed, I glance down at the white cotton sheet that has fallen away from my body, exposing my completely naked torso. Oh God! How the hell did that happen? Making sure I always take off my makeup after a night out, my only other hard-fast rule is button-down pyjamas. How out of it was I? Quickly covering my modesty so not to traumatise Jac with my free-swinging tits, it strikes me, like lightning, that the bed I'm sat up in doesn't appear to have the same comfort levels as an 'M' standard luxury pocket-sprung mattress… Squinting round the room, I see that the familiar whitewashed and minimalist decor I've also been accustomed to has disappeared too, replaced instead with exposed wooden ceiling beams and a terracotta floor. Eyes now fully adjusted, and with nervousness coursing through my veins, I take a minute to absorb the scene of absolute carnage surrounding me. Fragments of a shattered lamp are scattered across the traditional tiles, the whiteness of its hand-painted clay a stark contrast against the burnt orange of the classical Spanish ceramic. Empty bottles of red wine lie dotted on various side tables and, right by the door, a bra and knickers, presumably mine, have been frantically discarded in a heap. On the wall adjacent, looking at me with a face of smug judgement, is a very skewwhiff and precariously balanced picture of George Michael. Oh God… It wasn't a dream, I realise, with stomach-lurching clarity, I'm still at sodding Smiths!

'Cara! Cara Carmichael! Are you in there?' Amy's voice booms through the door as she batters against the wood like she's here to collect on a six-month-overdue mortgage repayment. Shit! Shit! What the hell did I do last night? Or more importantly, who did I do? Was it Javier? Where is he though? Bar the two empty wine glasses, there's no sign of another person having been here – no luggage, no clothing, no nothing. Has he bonked and bolted? The audacity! Ok, I really need to remember what happened last night. Think Cara, think! Focusing my brain, the last clear image I have is of Connie and me sitting out in the gardens, putting the world to rights, plotting the demise of husbandkind, and then… oh shit, the tablets. Fucking Camilla! Ecstasy? Of all the drugs she could have slipped us, she went for sodding MDMA. She couldn't have given us both a bit of space cake, could she? Not our mother, no: too many calories. Instead she decided to go straight for the mind-bending, psychoactive, diet-friendly Class A narcotic choice of hardcore nineties ravers. Oh my God! I don't even take paracetamol with caffeine in. What's going to happen to me? MIGHT I DIE?! My heart starts to race, and the room is suddenly 1000 degrees as I start spiralling into a hypochondriac decline. My mind is such a mess, I can barely even put one foot in front of the other as I stumble towards the door with my bedsheet wrapped around me as though I'm modelling bridal wear for the 'Dirty Stop-Out' edition of *You and Your Wedding* magazine.

'Amy, is that you? Are you on your own?' I shout through the door.

'Yes, slag-bag, now open up! Not your legs, I'm presuming you've already done that…'

With one arm holding my home-made toga to my chest, I yank open the weighty oak door and shuffle backwards into the room as my cousin barges her way in.

'No fucking way! You know whose room this is, right?' She gently shoves me to one side so she can better take in her surroundings.

'Er, Javier's…?' I say, very much hoping I'm right and a twenty-year-old Essex boy isn't about to come strolling out of the loo.

'It's fucking George Michael's!'

'What? I thought he was dead, and gay?!' My voice is about four frequencies above the highest level of sonar.

'Yes to both, dickhead. This was the room he always stayed in when he came here. So fucking cool. Oh my God, the bed!' She rushes over to the four-poster and bellyflops on top of it, then takes her phone out of her pocket and snaps a selfie. 'Wow, you can even still smell the sex…'

'Oh, right, yes…' I shuffle awkwardly on the spot, very conscious of my lack of clothing and dishevelled hair that makes me look like I've been shagged through a hedge backwards.

'No judgement here, Cara,' she says, with a knowing wink, 'it's what he would have wanted.'

'Wait a second,' I say, my mind still playing catch-up, 'if you're still here, does that mean that everyone is? No one went back?'

'No. That's why I'm here. Put your knockers away and your knickers on, babes, we've got ourselves a teeny tiny problem.'

22

Special K

'A *teeny* tiny problem?' I say in disbelief, standing (minus my top) in a completely different hotel room within the Smith's complex. To my right, a giant floor-to-ceiling framed picture of Grace Jones adorns the wall; to my left, sitting upright in bed and hyperventilating into a Jamon Ruffles bag is my sister. In front of her, and face down on the floor, is Camilla.

'Where the bloody hell have you been? And where are your clothes?' Jac demands to know, assessing my bra and skirt combo, having stealthily crept up behind me with the serial killer prowess of Freddy Krueger.

'Jesus, Jac! You scared the crap out me!' I yell, my heart coursing with adrenaline. I choose to ignore her questions, and the mortifying fact I found most (but not all) of my belongings scattered around the hotel grounds on the way here. Pointing to my mother's motionless body on the ground, I say, 'Holy fuck, is she… is she dead?!'

'Oh, she's fine…' Amy answers nonchalantly, opening up the mini bar and pulling out a can of Coke. 'We all know the only thing capable of finishing off Auntie Cam is either a wooden stake through the heart or a trip to Primark. No, I think you'll find she's currently down a very deep "Special K" hole.'

'A "Special K" *hole*?' I repeat, not having a clue what that means. 'Like the cereal?'

'Jesus, Cara – how are we even related?' She scowls, taking an exasperated swig of her drink before letting out a belch capable of waking the dead, but seemingly not my mother. 'She hasn't overdosed on fibre and refined sugar, she's taken too much keta-mine – she'll be out for hours.'

'As in the shampoo?'

'No, that's "keratin". Wow, you're so straight-laced it kills me. Ketamine – as in the anaesthesia. They use it on horses, Thai football teams stuck in caves, and apparently pensioners unable to let go of their youth – who knew? Anyway, turns out walking around a renowned drug den asking if anyone knew where she could find "Mollie" didn't result in finding her best friend, it found her something much more hardcore than a wrinkly pensioner in Lycra…' she adds, nodding towards my dribbling mother.

'How did she even get here?!' I ask her, squatting down close to my mother's face – slightly more reassured by seeing the slow rise and fall of her chest.

'Found her outside on a sun lounger while I was on my way over to see what the fuck was wrong with this one,' Amy explains, nodding towards a mid-panic attack Connie. 'She came wander-ing out of here bawling her eyes out and screaming for you – I thought you were dead! Turns out you were just missing, and not too hard to find either – only had to follow the trail of sensi-ble mum clothes from the swimming pool to the room I found you in. Naughty girl.'

'Where had *you* been though?' I ask but, before Amy has a chance to answer, I'm interrupted by the frenzied wails of Connie.

'C-Cara! C-Cara!' she whimpers. 'I've done s-s-something awful.'

Wow, the come-down is hitting her *hard*. I've never seen her like this before. Grey and clammy, from behind her crisp packet she looks bloody terrible.

'Yes, it *was* awful, but this time, for once, it wasn't *quite* your fault, Connie,' I admit reluctantly. 'I think we can safely put the blame into Camilla's hands for whatever the hell happened last night.'

'No, n-nno, I need to tell you something,' she mumbles breathlessly from within the greasy foil. 'I've done a bad thing…' but as she pulls the bacony bag away from her face, her attempts to expand any further are thwarted by my involuntary sharp inhale of pure horror.

'Connie, your face! What the hell have you done to your jaw?' I ask, aghast at the living, breathing and crisp-covered interpretation of Edvard Munch's *The Scream* painting staring back at me.

Panicking, she stammers, 'What-what do you mean?!' She drops the Ruffles and hurtles out of the bed and in the direction of the bathroom mirror. 'I haven't done anything to my— OH MY FUCKING GOD! WHAT IS THIS?!' She howls, slapping at her cheeks to try to dislodge her off-centre and protruding jaw back into the middle of her face.

'Ah, the ecstasy gurn,' Amy says knowledgably. 'Happens to the best of us. She'll be alright in a few hours… but until then she'll be looking like someone's hit her in the face with a comedy frying pan.'

'Amy, we need to call someone!' I fret, starting to fish for my non-existent phone in the imaginary handbag I don't have with me. 'Shit, where's all my stuff?' There was nothing in the room when I left. Did Javier do me over in more ways than one? If that's the case, the man put in a *lot* of graft for an old iPhone 10, a debit card to an empty bank account, and three emergency tampons.

'Who you going to call, Cara? Gurn Busters?' Jac jumps in, taking control of the situation. 'Drugs mean police, and police are not what we need right now. They'll take one look at the state of you,' she gestures to all three Carmichael women (and Amy), 'and throw us all in an Ibizan prison cell!'

'We can say it was an accident,' I insist innocently, hoping the white powder I can see scattered across pretty much every surface is down to the original occupier's unfortunate dandruff affliction. 'We'll tell them we've all been spiked and we're the victims. Surely we won't get into trouble for that?'

'I'm not prepared to take that risk. Anyway, there's something else. Connie, do you want to fill her in, or should I?' Jac asks my sister pointedly.

Connie, staggering out of the bathroom, is in no fit state to answer. The only form of communication coming from her swinging gob is a morse code of snotty sobs and wheezes as she struggles to compose herself enough to string a sentence together.

Jac, highly agitated and clearly on the edge, evidently has no time or tolerance for her antics. 'Connie, take a deep fucking breath and calm yourself, will you? We need to move quickly, before it's too late.'

'Too late for what?' I ask with a cold sense of foreboding. They're beginning to scare me.

'Well…' Amy steps in, happy to grass my sister up in a heart-beat, 'it seems Camilla's K hole isn't as deep as the one Connie has managed to get herself into, ain't that right, Con?'

Dropping dramatically to her knees, in the fashion of Michael Jackson's 'Earth Song' video, Connie's tears start once more, as does some only semi-comprehendible muttering about going to hell and a man called Giles.

Right, that's it. Enough is enough. Throwing myself down onto the tiles in front of her, I demand to know, shaking her violently by the shoulders. 'Connie, what have you done? And who the hell is Giles?'

'Wait, you don't know who Giles is?' Jac asks incredulously. 'But you spent most of your night with him and some random woman called Linda.'

Confused, I pull away from Connie. Giles and Linda? My mind draws a blank. I have literally no recollection, unless… 'Wait, is *he* the drug dealer guy from the Irish bar, and the beach?'

'What, the heavily tattooed, mostly made of metal and steroid injections guy in a muscle vest?' Jac snorts. 'No babe, that is not Giles. Think fewer gold chains and more beige chinos… massive fan of socks and sandals. Linda was dressed like Mel C and looked like she'd never used a drop of SPF in her life – the woman had more wrinkles than a Shar-Pei.' With my face still acting as a blank canvas of bewilderment, she adds, 'They were cutting lines of coke with their Halifax savers cards?'

'Oh! Giles and Linda!' I vaguely recall, as two blurry faces begin to re-emerge in my short-term memory bank. 'Were they, like, *really* old?'

'I'm going to puke,' Connie declares, reaching for the waste paper bin from underneath the dressing table and noisily emptying her stomach into it.

Over the cacophony of Connie's dry heaves, Amy says, 'I didn't see them, but from what I've heard, definitely heading towards their best before dates.'

'Didn't stop them partying hard with you guys, though,' Jac tells me. 'When I eventually found you both, Linda was teaching you how to snort a line with a twenty, and Giles was copping off with Connie.'

Wow. Ok… What else did I do last night that I have no recollection of? Feeling our story will be used for years to come as an educational case study of why not to take drugs, I mentally park mine and Snorty Spice's activities for the time being and focus on Connie's extramarital make-out session. Puckering up with a pensioner sounds pretty horrendous. I'd be rocking in a corner too if I'd made a pass at someone who already had a free one… for the bus.

Relieved that Connie's 'bad thing' is only a poorly judged act of unfaithfulness, my anxiety levels fall. Why is everyone being so melodramatic about it, though? Yes, she cheated, but it wasn't quite in the spectacular fashion of her husband-to-be: if you ask me, he was due a little payback. Personally, I'm delighted. What a lovely kick in the ball sack to realise your young fiancée has gone behind your back with someone whose ball sack scrapes the ground.

'Well…' I conclude, 'there are definitely some things to unpack at that much needed post-Ibiza therapy session, but all in all, it's not the worst thing she could have done, is it? I think we can all step down from our panic stations – it's not like anyone's going to find out. What happens in Ibiza, stays in Ibiza, right?' Feeling ridiculous for thinking something truly awful had happened, I pick myself up off the ground and stroll over to the mini bar to grab a much needed hair of the dog. Opening an ice cold San Miguel, I chuckle. 'Geez, you lot had me shitting bricks there for a minute! The way you were all carrying on, I thought she'd bloody killed someone or something.'

No one else laughs. In fact, the room is eerily silent, bar the faint snores of a comatose Camilla.

'Cara,' Jac says solemnly, passing me a folded scrap of paper. 'You probably need to take a look at this.'

I take the note from my deadly serious friend and open it up. The tension in the room is palpable as I slowly inspect the scrawling black cursive.

'Shoot To Slay: The Ultimate Revenge Package,' I read aloud. 'No refunds, no retractions, no repercussions... Deposit taken.'

Casting my eyes from the note back to my best friend, who has her head in her hands, I'm struggling to connect the erratically placed dots. 'Jac, what the bloody hell am I looking at here?'

Sighing, she stands up and takes the note from me, stuffing it inside a pocket of her denim jacket. 'Cara, it's a receipt.'

'A receipt? For what? A dodgy straight-to-DVD spy film starring Pamela Anderson?'

'For retribution,' Connie mutters, wiping a trace of vomit from the side of her mouth. 'He left it for me, on the bedside table.'

'Wait, who did? Oh God, don't tell me this is his room, and you got jiggy with *the geriatric*?'

Refusing to lift her gaze to meet mine, she says, 'Worse... I don't know what I was thinking. Well I probably wasn't – off my face, wasn't I? But he was so nice and understanding – he told me I could trust him and that he had the power to make all my problems go away. So, I told him, Cara.'

My sister's tone is more than a little ominous, and I don't like the sound of it, not one bit. 'Told him what? Connie, you're making me nervous here.'

'About how much *we* hated him, how he hurt everyone he came into contact with, about how *we* wished he'd disappear out of our lives forever and the only way for that to happen would be if he was, well, dead...'

'Connie, why do you keep saying *"we"* like that?' I ask, my blood running cold. 'And retribution for who? What have you done?'

'I've stopped him, Cara,' she whimpers, collapsing into the foetal position. 'Dom. I've stopped him... forever.'

23

SlayDom

A hitman? A bloody hitman! Sitting on the hotel room's cool, hard floor, I dangle my head limply between my knees as I try to block out the claustrophobic sensation of the ceiling and walls closing in on me. Having already vocalised every swear word I've ever heard in my life in very quick succession, I no longer know what to say or do. My world, much like my mother, is the wrong way round.

'To clarify...' I recap, as if by saying it out loud it'll suddenly make sense, 'Connie, shock horror, has fucked up once again. This time, however, rather than shagging my husband, she's enlisted an ageing coke addict assassin in nylon slacks to kill him instead.'

'She *thinks* she has,' corrects Amy, casually dabbing her finger in what I hope is cocaine residue, not hitman scalp flakes, and rubbing it into her gums. 'Not 100% sure.'

'And now,' I continue, 'based on her unreliable hazy drug memory, the general consensus is that this man, Giles, is on his way to America to take out Dom, presumably with either his walking stick or an incredibly boring story about growing up in post-war Britain? There's no way of contacting him, and she has no idea what time he left, or when the hit is going to take place? In fact, the only proof we have that this might actually be legit is because she has a vague recollection of paying him with her credit card, for which he rather considerately left a receipt on the bedside table after she passed out – because we *all* know murder for hire is a tax deductible expense.'

'Very progressive of him to have a card reader...' Amy praises, shuddering at the potency of the powder. 'My dad doesn't even have a bank account. He buries his money in biscuit tins around the farm. When he kicks the bucket, I'm going to have to dig the place up like I'm searching for fucking Fantastic Mr Fox.'

'Exactly!' I say, raising my head from my crotch to finally make eye contact with the girls. 'Sorry, but this is bullshit! Old people can't even use their mobile phones. There's no way the man was packing a portable card reader in his bumbag on the off chance of picking up some extra blood money from Car Crash Connie over here!'

'Ok, there's an easy way of determining this,' Jac paces the room pensively. 'Connie, where's your handbag?'

'Oh, I know!' Amy gets on her hands and knees and rolls my mother's body away from the bed. 'Saw it before while I was checking Auntie Cam for signs of life and spare euros.' With a triumphant smile, she quickly digs around under the bed and pulls out a dust-covered black clutch bag.

'Excellent! Pass it here, will you?' Jac instructs. 'You have internet banking, I presume?'

Connie nods in acknowledgement.

'Right, if you did use your card last night, we'll be able to see, won't we?'

As Jac opens the bag, I say a silent prayer to any god that might be particularly forgiving of accidental drug-taking, out-of-wedlock sexual liaisons, and potential contract killing scenarios, that Connie simply has incredibly vivid drug-induced dreams about violent old men.

'Ok, what have we got here?' Jac says, rummaging inside. 'Three emergency tampons, a battered HSBC debit card, and one smashed up iPhone 10 with… oh shit.'

'What?' I ask, as the colour drains from Jac's face.

'With a screensaver photo of Nancy and Ben,' Jac finishes slowly, holding up the phone to show me the smiling faces of my two baked-bean-and-ice-cream-covered children.

Oh no. Oh no, oh no, oh no. Not good, not good at all.

'CONNIE!' I explode, as she looks at me in befuddlement. 'This is my bag! Where's yours?'

With Jac and Amy silently exchanging 'WTF?' faces, I leap into action, ransacking the room with the expertise of a five-year-old on a play date. 'Don't stand there gawping!' I yell at the pair of them. 'Help me look for it!'

Five minutes later, standing in the midst of the upside down room, cushions and bedding sprawled all over the floor, I'm forced to accept that Connie's matching bag is nowhere to be seen.

'No… please, no,' I ramble to myself, grabbing my phone and bringing it to life with one solitary click of the home button. 'Connie if you did do this, you didn't use your bloody card, you used mine!'

'Oh, for fuck's sake…' Jac groans. 'That would makes things ten times worse…'

'How did you even know my pin?!' I screech at her, waiting for enough Spanish 4G to log in. 'Did you extract it from me while I was under the influence? You must have, because I'm pretty sure whatever you've paid for actual *MURDER* wasn't under the contactless limit.'

'What do you take me for?!' Connie shouts back, highly offended.

'I don't know...' I cackle manically, 'the type of woman who sleeps with her sister's husband, agrees to marry him and then hires a hitman to kill him off?'

'Fair dos,' she agrees, sitting herself down on the unmade bed. 'For what it's worth, the only pin I know is my own: 1,2,3,4.'

Arms crossed defensively over my chest, I curse the Carmichael women's disregard for credit card security and our parents' lack of ingenuity when creating the number for their home alarm system. 'Oh, right then... same as mine.' I'm annoyingly forced to backpedal.

Seeing the app has finally loaded, I nervously enter my login details and head straight to my recent transactions. Scrolling through an abyss of Costa Coffee, B&M Homewares and Bargain Booze payments, nothing immediately strikes me as untoward.

'It's not there!' I scream, getting ahead of myself and literally jumping for joy. 'Connie, you batshit crazy bint, you bloody imagined it!'

'Cancel the card, babe. Cancel it right now,' Jac instructs. 'To be on the safe side. No payment equals no link. No link means no jail time.'

'Yep, yep... on it,' I say, as I flit through the neverending stream of my caffeine, cleaning and cocktail problems. 'Wait a second...' I click on the glowing 'pending' tab in the right-hand corner of my screen. Straight away, I wish I hadn't. There, right before my eyes, is one lone payment... made at 4.30am today, most definitely not by me, and destined for the bank account of GShot Holdings Ltd.

'Shit, shit!' I begin to unravel, hopping up and down on the spot like a toddler needing a wee. 'There's something here! It's small though, £150. That can't be it, can it? CAN IT?!'

'Oh, he's bloody smart,' Jac remarks, snatching the phone from my hands while digging the receipt out of her jacket pocket. 'The deposit, of course! He's taken a small amount for now, to fly under the radar, and then he'll cash in on the full amount when the job is done. Very trusting of him, I have to say, but then who's going to be stupid enough to try and screw over a contract killer?'

Talking of idiots: 'Ooh, he's like the Klarna of the killing world!' Connie pipes up enthusiastically. 'Murder now, pay later. Quite handy, really.'

'Yes, super handy… in guaranteeing a criminal conviction,' Jac retorts, her voice dripping in sarcasm. 'Absolutely nothing suspicious about Cara's debit card making a transaction to what I imagine is an offshore and untraceable bank account potentially days before Dom pops his Christian Louboutin clogs. Not to mention the same scorned ex-wife very publicly cavorting with his recently humiliated fiancée, and a man who is probably at the top of every major crime agency's most wanted list. You look as though you're in cahoots, that you've both planned it. Trust me, if he dies, it's not going to take long for the police to put you on their "hit list" – the pair of you will go down faster than the bloody Titanic.'

I can't believe this! Of course she's made me complicit in her cocked-up criminal activities. We already share so many things in life – DNA, a man, why not a prison cell, too?

Absolutely livid at her imbecility, I yell, 'Connie, you fucking liability!'

The thought of losing my babies and them being raised by Camilla is too much to bear. Nancy's tenth birthday celebration is likely to be a Botox-and-binge-drinking pamper session. 'How could you do this? You've ruined my life AGAIN, and not only mine but my children's. There you were last night, bleating your heart out about never feeling good enough to be my sister and how awful *I* was for making you feel you were never wanted. Well, guess what? I most certainly *don't* want anything to do with you now. You're out, you're history, as dead to me as Dom is going to be in a matter of hours. You're right – I wish you'd *never* been born!'

I clearly hit the rawest of nerves, because Connie is up off her feet and inches away from my face in a matter of seconds. 'Fuck off, Cara! Stop acting so bloody righteous like I'm entirely to blame for this. What happened to "we could always kill him off and split the life insurance"? If memory serves, I'm not the only one who wanted him six feet under. You gave me the idea!'

At this revelation, Jac and Amy gasp in shocked unison, hands flying to their open mouths as though they're watching a live theatre performance of *Dynasty* unfold.

'I was joking!' I fume, fists clenching at my sides as heightened ecstasy emotions threaten to overflow into physical violence. Of course I've had moments of pure unadulterated hatred towards the man, but to wish a grisly demise on the father of my children is a step too far for even the most vengeful of wives – isn't it? 'Anyway, if I did want him dead, *I* would never be stupid enough to do anything about it – nor would I be sloppy enough to leave a sodding paper trail! This is just so *typically* Connie. Act first, think later, then try to absolve yourself of any sort of responsibility!'

Connie rolls her eyes haughtily. 'Oh well, of course *you* wouldn't ever do anything like this, because taking decisive action against a man as deceitful, devious and evil as Dom would involve actually having a backbone, self-respect, and the ability to stand up for yourself – all qualities a certain *someone* is clearly missing.'

The pure malice spewing from Connie, of all people, hits like a sucker punch to the throat. I can't believe, only hours ago, she somehow hoodwinked me into feeling sorry for her. Her manipulativeness manifests deep within my core and, without warning, a veil of burning hot anger descends. In a moment of madness, spurred on by years of pent-up aggression, I lose control of my fractured faculties and lunge at her. A voice, not even recognisable as my own, screams like a woman possessed – and obsessed – with revenge, 'YOU BITCH! WHY DO YOU ALWAYS RUIN EVERYTHING? EVERYTHING!'

Yowling like a vexed alley cat, Connie claws at my wrists and lashes out with her legs as she tries to free herself of my clutches. Unaware she's up against a woman channelling her inner She-Ra, after a few too many pints of Stella Artois, she fails miserably.

'How's my backbone looking now?' I hiss, as she wrestles against my weight. For once, being the fatter sister is playing to my advantage. This success, however, is short-lived as her many trips to the gym suddenly kick in and she manages to flip me, with WWE skill, onto my front and into a choke hold.

'Enough, you two!' Jac jumps in, hauling Connie off me, and restraining her tightly as Amy strolls over and sits on me. 'A cat fight isn't going to help right now, is it? We're all in this together whether we like it or not. All of us are complicit in some way or another – so let's calm the fuck down before you two are adding sororicide to the list of highly messed up shit to go down this weekend. Do I make myself clear?'

Completely out of puff, and with a potential hamstring injury, I raise my hands in the air to indicate my surrender.

'Jac, what do we do?' I beg her from under Amy, who is show-ing no signs of releasing me just in case I decide to manually correct Connie's gurn with the tray containing the Nespresso capsules. 'Should we call the police? Tell them what's happened? Maybe they can get word to Dom – warn him before anything happens? If we explain it was a massive misunderstanding then we might get a warning, a slapped wrist for being idiots? It can't be too late, can it? Maybe if we all get in a cab to the airport now, we can find Giles and stop him before he leaves. He's old, for Christ's sake, how fast can he even move?'

'Ok, first off...' Jac's voice is hushed as if the fuzz are already onto us and tracking our every move. 'This shit right here is conspiracy to murder, which in the UK can carry a maximum sentence of life – even if the fucker doesn't die. So no, a slapped wrist is not an option for you, ok? You are not Bridget Jones, Cara. Mark Darcy isn't going to come flying to your rescue and liberate you from a Spanish Alcatraz. You will not walk out of jail having had a lovely life-affirming moment dancing around in your Wonderbra. You'll hobble out in thirty years, a wizened shell of your former self with finely honed skills in maiming people with sharpened toothbrushes – that's if you even make that far. Cara, no offence, you probably wouldn't last a week. Secondly, from what I know about hitmen, which is mostly derived from Netflix, he'll be an expert master of deception and disguise – there's no chance we're going to coincidentally bump into him at the Ryan Air bag drop.'

Oh, it's bad, it's really bad. I'm spiralling once more.

'Maybe Giles will make it look like an accident?' Amy suggests. 'If there are no suspicious circumstances, then there's no reason to think Connie and Pied-off over here had anything to do with it, right?'

'See the previous note about the payment from Cara's bank account,' Jac reminds her. 'Doesn't matter if you've paid him one pound, a million, or whether you've signed up to a 0% interest bank holiday hitman deal: money has been exchanged and a contract agreed. The deal still stands and we're still screwed. We need another way.' Sitting down on the edge of bed, she tries to collect her thoughts while I begin my evolutionary transition from mother hen to flapping headless chicken.

'Javier!' Jac suddenly shouts, inspired. 'You said he was in international law enforcement, didn't you? That it was his job to find people who didn't want to be found?'

'Yes, but Jac, what happened to not involving the police?' As appealing as Javier putting me in handcuffs sounds, I'd much prefer for it to be in a kinky bedroom scenario rather than when I'm being thrown into a van on the side of the road with a bag over my head.'

'I meant the local police, not the big hitters. If we're talking Interpol, or a security service, a known and wanted hitman is going be pretty high up on their list of kudos criminals to catch. If we have someone we know and trust on our side, who we can cut a deal with, then that's a completely different story.'

'Yeah, I'm not entirely sure we'll be able to go to him…' I begin.

'On account of him not waking you up before he "go go–d" this morning?' Amy quips, suppressing a smirk. 'And in George Michael's room, of all places. Talk about "Wham" bam thank you mam!'

Amy's right, though. With no goodbye, no note, and no means of contacting him, all evidence points towards him wanting to avoid being held to another night of pleasure with me as much as I want to avoid being held at His Majesty's.

'The problem is, Jac, I don't know where he is or how to get hold of him,' I admit, blushing and feeling both a fool and a floozy. 'He has a knack of appearing out of nowhere when I'm least expecting it. I can't very well put out the bat signal and he'll come running. In all reality, I've probably got more chance of locating my ex-husband's morals…'

'Cara, that's it!' Jac raves .'We know Giles was still in Ibiza at 4.30am. It's now 10am.Unless he's a bloody geriatric Superman, there's no way he's going to get from here to Las Vegas quickly. If we hustle, and get our arses into gear, we *might* be able to get to him in time…'

'But you said we'd never be able to find Giles, that he's basi-
cally' – and Amy sings these last four words to the tune of Abba's
'Voulez Vous' – 'a "master of the scene".'

She then turns her attention to filling her pockets with tiny
bottles of booze from the mini bar.

'He is,' Jac says, dragging Connie to her feet and snapping her
fingers at me to start walking towards the door, 'but I'll tell you
who isn't… Dom. Wherever he is, that's where Giles will be
heading. Ladies, it's time for us hens to take to the sky. Flutter
your tailfeathers – we're going to Las Vegas.'

Having haphazardly wiped our fingerprints off every surface in
the room, and with Camilla slumped lifelessly between Amy and
Connie, we make our way outside. My top and, randomly, my
left shoe aside, I've got a strange and unshakeable feeling that
I've left something behind – but what?

'Does anyone else feel like they're missing something?' I ask, as
Amy struggles under the weight of my mother's immobile body.

'Yeah, Wonder Woman's lasso,' my cousin complains. 'Jesus,
how can someone who hasn't eaten solid food since 1984 weigh
so much? When she had her hip operation, did they replace it
with lead?'

Fortunately, it's far too early in the morning for any of Smiths'
drug-taking connoisseurs to be awake and compos mentis,
meaning there are no witnesses to observe our strangely
comprised party of topless, jaw-swinging, stolen-booze-clinking
granny-draggers making its way towards the hotel's exit. As we
conspicuously slope past the swimming pool, I spot a palm leaf
mass of material lurking at the bottom of the turquoise-tiled
deep end. I kiss goodbye to my mumsy purchase, and we reach
the top of the treacherous terracotta staircase.

'Cara, grab her legs,' Amy instructs, as we clumsily bump
Camilla down the steps like she's a baby in a pushchair manned

by four highly irresponsible mothers with questionable blood toxicology reports.

'I've got her legs, but someone get her bloody head!' I order, as Camilla's noggin lolls to one side, threatening to roll completely off her shoulders. 'It's swinging more than a Friday night at Unicorn Utopia.'

Reaching the wooden arches at the bottom without accidental decapitation, we pause for a moment to catch our breath while Jac scans the carpark for a vehicle to commandeer.

Watching Amy and Connie prop a slumping Camilla against a wall, my attention is drawn to a buzzing sound that seems to be emanating from somewhere deep within our group. 'What's that noise?' I smack my ears to check it's not coming from inside my head. 'Can anyone else hear that? Sh! Is it a mobile?'

Everyone pauses to listen, and I hear it again. It's quiet but it's most definitely there.

'Not me,' declares Amy, taking out a pilfered mini bottle of vodka from her pocket and downing it in one.

'And I don't have mine,' Connie reminds me, with a passive shrug of her shoulders.

'Well, it's not mine, either,' I say, pulling it out to check. 'So, whose is it?'

With Jac wandering around the carpark, and not in close enough proximity for it to be hers, we turn to face Camilla.

'Where's she hiding it?' Amy asks, eyeing her up. 'No handbag, no pockets.'

All three of us edge our way closer to her, ears pricked in the direction of the electric humming sound – which on closer inspection, seems to be coming from... her crotch.

'Well, no wonder it sounds "*muffled*," Amy observes. 'Who's going in for it? Bagsy not it. There's naff all chance you're getting me to put my hand near anything that's vibrating and in close proximity to your mother's minge.'

'Don't look at me, either,' I'm quick to add. 'Connie, it's probably Ray calling to make sure she's alive. You know what he's like – doesn't trust her bony arse as far as he can throw it. You'd better answer it because if you don't he'll have the coast guard and army out looking for her, and I think we can all agree that's attention we don't need right now.'

Seeing no point in voicing her objections, Connie accepts her fate with a disheartened groan, takes a deep breath, and plunges her hand down into the waistline of Camilla's sequined hotpants. Grimacing as she fishes about, it takes her a few seconds to locate what we all hope is indeed a mobile.

'It's not Dad,' she says with a gag as she removes the buzzing Samsung and passes it to me. 'Some random Spanish mobile number.'

Shooting her a 'why me?' look, I reluctantly take the phone and, trying to hold onto as a little of the overly warm device as possible, hit the green button to accept the call.

'Hello…' I answer, as Jac walks back towards us, shaking her head and chundering something about the lack of taxi services available in the arse end of the Ibizan countryside. Her rants, however, float around me like an oil slick on an ocean – I'm too busy listening to the oddly familiar accented voice on the other end of the line calmly giving me instructions and issuing demands. The one-sided conversation lasts only a matter of seconds, but in that time the heart-stopping realisation of what exactly it is that I've forgotten turns my stomach upside down and inside out.

Hanging up and turning to face the group, I ask coldly, 'Connie? Who is Ramón? And why the bloody hell has he kidnapped Debs?'

24

Cruel Summer

The finger-pointing has been going on for the best part of fifteen minutes. I'm blaming Connie; Connie is blaming Camilla; Amy is blaming Jac. And Jac? Oh, she's blaming everyone. And to be fair, she has a point: this is her hen do, and between us we've somehow turned it into an episode of *Murder, She Wrote*.

'If you two hadn't been completely off your skulls, this would have never happened!' she rants at Connie and me, pacing the carpark and throwing her hands to the sky in despair of the girls' trip gods. Long and short, no one has seen or heard from Debs since an undetermined time last night. My memories are vague at best, but I'm pretty sure our last interaction was just before I went outside to go and find Connie. Amy and Jac, however, are little a sketchier on their timeframes and whereabouts.

'Ok, where did you have her last?' I helpfully try to jog both of their memories.

'She's not a sodding pair of car keys, Cara,' Jac snaps at me. 'We're not going to find her down the back of the sofa.'

'Listen, does it actually matter where anyone saw her last?' Amy points out, and she's right. We know where she is, or where she's meant to be, at least.

Ramón was very clear in his message. 'Eivissa Harbour, 1pm, do not be late.'

If Connie turns up with what he wants, Debs will be returned to us unharmed. The good news is that, at the very least, we seem to finally have a name to match the tattooed face of the shady dealer man. The bad news is that we now know why he's been so keen to track Connie down.

After some persuasion (Amy holding her in a headlock while Jac threatened to delete her Instagram account) Connie eventually spilled her guts (what little of them were remaining) and filled us in on the whole sordid ordeal. I'll give it to my sister: when it comes to royally screwing up, she excels herself in committing to the calamitous cause.

'It all started the summer I left the *Love Island* villa. I'd gone all that way, lost all that weight and spent all that money on my lips, only to be out in two weeks. The injustice! Two weeks! That's all I had. It takes me longer to pick the perfect outfit for a night out. What chance did I have of finding love?' she grumbled, clearly still irked at the memory of her disastrous television debut.

Sadly for Connie, her five minutes in the sunlight didn't quite result in the fame, fortune, and free holidays to Dubai she'd initially anticipated as a result of becoming a prime-time reality TV star. Off she'd naively jetted to Spain, really thinking she was going places – not realising it would be swiftly back to Manchester on a Ryan Air flight. Yes, the only dealings with 'Boohoo' she'd be having were the tears falling out of her face in a two-star Majorcan self-catering apartment waiting for a junior producer to do her online check-in.

'I wasn't ready to go back home; couldn't face the embarrassment, the headlines, or the relentless trolling. Honestly, some of the messages were just awful… Mum has such a nasty way with words sometimes. So I decided to stick around a little bit longer on the island; got myself a hotel, and a couple of my friends came out to join me. Love or no love, I was determined to have the best summer ever.'

Something Connie hadn't been counting on, however, was the arrival of Ramón in her life, or the dire consequences a chance meeting at a swanky, super-glam, beach club in Palma would bring.

'You should have seen this place, a millionaire's playground,' she recounted. 'It had this infinity pool that was dug into a rocky peninsula – made you feel like you were at the edge of the world. Nothing else surrounding you but ocean, and money – tons and tons of the stuff. The joint was positively oozing with slimy men just asking to be taken for a ride. Our modus operandi: shake our asses until we landed ourselves a sheik and an invitation into the exclusive VIP area. It didn't take long for the biggest bottle of Laurent Perrier you've ever seen in your life to arrive at our table; quite an upgrade from the Jacob's Creek we'd smuggled into our water bottles. The waitress pointed to this muscly tattooed bloke in a roped-off booth, flanked by security guys and dripping in diamonds. She said it was a gift from Ramón De Leon and would I like to join him.'

Knowing my sister like I do, this would have been like catnip to her pound-sign peckish pussy. Give her a whiff of nice expensive things, and not having to pay for them, she'll be over you faster than wasps on a sticky child.

'You know I've always liked a bad boy, Cara,' she explained. 'Tats, chains, and more metal in his mouth than a James Bond villain. You should have seen this watch he was wearing. The thing had so much bling you'd be able to spot it from space. The minute we met, I felt the power he exuded – it was all-consuming. I wanted him, and he wanted me, too – who wouldn't?'

I thought it probably wasn't conducive to the conversation, or to getting Debs back, to remind her that literally none of the occupants in the *Love Island* villa had wanted her.

'After the beach club, he came on fast and furious,' Connie continued, 'telling me he was the son of one of the wealthiest and most revered men on the island, and he'd love nothing more than to whisk me away on his superyacht and treat me like a queen.'

As she filled in the blanks, vague recollections of her mentioning a Spanish boyfriend entered my mind. As she was never overly forthcoming on the details, not even a name, I'd presumed she'd made him up to save face after her very public ejection from the villa. Unfortunately for all of us, specifically Debs, that was very much not the case.

'It was such a whirlwind romance,' she sighed wistfully, as though recounting a scene from *The Notebook* – if Ryan Gosling has been replaced by a shit-scary muscleman who is partial to string vests. 'He was attentive, adoring, and super-generous. Every day a different designer handbag or dress turned up on my doorstep. I swear the man had shares in Gucci. I'd never seen so much bling in my life. True to his word, he treated me like royalty because, to everyone around us, he was a king. Money, respect, and power – it was everything I ever thought I wanted in a man, until it became clear what he was, who he was.'

It transpired Connie's 'king' was actually more of a lord, and a drug one, at that. His father, Carlos De Leon, was head of the infamous 'De Leon' cartel – possibly the most powerful narcotics-dealing gang in western Europe. Ramón was a dangerous man, with a formidable family and an even fiercer temper.

'The warning signs were there, but I guess I was so swept up in the lifestyle and excitement of it all, I'd managed to overlook them. We'd only been together for a couple of weeks when he insisted I send my friends home and move into his villa – taking away my phone and passport for "safekeeping". After that, it didn't take long for things to unravel. Doting one minute, hurling abuse the next – I didn't know if I was coming or going, apart from the fact I couldn't actually *go* anywhere. He was so paranoid about someone taking me away from him that I wasn't even allowed out on my own without his goons keeping tabs on me – although one was pretty hot, so that could have been worse.'

Typical Connie, being held against her will but still finding time to appreciate some oppressive eye candy.

'Turns out, I was being groomed, and not in a nice-trip-to-the-hairdresser's kind of way,' she explained, as if we were a right bunch of thickos who didn't know what the word meant. 'In exchange for his generosity, Ramón had a job he wanted me to do for him. I was expected to fly out to Colombia to collect a new product he was going to be selling – in a sort of "try before buy" deal. My assignment was clear: collect the gear, don't try to run, don't get caught. I mean, me, a drug trafficker! Can you imagine?'

No, I could not. I've been in the company of my sister in an airport when she rather shiftily, and unsuccessfully, tried to smuggle a 200ml bottle of Chanel perfume through the x-ray machine. A smooth criminal, she was not. No, the only way Connie was ever going to have a condom shoved down her throat was if it was attached to a penis.

'Oh my God, so what did you do?' Amy asked, sitting cross-legged by Connie's feet, as enthralled as a small child being read an incredibly farfetched bedtime story.

'Well, I totally panicked, naturally. That night, I packed my things and hopped out of the bedroom window. Didn't get very far though… His guys picked me up about half a mile down the road, brought me back to face his fury: a couple of broken ribs and a black eye. Ramón did not like to lose his possessions, and that was exactly what I was to him.'

How could I not have known this? Connie had been groomed, assaulted, and effectively imprisoned. Where was I when she needed me? Probably at home whingeing about going on the school run and how many snacks my kids get through in a day. She was right about me: if ever anyone was looking for a shining example of an awful big sister, there I'd be, my name up in lights, and giving zero fucks.

'He decided to teach me a lesson,' she told us, with tears pouring down her face. 'The following evening we were meant to be going out for dinner, but on the way we took a diversion to go and see one of his dealers. I didn't know at the time, but this guy was stealing from him, skimming from the profits. Nothing could have prepared me for what went down. He bundled the bloke into our car and we drove to a secluded dock outside Alcudia. The whole way, this guy was begging for forgiveness, for his life. He got neither. Ramón broke both his arms, shot his knee caps out right in front of me, then kicked him into the water to drown. It was a message, loud and clear. This is what happens to people who betray me. Do it again, and face the consequences. The only escape from him was death.'

'So, how did you get away?' I asked, astounded that Connie, the woman who once got trapped in a multistorey carpark for three hours trying to find the exit, had managed to Houdini herself to freedom.

'That same night the psycho insisted we still went out for dinner, can you believe it? Sea food, ironically. What could I do? I could hardly tell him no and leg it. There was no way out, or so I thought, until I walked into the restaurant bar.'

Enter stage left… my darling ex-husband. Of course. He had to make an appearance at some point. I'd never really known the full 'ins and outs' of how it all started, the affair. They weren't keen to dish the dirt and I wasn't exactly mad keen to hear it; but I knew the timings must have coincided with her Spanish escapades. What I didn't know was that Dom's annual Majorcan golfing trip with the boys happened to overlap exactly with Connie being banged up abroad, banging mob bosses.

'Never in a million years did I expect to see him. I didn't even know he was on the island. But there he was, larger than life, strolling over with a grin on his face and arms wide open ready to hug me. It was in that moment, while I was holding out for a hero, that I realised he was my only way out. Dominic Stringer was my guardian angel.'

Yeah, with the heart of a devil, I thought. That ex of mine could be described as many things but a protective servant of God, he was not. A testament to this was his immediate rapport with stone-cold-hearted killer Ramón, the pair of them, apparently, getting on like a house on fire. A sociopath and a psychopath walk into a bar... who'd have thought? With a mutual love of the beautiful game, and even more beautiful women, they were a match made in bad guy heaven.

'When Ramón invited Dom back to the villa with us, I thought my luck was in – that he'd be able to help me escape, or at least alert the authorities, send in the Navy Sealions or something,' Connie told us earnestly. 'But once he'd sampled some vintage lines and laid eyes on the bottomless munch menu from the all-you-can-eat stripper buffet, Dom was so far up Ramón's arse he was practically swinging off his tonsils.'

With more white powder up his nose than Frosty The Snowman, Dom wasn't quite the streetwise Hercules she was hoping for, and – to make things ten times worse – Connie wasn't the only one with a half-baked plan up her sleeve. Suspicious of Dom's motives right from the get-go, and convinced a cockney undercover narcotics cop had infiltrated his operation, Ramón may have lured Dom back to the villa under the pretence of prossies and pharmaceuticals, but what he actually had in mind was a little less gang-bang and more of a straightforward bang-bang... with a big fuck-off gun. With him furious and wanting answers, this was a Spanish Inquisition nobody expected.

'Everyone else had either gone home, or had sloped off to the guest rooms – it was just the three of us out by pool. They were both in the hot tub. I stayed on the side. No way I was getting in: absolute germ pits filled with faeces and spunk. Anyway, they were laughing and joking, seemingly having a great time then BAM! Ramón had a gun pointing in our faces and was demanding to know who we were working for. My life flashed before my eyes, honestly: it was mostly handbags and all the carbs I'd never allowed myself to eat, and I started to scream and scream. I thought that was it, game over – I was going to meet my maker, and what had I achieved in life? Not even a social media blue tick! But then Dom looked at me with this expression that immediately calmed me. It was this magical moment between us and I simply knew he would never let anything bad happen to me. That's when things sort of... escalated.'

Turns out Connie's interpretation of the word 'escalated' is slightly different from my own, which, when faced with confrontation, involves me counting to three and threatening the use of the naughty step... not blunt force trauma with a heavy object.

'You attacked him?' I asked in disbelief. 'With what? A set of press-on nails and a tourniquet made of hair extensions?'

'Dom had pounced on him, and they were grappling in the tub. Ramón, who clearly hadn't expected a counter-attack, dropped the gun in the water. Dom's head was suddenly completely submerged. I thought he was drowning and, if he was dead, who was going to rescue me?'

A classic Connie-ism, if ever I heard one. It reminded me of when I'd had to teach the kids about calling 999 in case they ever found me unconscious; Nancy was less concerned by the prospect of finding Mummy's head caved in at the bottom of the stairs, and more alarmed about who was going to cook her fish fingers.

'I acted on pure natural instinct,' she pleaded. 'I looked for the closest thing to hand, which happened to be some big ugly painted plant pot.'

'A plant pot?' I'd repeated incredulously, unsure Ramón sounded like the kind of guy to have a keen interest in the cultivation of chrysanthemums.

'Yes, a plant pot. Needs must, Cara. I grabbed it, and whack! Smashed it over his head. It's funny, because in films when that happens, people just pass out, don't they? Not really the case in real life, though. It only stunned him, so I had to think quick and move on to something heavier.'

'Heavier?' I wondered whether she'd next taken aim with his granite garden gnome collection.

'Yes, heavier. Will you stop interrupting me? I didn't know what else to do. I had to think on my feet, and then it struck me… my actual feet! I was wearing my Versace platforms, and those things weigh an absolute ton – so I swung me feet over and started kicking Ramón in the head repeatedly.'

Wow. Talk about being a fashion victim.

'It wasn't murder, it was self-defence!' Connie proclaimed, after telling us how, once she'd finished platform-pummelling Ramón to what they both assumed was death, the pair of them pulled the jacuzzi lid over his lifeless, floating body and fled the scene.

'Connie, a word of advice,' Jac said condescendingly, while Amy and I silently ogled her in astonishment. 'If you must insist on booting dangerous drug lords to death, might be worth

making sure you've done the job properly, because evidently
Ramón is very much still alive, understandably fucking fuming,
and out for blood unless you return something you took from
him which evidently wasn't his life!'

'Yeah, about that…' she told us, squirming awkwardly on the
spot. 'Potentially a little bit tricky.'

25

Hot Tub Time Machine

Midday and, having finally found a taxi driver willing to pick up our motley mum crew and shove Camilla in the boot, we're on our way into Ibiza Town to try and stop Debs becoming Ramón's next seafood special.

'How could you be so stupid, on so many different levels?' my tirade at Connie continues. 'If murder wasn't bad enough, you decided to add grand larceny to the rap sheet as well!'

As she was about to flee the murder scene, my sister had remembered one crucial thing that would not only hamper her escape back to the UK but would also lead the De Leons, and anyone investigating Ramón's watery grave, directly to her door.

'I didn't mean to!' she says, as we make our way along the cross-island, tree-lined C-731 highway towards Eivissa Harbour. 'The plan was to get my passport and then to leg it out of there as fast as possible. I knew the safe was in his bedroom, and was pretty sure of the code because I'd clocked him putting his coke cash in there the previous evening. So, while his security guards were busy swapping joints and strippers, we made a sneaky dash for it.'

Their rushed, and not very well thought out, am-dram re-enactment of *Ocean's Eleven* might have initially involved the swift retrieval of Connie's ID, but, once the vault was cracked and its brimming bounty revealed, it was Dom's fingers, not his feet, that were moving at the speed of light.

'He was shoving cash and jewellery into his pockets so quickly that, for a moment, I thought he was flossing,' Connie tells us, before placing her hand condescendingly on my arm, as though I'm a ninety-five-year-old nana, and whispering, 'Cara, that's a dance, by the way; nothing to do with oral hygiene.'

Here's the thing about my ex-husband: some guys are into collecting cars, fine wines, modern art. Not Dom. No, his thing was always watches. I can only imagine he'd have positively creamed his pants with excitement on discovering the safe was not only home to countless gems, gilded glitz and thousands of euros, but the very watch Connie had spotted on Ramón's wrist the first time they met. We're not talking about any old watch here. This thing was the highly sought-after, one-of-a-kind, and incredibly pilferable Jacob & Co Billionaire watch. Adorned with 252 Ashoka-cut white diamonds and hand-set in 18k worth of white gold, this V&A-exhibition-worthy time-piece could rival the bling of a Fabergé egg –with a price tag to match.

'I still can't believe the pair of you stole a 16 million quid watch!' Amy exclaims, sounding considerably more impressed than outraged, which in all fairness is understandable because between them they had pulled off a jewellery robbery to rival the Hatton Garden Heist. 'No wonder you ran off together. I reckon I could be convinced to do a bunk, and a bonk, with Boris Johnson if I knew eight million was on the cards.'

High on murderous and thieving adrenaline, and with the boundary between right and wrong completely smashed to shit, their affair had begun immediately. What was one more sin to add to their increasingly growing list of misdeeds? In a weird way, it was nice to know it wasn't simply a dazzling smile and a pair of fun bags that turned my husband's head, it was also dazzling diamonds and great big cash bags.

'I think it was a great philosopher who once said never to start a relationship under intense circumstances because they never work out.' Connie stares out sadly at the blurry green scenery as our taxi trundles towards what I hope isn't going to be our final destination. 'But I thought we'd be different, that we were destiny. After all, he'd saved my life and helped me hide a body. We'd done some pretty bad, messed up shit that kind of bonded us for life, do you know what I mean?'

I do not. The closest I've ever got to that level of solidarity was when Debs wet herself sneezing in Nandos and I had to pretend to the waitress that I'd spilt my Fanta on the floor. Not entirely the same, I imagine.

'There'd always been an attraction there. I'm sorry Cara, I really am. Everything I told you last night was the truth, though. Dom saw me at my worst, for who I truly was, and still wanted to be with me. How many other men would do that? He told me there was a darkness to my soul that only he could ever love, and he was right. Who else would want me if they knew what I'd done? What I was capable of? It had to be him. There was no point in fighting it any longer.'

'Ok, firstly – the relationship advice wasn't Aristotle, it was Keanu Reeves in the movie *Speed*.' Amy informs her, nineties films being her pub quiz category of choice. 'Secondly – I'm pretty sure the definition of romantic destiny isn't being gaslit into running away with a high-cheek-boned fuck-boy who's essentially saying you're a repulsive she-devil destined to die alone – regardless of how true that might be.'

'Amy's actually right, for once,' I jump in. 'Not only the she-devil stuff, but about running away. With all that cash, you could have easily disappeared, but instead you opted to come home and live in the very plain sight of your scorned sister *and* the De Leons. Why on earth would you do that? Surely you'd be worried about one of us taking you out, eventually?'

Connie and Dom were either incredibly ballsy or incredibly stupid – my money being on the latter. If I was wanted by one of the world's most deadly gangs, the last thing you'd catch me doing would be publicly flogging hair driers on QVC. I'd be more concerned about my brains being blown out than my bangs.

'Well, obviously, Ramón wasn't dead,' Connie points out, wryly.

Obviously, indeed. The man was very much alive, kicking and kidnapping – my sister proving that, when it comes to finishing off men, her skills lie mainly in the bedroom.

'According to the Spanish media, he was in a coma,' she continues. 'Multiple brain injuries, and highly unlikely to ever wake up.'

'Lucky for you,' Amy says, then asks the driver, 'Davíd, donde esta the club classics? And any chancio of stepping on it?' She's clearly infuriated by his musical tastes in 'easy listening', which is as slow as his driving.

'Not quite,' my sister replies, savagely. 'It would have been significantly better if he'd pegged it. Something that did turn out to be lucky though was Daddy De Leon thinking it was a targeted attack carried out by a rival cartel and, with their number one witness lying in ICU with his jaw firmly wired shut, who was going to tell them otherwise? No one was looking for us. We were off the hook with an absolute fortune in our hands. The world was our oyster...'

For my sister, a fairly simple creature, their newly acquired pot of cash meant being able to buy new boobs – along with a social media following worthy of that illustrious blue tick. For that sneaky ex-husband of mine, however, his new-found fortune meant one thing and one thing only: fulfilling his life-long, and very literal, career goals. As Connie confesses all, so much of the puzzle clicks into place. I bloody knew there was no way Dom could have blagged his way into one of the top jobs in football on merit and schoolboy charm alone – he needed an 'in', a favour to pull, or in Dom's case a ton of illegally acquired money he needed to shift and a sporting director with gambling debts up to his eyeballs to exploit.

'I knew you two were up to something!' I shout victoriously, thrusting my fist skyward in triumph – my sudden outburst taking ten years off poor David's life. 'There was no way he got that Manchester United job legitimately – of course he paid someone off. OF COURSE HE DID! Everyone thought I was just the bitter and twisted ex-wife, but I was right. Didn't I tell you, Jac? Didn't I tell you!'

'Yes, you did indeed tell me, Cara,' she recalls, reaching across Connie and dragging my arm back down to my side. 'I believe your exact words were "shifty pair of fuckers", and, wow, ain't that the truth. Connie, you two really pulled a swift one, didn't you? Practically the perfect crime, apart from the small, teeny tiny matter of Sleeping Psycho waking up.'

Battered and ego bruised, one can only assume that on opening his eyes Ramón was absolutely hopping – once his coma-induced muscular atrophy was no longer an issue, of course.

'I couldn't believe it when I saw him at the beach club yester-day,' she tells us, the colour draining from her face at the mere recollection of it. 'He was meant to be brain-dead. We both kind of assumed someone had gone in and switched him off, like a

TV on standby, but no, there he was – larger than life, and pissed as hell. I have no idea how he even found me.'

'Tagging your location on the million Instagram selfies you were posting every day probably made things somewhat easier for him,' I retort, wondering who out of the two of them was supposed to have the mentally-impaired noggin. 'Anyway, if he's that fuming, why didn't he finish you off there and then?'

Taking a break from anxiously biting off one of her glossy fake talons, Connie continues, 'Ah, here's the thing – never underestimate the power of fragile masculinity. Imagine having to tell your shit-scary dad, who's waging war on half of Europe's bad guys on your behalf, that the person who beat you up and then stole the family heirloom was actually little old me. Talk about awks. No, he wants his watch back quietly and quickly, and, if I wash up on beach with a hole in my head, there's little chance of that happening. He gave me until 1 pm today to return it. I assume he took Debs as a down-payment because, for some reason, he doesn't trust me.'

'But you flogged the watch! It's a goner – along with Debs, unless we can think of a way out of this.' I'm absolutely dumb-founded by Connie's lackadaisical calmness surrounding gunshot wounds and a one-way trip to Davy Jones' locker.

'Who said we sold it?' Connie declares, winding down the car window and flicking particles of acrylic into the roaring wind. 'That thing was harder to get rid of than herpes. We may as well have had a glowing "come and get us" target on our backs for the De Leons. It was an actual ticking time-bomb. No, we flogged the other pieces of jewellery from the safe – less traceable and valuable enough to pay off the Manchester United guy with change left over for my tits.'

'Oh my God, Connie,' I gasp, remembering the OTT glitter-ing timepiece on her arm that ill-fated Christmas Day I nearly tore her face off. 'Please tell me you still have it, preferably in Ibiza, locked up in your hotel room and not in the handbag you misplaced while smacked off your tits?'

Snorting sourly, she raises her eyebrows at me . 'Cara, and here I was thinking you were the smart one out of the two of us. No, I do not have it. Dom doesn't let me leave the house with it anymore, never mind the country. I'm a flight risk, apparently. He's completely lost the plot, thinks I'm going to do a runner with it, despite going to great lengths to ensure I'm stuck with him until death us do part…'

'What do you mean?' I'm surprised by the disdain for him in her voice. 'You made your seedy little bed. How long have you not been enjoying lying in the sticky side?'

'As I told you last night… it's complicated.' She flicks glossy hair over a shoulder, haughtily.

'Complicated' is probably the understatement of the year when it comes to anything to do with my sister. I've had conversations with the kids about where babies come from that have been more straightforward – and they involved metaphors about magic wands and flying tadpoles.

'So, if you don't have it,' Jac pushes, 'and you didn't sell it, that means…'

'Dom has it,' Connie finishes, 'in Las Vegas, I assume.'

Slamming my hands into the headrest in front, I yell, 'SHIT! SHIT! SHIT!' As if today couldn't get any worse, the one thing we need to save Debs is thousands of miles away on the arm of a soon-to-be dead man. Not that I'm questioning Giles' integrity or anything, but if I were an unscrupulous hitman tasked with taking someone's life for money, I'd probably have no qualms in taking the highly valuable lovely sparkly watch from his cold, dead arm also.

Looking down at my phone, I moan: we only have half an hour before Ramón's deadline.

Infuriated by our driver's rigid regard for highway safety, I shout, 'Venga, VENGA!' Sweating profusely, we're about as close to formulating a plan to save Debs as we are arriving on American soil to rescue Dom. Placing my throbbing head into my now equally throbbing hands, I wonder if Connie has packed her pulverising platform shoes, because Davíd might not be the only one who's forced once more to put his foot down.

A haunting dance cover of Nancy Sinatra's 'Shot Me Down' booms around the otherwise silent cab, Amy having finally got her way with the radio station. The four of us are sitting in deep contemplation of how on earth we're going to get out of this with all of our limbs and lives intact when my cousin suddenly whips her head round to face us with a startled gasp of inspiration. 'Davíd, how fario esta le Muh hotelio fromé le harrrbour Eivissa pelvic floor favour?' she asks excitedly in some kind of broken GCSE Spanglais, hitting him repeatedly on the arm before turning to face us with a wide grin. 'Ladies, hold onto your panty liners, I've got an epic idea...'

26

We're Going to Need a Bigger Boat

Ibiza marina 2.57pm. We've made it by the skin of our teeth, having had an incredibly quick pit stop at the hotel, as per Amy's request, which also gave me a chance to grab a top and some shoes. I love my friend dearly, but there's no way I'm hobbling into a mob meeting in my ill-fitting and slightly greying M&S strapless bra – despite it being thick enough to take a bullet. The rough plan, as it stands, is to appeal to Ramón's better nature/ embarrassment at being beaten up by a girl, then blame Dom for everything and beg for more time so we can get to Vegas, save knobhead, get the watch, and then fly back to Ibiza with it. Simple. Kind of. There are, obviously, quite a few logistical issues we need to work out, but all Ramón needs to know for now is that Connie's sorry and he can trust us.

'He's not going to buy it,' Amy argues, breathlessly folding Camilla's conked-out body into a trolley she's pinched from a nearby mini-mart. 'He doesn't seem like the reasonable type, that's all. I'm telling you, we'd be better off with my plan.'

'But you won't tell us your plan,' I point out narkily, the heat of the midday sun causing stinging beads of sweat to make their way down my forehead and into my eyeballs. 'The 'element of surprise' is all very well and good but you've got previous when it comes to the preposterous – so this time we're going to do things my way, ok?'

With a grunt of annoyance, she waves a dismissive hand in my direction and begins to push Camilla down the jetty towards the rows of gleaming white yachts bobbing away rhythmically in their moorings. Maybe it's down to my chronic sea-sickness, but I've never seen the appeal. I could have all the money in the world and I'd still opt to spend four hours at a soft-play centre over an afternoon on the high seas, and that's saying something.

Cautiously making our way down the boardwalk, I take stock of our very public surroundings… a smiling old couple playing bridge on the decking of their uber-swanky pleasure boat; a group of beautiful girls brandishing peace signs posing for selfies in front of a ship big enough to rival the Dover to Calais passenger ferry. Nothing about this hustle and bustle, broad daylight set up is giving off the 'public execution' vibes I was expecting. No, I can't help but feel there is something more sinister planned for us. As we reach the end of the dock, dazzling rays of UVA light bounce off the Med's dancing waves – obscuring the faces of the three suited and booted figures waiting for us.

'Right Connie, get your "on the game" face ready.' I squint with the glare as we approach our waiting entourage. 'Remember, doe-eyed and remorseful, ok? Say you're sorry, maybe offer him a blow job – and tell him we'll get his watch back within seventy-two hours. It'll be fine, absolutely fine…'

'Why does it sound like you're trying to convince yourself more than me?' Connie hisses out of the side of her mouth, at the same time as sucking in her waist and sticking out her tits.

Strutting towards us like a heavily tattooed peacock, Ramón enthuses, 'Ladies, welcome.' His red silk shirt hangs open just enough to display an eerily familiar four-headed feline inked onto his chest – a matching cat from the same mutant litter adorns his veiny and bulging neck.

'Ramón,' greets Connie coolly, as his two gigantic goons advance and indicate for us all to lift our arms – presumably for a pat down, not a group rendition of the 'YMCA'.

Amy, clearly unimpressed at such a violation, has her fists clenched and is sporting a look of displeasure normally reserved for old people driving slowly. 'Mate, the only wire you'll find in there is the scaffolding supporting my post-breastfeeding baba-lons,' she informs the man mountain attempting to frisk her. 'And if you think I'm going to allow your fingers anywhere near my nibbled-on nips, you're dafter than the dribbling one in the trolley looks.'

'Whoa, whoa, take it easy, chica,' Ramón laughs, indicating for his rent-a-muscle to step down. 'Fernando, please, respect the lady's wishes. She's right – this is no way to treat our guests. Especially my special VIP. So good to see you again, Connie, and this time you've brought me friends, so kind. You know how much I enjoy female company.'

Eyeing me up lecherously, a lazy grin spreads across his intri-cately art-worked face. 'Ah, and this must be your sister? I believe we've had the pleasure once before...'

As I shake my head in nervous disagreement, Ramón takes my hand and kisses it slowly, sensually. 'My apologies, for *some* reason I seem to be having a few problems with my memory of late...' He shoots Connie a withering glare.

'Yeah, about that...' Connie begins, in a vain attempt to smooth over the small act of nearly beating a man to death with a costly clodhopper. 'As I told you yesterday, I was checking out that cool plant pot and, well, those tiles of yours are extremely slippery when wet – it was simply incredibly unfortunate you happened to be right underneath when I accidentally... dropped it.'

'Yes, *incredibly* unfortunate...' he repeats, his Spanish accent bristling with frostiness. 'Also, that *vase* you *"dropped"* was my father's, a fifteenth-century Ming—'

'Oh, I'm so glad you thought it was minging too!' She cuts him off mid-sentence. 'But, obviously, I'm more than happy to replace it. IKEA have some lovely ones...'

With a caustic sneer, and slight trace of an eye twitch, he summons forward Goon One and Goon Two with an impatient click of twitchy fingers.

'Ladies, if you'd like to join your friend Deborah, we can get this party started!' Ramón says with a disconcertingly joyful clap as we're ploughed towards the water's brink by hands the size of snow shovels.

Approaching the deserted edge of the jetty, I glance down into the water and my heart soars with joy. There – sat in the same RIB as I saw Connie in yesterday – is a hysterical, gagged and incredibly sunburnt, but otherwise still in one piece, Debs.

'Fucking hell, you monster! Would it have killed you to slap a bit of factor fifty on her?' Amy yells at a pushy Fernando while attempting to fend him off. 'The poor girl's a strawberry blonde. She wasn't built for direct sunlight, you bastardo!'

'Ladies, please a sense of urgency would be preferable!' Ramón barks, gesturing towards the small and not particularly seaworthy-looking inflatable.

'Thanks, but no thanks,' I politely inform him, quickly dismissing his offer of what I imagine is going to be a little more bruise than booze cruise. 'Sorry, I get horribly seasick, and we actually have somewhere we need to be – which, if you'd let us explain, might be of great interest to you.'

Ramón starts to laugh, quietly at first before rapidly ascending into a full on crazy person raucous crescendo. 'Senoritas, I think there has been some confusion over what is a request, and what is a non-negotiable demand,' he says with a distinct air of agitation. 'Fernando, Jordi, please can you offer some clarity on the situation?'

Without saying a word, his henchmen simultaneously pull out matching revolvers and wave them threateningly at our faces.

'Get in the fucking boat, now!' Fernando yells, sending dollops of spit spraying all over my fear-frozen face.

Hands raised in the air to indicate our reluctant compliance, the four of us begrudgingly shuffle in the direction of the dodgy dinghy.

'Boss, what about this one?' Jordi asks, pushing my still-trolleyed, in more ways than one, mother towards the boat –her lolling head not fairing too well on the uneven surface of the wooden boardwalk.

'Just tip her in,' Ramón instructs. 'And take her wheels back to Pep at the supermercado before he loses his shit.'

Having been forcibly pushed down into a seated position, I share a highly alarmed, 'WTF are we going to do?' glance with Jac. It dawns on me I'm never going to see my babies again; this is the end, murdered in the middle of the Mediterranean by a madman with an axe to grind – hopefully not into our skulls. Will they ever find my body? More importantly, who will find the vibrators in my bedside table? Ray?! My poor soon-to-be orphaned kids?! I should never have left them… the battery-operated ones could have fitted in my hand luggage. Throwing our arms around Debs, I pull the gag out of her mouth and inspect her for signs of injury, aside from the skin damage.

'Babe, are you hurt?' Jac asks. 'What did he do to you?'

Sobbing with relief at our arrival, or possibly at the prospect of her skin shedding like a king cobra, Debs is awash with snot and tears. 'I'm ok, I'm ok. But what the fuck is going on? Is it because of the mini knives and forks?' she cries, between gasping gulps of air. 'One minute I was outside in the garden FaceTiming the baby, and livid with Will for feeding her a bag of Cadburys buttons. The next thing I know, something's over my head and I'm being dragged backwards into a van. Everything went black, and when I woke up I was here.'

'Can I just say,' Ramón interjects, jumping in alongside us, 'we didn't hit her or anything. She simply passed out – wouldn't wake up. I'm no medical expert, but I really think she needs to get that checked.'

The sound of the boat's engine rumbling to life fills my heart with dread, and my stomach with its own waves of queasiness. Foaming salty water froths and spits up around us – causing schools of fish to dart away from the spinning propeller's blades. Lucky little bastards, I think as I watch them dive to safety. What if we all jumped and made a swim for it, too? What would he do? Camilla would be left behind, of course, but I'm sure she'd manage to find a way out of it once she regained full function of her limbs.

With six of us now onboard, there is only enough space in the boat for Ramón and his enormous ego.

'Fernando, Jordi – wait for me in the van,' he instructs above the roar of the motor. 'I think I'm more than capable of taking on this many women on my own. Wouldn't be the first time, would it, Connie?'

As we begin to pull away from the marina with speed, I watch numbly on as the shoreline of Ibiza old town, with its formidable sixteenth-century bastions of Dalt Vila, rapidly fades from view. I wonder whether I'll ever get another chance to see its fortified walls, rustic buildings, and picturesque paved streets in the flesh? Looking at the vengeful expression on our tour guide's face, I'd say he's more interested in showing us ocean floors over cobbled ones. I don't feel well… I've not eaten since last night and the combination of hunger, bouncing waves, and fear is proving to be a bad one. Swallowing down a mouthful of bile, I try to look at the positives. At least I get to see the pure beauty of Ibiza from afar – its glowing white sandy beaches, towering green mountains and glistening white villas nestled neatly along the jagged coastline. Passing the sand-coloured and crumbling remains of what looks like an ancient defence tower, we continue round the island's most southerly tip until an ominously imposing rock comes into view on the brink of the horizon.

'Es Vedra,' Ramón informs us, in awe. 'Isn't she beautiful?'

I nod in anxious agreement as we charge towards the majestic limestone peak proudly protruding from the inky blue like a colossal and craggy iceberg.

'The third most magnetic spot on the planet,' he continues. 'Birthplace to the goddess Tanit, and home to sirens of Greek mythology. Those sexy bitches have been luring sailors to their deaths with their song since ancient times.'

'Fucking hell, they left that out of the *Little Mermaid*, didn't they?' Amy mutters, apprehensively peering over the edge of the boat.

Without warning, Ramón cuts the RIB's engine. 'It seems a lot of people like to leave the important details out of their stories, wouldn't you agree, Connie?' he says, towering over her menacingly. 'Like the fact you don't actually have my watch, despite telling me you did and you'd return it to me today. You see, I know it is not at your home in Manchester. My men have searched it extensively. They also tell me it is not in your possessions here in Ibiza. Ramón knows everything, my beautiful girl.

You see, I have it on *very* good authority that it's actually on the arm of that cockney coño of yours currently in Sin City. The very same one you brought to my home, and who helped you with your pathetically executed plot to execute me. He will pay the ultimate price for taking my watch, and my woman, make no mistake. I will see to that personally. People who double cross me, oh they do not make that mistake twice. They never escape my wrath. It is a lesson you will learn the hard way.'

Realising her jig is up, for a moment or two, Connie does not speak – instead she stares solemnly out towards the jagged, grey-scale terrain of Es Vedra, seemingly captivated by its mythical energy.

'You're brave, aren't you?' she finally mumbles, without breaking her gaze from the ancient rock. 'Bringing a lying and manipulative siren such as myself to a notoriously deadly spot – especially one where so many men have already lost their lives...'

'Connie, Connie ...' he chuckles deeply and sadistically, 'you've already had your chance to kill me. Sadly, for you, el Diablo has many lives – and none of them can be taken by the power of pottery, or platform shoes. The reason I have brought you here is because you stole something very precious from me, so, in return, I'm going to rob you of something truly valuable too.'

Quick as a flash, Ramón pulls a pistol out from behind his back and points it directly at my forehead. 'Nothing is more sacred than family, no? Cara, many apologies, but I had to take your friend in order to ensure *your* attendance at our little gathering. And as for your mother...' he says nodding towards an unbelievably still dozing Camilla. 'She has been more helpful than you'll ever know.'

'I presume it was you who drugged her, then planted the phone – you needed a way to reach us, right?' I piece the puzzle together. 'You're disgusting, rummaging around in a pensioner's pants like that. There are special registers reserved for people like you!'

Above the blustering howl of the rising sea wind, the audible click of the gun's safety being released quickly shuts my gobby trap.

'It pains me to say this, Cara – our short yet intimate journey together has been incredibly special to me. You are one hell of a woman, but sadly it's time for us to part ways...'

Fuck. Fuck, fuckety, fuck! Also, what's he on about? Our highly special time spent with him holding me hostage? The bloke's clearly off his rocker. Speaking of unhinged: my sister, cool as a cucumber, has not flinched once during this exchange. Looking between Ramón and me in contemplative bewilderment, she blinks slowly, totally taken aback, then... tears of laughter, not sadness at my imminent demise, start to free-fall down her face. Bitch.

Cackling maniacally, she says, 'Cara? You think *she's* the most precious thing in my life?' She sneers, wiping away leaking droplets of her evil soul from her cheeks. 'God, for a minute there, I thought you were going to cut my face or something!'

'Are you kidding me?!' I yell, shaking like a leaf as I clamber to my unsteady feet. 'After everything you've put me through, you're going to do me dirty like that? THANKS A BLOODY LOT!'

As our stomach-turning chariot lurches from side to side in the increasingly choppy surf, I'm not sure whether I'm going to slap her or puke on her.

Jumping up to throw herself directly between Ramón and me, Connie's facial expression is no longer amused, but full of determination and fury. If looks could kill, the man who turned her world upside down wouldn't be six feet under – he'd be 600 feet... under the boat.

'Here's the thing, Ramón, you do not know *everything*,' she gloats, 'and it's about time someone took your Cuban heels down an inch or two.'

Intrigued either by her brazenness, or plain stupidity, he lowers the gun. 'Is that right, Connie?' he asks, with face-pummelling arrogance. 'And, let me guess, you think *you're* the big woman to take down this big man?'

Smiling sweetly, like butter wouldn't melt, she says, 'You may give it Larry Largepants with all your guns, power, and daddy drug money, but in reality you're a little man – a little man with a tiny cock and…'. Then, with the reflexes of a cornered street rat, Connie lunges at Ramón's hairline, pulling something off his scalp that's reminiscent of how my pubic region looked in pregnancy, and brandishes it wildly in the air, 'a toupee!' The force of her snatch, timed perfectly with the impact of a fairly large wave, knocks Ramón off balance – sending him tumbling to the deck and his gun flying overboard.

'Newsflash, dickhead,' Connie screams, as he tries to right himself against the ocean's furious turbulence, 'the watch isn't in Vegas, it's right here, and if you want it, you're going to have to get it. Amy, NOW!'

On Connie's instruction, Amy, with lightning-fast reactions, reaches down, pulls out a dazzling, diamond-covered object from her pocket and lobs it overarm, with the enthusiasm of an Olympic shot-putter, straight into the water.

'Nooo!' Ramón screams, as it touches down into the brine with an impressively dramatic splash. His tattooed face contorts with rage. 'Bitches! What have you done? You'll pay, you'll all pay!'

'Oh, will we now?' Amy whips out a gun of her own and directs it straight at Ramón. Glancing up at the rock-steady hand of my grinning cousin, his initial reaction of shock and anger quickly gives way to bemused confusion. 'Wait… is that a penis?'

he asks, eyes struggling against the glare of the sun to see the pistol in her hand.

'No mother fucker, it's a cock glock!' Amy tells him with cool, calm collection. 'Now put your hands where I can see them, or you're going to face the full force of this fully loaded weapon.'

It's at this point my churning stomach can take no more of the day's highly eventful activities and promptly decides to empty itself all over Ramón's Gucci shoes. Clearly having one hell of a bad day at the office, and distraught at losing sixteen million to the deep, he has understandably reached his capacity for empathy.

'La perra!' he roars, lunging towards me, hands outstretched and directed at my throat. I feel the weight of his body upon me, the tightness of his fingers wrapped around my throat and the warmth of his breath in my face – and instead of thinking 'Oh shit! I'm going to die,' my mind says, 'Oh shit, this feels familiar.' As gooey lick-pool eyes, as deep as the water we're floating on, bore into my own, X-rated memories of the night before come flooding back to me.

'You!' I splutter in horror, as I realise what really happened at Smiths.

'Hola, chica,' he whispers nastily into my ear, running his tongue down the length of my face while my own trembling hands desperately try to claw his away from my trachea. 'It turns out I have quite an obsession with the Carmichael women – which is why, against my better judgement, I spared you last night – but today is a new day, and who is your saviour now?'

With darkness beginning to flood over me, I feel myself having an out-of-body experience. It's as though I'm watching a highly OTT theatre version of the end of my life unfolding before me. Taking one last look at last night's one-night stand – a pantomime villain minus his wig – and with what feels like my final breath, I manage to mutter, 'She's behind you…'

Turning his head slightly, there's little time for Ramón to react to Connie's incoming blow.

'Oi, dickhead! No one gets to put my sister in a chokehold apart from me!' she roars as the oar comes crashing down onto the back of his head.

Warm, viscous blood cascades down over his bare scalp and onto my face. Feeling his fingers relax around my throat, I greedily gulp in gigantic mouthfuls of sweet and salty ocean air. Staggering to his feet, hands instinctively behind his head, he's too preoccupied with attempting to stem the oozing flow to notice the pool of my vomit coating the boat's slippery floor... One misjudged step backwards is all it takes to send him, Gucci loafers and all, tumbling overboard with a blood-curdling scream.

'Shit, how many blows to the head can that man take?' Amy asks, while the rest of us watch in stunned silence as a flailing Ramón thrashes about and shouts obscenities.

'Shall we help him, do you think?' Debs asks, a little too compassionately for someone who, because of him, is soon going to be flakier than a social recluse who's agreed to a night out. 'I think his chains might be weighing him down...'

'And what do you think is going to happen if we let him back on, babes?' Amy responds, slapping his hands away from the RIB like she's playing a game of Whac-A-Mole. 'He's going to murder us and chuck us overboard. You know those fish foot spas that creep you out?' Debs nods, with terror in her eyes. 'Like that, but a *million* times worse.'

'Er, ladies...' Jac points into the distance. 'Speaking of fish... is that... is that... a fin?'

We whirl our heads round to follow the direction of her shaking finger and, sure enough, effortlessly slicing its way through the waves towards a heavily bleeding drug lord succumbing to the current is the hauntingly triangular shape of a grey dorsal fin.

'Oh my God, SHARK! SHARK!' Debs cries out, flapping so much she's in danger of rocking the boat over.

'Debs, stop it! You're going to tip us in! It's probably just a friendly dolphin wondering what all the commotion is about...' I tell her as we watch the speeding creature disappear from view, leaving behind a rippled wake in the water.

'When we were kids, you told me dolphins could kill... food for thought,' Connie says, only adding to Debs' hysteria.

'Listen, dolphin's don't eat people, and you don't get sharks in the Mediterranean – so everyone calm down, ok?' I try to reassure the pair of them.

'Well, not *entirely* accurate,' Amy says. 'According to *Shark Week* on the Discovery Channel, my favourite week of the year, the Mediterranean is thought to have on average forty-seven different shark species, including the angelshark, blue shark, longfin mako, scalloped hammerhead, thresher shark, and, of course... the great white shark.'

'WHAT?!' I cry, looking down at the now semi-submerged Spanish blood sausage whose busted nose is rapidly turning the blue water around him a pretty shade of crimson. 'Help me pull him in!' I shout frantically to the girls.

'*Or* we *could* just leave him...' Connie proposes, with a suggestive shrug of her shoulders. 'It would make life much easier, for all concerned.'

Actually, she's right. What *am* I doing? We should just leave him – shouldn't we? When it comes to Ramón De Leon, it's not like heaven's missing an angel. Shit, I can't believe I shagged him. Connie's never going to let me live this down. Of all the people to pop my post-marriage virginity with, I picked the most awful human being in the world – next to my ex-husband, that is. What is wrong with the pair of us when it comes to picking men? The same men, at that. If I let him die, however, does that make me equally as awful? I'm a good person, aren't I? Aside from emotionally bullying my sister for most of her life, hating my mother, not speaking to Ray, and telling my children our burglar alarm's motion detectors are cameras so Santa can spy on them. What am I thinking? I can't kill somebody; I'm a mother, a respectable member of society – I have a Waitrose membership card, for Christ's sake!

I spring to decisive action and extend the oar over the side of the boat. 'One of you help me, will you! Amy, hold my legs! Ramón! Grab the—

'AHHH!'

My moment of good Samaritanism has come too little, too late. In a sudden eruption of bubbles, he's snatched below the surface with a gurgle of terror.

'Wow, I guess Flipper the Friendly Dolphin isn't quite as chummy as he's made out to be,' Amy muses as she hauls me back to safety.

'SHIT! Maybe he swam under the boat? I'm sure he'll reappear any second now...'

Ten minutes later, there's no sign of Ramón and we're sat in silence – mouths gaping, hands slapped to our cheeks and sporting identical 'screaming face' emoji expressions.

'He could be part of the Spanish free-diving team?' Amy suggests, her eyes searching the shimmering seascape. 'You know, can hold his breath for a *really* long time...'

'*Or* he could be digesting slowly inside Jaws, and we can all go on with our lives without worrying about the De Leons coming to murder us,' Connie adds.

'Wait... wait!' Debs shouts. 'I think I see him! Turn the engine on, he's over there!'

Shuffling to the back of the boat, Amy pulls firmly on the engine chord, starting the RIB with a sputter of diesel fumes. 'Luckily for you lot, I learnt how to do this shit in the Girl

Guides,' she says as she steers us towards where Debs thinks she's spotted Ramón.

'There!' Debs points towards where a tattooed hand has broken the surface. 'Grab him and pull him in!'

'I've got him,' Jac says, reaching down and yanking his arm out of the water... minus a body attached to the end of it. 'OH MY GOD!' she screeches, dancing around on the spot like she's doing the jive with Thing from *The Addams Family*.

'Throw it back in!' I yell at her, vomit once more pouring out of my oesophagus and acting like chum. 'THROW IT BACK IN!'

'AMY, GET US OUT OF HERE, NOW!' Debs screams with such guttural energy I'm surprised she hasn't expelled her pelvic floor onto the actual floor.

'Aye, aye, captain!' Amy pushes the engine to full throttle, catapulting us across the waves back towards the mainland at breakneck speed.

'Holy shit,' Connie shouts above the wind, while we cling to the edges of the raft for dear life. 'I wonder how many lives el Diablo has left now?'

'Fuck!' I scream back. 'Did we just kill a man? Does this count as murder?'

'Survival of the fittest, babe,' Amy replies, philosophically. 'Think of it as divine intervention. God wanted him to be horrifically mauled to death in the most vicious and brutal way. After all, he does work in mysterious, and totally barbaric, ways.'

'And what about Dom?' I yell back at her over the din of the boat, my stomach still feeling like it's been surgically removed from my body and placed inside a tumble drier. 'We're hours behind schedule. There's no way we're going to get there before Giles. We're too late!'

'Leave it with good old Amy!' she shouts back at me with a twinkle in her eye. 'I've got a plan!'

Having very recently lived through the hatching out of one of her strategies, I dread to think what she has up her sleeve this time.

Willing to let her response slide in the name of the greater good, I ask, 'What the hell did you throw into the ocean anyway?' fairly convinced that, unlike the old lady at the end of Titanic, not even she would be daft enough to sink sixteen million pounds.

'Oh, glad you asked. When we get home, your sister owes me a brand spanking new diamanté butt plug,' Amy says, deadly serious. 'And believe me when I say, if she doesn't come up with the goods, I'll lose my shit.'

27

The Second Coming

Bouncing over the waves back towards the Santa Eulalia coastline, I can't help but wonder what branch of Girl Guides Amy attended as a child. The one I went to involved getting badges for baking scones, visiting old people in retirement villages, and doing Irish dancing. I must have been ill the day they did the Royal Marine orienteering badge. As the yellow window blinds of the M hotel come into view, I can just about make out a figure standing on the beach signalling for us to head towards them.

'No way!' I yell, squinting at the familiar face of a person who is waving with one hand, and holding a plate of what I can only assume are courgette fritters in the other.

'Is that Guthrie?' I ask, totally confused as to why modern-day Jesus is waiting on the shoreline – unless he's about to turn seawater into wine, because it's pretty fair to say we could all do with a BIG drink right now.

'Sure is!' Amy replies, rather smitten.

'What the bloody hell is he doing here? And, bar offering a nutritious vegan snack, how is he going to help us in our current predicament?'

'Cara, what is it you're always saying to the kids, hey? Never judge a book by its cover.'

'Yes, this is true, Amy but, generally speaking, the book in question isn't the bloody Kama Sutra.'

Laughing in agreement, she steers the boat towards the beach – enthusiastically waving back to Guthrie like a love-sick teenager., 'Boy, does he know his way round that book though...'

'Wait a minute,' I say. 'How would you know?!'

'Oh, we're a thing now,' she replies, super-casually.

'What? Amy, when did this even happen?'

'I left him my number at the retreat, didn't I? I wanted *in* on that multiple orgasm shit. Anyway, he called me while we were at Smiths and, as you and Connie were off doing your thing, Debs was having a nap/kidnap, and Jac had gone to Pacha, I invited him over...'

'Sorry?! Amy, hold that thought. Jac, you went to Pacha, without me?' I ask my bestie, utterly heartbroken at her betrayal. How could she do that to me? It was always our dream to go together – like Thelma and Louise; but instead of going over a cliff, we'd probably drunkenly fall head-first off a podium.

'Don't make this a thing, Cara,' Jac warns. 'I feel bad enough as it is, ok? If I had stayed with Debs, she wouldn't have been snatched. I got talking to a bunch of people who were going and as it was *my* bloody hen party and *you* were nowhere to be seen, I thought, fuck it, I'm going. Anyway, I was back a few hours later – place doesn't get going until 3am and I was tired, my feet hurt and it was full of young people in bikinis. You seriously didn't miss much.'

Huffing at her grumpily, I decide to let it go in the short term (especially since I'd apparently abandoned her in favour of shagging a marginally sexier version of Pablo Escobar) but I draw up a mental Post-It to remind her of her treachery when this is all over.

'Fine,' I tell her sulkily. 'Ok, Amy – back to Girthrie, I mean Guthrie.'

'Well, one thing led to another,' she explains, innocently, 'and we had one hell of a night. He does the most amazing thing with his tongue, by the way, like a snake scooping out the contents of a Cadbury's Creme Egg…'

'Lovely, thanks for that,' I say, with Easter now ruined for life. 'What I want to know is how Guthrie's going-down skills will prevent us from going down… for life.'

'Remember, I told you the retreat was super-exclusive, totally bouji? Well, I wasn't lying. Branch put a price on rooms to rival a return trip on a SpaceX flight. Turns out he only let us in because he wanted a bit of me, of course he did. Anyway, post-coital, Guthrie happened to tell me what he did for a living…'

'Annoying charity person with clipboard?' I guess, knowing I've ignored at least ten blokes who look just like him outside my local Tesco Express alone.

'Wrong!' she says, revelling in what she's about to tell me next. 'He's only the CEO of one of London's biggest hedge fund firms. Can you believe it?'

No, I seriously cannot, although it might explain his fondness for bushes.

'If he's so rich, why doesn't the bloke own any shoes or clothes?'

'Just fancy rich-person bullshit, isn't it? You know, poverty appropriation – makes them feel more grounded or some bollocks. Anyway, I imagine he likes to walk around without shoes because he particularly enjoys leaving behind a footprint… especially a carbon one. That's right, ladies, he might not have brought a t-shirt with him to Ibiza, but I'll tell you what he did bring… a motherfucking private jet! One that's prepped, primed and ready to take us to Vegas in thirty minutes.'

As Amy expertly manoeuvres the boat onto the beach, tears of relief slide down my face. 'Bloody hell, babe,' I say in utter admiration of her incredible resourcefulness, 'you must be one hell of a shag!'

'Yes, Cara,' she says, proud as punch. 'Yes I am.'

28

Sin City

Fourteen hours into our race around the world to try and foil a fatal old fogey, and we've finally touched down in the U S of A. Dirty, dishevelled, and disorientated – I have no idea of the date and time, whether I'm living in the future or the past, or if Dom's even still alive. Staking out the entrance to the swanky, five-star, Brynn Hotel from behind a somewhat less glamorous bin, this much I do know: even by night, Las Vegas is hotter than Satan's crotch after a spin class. Between Ramón and the watch, Amy and Guthrie's permanent residency in club 'mile high' for the entirety of the flight, and a massively freaked out Camilla eventually waking up over the North Atlantic Ocean and attempting to skydive out of the emergency exit – I'm in dire need of a lie down in a dark, air-conditioned room with a tequila-soaked flannel on my face.

'Mum, get down, will you!' I shout to my mother, who's managed to shimmy herself a couple of feet up a neighbouring palm tree and is clinging on like a shining crack-head koala bear example of why never to do drugs. 'What part of stealth do you not understand? He's going to see you!'

'On it!' calls Amy, strolling towards the tree and lobbing an empty Coke can at her head 'Sorted,' she says, watching a babbling and crazy-eyed Camilla come down harder than the post-Special K crash she's currently experiencing.

Despite the luxurious glass-fronted hotel being set back from the hustle and bustle of the main attractions, the pulsating buzz of the adjacent strip is practically palpable. Man, what I'd give to be a pepped-up reveller taking in the famous sights right now – throwing my life away by gambling on the slots instead of being embroiled in murder-for-hire plots.

'Wow, would you look at that?' Amy says, scanning a leaflet she was handed as we hurried past the neon-lit boule-vard's impressively accurate replicas of Saint Mark's Square, the Eiffel Tower and Empire State building. 'You can order hook-ers to your hotel room like takeaway food. DeliverFoo, I guess…'

I wonder whether I'd be able to hire one to sit with crazy Camilla for a couple of hours while we track down Dom?

'Jac's back.' I watch my friend jog across the valet parking bays and towards our not so inconspicuous hiding place.

'Ok, so the good news – Dom's still in the land of the living,' she tells us, with a 'yay, we're not going to prison' thumbs up. 'The bad news – he rolled out about twenty minutes ago, and the receptionist is refusing to tell me where he went – guest confidentiality, apparently. Even worse news – she asked if I was with the gentleman who also just came in looking for him.'

'Shit! Giles?' I ask, my head swivelling around as if one of us is about to take a sniper shot to the face. 'Ok, we need to find Dom stat! But how? Vegas is bloody massive – there are thou-sands of possibilities where he could be.'

'Cara, why don't you message him?' Connie suggests. 'I'm sure, if you said there was a problem with the kids, he'd reply – wouldn't he? Then you could casually ask where he is.'

'NO! Do not message him,' Jac says. 'Imagine if he gets his head blown off and there's a data trail of text messages with him telling you his *exact* location?'

Without saying a word, Amy stands up and strolls across the tarmac towards the lobby of the Brynn's curvaceous bronze tower.

'Where's she going?' I ask Jac, who raises her eyebrows. 'Amy, where are you going?'

Having walked away, completely ignoring my question, she returns after only a matter of minutes. 'Fortunately for you ladies, I missed my calling in life as a MI6 agent,' she says smugly, picking something threadlike out of her front teeth. 'And bellboys will tell you *anything* with the right kind of incentive.'

'Amy, you didn't?' I gasp. 'But… if you did, and you happen know where he is, then we'd all be *very* grateful – probably not as grateful as the bellboy, but you know… thankful for your contribution to the cause.'

'What are you on about? I offered him twenty bucks and he told me what I needed to know in a heartbeat, then I swung by the bar for a quick Bloody Mary. Damn celery, so stringy. Anyone got a toothpick?'

'So where is he?' I ask impatiently, watching, out of the corner of my eye, Camilla licking the inside of a discarded KFC box.

'Come on, Cara, this is Las Vegas!' she replies, like I'm an absolute idiot. 'Where on earth do you *think* he is?'

Standing outside a 'gentleman's club' called Sapphires, six very awkward and out of place women are wondering how on earth they're going to sneak in, incognito, without anyone wondering who invited mums on tour to the party.

'Maybe I should go alone, do a recce?' Amy suggests. 'Dom's going to spot Connie and Cara a mile off, and the rest of you are going to stick out more than the strippers' tits.'

In all fairness, she might have a point – Debs is sporting a pair of M&S linen culottes; Jac has brought her sensible cross-body

Radley bag, complete with a copy of *The Thursday Murder Club* sticking out the top; and, despite a sink wash, Camilla has an air of Wetherspoons urinals on a Sunday morning about her.

In a bid to avoid the front entrance and any potentially damning CCTV evidence that could be used in court against us, we decide to take a leaf out of our Passion Beach break-in book and slope around the back to see if there's a less conspicuous way of entering the club. Weaving between industrial-sized bins, a couple of used condoms, and sidestepping an inconsiderately parked black motorbike, our luck seems to be in as we spy an unmanned performers' entrance.

'Ok, once we get in there, we're going to need a disguise,' I whisper, the six of us lurking in the shadows as we wait for a group of feather-donned dancers in skyscraper heels to finish their fags and head back inside. 'As low-key as possible, do you understand? All we need to do is find Dom, drop the note on his table and then leave. Absolutely no funny business. Get in, get out – and we leave no woman behind, ok?'

The note was Jac's idea: an anonymous tipoff warning him his life's in danger and that he needs to get himself somewhere safe immediately and alert the authorities ASAP. Simple, straight to the point, effective, and most importantly – non-incriminating.

With the girls' cigarette break now over, we watch as they stamp out their butts and head back inside to get shaking them. Putting our heads down and edging towards the door, I manage to get my foot to the corner of it – catching it in the nick of time before it closes fully behind them.

'Go! Go! Go!' I usher our group through like a paratrooper captain shoving his soldiers out of a Black Hawk helicopter. It's time for us hens to hustle.

Slinking along the grubby, dimly lit corridor behind our oblivious tour guides, I try my best to be a Cara Cara Cara Cara Cara

Chameleon and seamlessly blend into our surroundings – tricky, however, when nipple tassels seem to be the fashion accessory du jour. Following the dancers through a 1960s beaded curtain and into a cheap-perfume-and-Redbull-scented dressing room, a whirlwind of beautiful women await us, all of whom are rushing around in various states of undress looking for shoes, earrings, and dental-floss-thick underwear.

'Oh, look at y'all!' a gorgeous Texan redhead dressed only in an impressively art-worked sleeve and patriotic thong purrs as she lovingly strokes Debs hair as though she's found an abandoned puppy, not a kitten… heel wearer. 'Aren't you the cutest!'

Not quite knowing how to respond to the compliment, or where to look, Debs replies all in a fluster, her face the same shade as the cowgirl's gloriously fiery mane, 'Great tits, I mean tats!'

'Crystal, they're here!' the semi-naked goddess shouts over to an equally stunning blonde bombshell, who's busy diligently plucking stray pubes out of her bikini line. 'The extra girls they hired for the creepy old dudes!'

'Thank fuck for that!' Crystal replies, quickly moving her tweezers from her bush to her brows without pausing for alcohol gel. 'What took you so long? There's a caravan exhibition on at the convention centre and we're absolutely swamped! You need to go straight to Carol in wardrobe. Now! Go!'

Dying on the inside from the brute force of the insult, but smiling politely on the surface, I'm about to inform them we're not who they think we are – old codger todger teasers – when Amy jumps in, size seven feet first. 'So, so sorry, dolls – traffic!'

'Amy, what the hell are you doing?' I ask while Debs, absolutely thrilled at being mistaken for someone hot enough to take their clothes off three months postpartum, enthusiastically waves them both farewell.

'What? You said we need disguises, and, bar an invisibility cloak right now, you tell me a better way of moving around this place undetected?'

She has an annoyingly good point.

'Good luck, ladies,' Crystal calls out, turning her attention back to her groin's five o'cock shadow. 'And watch out for the creepy English guy in the tweed suit. A big tipper, but going on the bulge in his pocket, his weapon is large, and loaded.'

'OMG, Giles!' I mouth to Jac, who nods nervously in acknowledgement as we hurry towards a stern-looking woman tapping her watch and holding up what looks like a crotchless carer's uniform. Fuck's sake, Cara, I think to myself as I start to peel my clothes off, get in get out – not get in, get your tits out.

'It's not that bad…' Amy attempts to convince Jac as we try to slip our way across one of the many floors of this absolutely humongous strip joint without any of its punters managing to slip into us.

'Fine for you to say, you look vaguely ok in your sexy air hostess get-up,' she fumes, pulling her fishnet body stocking out from between her arse cheeks, 'I resemble a Christmas ham before it's been cut out of its mesh.'

This might not have been in the original plan but, as far as disguises go, from a distance we're pretty unrecognisable under our assortment of brightly coloured wigs and inches of makeup.

'Over there!' Connie suddenly squeals, pointing just beyond an exotically, and erotically filled fish tank of prawn and porn stars. 'I think I see him. On that table at the far end.'

'Quick, come here!' I dive out of Dom and his friends' direct line of sight, and beckon to the others. 'Ok, we need to get closer without him, or Giles, seeing us,' I say, assessing the endless nooks and crannies, not only of the dancers, but of the dark and disco-smoke-filled club. Sapphire's vast layout, complete with concealed corners, is proving to be the perfect place for a hitman to lie in wait – he could be anywhere.

'What about on the other side of that stage?' Jac suggests, pointing to a gloomy booth tucked twenty feet or so behind where Dom and his friends are sitting. 'If we approach from the right, we'd be close enough to keep an eye on him, and an eye out for Giles. It's the perfect vantage point.'

She's right, it is. The only problem is getting there. We'd have to walk straight past Dom, risking the possibility of him clocking one of us – unless, that is, we took a short cut…

'Everyone, follow me.' I take decisive and, thanks to the latex, squeaky action as I move in the direction of the deserted stage.

'What are you doing?' Debs tugs at my arm, pulling me backwards. 'We can't go up there. One –someone will see us. Two – I physically can't move my legs high enough in this PVC catsuit to climb stairs.'

'Don't worry, it's not even being used,' I tell her, 'and it's pitch black up there. Come on – I'll give you a bump up.'

Having boosted Debs upwards with the finesse of a flapping salmon, we begin to crawl as fast as our fetish fashion will allow across the shadowed stage and towards the unoccupied booth. We're about half way across when the 1000 watt spotlight hits us.

'Uh-oh…' I mutter, caught in the glare, like an inmate making a break for freedom from a high-security prison. Rooted to the stage, a primal cacophony of whoops and cheers from leering male spectators rumbles up around us.

'What do we do?' Connie hisses, as the slow, sultry, thudding base of Alannah Myles' 'Black Velvet' kicks in.

She isn't going to like my answer because, aside from running, there's only one logical way out of this… Unsteadily rising to my feet in the manner of a newly born calf, if its hooves were six inches high and coated in rhinestones, 'Dance!' I order, under my breath, wobbling over to a set of sparkling poles that have risen majestically from the floor in front of us.

'No need to tell me twice!' Amy says, joyously leaping forward and contorting herself around the metal bar with the expertise of a Colombian Boa Constrictor.

'I can't, I just can't!' whimpers Debs, absolutely petrified, as if she's just been instructed to jump out of a plane.

'Babe, you've given birth in a room full of strangers. There's no way this is worse,' Jac tells her, grabbing hold of a pole and beginning to furiously rub herself up and down it like she's trying to use her crotch to light a fire. 'Just copy Amy!'

Glancing over at my cousin, I see her expertly working the pole like she's been doing this every day of her life since her teenage years.

'What?' she calls down from her fruit bat position. 'My gym does Pole Fit every Wednesday.'

While Debs begins to hop stiffly around the bar like a robotic morris dancer, I start working on some super-seductive moves of my own which, in my head, are a much sexier version of the Macarena but, judging by the disgusted look of a male audience member, clearly are not.

'Get your tits out!' he yells at me in frustration, while I roll my hips with the fluidity of a nana who's forgotten to take her cod liver oil.

Looking across the stage, I notice Dom's group has taken a rather keen interest in our peculiar performance. Well, why wouldn't they? To my right, Jac is attempting the Worm; to my left, Camilla, still totally out of it, has stopped for a quick toilet break, resulting in an alarmed Scottish chap in a Celtic Football Club shirt receiving a 'wee' added extra he hadn't asked for.

As Dom approaches our calamitous troupe, a worrying look of recognition spreads across that annoyingly fine face of his.

Shit! Have we been made? Trying to hide my own mug behind a Vogue dance move, I'm about to yell to the girls to make a high-heeled hobble for it when something peculiar catches my attention.

'Jac...' I say, shimmying over to where an undignified grub is struggling to get back up off the floor. 'Is it just me... or is Dom sporting a bindi?'

We both stop our awkward thrusting and take a second to study the curious red circular dot of cultural appropriation adorning the centre of his forehead.

'Oh my God, Cara, that's not a bindi!' she cries out, pointing to a thin crimson ray of light tracking across the stage. 'It's a bloody laser beam!'

I experience a crushing blow of realisation, and what occurs next feels like it's happening in slow motion. The high-pitched and hysterical warning of 'GUN!' has barely even left my lips when a bottle of Grey Goose vodka, carried on the shoulder of a topless waitress passing Dom at exactly the right moment, explodes in a violent eruption of glass and alcohol.

Screams and chaos ensue.

'Quick, this way!' I shout to the girls, dragging a still squatting Camilla across the stage and down the stairs to join the hundreds of terrified punters surging towards the exits. Above the rolling wave of worried willies, I can just about make out Dom's tower-ing frame fleeing in the distance – chivalrously throwing half-naked women out of the way in a bid to save his own fore-skin. What a gent.

As he clambers through the crowd, another bullet tears its way through the air – this time missing him by a matter of inches and careering straight into the decapitated and wall-mounted head of a stag that's already been through this drama once before. Fleeing in the opposite direction of the stampeding masses, we hurriedly head through the backstage exit, pure adrenaline allowing us to move faster in ankle-breaking stripper shoes than we'd normally be able to run in a pair of Nikes. Passing through the now deserted dressing room, we retrace our steps down the corridor, past a flapping bunch of feather-covered showgirls and straight out of the same doorway we entered less than an hour ago.

'Do you think that was Giles?' Connie pants, doubled over and gasping for air as her whole body convulses with the shock of being caught in the middle of a strip club shoot-out.

'Of course it bloody was!' I say in disbelief. 'Did you think it was only coincidental that a random lunatic happened to be taking shots at the man *you* paid someone to kill?'

We rush round to the front of the club in time to see Dom hotfoot it into a waiting black SUV before speeding off down the road into an oncoming sea of blue and red emergency services lights.

'Cara, watch out!' Jac yells, pushing me to one side so the racing motorbike roaring up behind us doesn't knock us over like skittles.

'It's Giles!' Amy shouts, attempting, to chase down the sleek Kawasaki as it hurtles past.

Watching the bike's leather-clad rider weave his way expertly between bins, people, and cars, before thundering down the road after Dom, a feeling of familiarity grabs me by the guts. Those broad shoulders… they seem too strong, too sexy, for a man of over sixty years.

'We need to follow that bike!' Jac searches desperately for a taxi or any road-worthy vehicle we can commandeer.

'Jac, it's pointless, we're too late,' I say in defeat, the pincers of realisation beginning to take hold of me. There's no way we're going to be able to catch up with either of them. Giles may have missed first time round, but he sure as shit wasn't going to make that mistake again, and, because we've failed to warn Dom those bullets were intended for him, he's a sitting duck: one whose pond is about to rapidly evaporate beneath him in the unforgiving heat of the Nevada desert.

'Over there!' Amy shouts, running across the road towards a promotional Sapphire club milk float, its accompanying pyramid billboard trailer showcasing an assortment of beautiful women who, unlike us, don't look as though they've just spent twenty-four hours in jail for solicitation and possession.

'Amy, what are you doing? We can't steal it. There are police everywhere!' Debs reminds her, pointing to the surrounding squad cars and armed officers flanking the club.

'We're not stealing it, Debs.' Amy disappears from view as she ducks under the dashboard. 'We're reminding the good party people of Las Vegas what a truly amazing time they could be having with fine women such as ourselves,' she says with a wink as the float sparks to life.

'YES, AMY!' I rejoice, my hopes of turning this shit show around freshly renewed. 'We are mums on holiday without our kids. We do not quit, and we do NOT go home early. Do you understand me?'

Nodding in brow-beaten agreement, everyone clambers in and puts their seat belts on. Safety first.

'Now, Amy,' I say, slapping my hands down onto the dash, 'follow that motorbike, and bloody step on it!'

29

Huns on the Run

'Will you stop shouting at me?' Amy demands, as we screech to a halt outside of the Brynn. 'How was I supposed to know these things only go at 15 miles per hour?'

Having chosen quite possibly the slowest vehicle in the history of high-speed chase scenes, we were not Fast, and I'm absolutely Furious. Vino Diesel lost Dom and Giles over thirty minutes ago. I honestly reckon it would have been quicker for us to pick up the milk float, put our feet through the bottom of it and Flintstones-run after the pair of them.

As the darkness of the night sky begins to give way to the orange and red hues of a spectacular Las Vegas sunrise, we race across the majestic mosaic floral tiles of the hotel's oriental-themed lobby. If this wasn't a life or death situation, I'd most definitely be stopping to take a selfie. With giant floral bouquets dangling from a gloriously glazed glass atrium, and two gilded-in-gold peacocks the size of Beefeaters watching protectively over the casino's entrance, this place is out-of-this-world incredible.

Very much hoping Dom decided to call things a night after nearly being shot in the head, instead of receiving it, we arrive at the reception desk, hot and sweaty messes.

'Good morning! Welcome to the Brynn Hotel,' an overly enthusiastic and, in stark contrast to our own stripper chic, impeccably dressed receptionist beams from behind her computer screen. 'How may I be of assistance to you ladies?'

Struggling to catch my breath, post frantic jog, I pant, 'We… need to… find… some men!' I'm struggling against my outfit's rather restrictive latex.

Looking us up and down dubiously, while still managing to maintain a beaming grin. 'Oh, we're not *that* sort of hotel, ma'am,' she says, super politely but also super bitchily.

'Oh, no…' I say, realising how that sentence sounded, especially given our current wardrobe predicament. 'No, it's not like that! I just need to…'

'Wow, this place has some impressive cocks,' Amy joins me at the front desk.

'I'm *so* sorry, but I'm afraid I'm going to have to ask you to leave,' the receptionist says through her painted-on smile. 'Security!'

With the click of her fingers, four suited and booted burly security men stealthily emerge, like Predator, from the foyer's impressive jungle-like foliage, and begin to manhandle all of us from the premises.

'No!' I shout, clinging on to a fairy-lit cherry tree as my legs are lifted from under me. 'SHE MEANT THE BIRD!'

'Thank you so much for visiting the Brynn Las Vegas, and have a great day,' the receptionist calls behind us as my fingers are prised free from the bark and I'm escorted, like an escort, through the rotating glass doors.

'Fuck!' I say, sitting down on the kerb next to Connie as we listen to Amy's tirade of verbal abuse being hurled at the hotel bouncers. I'm beginning to contemplate whether or not our next move is to jump a maid, steal her outfit, and go knocking door-to-door on the hotel's 2700 rooms, when a familiar face passes us by…

'Mike?!' Connie and I shout in unison, jumping to our feet at seeing Dom's best friend strolling past, arm in arm with a woman who is most definitely *not* the one he's married to.

'Connie, Cara?! What are you both doing here, *together*?' he asks, red-faced and quickly pushing his Deliverfoo order away as though he's just discovered a pubic hair in it (although she strikes me as more of a 'Hollywood' kind of gal). 'And what the bloody hell are you wearing?'

'Long story, Mike. Anyway, Yvonne's changed a bit since the last time I saw her,' I dig, enjoying watching him squirm. 'Don't worry, I won't say a word, it'll be our little secret – if you could do us a teeny, tiny little favour, that is. Don't suppose you know where Dom is, do you?'

Glancing from my sister to me as though it's a trick question, he says, 'For real? Or are you joking?'

'Not joking, Mike,' Connie informs him. 'Sadly, we're *deadly* serious. Why?'

'It's just that… well, I'd have thought *you* of all people, Con, would know, because you were the one who asked him to meet you. I'd get a move on too, otherwise you'll never make it before midday. Oh, and you won't be able to tell him you're running late, either – plonker forgot his phone.'

'Mike, I literally have no idea what you're talking about. Connie looks more baffled than my mother, who's found herself sat on a bench surrounded by pensioners carrying flasks and rambling sticks.

'The Grand Canyon?' he expands, as Connie and I maintain our blank expressions. 'He told me you'd texted about half an hour ago saying you'd flown in and wanted to meet him there at noon. Hey, are you ok? You look kind of more vacant than normal… Did you guys get caught up in the strip club shooting, too? It was wild, we only just managed to get out!'

'Yeah, wild… enjoy your shag,' I mutter, grabbing Connie's elbow and walking her away from Mike without even so much as a thank you or goodbye. I beckon the rest of the girls over. They leave Camilla looking like a right OAP (Old Age Prostitute) alongside an increasingly odd number of her peers. 'Right, we know where Dom is headed!' I tell them, as Mike flips me the bird and strolls into the hotel – presumably to give his female guest a good fingering too. 'The Grand Canyon, and we have to assume that's also where Giles is going. We're only half an hour behind them. We can still get there and stop this from happening.'

'I hate to break it to you, Cara,' Jac says, not wanting to burst my optimistic bubble, but also trying to be a realist, 'the Grand Canyon is named that because it's fucking massive. Even if we managed to get ourselves there, how are we going to track him down? It's not like we can ask Siri – sorry Amy.'

The mention of cavernous gorges sparks sudden inspiration. Pulling a now very sweaty phone out of my cleavage, I say, 'That's it, Jac! Siri might not be able to help, but one of her mates might. Connie, do you have 'Find my iPhone' set up?' I'm very much hoping my hunch is correct.

'Yeah, I think so – but how's that useful?'

Smiling, I hand her my device so she can input her login details. 'Think about it – you *last* had your phone in Smiths, and the *last* person you saw before we found you was Giles. He must have taken your phone in Ibiza and is now using it to lure Dom out into the open so he can shoot him in the face, then leave his decaying body in the desert to be picked apart by vultures.'

'Went a bit too far on the details there, babe,' Jac says, with a condescending pat of the shoulder.

'Ok, just waiting for it to load and… Oh my God!' Connie shouts with surprise. 'I'm moving! Well not me, but my phone – look!'

Sure enough, there on my screen is the blue blob of Connie's device rapidly making its way along Route 11, about to pass over the Hoover Dam and heading straight in the direction of the Grand Canyon.

'Cara! You genius!' Jac shouts, hugging me tightly. 'Now there's just the slight matter of actually getting there.'

She's right. It's 6am. There's not a lot of time, and it's going to be tighter than Debs' PVC, but it can be done: we only need wheels, and we need them stat. I'm looking to see whether I can order an Uber, when Jac's frantic flapping arm movements stop me in my tracks.

'Er, Cara… you're probably going to want to see this!' she shouts urgently. 'I could be wrong, but I think your mum's being abducted by those old people…'

Whirling round, I see my dazed mother being ushered up the stairs of a touring bus that's pulled up outside of the hotel. I'm about to leg it over and drag her back off when the vehicle's emblazoned orange logo catches my eye…

'Grandpa Canyon Rim Tours – Taking the Elderly to the Edge,' I read out loud, hardly able to believe our luck. 'Girls, I think we've found a way of getting there ASAP. Everyone, grab an OAP and get on that coach!'

Silently thanking Camilla for her unintentional brilliance, I introduce myself to a charming old chap wearing a 'Geology Rocks' T-shirt and escort him aboard. Listening to Amy and a woman who, according to her name tag, is called Miriam. wax lyrical about how much they both enjoy a good rim, I'm left very much hoping that, for once, someone thinks we're older than our years, *and* that this motor moves a hell of a lot faster than 90% of its passengers.

30

Ranger Danger

Just gone 10.30am and, after many an unscheduled toilet stop because of George's prostate and June drinking a thimble of water before leaving, we've finally arrived at the concreted and car-filled entrance to the south rim of the Grand Canyon National Park.

'Bye, Miriam! Thanks again for the swap. You're a crotch saver!' Amy says, waving goodbye to the eighty-year-old pensioner dressed in a sexy air hostess outfit and a pair of orthopaedic sandals. 'What a legend!' she says to us, admiring her new get-up of a shin-length floral smock. 'Really lets the air circulate...'

Sheltering from the already roasting late-morning heat in the protective shade of the Visitor Centre Plaza, we anxiously wait for the app to refresh on my phone.

'Shit, the signal's bloody awful,' I say, wandering round with my arm in the air, as if holding it an extra foot above my head will somehow improve the strength enough for us to track down Dom, and do my Tesco big shop from the middle of the scorching wilderness.

'Here you go,' Jac says, returning from the gift shop with a carrier bag of souvenirs. 'They only had ranger's shirts and hats – but I thought they might help fend off some of the unwelcome attention.' She death-stares yet another gawping tourist getting more of a view than they'd bargained for.

Pulling on the XL khaki green shirt, I'm thankful it at least covers my arse, but the flip side is that all of us, bar Amy, now look like slightly sluttier friends of Yogi Bear.

'Ok, ok! He's back!' I squeal, waving for the others to come closer as I watch the stationary throbbing blue homing blob of Connie's phone on my screen. 'Looks like he's stopped... for now, somewhere called Powell Point on the south rim trail?'

'Let me look.' Jac snatches my phone and compares it to a map she's holding. 'According to this, it's about a four-mile hike from here!'

'Don't mean to be a literal Debby downer,' Debs says, 'but that's four miles in weather you could slow roast a shoulder of pork in. We're all wearing stilettos, and we have... well, Camilla with us.'

With my mother now doing interpretive dance to a tannoy announcement warning visitors not to take selfies with a particularly volatile-sounding rock squirrel, I decide to make a decisive leadership call. 'Listen, there's no need for all of us to risk our souls, and soles, trying to sort this mess out. Debs, Amy, Mum... you stay here. Connie, Jac and I will go.'

'Whoa, whoa, whoa!' Connie says, edging away. 'Don't you think I should stay here with Mum?'

'No I do not. You got us into this, so you can bloody well get us out. Let's go.'

11.47am: shoes in hand and blisters as wide as the ten-mile ravine itself – I might be knackered and on high alert for deadly assassins, but one thing's for sure – the Grand Canyon certainly lives up to its name. Approaching Powell Point, I stop to catch my breath and fully absorb the magnitude of this natural wonder. Having left behind the vast majority of the crowds at the lookout stop closest to the coach park, I stand on the top of the near-deserted and colossal cliffs, and the vista is unlike anything I've ever seen. Vast and spectacular, it's as though the undulating layers of red and orange rock are a tangible mirage – a panoramic magic-eye picture you could reach out and touch. The kids would love it here. Taking a quick picture, I decide to bring them both back here, one day… when I'm out of prison and they're old enough to not try and shove each other over the edge, that is.

'Something else, isn't it?' Amy asks, as she strolls dangerously close to the edge, puckering up and taking a 'peace' selfie.

'Sure is…' I say, before jumping backwards in fright. 'AMY! What are you doing here? You're meant to be back at the visitor centre!'

'Wowsers!' Debs announces, tottering towards us from a slightly elevated trail running adjacent to the one I'm standing on. Camilla is following behind her on a child's wrist-leash fashioned out of a push-up bra. The pair of them weave their way between prickly pear cacti and the dark brown bark of pinyon pines towards us.

'Debs? For fuck's sake, you lot! The whole point of you staying back at the entrance was so you'd be safe.'

'Like you said in the strip club, Cara: leave no woman behind. As if we were going to let you stroll up to a hitman without backup. Flab Four for life! Plus a couple of late additions to the line-up…' Debs nods towards a still dazed Camilla.

Touched by their sisterly solidarity, and wondering how long my mother's muteness is going to last – surely whatever she took should have left her system by now? – I ask, 'How did you even get here so quickly?!'

'On the shuttle bus...' Amy answers, looking at my sweat-soaked shirt with a disgusted wrinkle of her nose. 'Air-conditioned, and they come, like, every thirty minutes. Much easier on the legs than the yomp you three have just done.'

Of course there are shuttle buses. This would have been much more helpful to know over an hour ago, and would explain how Giles has been able to get here without having a stroke or both his hips giving out.

Now fully reunited, our mismatched mum tribe continues on its hike, hearts thudding from both the cardiovascular type of HIIT, and the impending murderous kind, until we reach a weathered wooden signpost indicating the turning for 'Powell Point'. There, obstructing the entrance to the veering footpath, a suspiciously convenient 'closed due to high wind' notice rests against one solitary traffic cone. Looking around to make sure we're not being watched, or followed, like the group of rule-breaking rebels we now are, the six of us intrepidly slope our way past it and down the narrow, rock-lined spur, towards the canyon's protruding edge.

As the gentle winding path, with ever so slightly less tame sheer drops on either side of it, leads us further out towards the multicoloured horizon of lime and sandstone strata, an imposing granite structure, set within a circular cul-de-sac, comes into view. With the wind beginning to pick up, I brush strands of knotted hair away from my face as we approach what must be at least a twenty-foot monument which, from where we're standing, looks like it's teetering dangerously on the brink of the canyon's crumbling walls. It reminds me very much of an Aztec temple, with its blocky pyramid shape and central staircase. From ground level, a bronze plaque celebrating the many achievements of one John Powell is visible at the summit. Directly below the engraved homage, in dedication to the many failings of my ex-husband, bound, gagged, bleeding, lies a significantly less celebrated figure: one Dominic Stringer.

Before I even have time to determine if he's still breathing, or assess what dangers may be lurking in the peripheries, I'm stopped dead in my stilettos by the chilling sound of a pistol cocking directly behind my head, followed by two little words that make my blood run cold.

'Hola, Cara...'

31

Time to Kill

'Javier!' Connie says in astonishment, as I turn with my hands raised in surrender, unable to take my eyes off his impressively large piece.

Without lowering the gun, he smiles that delicious womb-wilting smile of his, and says, 'Connie, Cara… honestly, we *really* need to stop meeting like this,' in a flirtatious, but 'move and I'll blow your head off' kind of way.

With no idea of what's happening right now, several things are running through my mind. How does Connie know Javier? Is Dom still alive? Where's Giles? And more importantly, how's my hair? If I'm about to be shot, or put in cuffs, I'd still quite like to look cute. As Dom whimpers pathetically from the top of the stone monument, at least one question is answered: he's still in the land of the living… for now.

'What on earth are you doing here?' I ask, as my eyes dart questioningly from my flabbergasted friends to Javier's loaded gun to the crooked pine trees precariously clinging to either side of the slim peninsula –in case the rest of Interpol, or an old dude with a tactical assault rifle disguised in a walking frame emerge from behind them.

'I came here to bring a mutual friend to justice,' he replies, as Dom, now crying harder than Nancy the time I unreasonably refused to let her put her hand in an open flame, scoots into a sitting position and attempts to wriggle free.

'Oh my gosh! You were tracking him down too, this whole time? That's why you were in Ibiza?' I ask, semi-thankful Javier has at least apprehended Giles and that this whole debacle is kind of over, but also wondering why he's left a now praying Dom up on the observation deck like a sacrificial lamb. Anticipating being immediately arrested for our part in Dom's botched bumping-off, I begin, in a last-ditch attempt to save our skins, 'Listen, I know we should probably wait for a lawyer, but so you know, it was a total accident on our part, ok? Connie didn't mean to. My mother slipped us both a—'

'Shhh,' Javier says, walking to me and placing a warm, salty finger in my mouth –enforcing my right to remain silent and not incriminate myself any further in the most tantalising, yet slightly unhygienic, way imaginable.

Retracting what I hope isn't too much of a dirty digit, he takes a step backwards and seductively lifts up his skin-tight T-shirt like he's about to drop to the dusty floor and dry-hump it, Magic Mike style. The sight of what lies beneath the black, clingy material is enough to make me go weak at the knees –and not *just* because of his rock-hard abs (although they are a contributing factor). There, tattooed above his left nipple, is an image I've already seen up close and personal twice too many times on this trip, an image that seems *especially* out of place on a respectable officer of the law.

'Gato de cuatro cabezas; *the four-headed cat*,' he translates. 'The official mark of the De Leon family. Ramón sends his regards.'

'Unlikely,' Amy splutters through a cough.

Then, only the sound of a screeching hawk in search of prey is audible in the ominous silence that descends between us.

'I… I don't understand,' I eventually say with an uneasy feeling I too am a small and vulnerable woodland creature about to be demolished by a blood-thirsty predator.

'I'm here on behalf of my big brother, Cara,' Javier says coolly, unblinking and intense eyes boring straight into my own disbelieving ones.

'Your brother?'

'Yes, Ramón,'

'*Awkward*,' Amy coughs again.

'Ramón?' I ask, very much hoping Javier does not notice Amy's suspiciously timed upper respiratory infection.

'Yes. Ramón. You see, Cara, you are not the only one with an impulsive, problematic sibling constantly requiring you to clean up their messes. When he told me about his antics with Connie – I had no choice but to step in before my father found out,' Javier explains. 'My role in the family is to fix things quickly, efficiently… permanently.'

'So, you're not related to Giles?'

'Giles?'

'Yes, Giles! Giles the hitman?' I snap, infuriated by our circular to-and-fro. 'We tracked him here through Connie's phone. He took it in Smiths the night she asked him to kill Dom? Although, now I'm incredibly confused…' I say, trying to connect the dots.

Looking at me as though I've lost the plot, he says, 'Cara, I have got no idea what you are talking about. It was *I* who took Connie's bag. You followed *me* here. The only Giles I know is the old guy who lives at Smiths. He's married to the manager, Linda. He is what I think you Brits would call a "knob head" – runs a detoxing weight loss company that he's always trying to get people to buy into when they've taken too many drugs. Thinks he can solve all of their problems with shots of ginger, or some bullshit.'

'Ohhh…' comes Connie's voice of realisation from behind me.

'What do you mean, "*ohhh*", Connie?' I bark at her, as the image of the 'GShot Holdings Ltd' transaction from my bank statement slaps me firmly in the face.

'Yeah, now that he's said it, that *does* kind of ring a bell.'

'What? Are you for real? Do you mean to tell me that I have travelled thousands of miles across the world, risked life and vaginal lip in latex, spent hours on a coach trip listening to an old man tell me an excruciatingly long-winded story about tectonic uplift, and now have a gun pointed to my head because the "*Shoot to Slay* Ultimate Revenge Package" *YOU* bought was something to help you look better in a bikini?'

Gurning awkwardly, she silently mouths 'sorry' at me, before sidestepping behind Jac who, having had her hen party completely ruined, does not look like a much safer option at this point.

With an exasperated sigh I turn back to Javier. 'To be perfectly clear, *this*…' I say, flapping my arms in the direction of a moaning Dom, the Grand Canyon, and my utterly ridiculous hat, 'is *all* about the watch?'

'It's not just *any* watch, Cara.'

'I know, I know!' I shout, absolutely sick to death of hearing about the bloody thing. 'It's a sixteen million quid, white gold, pebble-dashed in a shit load of diamonds Jacob & Co Billionaire watch. It's the Marks and Spencer's Foodhall of watches, I get it!' Still piecing the puzzle together, I crane my head over Javier's shoulder to where my sister is cowering. 'Connie! I'm guessing this was Ramón's sexy security guard who was keeping tabs on you in Majorca?'

'Sí, see! Total hottie!' she calls, with a thumbs up from behind Jac's back.

I turn back to Javier. 'And the "associate" Ramón had search Con's house in Manchester, I take it that was also you?'

He nods.

'But you couldn't find it, which is why you were at the airport – you thought she had it on her in Ibiza?'

Another nod.

'Wait… Where do I fit into all of this?' I say, a self-esteem-crushing penny dropping. 'Was I a mark?! Were you hoping that if you flashed this pathetic divorced mum of two an overly whitened and veneered smile she might drop her sister in it and tell you where the watch was? Oh, I knew it was too good to be true. There I was thinking you wanted casual sex and to objectify my body, but nooo. You were using me… for *information!*'

Lying, thieving, drug-toting, murdering maniacs. I really need to have a serious think about my taste in men and, if I ever get out of this alive, some kind of therapy. No better than my sister when she fell for Ramón; all the warning signs had been there, but I'd chosen to gloss over the details in order to create a narrative to match my holiday shag agenda. I'd wrongly assumed that 'international investigations' meant working for the good guys, flushing out James Bond pussy-stroking villains and thwarting terrorist attacks etcetera. I feel what's left of my dignity draining away, which is already precious little considering I'm being held at gun point dressed like a park ranger who's *on* the game instead of looking after it.

'Cara… you need to calm yourself down,' Javier says, clearly oblivious that this sentence, along with '*do you think it's just your hormones?*' is up there as one of the worst things to say to an angry woman. 'Believe me on two things: I would have very much loved to have had casual sex with you, and, no, you were never part of my plan. I knew you had nothing on your sister, but I liked you. You were interesting to me – a pure heart, with a dirty mind. What was not to like?'

'One – why are you talking about me in the past tense?' I'm not liking where this is going one little bit. 'Secondly – if you still want that bang,' don't you think that waving something that actually goes bang in my face might be the wrong way of going about it? I'm not armed. What am I going to attack you with, my stripper shoe?' Trailing off, I realise that, given the Carmichael women's history, that's probably exactly what he does think.

Acknowledging that holding an unarmed woman at gun point could come across as somewhat excessive, in an act of goodwill he lowers his weapon. Taking my opportunity, and skills learnt from the one high school self-defence class I attended, I aim my very spikey foot straight at his crotch and… miss completely. Shit. On top of the therapy, I really need to book in a trip to the opticians.

'Quite finished?' Javier asks, stifling a laugh while still attempting to hold some authority over the situation.

'Yes, thank you,' I say, smoothing my shirt back down over my arse, as I try to claw back a little shred of self-respect. 'Tell me something: how did you and Ramón know Dom had the watch in Vegas and that Connie hadn't squirrelled it away somewhere for safekeeping?'

'Ah, well …' he says, taking me by the shoulders and spinning me round so that I'm facing Connie, Debs, Jac, Amy, and my mother. 'It seems I have been betrayed by one of your acquaintances, Cara, as have you…' and, with that, Javier turns the gun on them. 'Time for you to find out who the fox in the hen-house is.'

As four members of our party gasp in fear and disbelief, another, as cool as the cucumber she has in her gin, reaches into her handbag for a cigarette. Placing it against her lips and lighting it, she stares intensely at Javier before taking a long and deep drag.

'Sorry, darling,' Camilla says, opening her mouth to speak for the first time in over twenty-four hours and apparently perfectly alert. 'This is going to sting a little...'

32

Mum's the C Word

And the Oscar for best supporting villain in a calamitous biopic of my fucked-up life goes to… my mother.

Camilla and Dom's affair had started years ago, it turns out, long before he hooked up with Connie, before we were even married. The woman let me walk down the aisle knowing full well that my husband-to-be had already been up one that morning – hers. What kind of mother does that to her own child? Her flesh and blood? 'We can't choose who we love' was her pathetic attempt at justification – an excuse I'd heard before, and one I wasn't buying.

'You don't know the meaning of the word love!' I ranted at her, as she reluctantly revealed the true extent of their deceit – which, unbelievably, had been rumbling on and off undetected by anyone for years, only coming to an end after Dom unceremoniously dumped her for my sister. 'What about the love you were meant to have for me? The whole point of having children is to give them every ounce of goodness and adoration you have inside you. You are meant to protect them, sacrifice yourself to ensure their happiness – not absolutely destroy their lives because you think their bloke is a bit of hot stuff. Jesus, WHAT IS WRONG WITH YOU!'

Where most people who had done something so callous and calculated might have started with an apology, Camilla had begun: 'Darling, I feel like you're being a *little* hysterical over something that's old news now… you'll give yourself tantrum tramlines', showing about as much empathy as a brick wall. 'We first met *years* ago, before you were even on the scene. I mean, technically, it was *you* who stole him from me! Anyway, things weren't great with Ray at the time. He could be such a terrible bore. Marrying him had seemed like a good idea – you got a father, and of course he gave me Connie – but he's not the world's most exciting man, is he? He was going through his "devout Christian" phase – do you remember? He wanted to quit his job as a solicitor and become a man of the cloth. Me, a vicar's wife? Can you imagine?'

I could not. What I could imagine, however, is how being married to Camilla can drive someone to do a lot of things, religion probably being the milder of the outcomes. Poor Ray. While he was trying to find God, there my mother was finding other men, specifically Dom.

'I'd been on a theatre trip to London with some friends. We went to a bar afterwards and there he was. This young, fiercely confident thing who had the gift of the gab and a gorgeous face to go with it. He was everything I was looking for, everything your step-father was not – a bit of fun that made me feel desired, beautiful… young again. It was never meant to last more than a weekend, but you know how terribly compelling he can be.'

Yes, I did – mainly because everyone he's ever rampaged through, like a devastating love locust, keeps telling me.

'Honestly, the day you walked into our home with Dom on your arm and introduced him as your new boyfriend was the worst of my life. How could he do that… to me? It was like he'd purposefully pursued a younger, hotter version of myself – well, until you had the children that is, sweetheart. Pregnancy really was *not* your friend.'

Now, most husbands I know can't wait to get shot of their mother-in-laws. There are thousands of awful wedding speech jokes dedicated to just that. Not Dom. No, never happy with his lot in life, he decided he wanted to have his cake and eat it – constantly keeping Camilla waiting in the wings with promises of running away together and living happily ever after. That was until Connie happened. We were the female equivalents of iPhones: the man just kept upgrading to the newest and trendiest of the Carmichael women until he found a model that had the most impressive silicon parts.

'Oh, when things started up with Con it wasn't like how it was with you. She was special, ready to do anything for him. He dropped me faster than I shed carbs before Marbs. I tried to get him to end things with her, but he was having none of it. We were over, and he was gone.'

Sadly for Dom, something he had not taken into consideration when casting Camilla aside is that we Carmichael women are notorious for a few things in life: alcohol consumption, our fear of ageing, and holding a grudge…

As they stand side by side at the cliff's edge, the wind buffets Camilla and Dom's faces, and the rest of us struggle to keep our balance in the sweeping gusts of warm desert air. Javier paces in front of them, his gun expertly flicking between their skulls. I'm too numb with shock do anything other than stare on in silent disgust.

'One of you is lying to me,' Javier says casually. 'Camilla, you came to me at Smiths to tell me Dominic here had the watch.

Yet, Dominic is *very* insistent you are the one who now has it, and that you stole it from him.'

Of course. The blonde woman on the balcony, it was her. She'd snuck off to fill Javier in on Dom's whereabouts, and to tell him he had the watch – but how did she even know about it?

'I am a very patient man, but my willingness to endure this charade any longer is beginning to wane. So, we're about to play a fun game! You're familiar with "Truth or Dare", yes?'

They both silently nod.

'Excellent!' Javier rejoices. 'These are the rules. You tell me the truth, or I dare my beautiful assistant Cara to push you straight off this ledge. She looks pretty pissed off, don't you think? I wouldn't mind betting that she'd do it.'

He's not wrong. I'm so enraged I very well might. I've never felt anger like it in my life. Fuck it, why stop at one? I might chuck the both of them over and be done with it. Now there's no link to 'Giles the hitman', who would know?

'And if she gets a horrible case of "good conscience", not that she will considering how much you two have fucked her over, I will shoot Connie in the head and then push both of you over myself. All in all, a pretty good result for Cara. Everyone clear on the rules?' he says as though he's hosting a Saturday night prime-time quiz show.

Ok, they aren't quite the rules I remember from my school days but, as I'm not the person holding the gun, I'm reluctant to nitpick.

Connie, on the other hand, never really one for family games, turns to run. With lightning-fast reactions, Javier spins on his heels and shoots at the ground behind her – immediately rendering her motionless in a cloud of dust. 'I wouldn't, if I were you... Come on, Connie, you started all of this – did you really think I'd leave you out?'

As he beckons her back like a puppy, she shakes her head in terrified acceptance and skulks over to his side.

'Ok, here we go – time to sound believable!' Javier says, possibly enjoying this a little too much as he turns his attention back to the terrible twosome.

'Dominic, for the last time… where is the watch?' he demands to know, with the slightest hint of tension beginning to show in that strong square jaw of his.

For a man so renowned for 'Billy Big Bollocks' backchat and his macho 'man's man' persona, it's strangely disconcerting to finally see my ex-husband so small and broken. 'I've told you already,' he whines pathetically, 'I *don't* have it. This bitch here got Connie to take it from me. She's the one who's lying!'

Turning his gun around so that the barrel is in his hand, Javier whips Dom across the face. 'Dominic! Show some respect, please,' he says. 'That is no way to talk to a lady – especially an elderly one.'

Camilla's face is an absolute picture of fury, and I can't help but smirk at the insult. Sexy and spicy, he's the gift that keeps on giving… death threats, assault, and horrific cliff-based 'would you rather' ultimatums aside.

'Fucker!' Dom says, adding a crimson layer of saliva to the already russet-coloured earth, while waving an angry finger at him. 'You Spanish shithead, just wait until I get my hands on you!'

Evidently not impressed with Dom's sudden show of bravado, without warning, Javier takes aim and shoots his wagging index finger clean off – sending it spinning into the 1.8km deep void behind him. As we all scream, and collectively cover our faces, ears, tits and bits, Dom drops to the ground, writhing around in agony.

'Well, there's one less hand to worry about, so I think I'll take my chances,' Javier says unflinchingly, while Dom howls like a wounded animal caught in a hunt. 'Here's the thing though, Dominic, from everything I've heard about you, I don't think you can be trusted, and so I'm not *entirely* sure I can believe you.'

'You can, you can!' Dom pleads hysterically. 'Please!'

'Nope, sorry!' Javier says, pressing the pistol firmly into the side of Connie's temple. 'Ok, Cara, over to you. Think of this as your ultimate revenge. Time to decide who of your awful family gets to live, and who gets to die. I'd hate to be you right now. Talk about a tough call.'

Convulsing uncontrollably with shock and fear, I'm unable to string a sentence together right now, never mind decide who I'm going to murder today – direct DNA matches, or the father of my children. Desperately, I look to the girls for help. It proves to be a pointless venture. The stress of the situation has Jac vomiting in a bush, so she's out; Debs has fainted or is having another badly-timed nap; and Amy is mouthing, 'Did anyone bring a snack?'

'Cara, push her. Push her now!' Dom chimes, hauling himself up to my eye level. 'What kind of mother would sleep with her daughter's husband?' He's attempting character and actual assassination at the same time. 'She never thought about you once. I tried to leave her, but she kept telling me it was pointless, that the damage was done. She didn't give a fuck, Cara! Come on, you know it's always been you. I've loved you from the minute I met you. I was going to leave Connie anyway– we could try again, I know that's what you want deep down. We could get past this. Your mum never meant a thing to me, I mean – look at her! Some hag who's still dressing like she's twenty-five – so angry she doesn't have her looks any more that she's willing to throw her own daughters under the bus to still feel attractive. She's as toxic as the shit she pumps into her face and you know it! Shove the old witch off, and we'll go home to the kids – just you and me, how it used to be, how it should always be.'

Dom is so invested in his performance, so caught up in trying to convince me not to push him over a cliff, that he doesn't see the impending danger of a bitter and twisted Camilla approaching from his right.

'*Toxic*?' she spits, spiralling into deepening madness. '*Hag*?! You spineless, loathsome excuse of a man. I gave you years of my life, and love, and this is how you repay me? BY CALLING ME OLD?!'

Possessed with the fighting spirit of a drunk girl in a chicken shop at 3am, she charges at him with her hands outstretched. Instinctively, Dom takes a misjudged step backwards to dodge her savage advance. It is a grave error on his part, and one he immediately realises but is unable to do anything about. Feet slipping on the loose shale-like stones of the canyon's ridge, a distraught look of alarm disperses across his face. He reaches out in an attempt to anchor himself to safety, and time stands still as my mother's fingers fleetingly graze against his own four remaining digits. Camilla's frenzied expression momentarily flickers from enraged to contemplative as the full impact of her deadly actions hits home. In that moment, I think she's going to pull him back in, and the small remaining fragment of her dead heart will begin to beat once more just in time to rectify her crime of passion. I am wrong. Overestimating her compassion, and underestimating her hatred, Connie and I watch on in stunned silence as, right at the last second, with a chilling smile Camilla retracts her hand and Dom slips from view with a blood-curdling scream.

Legs collapsing underneath me, I sink to the dry earth. He's gone, I can't believe he's actually gone. Well probably not yet; it's one hell of a drop to the Colorado River below, via a few head-crushing ridges and body-mangling mantles. My senses are all muted. I feel as though I'm being held under murky water. Not knowing whether to laugh or cry, all I can think of is how I'm going to tell the kids that they'll never see Daddy again because he shagged Nunnie and then she shoved him off the Grand Canyon. To be fair, I imagine they'll probably react similarly to when their hamster died: look at me wide-eyed then ask for a chocolate chip brioche.

'Mum!' Connie screams, her rigid body rooted to the spot in traumatised incomprehension. 'What have you done? What have you done?!'

'I took decisive action, sweetheart,' Camilla says calmly, with warped satisfaction. 'It was for the best. He had it coming, you know he did. Look what he did to me, your sister, to you. Now he's gone, we can all move on.'

'But that wasn't the plan!' Connie cries, tears streaming down her face. 'I didn't agree to this!'

'Connie…' Camilla says, eyeballing my sister sternly, and, if looks could kill, it wouldn't only be Dom with his head cracked open like Humpty Dumpty right now. 'Not now, dear, you're being hysterical. Be quiet, we'll talk about this later.'

'Stop telling me what to do!' Connie screams, unperturbed by our mother's sinister warnings. 'You've been controlling me every day since I was born, and I've had enough – do you hear me? I'VE HAD ENOUGH! You killed him! I didn't want him dead. That's why I came all this way – because I thought I'd done a bad thing, and I tried to fix it! Unlike you, I'm a good person. Yes, I wanted to hurt him, but not like this!'

'Sorry,' I say, shakily getting to my feet with a feeling of dread building inside of me as deep as the valley below. 'What *plan*?'

'Yes, ladies. What plan?' Javier asks curiously, gun still aimed squarely at Connie's head. 'Oh, don't tell me, a double cross? You Carmichael women are *too* much! If millions of euros weren't at stake, I'd totally be here for this drama. *But* – I want my shit back and to get out of this fuck-awful heat sometime this year. So, who has the watch?'

'She does,' Connie says, pointing to Camilla quicker than Ben snitching on Nancy for taking the Sharpies.

'Connie! *What* are you doing? You idiot! God, I should have bloody shoved you over as well,' Camilla fumes. 'Do you ever actually engage that supposed brain of yours? Giles, case in point. What the bloody hell was that? There I was doing my best to get the De Leons off our backs by sending them here, and what are you off doing? Hiring imaginary hitmen and dragging us even further into the shit than we were before. I take my eye off you for one minute, mix a bit too much ketamine with my menopause pills, and wake up on a plane heading straight back into their bloody path! We were home free. All you had to do was keep yourself together, and get through three days in Ibiza without being a total screwup!'

'Without me being a screwup?! If you didn't want me to do stupid shit, mother, how about not slipping me mind-altering substances? Speaking of which, when the bloody hell did you regain enough control of your limbs to MURDER somebody?! Oh my god, you're like the bloke from the *Saw* movie – quietly watching the chaos go on around you and then rising from the dead to destroy us all!'

'Connie, what is she talking about?' I demand to know, feeling like I'm living in a strange *Scooby Doo* alternative universe where the monster's mask has been removed to reveal an even more terrifying, heavily Botoxed and soulless ghoul who totally would have got away with it if it wasn't for her meddling kids. The wind has picked up so much, it's getting hard to hear a single thing over its rushing howl. 'And, if I were you, I'd explain now before I take that gun off Javier and shoot you myself.'

'Connie, don't you dare…' my mother warns.

But Connie is ready to sing like a canary. 'After the *incident* with Ramón in Majorca – *so* sorry about that by the way –' she shouts over to Javier with an apologetic smile, 'Dom was out of control. Snorting endless lines of coke, taking the money we'd stolen and using it on whatever he wanted, without consulting me – fast cars, even faster women. It was like I was nothing to him, another possession. He was no better than Ramón. By the time I realised my mistake, it was way too late and I was in way too deep. He wasn't the man I thought he was, and Cara, I felt awful about what I'd done to you and the kids. When I tried to leave, he threatened me. Who knew that Dom was quite the David Bailey? He had a rather incriminating photo of me... with Ramón, time-stamped about five minutes before I, well, stamped on his head. He said he'd send it to the De Leons and they'd kill me if I dared walk away.

'I was a total mess and so I confided in the one person I thought I could trust, the one person who should have had my back... mum. I told her everything, about the affair, Ramón and the watch. She was amazing, so understanding – completely took control of the situation and formulated a plan. We were going to hit Dom where it really hurt, by stealing the watch from him and selling it ourselves. All I had to do was ride it, and him, out – keep him happy, go along with everything, and not make him suspicious for as long as it took for us to find a buyer. "Make him believe you love him," she told me, "so that when you go, it will hurt him even more".

I had no idea it would take so long, and when the marriage proposal came – I could have died. I was desperate to leave and he knew it. It was just another way of tying me in – that's why he was pushing for it all to happen so quickly. A couple of weeks ago though, mum found someone, a friend of a friend of Aunt Mollie's son – Craig the Convict – and it was all action stations. The timing couldn't have been better. I knew Dom wouldn't take it to Vegas, in case he got stopped at customs, so the night he left, I took it from the safe and brought it with me to Ibiza the next day. Silly bastard. I knew after all of those years of living with

Cara that his combination would probably be 1,2,3,4. The plan was to carry on like normal, not to raise suspicion – after all, I had his sister Gemma with me. I was to have one last blow-out with all my friends and then we were just not going to go home. By the time he'd have got back and realised it was missing – Mum and I would be in Venezuela, cash and piña colada in hand. Not for one minute did I question her vendetta towards Dom, I just assumed it was because she was trying to protect her daughters. Little did I know I was just a pawn in her plan of revenge. I thought she was looking out for me, why wouldn't I? I swear to God, Cara, I didn't know about her and Dom and that she formulated this whole plan just to get back at him for dumping her – you have to believe me!'

'But why did he tell Javier that Mum had the watch?' I ask, not understanding how Dom had jumped to that conclusion without having returned to home to find it missing.

'Ahh, well… that *might* have been my fault, I've always been a bit of a nightmare for drunk texting. After the stripper story broke, I was absolutely raging. I didn't love him… but that didn't mean I wanted to be publicly humiliated. He thought he could do whatever he wanted, and I'd had enough! One of the last things I remember before Mum slipped us the ecstasy was sending him a ranting text saying she had the watch and he was never going to see it again…'

In the midst of this *Judge Judy Sibling Special*, out of the corner of my eye I can see Amy and Jac frantically waving in my direction, trying desperately to get my attention. Unable to hear them above the din of the gale, it looks as though they're mouthing the word 'BOMB,' at me. Shit, who has a bomb? Surely not my sister or mother, and I've seen under Javier's shirt – so it's not him. What are they on about?

'Are you quite finished telling everyone *everything* now Connie?' Camilla asks bitterly, as foliage and dirt whip at our bodies. 'What do you think is going to happen next? We're going to tell him where the watch is and he's simply going to let us go? You stupid girl – we're going to be joining Dom in hell!'

'Speak for yourself, Camilla,' a voice rings out to her right. 'I'm not fucking going anywhere!'

Standing there bloodied, bruised, and evidently not having fallen as far as we'd thought, is Dom. Catching Javier completely off guard, he rushes at his knees, and aggressively rugby-tackles him to the ground.

'How do you fancy your chances now, hey?' Dom shouts, repeatedly punching him in the face with his good hand – sending the gun flying into the shrubs behind. With Javier startled and disarmed, Dom makes a play for the weapon. Surprisingly nimble for a man who's just scaled a cliff with only nine fingers, he's no match for the speed and athleticism of the Spaniard who clambers on top of him and starts dishing out body blows. With both her nemeses rolling around on top of each other in the brush, trying to kill one another and not her, Camilla decides now is the perfect time to scarper.

'Good luck, darling,' she says to Connie as she makes an ill-timed run for it, scurrying past the grappling duo at the precise moment they both manage to get a finger to the trigger. It happens in the blink of an eye. One minute she's up and running towards the monument, the next she's face down in the dirt with a bullet in the back.

Screaming, Connie and I rush to her side.

'Mum!' Connie cries, turning her over and pushing that perfect platinum-blonde hair of hers out of her face.

Coughing as blood begins to ooze from between her shoulder blades, Mum pulls me close to her face for what I presume are going to be the deeply moving and sentimental last words of Camilla Carmichael. 'Cara,' she rasps, as her eyes begin to close. 'Don't ever forget… when I'm gone… stay away from pastry.'

Brilliant. Of course that's her parting shot before she leaves these earthly planes. God, there's going to be so much to unpick in those upcoming counselling sessions.

'One more thing,' she croaks, suddenly opening her eyes again as Connie weeps like a willow beside her. 'Make sure you send a good photo of me to the newspapers...'

And with that, she's gone... for all of three seconds before she pipes up again. 'From when I was twenty-five... and put a filter on it.'

With her lids firmly closed, I'm waiting for her to once more rise from the dead like a slightly more sun-tanned Michael Myers, when the sound of a second shot reverberates around the vast canyon walls. As birds scatter into the perfectly blue sky above us, I turn from Camilla and rush to where another body lies on the floor. With tears stinging in my eyes, I look down queasily at the bloody, convulsing wreck of a man lying on the ground in front of me.

'Jesus Christ!' I say. 'Has he...?'

'Sí, Cara,' Javier pants, bending down to retrieve his weapon from Dom's quivering hand, 'he has shot himself in the cock.'

'Just out of interest,' Amy says, appearing over my shoulder and gawping in morbid fascination, 'was it with a glock?'

33

Crime of Pacha

'You weren't wrong when you said it doesn't get going until 3am!' I shout over to Jac as the deafening base of Avicii's 'Levels' rocks the core of Pacha's heaving dance floor. Closing my eyes, I let the endorphin-releasing beats of this legendary dance track infiltrate my mind, body and soul.

After a whirlwind twenty-four hours in Las Vegas that I never want to relive, I can hardly believe our little flock of mother hens, along with their newest recruit Connie (on a trial basis only), are finally on our night out to end all nights out.

'I feel so guilty for having fun,' my sister admits, glow stick in hand, and looking as though she's having the absolute time of her life. 'You know, after Mum, and Dom, I feel like we should be more sad.'

'Really?' I ask without an ounce of remorse in my body. 'I wouldn't if I were you, after everything they've collectively done. They got what they deserved. Anyway, they're both going to be totally fine, the medics said. Flesh wounds, the pair of them. Mum's always been an absolute drama queen – we should have known her heart's so small the bullet would have missed it by a country mile. And Dom? Well, let's just hope his reconstructive surgery works – because if he loses his shagging ability, it truly is a fate worse than death. It's Ray I feel sorry for, knowing everything Camilla has done and still having to fork out for her medical bills. He's going to have to use her filler fund just to get her home.'

'I still can't believe we're here together!' Jac screams, absolutely in her element, and finally enjoying the hen party she deserves. Smiling, I watch on in joy as she completely loses herself in the deafening pulse of the electrifying music. Truth be told, nor can I. It's a miracle that can be attributed directly to the son of God himself, Guthrie… and his private jet, along with the incredibly convenient air strip located at the canyon. One quick SOS call from Amy had him ready and waiting to whisk us away in no time at all. He'd even radioed in a report of an illegal poacher accidentally striking two civilians while on the hunt for, ironically, a wild stag – summoning a rapid-response crew of air paramedics to deal with the injured we'd left in our wake. The flight back had been another eventful journey. Having agreed to take Javier along with us in order to retrieve the watch that the worst criminal masterminds in history had hidden in a shoe at the bottom of Camilla's suitcase back at the hotel – Amy and Guthrie weren't the only ones who gained their mile high wings.

'I have to say, Javier took the whole watch thing a whole lot better than I expected,' Connie says, bopping away in her hot pants and crop top – blending seamlessy into the throngs of happy go lucky clubbers. The rest of us, on the other hand, look more like parent chaperones on a school trip – but after everything that's happened over the past seventy-two hours, I really couldn't care less. 'He's a good egg. I actually quite like him, apart from the whole threatening to kill me thing,' she continues, 'and you know… I am in the market for a new brother-in-law!'

Stopping dancing to inflict my most crippling death stare on her, I warn her: 'Too soon. Too bloody soon.'

'Ok, fair enough!' she laughs with a flick of her fake hair. 'Anyway, when are you going to tell him about our little fishing trip with Ramón? I imagine that's going to be a bit of a buzz kill, isn't it? No pun intended. Oh, and your *escapade* with him in Smiths? By the way, just offering up a bit of friendly, sisterly, advice here… relationships based on intense experiences never actually work out.'

Choosing to ignore Keanu Weaves, I'm very much hoping Ramón doesn't come up in conversation before we leave the island tomorrow. If he does, however, I might be able to use the explanation of justifiable self-defence to appease Javier – along with the pretty good trump card that he tried to kill my mother and sister. Anyway, I don't know what, if anything, the future holds for us – after all, what happens in Ibiza (and over the north Atlantic… twice), stays in Ibiza. What I do know is that I'm most definitely not the same Cara Carmichael I was when I left Manchester what feels like an absolute lifetime ago now. Rejuvenated, reinvented and no longer revenge-thirsty, I feel the weight of the world has been lifted from my shoulders. A new and improved woman, I'm actually excited to get back home and start living again. Who knows? Maybe I'll even take those carp-holding, aubergine-emoji-sending weirdos on Fumble up on their offers of going out for Greek food.

'Oh my God, this is amazing!' enthuses a suspiciously alert for this time of night Debs, jumping up onto a nearby podium and using some of her newly found confidence from Sapphires to give one of the professional dancers a run for her money – proudly shaking her boobs, along with mooing double breast pump.

'Girls, I've found someone I want you all to meet. Connie, I believe you're already familiar with his work,' Amy says, bopping her way over to us with a man in a green checked shirt and pair of khaki chinos. 'Everyone, this is Giles! Giles, this is everyone!'

'Connie, always a pleasure,' he gushes, reaching over to kiss her hand. 'Let me know when you're ready for a top-up of those groovy ginger shots, yeah?'

'Oh *wow*,' I say to my sister, 'he's *so* much older than I thought he'd be.'

'His head looks like a scrotum,' Amy whispers as Connie gags and swiftly heads off in the direction of an attractive man dripping in Balenciaga she's spied in the VIP area.

'Never learns, does she?' Amy says, fondly.

'Nope.' I watch her sashay off into the crowd. 'She really doesn't.'

'Girls, can I just say…' Jac begins, shimmying her way back to us, absolutely smashed on vodka Redbulls. 'This might not have been the hen party I, or any of us, expected, but I'll tell you something: wow, it sure as shit isn't going to be beaten. Look at us, a bunch of fucking mums! Look at what we did! Six nights, which admittedly should have been three, without worrying about nappies, after-school clubs, a weird rash that Dr Google tells us is a horrible child-killing illness, or moany teenagers with crusty sheets. We were our own people, and do you know what? That felt so good! Yes, we nearly died a couple of times, and broke a few laws that would definitely get me fired back home, but wow… "Mums On Tour" was EPIC, wasn't it?! I bloody love you lot. We should do this every year, don't you think? Maybe not exactly the same, 10% less drama, but definitely a crazy, girls-only vaycay. Deal?'

'Deal!' I agree, wondering who I'm going to get to look after Ben and Nancy – because after I unceremoniously dumped them with Aunt Sarah and Uncle Geoff for nearly a week, there's no way they're ever going to agree to have my kids ever again, and I think Ray has suffered enough.

'Cara, five o'clock!' Jac says, with a wink.

'Already? I thought it was about three?' I say, pulling out my phone to check the time.

'No, numpty, behind you – look!'

There's no need to look behind me. I feel his big strong arms wrap around my waist and the warmth of his breath on my neck as he nuzzles the roughness of his stubble into the softness of my skin.

'Hola, Cara'

'Hola, Javier,' I say with a smile as broad as his shoulders.

As the beat of Tori Amos' 'Professional Widow' kicks in and the crowd around us goes wild with excitement, I turn round and go utterly wild for him. Honey bring it close to my lips indeed.

Epilogue

I can't believe they've put us in a room together. I'm livid. I want to be nowhere near Dominic Stringer ever again, never mind stuck in a two-bed hospital ward with him. In the morning, when the nurses do their shift change, I'm going to speak with the matron – or whatever they call them over here in the States. I want to be moved as far away from him as possible. The indignity of it. He's lucky I still have my catheter in, otherwise I'd be out of bed and finishing him off – not in a sexual way, of course; he couldn't even do that if he wanted to. I believe that's what they call poetic justice. He hasn't woken up yet. They've still got him sedated. Maybe I'll hang around a bit longer, just so I can be here when he comes to and realises what's happened to his pride and joy.

Where is the nurse? I buzzed for my pain meds over fifteen minutes ago. I could do with a drink too, the proper kind. I'm about three hours away from having a swig of the hand sanitiser. Finally! The door opens. I hope they've brought the good drugs this time. You pay enough in the land of the free so it'd better be morphine. A male nurse tonight. I wonder where the usual one is?

In the darkness of the room, his sloping frame looks familiar but he's wearing a mask so it's impossible to tell what lies beneath. Shame, it'd be nice to have a lovely young chap to have a little ogle over. Odd he's locked the door behind him though…oh, and of *course he's going over to Dom first. Nice to see that chivalry is alive and well. I'll have a little close of my eyes while I wait, get my beauty rest in while he changes his drip. Only about another week or so in this place, and then I'll be home, back to normal life, and normal boring Ray. If he'll have me back. Perhaps I'll book myself in for a little Botox – to cheer myself up. Speaking of needles: at last, it's my turn. I really can't be bothered with chit-chat at this time of night. If I lie still with my eyes closed then he'll just shoot me up and leave. Ow! This one's a little heavy-handed for my liking. Not much of a bedside manner either. These drugs feel a little different from my normal cocktail too, not quite as warm and fuzzy as the last dose. Why does my arm feel so cold, and now my chest and neck? No, this doesn't feel right at all. Imbecile must have given me the wrong meds.*

Peeping through an increasingly heavy lid, I try to clock his nametag...but his back is turned now. My head throbs, and my lungs begin to burn. I call out to him to come back, so I can ask him what he's given me but he's slipped out of the room as silently as he arrived. As my eyes close and blackness devours me, I add him to my list of people to complain about in the morning. Honestly, you just can't get the staff these days. His face may not have been visible, but I'm sure they'll know who he is from what I could see. After all, how many male nurses can there be with weird feline neck tattoos and one arm...?

-THE END-

Acknowledgements

I've had three main ambitions in life, to date: meeting Dwayne 'The Rock' Johnson (and embarrassing myself horribly while attempting to invade his personal space), becoming Beyonce's best friend, and writing a comedy novel. One out of three ain't bad. There are so many people to thank for this particular aspiration becoming a reality. First off, my big kids, Jack and Evelyn ... my muses for writing about a child-free weekend in Ibiza, and inspiration for pushing myself to do better and be better. Follow your own dreams and work hard my babies, anything is possible if you want it enough. Sadly, this motivational TED talk does not extend to Haribo before bed. You will never mani*feast* that. I love you all so much, and will never stop trying to hold your hands in public – or asking if you've had a poo today. Sorry Mummy seems to spend so much time chained to her computer and chain-eating Jammie Dodgers as though she's competing for a Guinness World Record. One day I'll write a book that you'll be able to read before your 18th birthdays.

Big shout out to Nate, AKA Natey Chops / Chopples, the Big NC, and littlest of my littles. Your timing wasn't the best, if I'm being honest, but you were destined to be and you can't fight Destiny's Child – otherwise you'll never get to be mates with Beyonce. Sperm hit egg pretty much as pen hit paper, and I spent as much time with my head down a toilet as I did down plot holes – but you were totally worth it. For those still reading, for the record I do NOT recommend attempting to write a debut novel while pregnant – and then having to finish it postpartum because your baby didn't get the memo about not coming early.

Steve, thank you for not divorcing me. It's appreciated. We both also know it'd cost a fortune, and we need the money to pay off the sofas in the living room. Thank you for doing all the morning school runs after I'd stayed up until stupid o'clock writing, and for the snacks, along with the constructive criticism – despite me wanting to push you off a cliff for saying things like 'Don't you think it's a bit wordy?' You are one of a kind, and I'm lucky to have a husband who only raised one eyebrow when I told him I was off to get drunk in Ibiza for a 'work trip'.

Bringing me nicely onto Lucy … The best Momager on the block. You always have my best interests at heart, and never mute me (to my knowledge) on WhatsApp despite my constant bombardment of irrational thoughts. The most fun partner in crime to have by my side in Ibiza. Your cannonball will go down as legendary for centuries and will ensure we're never allowed back into a certain swanky beach club for just as long. I'm sorry your toenail paid the ultimate price for the laughs.

Speaking of agents – Jo, and Lauren! Thank you both for coming on this journey with me and for your unwavering confidence in my abilities, even when I'd completely lost my head (along with the plot) and would send wailing voice notes telling you how shit it was. I'm so very grateful you plucked me out of the social media abyss and encouraged me to turn my hand to writing.

To everyone at HarperNorth – another bloody book! As always, your continued belief in me as a writer means more than you'll ever know. You were also very understanding of a highly emotional and very pregnant author whose baby messed up our planned publication date. Cheers for not suing me for breach of contract. Gen, thank you for helping me to see the wood from the trees on many an occasion – and for the 'violence' checks. The book would probably have 90 % more 'fucks' in it too if it wasn't for your exceptional editing eye. You understood my vision right from the get go, I didn't want 'safe' or 'mumsy' – I wanted drugs and sharks attacks – and you just said, 'cool, write it how you want'. Legend.

Alice, Meg and the rest of the wider team – your behind-the-scenes efforts are also incredibly appreciated. There's so much time and effort that goes into making a manuscript a reality and you all do an amazing job. Lisa Brewster – thank you for my banging book cover! I realise a brief of 'chickens, murder, and summer holiday vibes' wasn't easy.

To my mum and dad. These characters are not based on you. Don't cut me out of the will. Thank you for baby holding and coffee making, and apologies for the number of times Nate puked on you in the process. Who'd have thought the BBC computer that used to sit in the corner of the dining room would be responsible for inspiring a creative writing passion that would spawn the term 'Glock cock.'

John and Amanda, thank you for grandchildren- and grand-dog-sitting. You took one for the team on many an occasion, especially with the dog… To all my friends who also had to live through my existential crises – you know who you are! Less 'Flab Four', and more 'Safe Six'.

Last but not least, my social media peeps! You guys are the best. Constantly supporting my ventures – whether it's books, David Attenborough spoofs, or my dodgy singing voice. I wouldn't be doing any of this if it wasn't for you.

Also, big up Instagram and TikTok for the *alllll* the procrastination.

What's next? I'm not sure, but I reckon Dwayne and Beyonce should be worried…

Harper
North

Book Credits

HarperNorth would like to thank the following staff
and contributors for their involvement in making
this book a reality:

Hannah Avery
Fionnuala Barrett
Samuel Birkett
Lisa Brewster
Ciara Briggs
Sarah Burke
Alan Cracknell
Jonathan de Peyer
Anna Derkacz
Tom Dunstan
Kate Elton
Heather Fitt
Monica Green

Natassa Hadjinicolaou
CJ Harter
Megan Jones
Jean-Marie Kelly
Taslima Khatun
Sammy Luton
Oliver Malcolm
Alice Murphy-Pyle
Adam Murray
Genevieve Pegg
Florence Shepherd
Emma Sullivan
Katrina Troy

For more unmissable reads,
sign up to the HarperNorth newsletter at
www.harpernorth.co.uk

or find us on Twitter at
@HarperNorthUK

Harper
North